GOLD TOWN

LYNNE CAIRNS

Quokpress

This historical novel is a work of fiction. However, as the fictional characters are placed in the historical setting of the Western Australian gold rushes of the 1890s, some real people do appear.   Find out about them on page 368.

ISBN: 978-0-6484376-4-2

Dedicated to the memory of my grandfather's uncle, James McHugh, and all those who, like him, died of thirst in their outback search for gold.

Chapter 1

October 1894

The sunset's glow gilded the trunks of the salmon gums and glittered on the hot stream of liquid splattering the thirsty red soil. Ants scurried among the scattered brown leaves and twigs, a lizard darting up a twisted tree trunk, stopped to cast a jewel eye at the intruder in his world, and the crow that had been content to mutter and croak in protest at the alien presence, took off with a harsh caw.

'I'll go get some firewood, Dad,' Jack Morrison called, buttoning his fly. But he hadn't got far when he stumbled, hurtling on for several paces before regaining his balance.

'Bloody roots,' he muttered. But it wasn't a root. It was a boot. A boot attached to a leg, to a body.

'Dad! Dad, come quick,' he called, 'There's a dead bloke here.'

Within seconds, his father joined him in observing the body.

'A new chum prospector, by the look of his clothes,' said Jack.

'Poor devil,' the old man muttered, 'Looks like someone crowned him with something sharp, probably a shovel.'

'What are we gonna do with him, Dad?'

'Well, we can't get him to a town, and can't leave him here, so I guess we'd better bury the poor bastard. Go get a shovel, Jack, while I see if there's anything on him to tell us who he is. And bring the gun, whoever done it might still be around. He's not been here long.'

Jack was almost back to their temporary camp, when a shriek of terror ripped through the silent bush. Rushing back, he found the old man sitting on the ground clutching his heart.

'What's the matter, Dad! Look like y' seen a ghost.'

'Thought I had! He sat up! Frightened the living daylight outa me!'

As they cautiously approached the crumpled body, there came a low moan.

'My God, Dad, he's alive,' said Jack. Bending closer, he went on, 'It's all right, mate. We're friends. What happened?'

'Canna remember,' came a trembling whisper. 'Where am I? Ma head hurts ... ma ear ...' he mumbled, clutching the bloodied side of his head. Sitting up, he looked around dazedly, feeling in his pockets as he did so, 'the bastard's ta'en ma money. Ma Miners Right too! And where's ma pack?'

'There's nothing here mate,' the old prospector said, 'we'd better get you back to our camp.'

That young Scottish prospector was luckier than some who came seeking their fortunes in Western Australia's dry interior in the early 1890s. The lure of gold attracted thieves, confidence tricksters, escaped criminals even the occasional murderer.

A week later, in Southern Cross, he sat in the police station trying to give a coherent description of his attacker, 'Well, he was about ma height, sandy hair an' whiskers. Think his eyes were blueish, greyish maybe. Just an ordinary sort of fella.'

Half the men streaming through the West Australian outback on their way to the new goldfields could be described as ordinary fellows, like the fair-haired young prospector who wandered into a canvas-walled saloon at the gold rush town of Hannan's Find three weeks later.

Only a few beers, he thought, *then I'd better be off.* News of the find would soon leak out now he'd registered his claim. Luckily, rumours of a rich find further east had set off a new rush. The town was strangely quiet and the bar almost empty. Just a few old-timers arguing about the direction of the best lodes, and a bloke in the corner reading an old newspaper.

'New in town?' asked one old chap, taking in the newcomer's clean dungarees and shirt.

'Been prospecting,' he replied, sipping his lukewarm beer. 'Got enough for some new britches,' he added, feeling the new clothes needed explaining.

'I was just saying to Joe here,' old Fred went on, 'it looks like we're in for another stinker of a summer. Last year, there just wasn't enough water to keep everyone alive.'

The nondescript digger in the corner idly followed the conversation at the bar as he perused the tattered newspaper. Suddenly he tensed, muttering, 'Damn. That bastard's still alive.'

He'd just been calling himself Sandy, but maybe it was time for a change. With a grim smile, he joined the group at the bar.

Six months later:

Nora Patterson settled into her seat on the train and pulled a small mirror from her bag to tidy her hair. Pinning up the honey-gold strands that had strayed from under her hat, she pushed away the concerns raised by friends and acquaintances. Ned wouldn't have asked her to come if it wasn't safe.

He'd sounded so excited when he wrote asking her to come west. Enclosed was a bank draught to pay for her fares. "We're going to be rich, darling," he wrote. "I'll buy you jewellery and lovely clothes, and when we've got enough out of the mine, we can go home to Melbourne and build a fine house. Just wire me when you're arriving, and I'll be at the coach stop to meet you."

It had been hard, him being so far away when her father died in debt. Knowing no one in Melbourne except for a distant relation who made her feel completely unwelcome, she'd found work as a trainee nurse. It meant taking off her wedding ring and pretending to be single, but the hospital nurses' quarters had seemed like a refuge, despite the irritatingly rigid rules. *They weren't enough to keep you on the straight and narrow, though*, she thought.

All through the stormy sea passage to West Australia, she had argued with herself about what to tell Ned. Soon she would have to decide. They'd always been honest with each other.

His letter couldn't have come at a better time. She needed to get away from Melbourne, try to forget what had happened and start again. But the only person who wasn't horrified at the idea of her travelling alone to some remote place on the other side of Australia was Mrs Riordan, an old lady who'd lived on the American goldfields in California. She had plenty of practical advice.

'Always give your clothes a good shake and check nothin's crawled into your shoes in the mornin', and get a good, strong pair of them elastic-sided boots. And a shady hat.

'You go, Nora,' she went on. But you'll need to be careful until you're safely back with your husband. There'll be hundreds of men. Most of them decent fellas, but all dyin' to get their hands on you. There'll be quite a few crooks, too. Gold attracts them like flies. So, bring me the wooden box you'll find in the bottom drawer of the lowboy, dear. I've got a little present for you. You said your dad taught you to shoot.'

'Only a shotgun, Mrs Riordan,' Nora replied.

The box contained a small revolver enclosed in a satin-covered holster, plus a packet of cartridges.

'Used to wear it under me dress,' the old lady told her. 'I padded the holster and put a slit in all my skirts so I could slip my hand in and grab it if ever things got out of control.'

She laughed. 'Well, as you're an experienced old married woman and a nurse and all, I suppose it's safe to tell you I had a colourful career on them fields, before Harry came along and made an honest woman out of me, the darlin' man.'

Nora had accepted the unexpected gift, though it stayed in her trunk. None of the hundreds of men crowded onto the ship had bothered her, but the women who shared her cabin were shocked to hear she was going all the way to the diggings. No decent women were to be found out there, they told her.

With a piercing whistle and a hiss of steam, the train rattled out of the Perth railway station, gathering speed as it left the small city and clattered over the wooden bridge spanning the Swan River. Nora was determined to enjoy the trip, despite the coal smoke and dust blowing in through the windows, left open because of the heat. She loved the scenery, all tall gum trees, as the steam locomotive puffed laboriously up through the hills east of Perth.

Then came some farming land, fields of parched stubble and ghostly ringbarked trees. It was dusk by the time they reached the town of Northam, just a pub, a street of darkened shops, a scattering of dimly-lit windows and a small station building, where she bought a cup of tea and a sandwich and waited what seemed hours before, with a mournful wail, the train chugged out into the darkness.

All signs of settlement had disappeared when the sun rose next morning. There was nothing to see but red soil, sparse scrub and scattered gumtrees, their trunks chalk-white or glowing shades of copper and salmon pink. Then the train's whistle warned passengers that they were about to arrive – somewhere. As scattered shacks merged into a busy, if ramshackle settlement, towering poppet legs and the rumbling, rhythmic thump of ore-crushers declared it a mining town.

'Southern Cross, end of the line,' the guard yelled as the train slowed to a stop beside a small dirt platform.

Clutching her carpetbag and purse, Nora climbed down into the overwhelming dust and noise, trying to control the tickling in her nose. Through the haze, she saw hundreds of camels, linked together in long trains, and dozens of wagons, drawn by horse teams or long strings of donkeys.

Her guess that they were there to collect freight from the train was confirmed when a gruff voice behind her said, 'They'll be loadin' stuff for Coolgardie and the rushes. Everythin's got to be taken up on these 'ere camel trains and wagons.'

A small, corrugated iron room was set aside as a ladies' waiting room, but the lavatories were a couple of tiny tin structures on the far side of the line. Hoping she had time to wait till the crowd cleared before venturing over there, she headed to the stationmaster's office to ask, 'Excuse me, but where do I catch the stagecoach to Coolgardie? And do you know what time it leaves? Will I have time to get something to eat?'

'You've got about an hour, Missus,' the man said. 'The coach leaves from right here after the mail is transferred, but they won't leave you behind.'

After a cup of tea and some cold toast at the station's tearoom, Nora joined the waiting crowd of men, and a large, jolly-faced woman, as a Cobb and Co coach appeared out of a cloud of dust.

The driver hopped down and touched his hat to the two women before helping them up into the coach, where they were quickly joined by six men of various shapes and sizes. Another six clambered up onto the outside of the vehicle, settling themselves on precarious perches as the driver flapped the reins, calling 'Gee-up' to his team.

When those inside were all settled into their seats, the big lady said, 'Well folks, it looks like we're spending the next day and night together, so maybe we need to get acquainted, I'm Mrs Kennedy, and this lady,' looking at Nora, 'is … ?'

'Mrs Patterson.'

'Percy Davis. Delighted to meet you, ladies,' said the fellow near the door, smoothing his neat moustache.

'Farrington, of Farrington and Farrington, mining consultants,' said the big man in the tweed suit, standing up suddenly and bumping his head on the roof.

'Todd, of Todd and Todd, gold grubbers,' put in the be-whiskered fellow in the corner.

'Fair go, mate. That's just how city folk talk,' said the old, bearded gent next to Nora, 'Pleased to meet you, ladies. I'm Bill Morrison.'

'Jim Blake,' came from the tall prospector with the large black moustache, and the full-bearded, lanky fellow opposite Nora introduced himself as Seth Rogerson.

It was stiflingly hot in the crowded coach. Some of the men had removed their jackets and Nora envied them. If only it was that easy to get out of her restricting clothes.

As the men discussed fluctuations in the price of gold, a subject dear to the heart of all miners, Nora let her mind wander to the worries she'd been trying to ignore. Would Ned have changed? She knew she had. Could she simply slip back into her old life as if nothing had happened?

After a couple of hours, she was getting accustomed to the stagecoach's bouncing and creaking rhythm. Some passengers were dozing, but no way could she sleep, squashed between the coach's side panel and old Mr Morrison.

'Been down the city for a few weeks,' he told her. 'Fell down the mine and broke me leg in a couple of places.'

It was a much more pleasant ride on the outside, he told her, and he'd have been up on top except for his bad leg.

'Now the roads are better, they claim they can do it in twenty-four hours,' he went on. 'Used to take three days an' we camped along the way. A bit rough, but is bein' cooped up in here day and night any better?'

Nora supposed they would have to stop and change horses, but when that time came, there was no friendly inn for the passengers to relax in, just a bough shed beside a campfire. After stomping their feet to get the circulation going, the men strode away amongst the nearest trees, unbuttoning their flies. With her own bladder about to burst, Nora looked at Mrs Kennedy, who beckoned her away from the track a bit.

'Usually it's ladies to the right, gents to the left,' she laughed, 'but those fellas were in too much of a hurry. Come over behind these trees.'

When they reached the small stand of white gums, she heaved up her voluminous skirts to squat behind the nearest bush. Nora slipped behind another one.

While Nora struggled with her drawers, Mrs Kennedy said, with a laugh. 'I learnt a thing or two about peeing in the bush from my old auntie. She always wore free-traders. I kept some of hers and wear them when I'm travelling. No one can tell with all these darned petticoats we have to wear.'

'What are free-traders?' asked Nora.

'You know, those drawers that are open underneath. Your granny probably wore them.'

'Oh!' came Nora's flustered murmur.

Having rearranged their clothing, the two women returned to the fire, where they were handed a pannikin of tea and a large corned-beef sandwich. Too hungry to be fussy, Nora wolfed it down.

'Here, come sit by me, dear,' Mrs Kennedy said as they climbed back into the coach. 'We women need to stick together. We're totally outnumbered out here.'

When the noise of the other passengers subsided, she went on, 'How far are you going dear? I'm headin' back to Coolgardie. My Mike decided he'll make more money selling grog to the diggers than scrounging after gold.'

'I'm going on to Hannans,' Nora told her.

'Ooh, it's a bit wild out there. There's hundreds of men and only a handful of respectable women. And there's no water. It was so bad that the miners were allowed to come away over summer. You know, they usually need to stay and work their claims.'

'Yeah, it was terrible last year. Blokes were dyin' of thirst out in the bush,' said one of the men.

'I hear prospectors keep stumbling on the remains of those poor fellows,' said Farrington.

'When me an' my boy Jack was prospectin' last year,' Morrison told them, 'we found this bloke lying in the bush. We was about to bury him when he frightened the life out of us by sittin' up an' swearing at us. Some bloke had attacked him, stole all his money an' papers and left him for dead. The bastard must have hit him with a shovel. Sliced his ear clean off. Bloody maggots were already crawlin' in the wound.'

'Did the poor man recover?' Nora asked.

'Well, we patched him up and took him up to Coolgardie. I've seen him in Hannans a couple of times and he's doin' all right. Bit deaf, though, without the ear. The town was pretty rough, Missus,' he went on, 'but it's different now. We've got shops an' pubs. Even some policemen.'

'I believe the water situation is much improved,' said Farrington. 'Several enterprising fellows are condensing fresh water from the salt lake, and there's been some rain. Most of the men who took advantage of the relaxed rules have gone back.'

'The government's making dams and puttin' up water tanks, I hear,' said Jim Blake.

'They're talkin' about building a pipeline to bring water up from Perth,' Rogerson said.

'Oh, that's just a pipedream! It'll never happen. It's nearly four hundred miles.'

'I don't know, they can do amazing things these days.'

Chapter 2

Water was still scarce in Hannans, but the place that began as a collection of tents and shanties was fast becoming a town, which the West Australian government had named Kalgoorlie. To most of the inhabitants, however, it was still Hannans.

A few saloons, stores and other businesses housed in tents or hessian shanties had appeared within weeks of the first rich finds. But now, the wide dirt road, where horses, camel teams and wagons constantly stirred the dust, was lined with a ramshackle collection of hessian stores, hotels, boarding houses, grog shops, brothels, tents and thatched brush shelters.

At sundown, as the incessant clinking of picks and the rattle of crushed rock in dryblowers and panning-off dishes died away, the pall of red dust settled back to earth and hundreds of weary men converged on the pubs to wash the accumulated grit from their throats, drown their sorrows or celebrate their good fortune, depending on the results of their hard day's work.

The rough bar of the Club Hotel, one of the first to be established in the town, was already crowded with men standing elbow-to-elbow, downing lukewarm drinks and trying to hear each other over the din of raised voices.

Outside, young Joey O'Callaghan was too busy polishing boots to do more than acknowledge Danny O'Hara's greeting with a wide grin. But his customer said, 'Young fella's doin' a grand job, Danny. Never expected t' see a shine on these old boots again.' Fumbling in his pocket, he handed the boy three pennies.

'Gee thanks, Mister.'

'You earned it laddie,' he replied, tousling the boy's shaggy red hair.

'Shouldn't you be headin' home?' O'Hara asked the boy.

'Ooh, yeah, Mum'll be wonderin' where I got to.'

'Want a hand to carry anything?'

'No thanks, Mr O'Hara. See, it all packs up into this box.'

'Well, say hello to y'r ma. An' if Ben's still there tell him I'm at the Black Swan. You comin' for a drink, Willie?' he went on turning to the other man. 'We usually go to the saloon. Too many blokes in the pubs.'

Gee, the time sure goes quick when y' busy makin' money, Joey was thinking as he hurried away, glad that O'Hara had reminded him of the time. The old fellow and his mate Ben Drummond had a mine just up the hill from where Joey lived.

They and several other miners had rallied around to help his mother after her husband's accidental death. They'd finished her little shack and clubbed together to send her and the boy for a holiday down at the coast. Joey liked being back in Hannans. There was no school yet. So he and his pal, Timmy O'Rourke, pretty well ran wild, accompanied by Timmy's dog, Splinter.

Joey was nearly home when he met Ben Drummond and his friend Bluey Longmore, who had just finished thatching a bough shed for his mother, Mary, and were heading down to town.

'Hey, Joey,' Ben called, 'Better hurry home. Your mum's getting worried.'

'Oh, hello, Mr Drummond, Mr Longmore. I been very busy an' forgot the time.'

'Off you go then, young fella.'

'Mary's got a good little bloke there,' remarked the redheaded Longmore as the two men sauntered on down towards the town. 'D' you think they'll be all right, Ben? Maybe she should have gone back east.'

'We'll just have to keep an eye on them, Bluey. What's all the rumpus down at the Club?'

'Sounds like a stoush,' his mate replied, stretching his long neck to see, 'Probably should avoid it, but... Hey! That doesn't look like a fair fight. Come on, mate. They're ganging up on some poor sod.' Then, his normally soft voice rose to roar of rage, 'Fair go, you bastards.'

As the two men rushed into the fray, the piercing shrill of a police whistle cut across the cacophony of cursing and they saw that the man backed up against the hotel wall by the angry mob was a policeman. The police weren't always popular on goldfields but there'd been no open hostility here.

Reminded of their civic duty, or simply eager for a fight, some of the bystanders surged forward, getting into each other's way and initiating separate punch-ups, but the two newcomers, supported by a few other level heads among the crowd, soon reached the centre.

With some sort of balance restored, most of the rowdy troublemakers slipped quietly away, leaving only the ringleaders either unconscious on the ground, securely held, or in one case, tied with his own belt and hobbled by the trousers around his ankles.

It was the lanky Bluey who finally dispersed the curious crowd. Standing on the hotel steps, he shouted 'as you fellas know, there's no jail here. So, these blokes are going to spend the night chained to that big tree down in the police paddock. Not very comfortable accommodation. If you don't want to join them, clear off.'

'You all right, constable?' his friend was asking.

'Yes, I think so. Where's my cap?'

'Here. It landed under the step. What are you going to do with these blokes? Don't think you'll have room for them all at the prison tree.'

'I'll have to arrest the ringleaders,' he said bending to check the two men on the ground. 'This one's coming around. I'd better get the cuffs on him.

'You three,' he went on raising his voice and indicating the other captives, 'are under arrest. If you come quietly, I might let you go home. Any trouble and the charges will be more serious.'

'You might need a hand to move them,' put in Ben, who'd noticed the young policeman wincing as he straightened his back.

'Here, I'll take this one,' he went on, bending to hoist the unconscious man up in a fireman's lift. 'You all right with the other bloke, Bluey?'

A couple of the other men who'd gone to the policeman's aid helped escort the captives back to the police tent, where the two ringleaders, now fully conscious and cursing, were quickly secured to the lockup tree.

'What was that all about anyway?' asked Longmore.

'Those two were throwing their weight around in the Club and I tried to eject them. I owe all you gents a big thank you, I'm Constable Purkiss. And you are?

'Dave Jessop.'

'Tom Briggs.'

'Bluey Longmore.'

'Ben Drummond, glad to help,' Drummond said as they shook hands. 'Why were you on your own, Constable? Haven't we got more officers stationed here now?'

'The corporal's escorting the gold coach; Sergeant Stokes is out chasing missing prospectors and the other constable's got a dose of dysentery. I hope he'll be back on the job tomorrow. I'd better get the names of those men and write out a report.'

'You don't think they're likely to cause any trouble?' asked Briggs.

'I'll keep my gun handy.'

'Righto. Well goodnight, constable. You fellas off to the pub?'

'Of course,' laughed Jessop, 'which one?'

'Club's nearest.'

'That'll do me,' said Longmore.

'I'm supposed t' be joining Danny at the Black Swan.' said Drummond. 'See you fellas around.'

'Did he used to be a policeman?' the constable asked the others, as the tall man walked away. 'That neat trick with the belts is something an old English bobby showed me.'

'Not as far as I know.'

⤞⟋⟍

The setting sun's fiery light glimmered on the gimlet tree trunks by the time Nora heard the welcome cry of 'Whoa, there,' from the driver. This staging post was more substantial than those at the other brief stops, with a roughly painted 'Hotel' sign and a tent where the passengers sat at a rough plank table to eat corned beef, potatoes and onions. Only Farrington bothered to criticise the cuisine before tucking into the rough meal.

When she joined the other passengers inside the coach, the strong smell of rum emanating from some of the men suggested they'd enjoyed more stimulating refreshments than the coach operators' strong black tea. Fortunately, after a slightly noisy argument between Todd and Davis, the affected men fell asleep, leaving the rest to desultory discussions about gold. Soon Mrs Kennedy dozed off and Nora didn't need to make conversation.

She wondered how anyone could sleep in the rocking, creaking coach, but was content to watch the moon-silvered scenery and enjoy the cool, gum-scented breeze that dispersed the fog of tobacco smoke as the coach rumbled on.

There were several stops during the night, when the passengers could relieve themselves while the horses were changed, but Nora and Mrs Kennedy only ventured out once, where a rough lavatory was available. The older lady went first, carrying a hurricane lantern. Nora, following close behind, had just decided the furtive figures dancing among the trees were only shadows cast by the moving light, when something swooped down out of the darkness. As the cry of 'booook, booook' faded away, Mrs Kennedy laughed nervously.

'Just a blooming owl,' she said. 'Almost made me pee myself in fright.'

'Me too,' Nora agreed as they reached the hessian-enclosed dunny.

Though they thoroughly checked for redback spiders or other insects lurking on the seat, back in the coach, it was hard to relax, wondering what other crawling creatures might have crept into her clothes.

After a few hours of restless sleep, she awoke at dawn, and was trying to stretch her cramped limbs when the coach rocked wildly.

'Whoa, damn y' bloody hides, Whoa!' came the driver's shout, and the coach lurched to a stop.

'Bloody Hell,' came a voice from the roof, 'Snowy's gone overboard.'

'It's all right, mate. I managed to catch the luggage straps. What happened?'

'Sorry for the sudden stop,' said the driver. 'I think the leader stepped in a hole. Didn't want her to do any more harm. You other blokes all right?'

'Yeah. Anything we can do?'

'Help with the rest of the team while I check the damage. I hope she hasn't broke her leg. Hate t' have to shoot her. She's a bloody good mare. In the meantime you might as well stretch y' legs.'

'Sounds like a good idea,' muttered Todd, pushing open the door. The other men quickly followed.

'I'm getting out too,' Mrs Kennedy said, 'I think there's enough light to find our way to those trees. I'm dying for a pee.'

'Me too,' Nora laughed, climbing out after her.

They returned to find the driver kneeling beside a trembling bay mare, whispering endearments as he massaged and prodded her left foreleg.

'Well, that's a relief,' he told the horse. 'Won't be having to shoot you, me old darlin', but we gonna have to take it easy from now on.'

Turning to the expectant crowd of passengers, he went on, 'Righto, folks, we'll be back in business soon as I rearrange the team and put Dolly here on a lead rope. But I'll be taking it slow; so don't expect to see the mighty city of Coolgardie any time soon.

It was late that afternoon, when Nora and the other weary passengers finally reached Coolgardie, where some two-storey corrugated iron buildings stood out from the shacks and tents that straggled along a wide dirt road. Everything was covered in a layer of red dust. Even herself. It was everywhere, in her hair and in her clothes. Even up her nose, she found after an attack of the sneezes.

'Thank goodness we got here before dark,' said Mrs Kennedy. 'I don't think I'd survive another night on the road. Not that the company hasn't been pleasant. Nora my dear, I think you'll find this pub is the best for ladies. I'm sorry I can't offer to put you up, we're still living in a tent.'

'Thank you, Mrs Kennedy,' Nora replied. 'It's been nice meeting you. I hope your husband's business does well.'

'I hope so too, but you never know with my Mike. I'm afraid he might drink all the profits. Then where will we be?'

Nora had no answer to that rhetorical question, so just smiled and prepared to alight from the coach.

The corrugated iron hotel had only one entrance, through a bar full to bursting with men, most of them drunk, and her heart sank when she was taken to her room. It was tiny, dark and stiflingly hot, with one small window and a rough plank floor. On a small table sat a tin dish, but when she asked for water, all she received was a couple of pints in a tin jug. She washed her face and hands as best she could, turning the water into a muddy red soup, before collapsing on the bed.

Chapter 3

From where the windlass stood on the heaped spoil around the head of the mineshaft, Ben Drummond could see a long way across the shantytown that was Hannans, and the flat that had been dug over by hundreds of diggers searching for alluvial gold. He chuckled to see young Joey O'Callaghan and his mate Timmy sneaking around the back of Courthope's store, peering at the ground, playing detective. Joey, not yet eleven, could read better than some adults and had become obsessed with Sherlock Holmes since the stories were serialised in some of the newspapers.

'How're you going, Danny?' Ben called, pushing a sweaty lock of dark hair out of his eyes.

'Nearly there, mate. Give us a minute,' the sepulchral voice echoed up from the depths of the mine.

Ben just stopped himself from saying 'be careful'. It wouldn't be appreciated, but he couldn't help worrying about his partner. It was hard work for an old fellow, but the Irishman was touchy. Any suggestion that he wasn't up to the work spurred him on to do more.

'Righto, mate. Haul her up,' Danny's voice echoed from down below.

'Goodoh! Stand clear,' he replied, grasping the iron windlass handle and throwing the strength of his back into winding the rope around the rough-hewn log. Muscles stood out on his arms as the heavy bucket of ore rose to the surface.

'All clear,' he called as he swung it aside and set it on the ground, 'You comin' up?'

'To be sure, mate. Reckon it's smoko time.'

As Ben tipped the ore from the bucket, glints of gold sparkled in the morning sun, suggesting that, though the last week's work hadn't resulted in much gold, the little mine still had a future. Danny was sure the reef wasn't petering out, and it looked like he was right.

'Looks promising Danny,' Ben said, as his mate clambered up out of the mine, his white hair and whiskers liberally sprinkled with red dust.

'Yes, I knew we were onto it,' he said, as he wandered over to the campfire where the water in the billycan was already boiling.

While Ben tossed a handful of tealeaves into the boiling water, Danny scraped the coals away to reveal the golden crust of a loaf of damper bread. Ignoring the heat, his tough old fingers dragged it clear. Thumping it on the hard ground a few times to shake off the ash, he slid it onto a tin plate and carried it to the rough table in the bough shed, then sliced generous chunks off while Ben poured the strong black tea into tin mugs.

'What do you want, Danny? Dripping or Cocky's joy?' he asked, opening the hessian-covered safe hanging from the rafters.

'I think I'll have a bit of that drippin' from the roast roo and onions. We can always get treacle.

'No, Seamus,' he went on in response to the hopeful stare from his shaggy grey dog. 'You had the bone.'

The haunch of kangaroo had been a gift from the local Indigenous people who sometimes camped at the far end of the lease, in exchange for a bag of flour.

'Funny buggers,' Danny said, liberally spreading the tasty fat on his bread. 'Don't know why they stay around here. There must be more of their tucker out in the bush. Hardly even see a roo around now since the scrub is all cleared away.'

'Maybe they've always come here,' Ben replied. 'It might be a special place for them.'

'Well it can't be because of the gold. They don't set no store by it.'

'Do you want another cup?' Ben asked lifting the billy.

'Don't I always?' Danny laughed, as Ben poured the inky liquid.

'Mind if I take a stroll down to the post office, Danny?' Ben said as his old mate tamped down the tobacco in his pipe and settled in for a smoke.

'Get the paper too, if it's in. An' those shirts Mary said she'd mend for us ought t' be dry by now. So drop them in at her place, on your way.'

'Righto,' Ben replied. Lifting the clean shirts off the rope that served as a clothesline, he strode away down the hill to Mary O'Callaghan's shack. He was about to knock when Joey called out from down the road, 'Mum's out, Mr Drummond.'

'That's all right, Joey,' Ben replied. 'She said she could mend these.'

'She'll be home soon. Do y' want to stop for a cuppa?'

'No, I can't stay. I'm just off to the Post Office. We've got a lot of work to do today so I need to get back.'

With a wave, he went on his way, thinking back over the conversation with Danny about the black people. Well aware that they had no reason to forgive white transgressions, he'd been wary of them at first. But, travelling around the bush over east, he was surprised by their tolerance and generosity. On the outback cattle stations, the black stockmen were more prepared to share their campfire and meagre supplies with a stranger than some whites.

The post office was still only a glorified tent, where postmaster Bob Humphries and an assistant tried to control the influx of mail. Much of it very inadequately addressed.

'Hello Ben,' Bob said, turning to rifle through an overflowing pigeonhole. 'There's a bundle of newspapers and a parcel for Danny. And a letter for Mrs O'Callaghan. Can you drop that off for her? Nothing for you, I'm afraid, mate.'

'Thanks Bob,' Ben said, resignedly as he turned to go.

'Got a minute?' Bob asked. 'You riding out anywhere on Sunday? Any chance you could take some mail out to Broad Arrow?'

'There's still no sign of the mailman you've been promised?'

'No, and we have to get rid of some of this stuff. We're going crazy here. The place is overflowing with letters and parcels addressed "Care of Post Office, Hannans". We don't know who these blokes are, or where they might have wandered off to. If some of them don't collect their mail, we'll be needing another tent just to store the stuff.'

'Glad to help,' the tall miner replied, accepting the bundle of letters. 'Might as well have a look out that way.'

He always appreciated an excuse to get out in the bush. To escape the teeming ant's nest that Hannans was in its first months, he'd got into the habit of riding out on the pretext of doing some prospecting on Sundays when everybody took a day off. The town was quieter now, but at times he still felt the need for solitude.

During the afternoon, he and Danny set to breaking up the rock. It had to be crushed very small before the dryblowing could start. It was tedious, boring work, so Danny was pleased to stop and put the billy on when Bluey Longmore dropped in to tell them one of their mates, Dave Jessop, was celebrating with a get-together at the pub.

'Not sure what,' he said, 'guess we'll find out when we get there.'

'Hey Ben,' Danny called. 'Smoko time, mate.'

'This lot's nearly done, Danny, I'll be with you in a minute.'

'You're keen,' Bluey said when the other man dropped the iron bar and came to join them at the fire. 'I'm glad of any excuse to stop dollying.'

'Bloody awful job,' Danny put in. 'But, hey! We're getting a public crusher.'

'When? Next Christmas?'

'The big companies are setting up their own, but I imagine they'll not be offering to put crushings through for the little blokes.'

'The Mt Charlotte's is pretty well set to go.'

'Even when we get a public one, the big mines will have great heaps of stuff ready. We might get a chance some time later in the year. I wouldn't give up on the old dollypot yet.'

'How's Steve going?' asked Ben. 'You said he was talking about giving it all away.'

'He was missin' his family, but now they're coming to join him. He's ordered some iron and hessian to build a proper house,' Bluey replied. 'Well, I'd better get back to the old grind or he'll reckon I'm slacking on it.'

'So long mate,' Danny said. 'Guess we'd better get back to work too.'

'It's about knock off time,' Danny called, when the sun dipped towards the horizon.

'Righto,' Ben replied, 'D' you think we've broken its back?'

'Yeah, broken mine too,' Danny groaned, putting down his tools and stretching, before going to stir up the campfire to boil water for another mug of black tea. As Ben joined him, Seamus threw himself down with a sigh.

'You'd think he'd been working hard all day,' Ben said.

'Oh, he has. He's been supervisin' us, y' know.'

It was Danny's turn to cook their dinner so, as the dog emitted a couple of gentle snores, Ben picked up a notebook and pencil to return to something he'd been trying to do for weeks. But Seamus stirred, lifted his head with a reproachful look in his yellow eyes then rose, shook himself and stalked away. Danny laughed. 'Caught you at it again, did he?'

'How the Hell does he know when I pick up a pencil? I thought he was asleep.'

'He feels you looking at him,' the other man said. 'Dogs got a sixth sense we human bein's lost long ago.'

'Better give up. The light's fading, anyway.'

'You're pretty good at drawin', Ben. Should get yourself some proper paper an' stuff.'

'Waste of money,' Ben grumbled.

That night, Ben and Danny wandered down to the ramshackle Club Hotel. Seeing Dave and Bluey at the bar, they wove their way through the noisy crowd.

'Hey, fellas,' Dave said. 'Glad you could come.'

'Pleased to, Dave. But what's the special occasion? You getting married or something?'

'Na, not yet anyway, Danny. Actually, it's my birthday, but I only remembered that because I signed the papers today to sell my mine. Got more than I ever thought I'd have. Enough to go home and buy myself a nice little farm, somewhere green and moist. Sick and tired of the heat and no water. Gippsland sounds promising.'

'Hey, Dave, How you goin' you old bastard?' A slurred voice interjected.

'I'm doin' grand, Jacko,' Dave replied. Then turning back to the newcomers, 'Better come get a drink before they drink it all. I'm shouting the bar.'

Over the din of raised voices, Ben asked if he was leaving Hannans straight away.

'As soon as the cheque's cleared and I can transfer the money to my bank back home. By the way, the buyers don't want my camp or any of my tools, so maybe drop by tomorrow and have a look. Might be some stuff you could use.'

'Thanks, Dave. Might do that.'

'Don't forget to write and let us know how you are once you get settled. Is there maybe a lady back there?'

'I'm hoping. I don't think she's got married or anything.'

'You should write and let her know you're coming back,' put in Bluey.

'I already have,' he laughed, before turning away and raising his voice, 'Hey, you fellas. Cut the racket.'

'Yeah,' a drawling voice cut through the noise, 'Shut the hell up. We can't hear ourselves think over here.'

'So,' came back from the rowdy crowd, 'Who are you tellin' to shut up?'

'You and your loud-mouthed mates, Bourke. You'll have the coppers pokin' their noses in, if you don't watch out.'

'Uh, Oh, Here comes one already.'

The noise dropped marginally as a constable stepped through the door, but Bourke was making it clear that he wasn't going to be told what to do. Leaning on the bar with his thumbs hooked into his belt, he was obviously looking for trouble.

'Would you like a drink, constable?' the barman asked.

'No thanks,' the young policeman replied. 'I'm on duty.'

'Evenin', Constable Purkiss,' Dave said, recognising the young policeman.

'Hello, Mr Jessop, Mr Longmore, Mr Drummond. Thanks for your help the other night. I'm just doing the rounds. All quiet in here?'

'Just a bunch of fellas having a good time,' Dave reassured him.

'What about that bloke?' the policeman replied with a nod towards Bourke. 'Thought he might be looking for a fight.'

'He seems to have cooled down,' Bluey said as the young fellow called for another drink.

However, as Ben had half expected, no sooner had the bobby left, than Bourke took his drink and strutted over to the group in the corner.

'Listen, you Yankee bastard. Don't go tellin' me what I can an' can't do. This is a public house. Public! Y' hear? That means you got no say in what anyone else does.'

'Yeah, so what y' gonna do about it?' the American asked, rising to his feet with his hand on the revolver stuck in his belt.

'He ain't gonna do nothin', the barman's roar silenced the crowd, as he rose from behind the bar with a shotgun aimed in the direction of the two men. 'I suggest you take your argument elsewhere, or shut up.'

The crowd, even the American's friends, scattered, leaving the two men alone to stand glowering at the barman, united in their resentment at the interruption.

'Well, come on outside if y'r not too lily-livered,' Bourke yelled, heading for the door.

The American went to follow, but was stopped by one of his mates. 'Better give me the gun, Tom. You won't need it to handle that young whippersnapper, an' I wouldn't like t' see you getting strung up if you use it.'

Shaking off the restraining hand, the angry man reached for his gun and the watchers gasped as he aimed at his unarmed friend for several seconds before, laughing, he flipped it over and handed it butt-first to his white-faced mate, before swaggering out the door.

As most of the crowd followed, the barman said, 'I guess that lot will make sure it's a fair fight. You fellas want another round, before I close up?

'Sure,' said Dave and Bluey in unison.

'No thanks,' Ben said. 'Think I've had enough. What about you, Danny? Ready to head home?'

'Better wait till that lot sorts 'emselves out,' O'Hara laughed, as loud shouting told them that the battle had begun.

A few minutes later, the crowd started to return, some laughing. Then there was a loud cheer as the two antagonists entered arm in arm, both sporting black eyes, and demanding everyone have a drink on them. Shrugging, Ben accepted the pannikin of lukewarm beer, not wanting to get on the wrong side of either of the two drunks.

Danny enjoyed lying in until sunrise on Sundays, but Ben was up at dawn as usual the next morning. After lighting the fire and setting the billy to boil, he whistled the dog and headed off to look for the horse he'd inherited from a prospector who died of typhoid. Ben, who'd survived the disease as a child, nursed the old man and promised to find and take care of his horse.

That was no easy task that first terrible summer, with horses dying of thirst and starvation because the owners could not provide for them. But old Walter learned to survive on the scrub and sniff out any water that could be found. Then, when the scorching heat dried up the last water holes, he'd wandered in one day, scarecrow thin. Buying extra water and feed for Walter was Ben's only extravagance.

Though he was allowed to roam free, Walter had a weakness for the bag of oats Ben kept in the brush-covered lean-to verandah, so never wandered far these days.

Danny had the billy boiling and was making johnnycakes for breakfast by the time Ben returned.

'Looks like you didn't have far to go, Ben.'

'No, he was heading home.' Then to the horse, 'Needin' some oats, eh, boy?'

'That old bag of bones will leave you broke one day if the gold runs out,' Danny complained, but admitted to himself that he also had a soft spot for the rangy gelding.

'Here, horse, have one of these,' he went on, holding out one of the johnnycakes that had been cooling on the stone by the fire.

'Don't mind if I do,' said Ben, helping himself to one of the small, scone-like dampers, as the horse lipped the other from Danny's hand.

'So, where are you off to?'

'Well, like I told you, Humphries wants me to deliver some mail out to Broad Arrow, so I thought I'd have a look around out that way.'

'It's been pretty much picked over, but you might find something. Take plenty water.'

'Yes, Ma.' Ben laughed. 'I'll take the two waterbags. You've trained me pretty well.'

'I know, but you might meet some other poor devil who's needin' a drink. Heard they found the body of another poor sod out near Siberia. You be careful, mate.'

'G'day Danny, Ben gone bush again?' Bluey Longmore asked, as he wandered into the camp some time later.

'He's takin' some mail out to Broad Arrow for Humphries. Want a cuppa? Billy's boiling.'

'Thanks Danny,' Bluey replied, settling his lanky frame on one of the logs beside the fire as Danny tipped tea into the bubbling water.

'You and Ben go back a bit?' asked Bluey, as they sipped the hot drink.

'Couple of years now. Met up on the track. I tell y', I was a bit nervous when this big bloke offered to push my barrow if he could put his pack on it, but I was tuckered out and, after a good sniff, Seamus gave him a character reference.'

'Doesn't talk about himself much, does he?'

'Well, no. But neither do a lot of blokes out here. Most of us have things in our past we don't want noised around.'

'No, I guess you're right,' the other man replied.

'I used to worry about him wandering out in the bush but he's like the old horse, always find his way home. I think he spent some time outback over east. How're you fellas goin'?'

'We're makin' wages. Steve's family will be here in a week or so, so we're busy gettin' his house ready.'

Bluey wasn't the first to ask questions about Ben Drummond. 'Suppose they think after working together for two years, I really know the bloke,' Danny chuckled to himself after the other man left. Most men sooner or later gave you some inkling of their former life, though he had to admit he'd kept very quiet, himself, about how he first came to this country.

But no, Ben was different. It had taken him a long time to be comfortable with other blokes. Remembering his own worst experiences, Danny sometimes thought his mate might have spent time in prison. He had the old lag's dislike of enclosed spaces. Like Seamus, he preferred to sleep out under the stars.

Lighting up his pipe, he settled back in his bush-timber easy chair and picked up his book, but found it hard to get back into the story. So, slapping on his battered old hat, he called Seamus and the two meandered down to the town, the dog frequently stopping to investigate scent-messages left by other canine residents.

As usual on Sunday, the town was full of men taking a break from digging, dollying and dryblowing, those not already in the pubs clustered in small groups arguing or swapping tall stories. After talking to a few acquaintances, Danny was heading for the saloon he and his mates favoured, when he was hailed by a big, sandy-headed man outside the makeshift barbershop near the Club Hotel.

'G'day, Danny. Remember me? Gus Svensson? How you keepin'?'

'Oh, hello Gus. Haven't seen you around lately,' he replied.

'Me and Peter, we have a little show 'bout twenty-five miles out. Was good at first, but easy gold gone. Main reef all tied up an' leaseholder not very friendly. We are thinking maybe to be finding some place better.'

'Well, I've heard someone's onto something pretty rich back towards Coolgardie a way. Could be worth givin' it a look.'

'Might be better than a dead horse to be flogging.'

'Can I shout you a drink?'

'Thank you, Danny but I am needing to be getting back.'

'Well maybe go to the warden's office first and ask about that new find.'

'Yah, I might just be doing that. Nice talkin' t' you, Danny.'

'So long, Gus. Give my regards to Pete.'

Several hours later, hearing a distant 'Cooee', Peter Andersen shaded his eyes and stared down the track. As soon as he recognized the chestnut mare, he put the billy back on the fire and it was bubbling away nicely by the time Gus drew rein and slipped out of the saddle.

'Hullo, mate,' Anderson called, 'almost didn't recognise you without the whiskers.'

'Got a shave an' haircut. Anyway, I am running into old Danny O'Hara. He tells me about a big new find, out on the Coolgardie road, about nine miles. Supposed to be good, so here I come back quick to see what you think. This claim's not doing us any good, yah? Maybe, we give up? Leave it all to the silly hatter on the hill. Everyone else give up long ago.'

'Well we were getting a bit, back then, but we can't follow the reef with him holding the lease. If we get too close he's likely to take a pot-shot at us. Well, you know what they say about hatters, "Mad as". Reckon he's gone off his head out here all on his own.'

'Let's go, Peter. Sure we won't be missing our nasty neighbour.'

⌒

The man on the hill watched his neighbours' preparations to leave with a grim smile. It was just as well they were moving out. *Saves me the trouble of dealing with the nosey bastards.* It would've been a pleasure, though, he laughed, picking up his rifle to casually take aim at the big Swede loading equipment onto the dray.

Deciding he'd better see they didn't steal anything, he boiled the billy and sat to drink his tea at the rough table inside the door of his shack, so he could watch without being observed. *I wish it were me getting out of this godforsaken place,* he was thinking as he slurped the hot liquid. But it wouldn't be wise. Not yet. Bored with watching, he picked up the framed photograph that lay among the clutter on the table. The woman's picture had helped make the lonely hours easier. But he was not in the mood for fantasising, today.

Chapter 4

It was about twenty-five miles to the little settlement known as Broad Arrow, but Ben was in no hurry. He enjoyed riding through the bush on those bright, clear mornings with the scented air full of birdsong. Though the Australian outback had seemed strange and alien at first, it had welcomed him in his time of need, and now, in this red dirt country he found a strange solace.

He'd even started feeling at home in the rough and ready goldfields community. Nobody asked questions, but mates looked after each other. So, mostly, he was fine but, on occasions, feelings of hopelessness overwhelmed him. Drink didn't help. Just made him maudlin, so he kept off it when he was down. But there was nothing else to do but gamble on the two up, or the races and football matches so, that's when he went bush.

After giving Walter a chance to stretch his long legs in a canter over the flat, open country north of the town, he pulled him back to a trot.

'Don't want to wear yourself out, mate,' he told the horse. 'Better stay fresh for the trip back home.'

For a long time, he'd wanted to explore some of the broken country on the west side of the track, so turned Walter's head to follow a dry creek-bed running northwest. White-trunked gum trees bordered the winding strip of sand that would become a flowing stream only if, and when, enough rain fell.

Walter's hooves made little noise on the sandy creek-bed and they surprised a group of emus coming the other way. The leader stretched himself to his full height to stare down this strange double-headed creature before, deciding discretion was the better part of valour, he turned to lead his flock away at a tangent, long legs covering the ground.

With most of the trees and undergrowth gone, and hungry diggers hunting alternatives to tinned meat, wildlife had almost disappeared from around Hannans. But out in the bush, the animals showed little real fear of men. Though he shot the occasional roo or bird for food, Ben hated having to kill these fascinating creatures.

As they moved on, the gully swung around to the north, widening into another sandy creek-bed, shaded by white gums.

'Good place for a smoko,' he told the horse. Dismounting, he poured water from the waterbag into his hat for the horse, loosened the saddle's girth and let him loose. Hanging the wet hat on a twig to dry, he quickly gathered enough fuel to make a small fire.

When the water in his little billycan came to the boil, he tossed in some tea and poured himself a pannikin of the bitter liquid. Finding it a bit too hot, he pulled a little notebook and pencil from his pocket and sketched a girl's face. The tea was almost cold before he stopped to take a sip and check his work.

The eyes weren't right. And the smile. 'Why can't I ever draw her face?' he sighed. It seemed like she was doubly dead, when he couldn't properly remember her face.

Topping up his tea from the still-warm billy, he gnawed the dry damper-bread, his mind preoccupied with haunted memories, until a questioning whinny from his equine companion recalled him to the present.

'You're right, matey. Time to get up off my arse if we're going to get there and back today.'

He reached Broad Arrow about midday, and when news got around that he had brought mail, a small crowd gathered.

'Any for McCrae?' asked a stocky Scotsman.

'No, sorry,' Ben told him, then went on, 'it's probably best if I call out the names on these letters. Martin, Johnson, Smithers, Buchanan, Johnson, O'Donoghue, Shultz, Howard, and S. Wilson esquire. Is that you, Sam?' he asked as the familiar white-whiskered face of Danny's old friend appeared at the back of the crowd.

'That'll be me, Ben. How are you and Danny goin'? Still makin' wages?'

'We're doing pretty well, Sam,' Ben replied, handing out the mail to the others.

'Come an' have some tucker at my place,' Sam said, 'Oh, an' I've got a couple of letters meself. Maybe you could post them for me.'

'No trouble, Sam. The post office is likely to be open today as the coach is due.'

Sam was interested to hear what had been happening in the 'new camp' as he called Hannans. Coolgardie being 'the old camp'.

'Y' never know,' he laughed, 'we might start giving you Hannanites a run for your money soon, the way this little place is goin' ahead.

'Yes,' Ben replied, 'I'm surprised how big the Arrow is now.'

He was also surprised at the meal Sam served up.

'Got a shot at this wild turkey,' Sam explained. 'He was sittin' out the back just asking to become someone's dinner. Bloody big bird, so I shared the meat with my mates. I been tryin' out some of them herby things that grow on the salt lake. Was worried I might poison meself, but so far, so good. So I put some in the stuffing.'

'It's really tasty, Sam. You ought to get a job cooking for one of the big pubs.'

'Couldn't stand livin' in town these days. The bush is the place for me. Have some more, lad. It'll just go off if I keep it.'

'I don't think I could manage any more, Sam. And I'd better start heading home. Where are the letters you want posted?'

'Here, mate. One each to my sister's girls. Well, they're not girls anymore. I think one's already a granny,' he added with a chuckle.

'You'll give my regards to Danny, won't you?' he went on, following Ben out to where Walter was tethered in the shade of a rough bough shelter.

'Of course,' Ben replied, lifting the saddle into place and fastening the girth strap. 'He'll be pleased to hear you're keeping well.'

After checking the bridle, Ben shook hands with the old fellow and swung into the saddle. With a brief wave of his hand, he turned Walter's head towards the Hannans track.

⌒

That morning, after a sleepless night trying to ignore the yelling, fighting and drunken curses on the other side of the thin, tin hotel wall, Nora had found a crowd of men milling about the Coolgardie Cobb and Co. office. But it wasn't until she was back in the coach that she realised they were all climbing aboard. News

36

of a rich find somewhere to the northeast had set off a new rush. Five men squeezed inside with yesterday's train passengers who were going on to Hannans and a dozen more were perched precariously on the outside.

The squash eased when the coach stopped to unload them and their gear at a lonely spot marked by some blazed trees and a rudimentary track, apparently leading somewhere. Their excitement was contagious and a couple of the inside passengers decided to join them.

'That's better,' said old Mr Morrison, sighing as he stretched out his injured leg. 'These coaches are only supposed to hold eight. Here, Blake, how about you move over this side so Mrs Patterson can have the window seat.'

Nora was glad to move. It was embarrassing to be squashed between two strange men and, tired out after the long journey and sleepless night, she was afraid she might doze off and wake with her head on one of their shoulders. Now that she could lean on the coach wall, her eyelids drooped and an hour passed before she awoke to hear they were nearing their destination.

Advertisements for hotels, stores and other businesses at Hannans had appeared in the Perth papers, but the only signs they were approaching a town were hundreds of tents, some with hand-written signs she couldn't read. A rough bough shed with a forge was obviously a blacksmith's shop. Then came a larger tent, surrounded by piles of tin dishes, picks, shovels and bags of chaff, which had a wooden sign proclaiming it to be a general store. The rambling canvas and hessian structure with crowds of men standing about drinking from bottles and tin pannikins could only be a pub. More tent shops, some larger and better appointed, trailed along either side of the road, and now came another hotel, the Club. Though mainly constructed of the ubiquitous hessian, it sported a tin roof and verandah.

There seemed to be hundreds of bewhiskered men wandering about, their clothes stained a uniform russet colour from the red earth, and Nora realised that Hannans was a bustling town, despite the lack of anything that looked like a permanent building.

With a loud 'Whoa, there!' the coach driver pulled his team to a halt outside a tent with a large Cobb and Co. sign, shouting 'Hannans', unnecessarily, as the dust-covered occupants untangled their stiffened limbs and prepared to emerge. Old Mr Morrison got out first and, with much creaking of arthritic joints, helped Nora down from the coach onto the soil of what would one day be known as The Golden Mile.

Thanking him, she looked around excitedly, expecting to see Ned. Surely he'd got the telegram saying she'd be arriving today. But there was no sign of him, so she stood waiting, aware that she was an item of interest to the crowd of men who'd come to meet the coach.

After a while, Jack Hughes, the Cobb and Co clerk, brought out a packing case for her to sit on, apologizing for it not being a real chair and for the fact that her trunk hadn't arrived.

'Is someone meeting you, Ma'am?' he asked.

'My husband. He was supposed to meet me here.'

'He'll be along soon, then. Word gets around pretty soon that the coach is in,' he assured her.

It was embarrassing and a little scary, sitting there with all the men watching her, and she got the feeling word had spread that a strange woman was in town so they'd all come to have a look. Most politely acknowledged her presence by raising their hats, but some stared as if they'd never seen a woman before.

After an hour or so, Hughes, surprised to find she was still there, came back with a worried frown and suggested she go to the post office to see if her husband had left a message for her. 'He mightn't be able to get into town today, if his lease is a long way out,' he said.

'I think it's near a place called Siberia,' Nora said, causing the man's frown to deepen and several bystanders to feel the need to crowd around offering advice. Looking up at them as they towered over her, their tall forms silhouetted against the sun, Nora felt intimidated despite their obvious good intentions.

'Siberia's sure a long way out,' said one.

'Lots of blokes got lost out there and ended up doin' a perish,' another man put in.

'Better try the police, Missus, if he doesn't turn up soon,' said a lanky redhead.

'The Post Office will be open, as the coach has just brought the mail,' said Jack Hughes. 'Check there first, Mrs Patterson. He might have left a message for you.'

Shaking off the other men's offers to escort her, Nora set off with a sinking heart, to where a sign identified another tent as the post office.

Ben leaned on the hitching rail outside the Post Office finishing his smoke, as the young woman passed by. *Must've just arrived*, he thought, as she disappeared inside. Her blouse was too white to have been very long at the diggings, where everything was soon turned to shades of pink by the red dust.

A glimpse of the red-gold curls piled under the girl's hat stabbed at his heart. But she was taller, with toffee brown eyes, not blue. Stubbing out the cigarette, he followed her inside in time to hear her asking, 'Do you have any letters for Mrs Edward Patterson? Or a message?'

'We haven't had time to sort the mail that's just come on the coach, Missus, but I'll see if there's anything already here,' said Bob Humphries.

After sorting through a pile of letters in a bulging pigeonhole, he came back holding three envelopes. 'None for a Mrs Patterson, but there are three for a Mr Edward Patterson, would that be your husband?'

'Yes. May I have a look? Oh these are my letters. Why hasn't he collected them? I sent a telegram care of the post office too, has he got that?'

'I'll have a look. Yes, here's one, from Fremantle – says you've arrived, and another from Perth the day you left. I'm sorry, but he hasn't received them either. Was he living here at Hannans? Might be out at one of the other diggings. Some men don't get to town very often.'

'But he was supposed to meet me here. Oh, what am I to do?' she asked with a catch in her voice.

'Try the Police Station, Ma'am. They might know his whereabouts,' Bob suggested, then watched her walk to the door with a worried frown, before turning his attention back to the other customers.

'Hello, Ben. Thanks for delivering that mail. Did you have any trouble finding all those blokes?'

'No, Bob. They're all still there, and Sam Wilson asked me to bring these letters in. Don't suppose there's anything for me.'

'Sorry, mate. Nothing yet.'

He hadn't really expected any, just hoped someone at home might reply to his letter. *After seven years, they might all be dead,* he was thinking as he mounted Walter and headed for their camp.

It was a welcoming sight. A shady oasis on the outskirts of the dusty town. Danny, who'd seen other goldfields devastated when trees were cut down to timber shafts or fuel steam engines on the big mines, had insisted they leave some untouched. The camp itself was just one big hessian-clad room, plus a bough shed thatched with mulga branches. They mostly lived outdoors, even in winter when the early mornings could be frosty, but the new corrugated iron roof extended out to make a narrow verandah, which was where Ben and the dog, Seamus, preferred to sleep most of the year.

Now iron's cheaper, maybe we can put up a fireproof kitchen, he was thinking. It wasn't safe to have a fire inside hessian and thatched buildings, so they still cooked on the outdoor campfire.

As he swung out of the saddle, Seamus gambolled out with a great doggy grin to prance around him. Big shaggy paws landed on his shoulders and a pink tongue sloshed across his face.

'Down, fella,' he said, 'No need to make a fuss. I've only been away since this morning.'

'Hey there, Ben,' Danny said, 'like a cuppa?'

'I sure would, Danny. Gets a bit dry out there. Sam Wilson's still at the Arrow. He sends his regards.'

By the time he'd unsaddled, fed and watered Walter, Danny had stoked up the fire and was tossing tealeaves into the boiling water. Armed with pannikins of the strong, dark liquid, the two men settled quietly beside the campfire, Danny on his bush armchair, Ben lounging on the ground with his back against a log.

For a while, only the sounds of the bush and the crackling of the fire intruded on Ben's thoughts. That was one of the things he liked about his old mate. He never bombarded you with questions about where you'd been. He'd sit quietly sipping his tea or sucking his pipe until you felt like talking.

'How was your day, mate?' Ben asked, finally.

'Not too bad. Been takin it easy. Took a stroll down town an' had a drink with a couple of mates. Ran into Gus Svensson, you remember him? Big Swedish fella? Sounds like their little show's a fizzog. Told him about that new rush.'

'I do remember him. Mate's name is Pete?'

'Yeah.'

Ben was glad not to be asked about his day. He'd been all right until he went to the Post Office. Maybe his letter had gone astray. Thinking about having to try to write again had stirred up the old memories he mostly managed to keep locked away.

Chapter 5

With some apprehension, Nora walked into the canvas police station to find a harassed constable standing behind a rough plank desk.

'Yes?' he asked, grumpily. Then seeing his visitor was an attractive young lady, he modified his tone and attempted a smile. 'What can I do for you Ma'am?'

'Hello Constable, I think my husband, Edward Patterson, has gone missing. I just arrived on the stagecoach, but he's not here to meet me, and he hasn't received the letters and telegrams I sent him.'

'Did he know you were coming? Most men don't expect to see their wives turn up out here.'

'Yes,' she replied. 'He wrote asking me to come and sent money.'

'Well, if you are sure he was expecting you, I imagine he'll be here soon. All I can do is put his name in our Missing Persons and Friends book. As you can see, a lot of people are trying to trace men who seem to have disappeared.'

Some don't want to be found, he was thinking, a barely-mapped goldfield is the perfect place to hide from your wife, your creditors, or from us. He didn't want to upset the young woman, but most likely the husband had done a runner.

'Where are you staying, Mrs Patterson? We can let you know if we hear of him.'

'I don't know,' she replied, 'I just arrived.'

'Try Mrs McPherson's boarding house. A couple of doors up from the Club Hotel.'

Annoyed that he didn't take Ned's disappearance more seriously, Nora stepped out onto the road, just as a camel team loaded with creaking bundles of corrugated iron sheets blundered past, filling the air with choking red dust. As she staggered back coughing, a hand grasped her arm and a gruff voice said, 'Easy Miss, it's only a camel train. Nothin' to be scared of.'

Then, as she wiped at her eyes and groped in her purse for a handkerchief, the voice went on. 'Copped a load of dust, did you? Gotta shut your eyes when a camel train goes by.'

Blinking and dabbing at her eyes, she turned to thank her rescuer. There was nothing memorable about him except for the pale blue gaze lingering on her chest. Fearing her blouse had come unbuttoned, she reassured herself with a quick glance, thanked him and walked quickly away to find the rambling hessian boarding house. She was eager to get inside away from the curious glances of so many men, but all the rooms were taken.

'I think Mrs Bunning might have a room, dear,' the landlady told her. 'It's about halfway down town on your left.'

So, once again, she was forced to run the gauntlet of male stares and hurry along the road, her heavy carpetbag bumping against her leg. Most of the men politely stepped aside, touching their hats, but a few seemed to go out of their way to confront her, or brush close as they passed. She was sure she felt a couple of attempts at a pinch through the layers of skirt and petticoat.

After failing to find something resembling a boarding house among the dust-reddened tents and humpies, Nora gave up and asked an old man sitting on a keg outside a particularly dilapidated tent where she might find Mrs Bunning's boarding house.

'Well...' he replied, stopping to remove the pipe from his mouth to point with, 'you'll be havin' to go back to the Coolgardie road, turn right and you'll find it up near the police tent.'

Thanking him, she retraced her steps, wondering how she could have missed it, then realised that it must be one of the hessian shanties she'd passed earlier without noticing the cardboard signs above some of the doors. Mrs Bunning's place was indistinguishable from the rest, except that its sign read "Full Board. Water Extra." A knock on the frame of the hessian door brought a small, round lady bustling to the entrance.

'Mrs Bunning?' Nora asked.

'Yes.'

'I've just arrived in town and need somewhere to stay for a few days.'

'We're really full up, but I could let you have my son's room for three nights, then he'll be back from Southern Cross.'

'Oh, thank you. I don't think I'll need it longer than that. My husband is supposed to be meeting me, but must have been held up.'

'That'll be fourteen shillings, please.'

As Nora hesitated about handing over most of her remaining money, the lady went on, 'That's twelve and sixpence for the room and all meals. Plus sixpence a day for water.'

'Water is extra?' Nora asked, 'Can I have a bath, then?'

'I'm afraid not, dear. I can only afford a few gallons each day. That's enough for drinking, cooking and a jug-full for each guest for hand-washing.'

As the comforting thought of soaking in a warm tub faded, Nora accepted the inevitable and paid up. She was shown into a tiny, lean-to room with a camp stretcher covered by a rough grey blanket, one chair and a small rickety table, on which lay a tin dish. Well, it was a refuge for a few days and surely Ned would arrive before she got thrown out on the street with only a few shillings in her purse. Relieved to be out of the sun and the public gaze, she plonked her bag on the bed. All it held was a sponge bag, a change of bloomers, a spare blouse, a nightdress and a small photograph of Ned. Everything else was in her trunk, which seemed to have disappeared *en route* from Southern Cross.

She knew she should keep looking for Ned, or at least go back to the coach office and leave a message to say where she was, but she was so tired. Sitting on the bed, she pulled off her boots, lay back on the hard mattress and was instantly asleep.

It was dusk when she was woken by the delicious smell of roasting meat and onions, and Mrs Bunning' voice calling that dinner was ready. Climbing groggily off the bed, she put on her boots, tidied her hair in the tiny mirror hanging on the wall and went out to meet her fellow boarders, who Mrs Bunning introduced as Mr Timms, Mr Griffiths, Mr Campbell and Mr Vernon.

Mr Timms, it seems, was a clerk at one of the big mines, while young Mr Griffiths worked at a general store. Mr Vernon explained that he and Mr Campbell were both in Hannans to work at the Mine Warden's office.

'The warden, Mr Jephson, has been given extra responsibilities on top of his mining work. He's now Resident

Magistrate, sub-collector of taxes, official stamp seller and local court magistrate, so we've been sent up here to help,' said Mr Vernon.

She went to bed early, but the uncomfortable bed and the shouts and cursing of drunken men outside her window kept her awake until well after midnight.

The glow of sunrise was seeping through the hessian walls when she awoke next morning to the rhythmic pounding of an ore-crushing battery. Unable to sleep with the noise, she got up. After washing her face in her small allowance of water, she brushed and put up her long hair before unpacking her clean clothes and getting dressed. The blouse she'd been travelling in was very dirty, the neckline and underarms stained with red dirt. Pulling on her boots, she went into the dining room, where Mrs Bunning was laying the table for breakfast.

'Hello Mrs Patterson,' said the landlady, 'breakfast won't be long.'

'Good morning, Mrs Bunning. I'll be going out for a while this morning. I need to go back to the coach office and let Mr Hughes know that my husband might come looking for me.'

'I hope he turns up today, my dear.'

'So do I, Mrs Bunning,' she replied.

'Well take a seat. Breakfast will be ready soon. I know it's a bit too hot for porridge, but the men like a big breakfast so I've made some. And there'll be bacon and beans. Sorry no eggs.'

'Oh, I'll be happy with some tea and toast, Mrs Bunning.'

As the other boarders consumed large servings of porridge followed by bacon and beans, Nora sat nibbling her toast and thinking of all the mishaps that might have befallen her husband. Surely he would come today.

Returning to her room, she pinned on her hat, took up her purse and stepped out through the front door of the boarding house. The air was clearer than yesterday with an early morning breeze blowing away the dust that lingered over the diggings. Lifting her skirt to avoid it dragging in the dirt, and keeping her eyes out for horse manure and dog droppings, she walked down the edge of the road. There was no footpath as such, only a well-trodden pathway safe from the constant stream of wagons and camel trains that clattered by, raising clouds of red dust. A lot of men were wandering around the town, but not the crowds that had been there yesterday.

The roadway was very wide and the trees that had been left in the centre supplied a shady place for dozing dogs and groups of men who stood talking. Even near the hotels, it was much quieter, with only a few drunks lounging around outside the one near the coach office.

When she knocked on the doorpost, Hughes looked up to say, 'Good morning. Mrs Patterson, isn't it?'

'Yes Mr Hughes. I wonder if my husband, Ned Patterson, came looking for me yesterday,' she asked hopefully.

'I'm sorry Mrs Patterson,' he replied. 'I haven't seen him, or anyone else, looking for you.'

'Well, if he does turn up, can you tell him I'm at Mrs Bunning's boarding house, please?'

'Of course, I'll be happy to do that,' he replied, though he was beginning to think maybe the husband had run off. It had happened before. Shame, she seemed to be a nice young woman, besides being very pretty.

After leaving her message, she went on to the Police Station, but there was no news of Ned. As she stepped out of the tent, a crow alighted on the hitching post, looked her up and down, then flew off with a derisive caw.

Back at the boarding house, she asked Mrs Bunning if she could get extra water to wash her blouse. 'It's very dirty after travelling for so many days, and I don't have any more changes until my trunk arrives. It must have been left behind at Southern Cross.'

'I can sell you some water, but I could put it through with the washing I'm doing this morning, Mrs Patterson. I won't charge extra. It won't make much difference to me, I've got a whole lot to wash. I can't guarantee they won't all be pink when they're finished, though, because of the red dust.'

'Thank you, Mrs Bunning. I'd really appreciate that. Can I help?' asked Nora.

'You could help me hang them out later, if you're not going out again.'

'I think I'd better stay here in case my husband comes looking for me.'

As the hours of the day dragged by with no sign of Ned, she was glad of the chance to help with the washing, as it took her mind off her worries. But as evening came with still no sign of him, she could no longer tell herself that all was well. With the evening meal over, she slipped away to her room to avoid having to make conversation. But getting to sleep was not easy, as increasingly alarming explanations for her husband's absence crept into her mind.

It was still dark next morning when she awoke, dozily thankful that she had only one more night of sleeping on the creaking camp stretcher, until reality struck and she sat up, wide awake.

'Oh my God,' she whispered, 'Tomorrow, I'll have nowhere to go. Oh, Ned, where are you?

Could he really have abandoned her? What if he was out there somewhere dying of thirst or sick with typhoid. Could he have taken his own life, knowing she had betrayed him? No! Who could have told him? But if something bad had happened to Ned, maybe it was her punishment.

I'll have to start looking for him. Someone must know where he's gone. 'And where in this God-forsaken place is my trunk?' she muttered as she shook out her stained and crumpled clothes.

She had no appetite for breakfast but forced herself to sit and eat some toast before hurrying down to the Cobb and Co tent, only to find it closed, as the next coach didn't arrive until Thursday. With no good news at the Post Office or the Police Station, she went into the busiest of the ramshackle general stores. It was jam-packed with all sorts of goods, from bags of flour and tins of kerosene to men's working clothes and heaps of tinned food. Several men in moleskins, who were buying stores to go prospecting, touched their hats and stood back to let her be first served.

'Oh, thank you, I won't take long. I just wanted to ask if anyone remembers my husband, Ned Patterson. I've got a picture of him here,' Nora said, handing the photograph to the shopkeeper.

'Can't say I recognise him, Ma'am, but then not many of my customers are clean-shaven. Do any of you fellas know this bloke?' he called, and the men all crowded around.

'Dunno. Give him a beard and a scruffy old hat and he'd look like a lot of blokes out here.'

'Looks a bit like that Freddy Cartwright, out at the Six-mile, don't y' think, Tom?' put in a tall man who was leaning over her shoulder to peer at the photo. 'Has y' husband got a wooden leg, Missus?'

'No.'

'Ah, well Freddy has, so it can't be him.'

It was pretty much the same story at all the stores. It seemed Ned looked a bit like a lot of men. Jackie Whatsit, Herb Something-or-other, or just Whatsisname out at Burdong.

She went back to the boarding house for lunch, feeling very downhearted. Surely someone must have seen Ned or talked to him. Though she could see the problem. Most of the men did look alike with half their faces covered in whiskers and identical dirt-stained clothes. Some were short and some were tall, with black, red, or fair beards, but about half were Ned's size.

In the afternoon, trying not to hear the comments, some admiring, some embarrassingly explicit, of the drunks lounging outside, she enquired at some of the pubs, but found no one who knew Ned.

'Ooh, What a looker! I think I'd remember him if ever I seen him,' said one of the blowsy barmaids.

Having asked at the shops and all but the most disreputable-looking hotels, by late afternoon, Nora knew Ned wasn't in Hannans. Maybe he was sick. She shuddered to think of him lying sick in a tent out in the scrub with no one to care for him. There'd been a typhoid epidemic on the goldfields, she knew.

But, if he didn't turn up, she had only one more night at the boarding house. Tomorrow, she must find somewhere else to stay. After counting the coins in her money purse twice, and frantically searching its folds and corners, she had to accept that she only had five shillings to her name. Anywhere cheaper than Mrs Bunning's place could hardly be suitable for a woman on her own in a rough town like Hannans. She'd have to try to find work, preferably live-in.

One of the bar owners had offered her a job as a "singing barmaid". The wages offered were far too good to be true. What were you expected to do besides sing? Walking back to the boarding house, she heard music coming from one of the hessian pubs and peered in through the open shutter. There was no window.

A scantily clad waitress was wandering about with a tray full of glasses, singing a rather bawdy song and pretending to avoid the pats and pinches of the already inebriated customers. So that's what a singing barmaid did! Nora shuddered. Surely, she could find something more respectable. Back at the boarding house, she asked Mrs Bunning about live-in work.

'Well, one of the mine managers might be looking for a housekeeper, or else look for a barmaid's job in one the better pubs.'

The thought was very daunting. She'd never been anywhere like this place. Everywhere she looked, there seemed to be dozens of unkempt men wandering about, many of them intoxicated, some staggering drunk, and all showing a frightening amount of interest in her.

She was too worried to really enjoy Mrs Bunning's tasty cottage pie, but the other boarders soon demolished extra helpings and the date pudding that followed. Afterwards, she got into conversation with the two men from the Mine Warden's office.

'Do you have records of all the mining claims?'

'Well, the warden's office should have them, but everything's still a bit unsettled. The office is just another of those hessian humpies. Was there a particular reason you wanted to know?'

'Yes, my husband wrote to tell me he'd found gold, so must have registered a claim. He asked me to come, but when I arrived, he wasn't here. He must have been held up, but I thought if I knew where his mine was, I could go out there. I'm a bit worried that he might be sick. I've heard there's a lot of fever around.'

'I think the police might have a copy of the register,' put in the other man. 'Perhaps check with them tomorrow.

Chapter 6

'Water's getting low Ben,' said Danny, bending to bail some from the bottom of their small tank to fill the billycan.

'Yes,' Ben said, 'I'd better take the cart out to the condensers and get some tomorrow. How much are they charging now? Have you heard?'

'I think it's gone down to fourpence a gallon, so two pounds should fill the tank.'

'Tell you what, I'll go down to Courthope's today and put in our order. That'll save having to talk Walter into being a carthorse twice in the same week. I can go and pick it up after I get the water.

Late that afternoon, he strolled down town, taking a wide detour to avoid two dogs who circled each other, legs stiff, teeth bared, cursing in low growls. Only a matter of time before a fight started, he was thinking, when a whip cracked and a yelping dog shot past, a bleeding stripe across its rump.

Poor bloody dog! No need for that. He turned to see who'd been responsible for the unnecessary cruelty. *That Yankee idiot, Tom Tucker.* A mate of one of Danny's friends, Ben had only met the man a couple of times and felt an instant dislike.

Hurrying on to avoid talking to the bloke, he almost collided with a young woman coming out of the store. Tipping his hat, he stepped back with an apology. As she hurried away, he remembered where he'd seen her before. She'd been in the Post Office the other day looking for someone. Oh yes, her husband. *Wonder if she found him?*

He walked inside in time to hear someone ask, 'What was that fella's name again, Mike?'

'Patterson,' replied the man behind the counter. 'Don't remember him, but we've had hundreds of blokes through the doors over the last few months.'

'Well, if I had a wife like her, I wouldn't want her wandering around a rough place like Hannans on her own.'

'Me, neither. Hello Ben, what can I do for you?'

'G'day, Mike. We need a bag of sugar, one of flour, two bags of chaff, one of cracked oats, and a tin of kero, thanks. Guess we'd better have a case of canned meat as well. I'll be back tomorrow with the cart to pick it up if that's all right with you.'

'That'll be fine, mate. We'll get it ready for you."

By the flickering light of the campfire, that evening, Ben attempted to read the Coolgardie Miner, while Danny, holding his book, Stevenson's *Kidnapped*, inches from his nose, followed the adventures of David Balfour until the fire began to die down.

Putting the book aside, Danny lit up his pipe, so Ben pulled out the makings and rolled a cigarette. As they quietly smoked, the only sounds were the crackling of the fire and the soft murmuring twitters of birds settling down for the night.

'Mind if I tootle a tune or two, Ben?' Danny asked, pulling a tin whistle from his pocket.

'No, of course not,' Ben replied, from where he reclined on the ground. 'Maybe something cheerful. I'm not sure I can take sad songs tonight.'

'Well, I'll see if I can brighten things up for you,' his mate said, launching into a merry tune Ben recognized as a very bawdy song. But he wasn't in the mood to hum along and after a couple of verses Danny put the whistle away.

'You didn't have to stop, Danny. I'm sorry I'm such a miserable bastard.'

'It's all right, mate. I think I'll turn in anyway.'

'I might as well hit the hay too,' Ben said. 'In the morning, I'll round Walter up and go out for the water first thing, then pick up our stuff from Courthope's. G'night, mate.'

Having checked the fire was out and accompanied Seamus on his nightly patrol, Ben sat on the bed watching the dog's bedtime ritual.

'You sure you've turned around the right number of times?' he asked, receiving just a grunt in response.

Stripping off his outer clothes, he lay back on the bed, watching the stars until sleep came, and the old dream.

'You have to go, dear.'

'I wish I didn't, sweetheart.'

'Don't worry, dear. Baby's not due for ages...'

As their lips touch, darkness falls on her face and her mouth opens in a scream. A scream echoed by others. Hoof-beats pound the earth. He runs to save the naked dark woman she's become. A sabre flashes in the dying light and the head is gone. Gore splatters, engulfing the still, white, bloodless body he holds in his arms.

'Ben! Ben, Are you all right, mate?"

As the voice penetrated the chilling horror, Ben woke, to hear himself screaming. Stuffing his fist in his mouth, he shook off his mate's restraining hands to blunder out into the darkness, Seamus padding after him.

Awakened by the touch of a cold, wet nose on his face, Ben opened his eyes to daylight and the concerned yellow gaze of Seamus.

'Mornin' old fella,' he murmured, draping his arm around the furry neck. 'I'm all right now, better get up. Got to get the water today.'

Some coughing and a loud yawn from inside warned him that his mate was awake. Would Danny say anything about last night? It wasn't the first time he'd had the dream, but mostly he'd managed to wake up before squealing like a stuck pig. Rolling out of bed, he pulled on his shirt and dungarees before going to stir up the embers of the campfire, then headed to the woodheap.

'Mornin' Ben,' Danny called, emerging from the hessian shanty as Ben returned with an armful of mulga roots.

'Mornin' Danny,' he said, avoiding his friend's eyes as he tossed the wood on the fire. 'I'll go get the water this morning.'

'Righto,' Danny said, putting the billy on the fire. 'Looks like another fine morning.'

Ben sighed, his hopes fading that the subject of his bad dream wouldn't be mentioned. When Danny started talking about the weather, he had serious things on his mind. 'I'm sorry about last night Danny,' he said. 'There's just some old miseries that creep up on me at night. I'll try not to disturb you again.'

'Well, from what I know of bad dreams, you don't have much choice. I've had my share of them in my time. So, if you need to yell, go ahead. Seamus and me, we don't mind. And if ever you want to talk about it. Well, we're here.'

'Thanks Danny.'

'I know you don't like getting drunk, mate, but maybe a shot of whisky at night might help you sleep better.'

'I don't know. Usually booze just makes me miserable,' Ben replied, tossing tealeaves in the billy. 'So, what will it be for breakfast, beans and bacon, or just plain beans,' he asked, trying to laugh.

When Ben dropped in to ask Mary if she wanted him to get her some water, Joey helped put their drum on the cart and jumped at the chance of a ride out to the condensers. As he'd hoped, Ben let him drive the cart.

'I like drivin' Walter,' he said. 'Maybe I'll be a wagon-driver when I grow up.'

'Well there's plenty work for drivers now, since the big mines started up. Lots of machinery arriving nearly every day.'

'Yeah, all them big wheels for the poppet heads, stampers for the rock crushers, an' boilers for the condensers. You'd get lots of money drivin' them wagons.'

'It's a hard job, though.'

'Maybe if I got really good, I could drive the stagecoach. That'd be a bonza job. Drivin' them teams an' not havin' to carry heavy, dirty loads.'

Having filled the drums and paid for the water, Ben took over to drive the heavily laden cart back to town and Joey returned to the subject of his future occupation.

'Timmy says he's going to work on a mine as soon as he's old enough. He hates workin' for his pa. But mining's too much bloody hard work.'

'There are worse jobs.'

'Yeah, his old man's talkin' about putting' in for the sanit'ry contractor job. His Ma reckons no one will buy her cool drinks if Pa Kenny's the dunnyman.'

'She could be right about that. But someone will have to do it. It's about time they did something about the stinking cesspits in town.'

'But there'll always be plenty work drivin' horses, won't there?'

'I don't know,' Ben replied. 'I saw in the paper that someone's invented a horseless carriage.'

'That'd be really weird, wouldn't it, t' see a carriage going along with no horses.'

'And they reckon they can make a flying machine too.'

'Maybe I could drive a flyin' machine's when I grow up. That'd be bonza.'

✧

After a sleepless night worrying about Ned and her own precarious situation, Nora awoke late, groggy and tearful. By the time she was dressed and had done her hair, she hoped her eyes were slightly less puffy. But Mrs Bunning, who was making early breakfast for her boarders, took one look and made her sit down with a cup of tea.

Forcing down a piece of toast, she returned to her room to pack up her meagre possessions. Pinning on her hat, she took up her carpetbag and stepped out onto the dusty street to continue searching for Ned and for some live-in work.

Her first stop was the Post Office, in the vain hope that a letter from Ned might have arrived since she last asked. But, as the man behind the desk explained, there was no regular mail from the outlying finds.

'Sometimes a returning digger brings a letter to post for one of his mates, but some of these places aren't even on the map.'

From there, Nora walked on to the police tent and was lucky to find the constable she'd met before, Constable Purkiss, manning the desk.

'Good morning, Mrs Patterson,' he said with a friendly smile, 'I'm afraid we have no news of your husband. But,' he went on, lifting a large book from under the desk, 'we do have records of all the claims around Hannans and it seems he did register one back in October. There's a description of its location, but it's a bit vague.'

Opening the book to a marked place, he peered at the crabbed writing, brows knitted.

'It's definitely out Siberia way, but the trouble is there are no marked landmarks. It says ten miles from the turn off to Reison's and 500 yards northwest of a line from the conical hill where there's a breakaway. Not very helpful. I'll see if any of the others can pinpoint it on a map.'

'How many conical hills are there out there?' Nora asked.

'Dozens I imagine. Not many prospectors have the skill to survey the area properly. If we work out approximately where it is, maybe one of us can find the claim next time we are patrolling out there. Trouble is, we don't even have enough officers to police the town now all the riffraff are moving in.'

Completely disheartened, she thanked him and wandered out into the glaring sunlight, startling a crow pecking at garbage in the gutter. She could no longer put off the urgent task of finding work. Taking a deep breath, she straightened her back and entered the hotel next door.

'I'm looking for work,' she told the barkeeper. 'Is the owner around?'

'I'm the owner, lassie,' he told her, 'but sorry, there's no jobs. My wife does all the woman's work. Y' could try the pub over the road.'

It was pretty much the same story there, and at all the hotels and taverns. There weren't many women in town, but neither were there many jobs for them, so all the respectable barmaid jobs were taken. She asked about cooking and other kitchen jobs but there was nothing. Many of the pubs employed Chinese or Indian men as cooks.

By midday, she was exhausted, thirsty and hungry. Afraid to spend any of her remaining cash, even a shilling for a drink of water, she was thankful that a friendly shopkeeper had given her a drink.

'I guess it'll have to be the singing barmaid job, she finally admitted to herself, but when she returned to the pub, that job was gone.

Chapter 7

'Whoa, boy,' Ben called, pulling up outside Courthope's store. As he tossed the reins over the hitching rail, a woman hurried past. Catching a brief glimpse of her face, he thought it was that Mrs Patterson who'd been looking for her husband. She didn't look happy, so maybe the bloke hadn't turned up. Shrugging, he walked into the store.

'G'day Ben,' the shop assistant said. 'You come for your order? Got it all ready.'

'Thanks, Mike.'

'Glad to see you're looking after old Walter,' Mike laughed, as he helped load the heavy produce bags into the cart.

'He's not happy today,' Ben replied. 'We've already been out to the condensers, and he thinks pulling a cart is beneath him. Don't you, mate?' he went on, giving the long nose a rub.

Back at camp, he called out to Danny, but no answer. Calling again, he ran to the mine.

'You down there?' he called.

'Yes, lad. Think I'm onto a new leader.'

'For God's sake, Danny,' Ben muttered, as he went to unload the stores. *I wish he'd not go underground when I'm not here.*

By the time he'd unharnessed and rubbed down Walter, he was relieved to see his mate's head pop up out of the mine.

'Found a good patch down there, Ben. Be a few bucketfuls to bring up after we've had a bite to eat.'

'Goodoh,' Ben said, 'I got a loaf of bakers' bread while I was down town, and some cheese.'

'Be a change from damper an' dripping.'

'The baker's selling currant buns too.'

'It's gettin' real civilised up here lately. We'll all be gettin' soft.'

'Not you. You're a tough old bugger.'

'That's from livin' on corned beef an' damper for years.'

'Might get more real meat now. The squatters are driving flocks of sheep out here.'

'Wouldn't think it'd be worth their while. If the poor things are livin' on scrub an' going without water, the meat'll be pretty tough and stringy.

For the next few hours, as Danny crouched in the bottom of the mine, working to expose the gold-bearing seam, Ben removed bucket-loads of spoil. It was midafternoon when he climbed out of the mine to raise the last load of waste rock and lower the empty bucket for Danny to fill with the precious new rich ore.

Leaning on the windlass, waiting for Danny's signal, Ben watched a wedge-tailed eagle riding the thermals, sharp eyes peeled for signs of prey. As it swooped to carry off some small marsupial, a movement down the slope drew his gaze.

What the hell's that bloke up to? There was something very peculiar about the way the man slipped from one group of trees to another, watching the men working on the mine down there. He looked like any other miner, ah, except the boots. *Now who would wear black riding boots to go poking around among the mullock?* he asked himself with a wry grin.

'Righto, mate,' Danny called, and Ben slowly raised the heavy load of ore.

'All clear,' he called as he swung the bucket aside, 'you coming up for a smoko? Billy's boiling.'

'Too right,' Danny's voice echoed from down below and he was soon clambering over the top of the shaft casing.

'What y' lookin' at?' he asked, noticing his friend staring down the hill.

'That fella. Think I know who he is. You mind if I invite him for a cuppa?'

'Go ahead. I don't mind company.'

'Good day, Constable,' Ben called. 'Have you time for a cup of tea?'

The young policeman jerked upright, before turning to wander up to the camp, looking embarrassed.

'Oh, it's you, Mr Drummond,' he said, removing his battered hat, 'Yes, thanks.'

'Have you met my partner, Dan O'Hara?' Ben asked. 'Danny, meet Constable Purkiss.'

'Timed that right, didn't you Constable?' said Danny grabbing another tin mug from the makeshift cupboard. 'Sit y'self down.'

'Thanks Mr O'Hara, I'll be glad to take the weight off my feet,' he puffed.

'New boots?' Ben asked.

'Yes and they pinch a bit, but my old ones were falling apart. We just got some new stuff.'

'Well maybe next time you go out in plain clothes, wear the old ones. Or better still, get hold of some that don't look like police issue.'

'Bugger,' Purkiss muttered, casting an eye over the offending footwear, 'Never thought of that.'

'I would've thought Corporal Williams might have. He's been around the fields for a while.'

'He's out of town. There's just me and Smith and I think he's only worked in the city, where the detectives handle that sort of stuff. We're chasin' the crooks who've been stealing gold from the big mines. Not really sure what I'm supposed t' be lookin' for.'

'I guess a bloke could slip a few specimens into a mate's dollypot if he was prepared to take the risk.'

'Yeah, we're watching blokes who work on the big mine but have their own claims. Thanks for the tea. Better be getting back to the station.'

'Seems a friendly young fella, for a trooper,' Danny remarked, wincing as he stood up. Watching him trying not to limp, Ben was glad the heavy work was done for the day.

'Think I'll give Bluey's shindig a miss tonight,' Danny said, dropping into his bush armchair as Ben stirred up the fire.

'You all right?' Ben asked with a worried frown.

'Just me old rheumatics.'

'I might stay home too,' Ben suggested, not in the mood for celebrating the imminent arrival of Steve Hoskin's wife and children.

'No, you go Ben. Steve's a good mate.'

On the suggestion of one of the shopkeepers, Nora walked up to the nearest big mine and knocked on the door of the only place that looked like a real house. The grand lady who opened the door quickly sent the girl on her way. She didn't want someone who looked like that hanging around her husband.

There were few mines that looked really successful. Where there seemed to be some sort of proper house, she knocked on the door but only one person answered and he apologetically explained that his partner looked after the housework.

Her bag seemed to grow heavier as the afternoon dragged on, her legs were aching and there was a blister on her left heel from her boot rubbing. To avoid a bunch of crows tearing at something unspeakable, she turned off the rough track and found a rock to sit on, overcome with weariness. But she couldn't give up.

It was late afternoon by the time Nora reached the furthest mine site. The manager's house was little more than a shack, but stood out from the surrounding humpies. At first she thought no one was home, but then received a curt, 'Come!'

The manager, who had been expecting one of his workmen, not a lovely young woman, asked what he could do for her, and Nora explained she was looking for work. Did he need a housekeeper? By the look of the room, he certainly did.

'Now, isn't that a coincidence,' he smirked. 'My last housekeeper was suddenly called away. How soon could you start?'

'Straight away, sir, if you wish,' Nora replied, keeping her fingers crossed behind her back.

'Oh, Jolly good!' the man said, going on to introduce himself as Mr McRoberts. 'And you are?'

'Mrs Patterson, sir. I'm new in town. I have references if you wish to see them.'

'We won't worry about them, Mrs Patterson. Welcome to the great metropolis of Hannans. Come, the kitchen's outside and here's your room,' he went on opening a hessian-covered door to reveal a narrow room with a bed, a rickety chair and a curtained hanging space in one corner.

'Sorry it's not more elegant,' he laughed, leading her out the back door, past a small water tank. 'The kitchen's just a tin shed, I'm afraid. It's got to be out here in case of fire.'

Nora was relieved to find there was a proper stove. But there wasn't much else, just a table, two chairs and a sort of cupboard made from the wooden cases that kerosene tins came packed in. A tin wash-up dish sat on the table with a stained tea towel draped over it.

'You'll need to get water from the tank and the woodheap is next to it,' McRoberts told her. 'I'll be out for an hour or so. Make yourself at home and knock up some dinner. There's only bully beef, potatoes and onions.'

As soon as he left, Nora went back to her room and collapsed on the narrow bed with a relieved sigh. She'd half expected to have to go back and beg Mrs Bunning to let her sleep on the kitchen floor. Leaving her bag on the bed, she went the woodheap for some logs and kindling. With the stove lit, she put the kettle on to boil, and then searched the cupboard, looking for tea. Not only was there some, but also an opened tin of condensed milk. After she'd scraped away the ants that had drowned themselves in it, there was enough to make a cup of strong, sweet tea, and to keep some for cooking.

With the limited supplies available, Nora put together a meal of mashed potatoes, fried slices of canned meat, gravy flavoured with Worcestershire sauce, and some flour and water dumplings in caramel syrup.

She felt quite pleased with the result. She'd even found a clean tablecloth. Mr McRoberts seemed to enjoy the meal and congratulated her on her efforts. She thanked him and went out to the kitchen to wash up, leaving him to drink his port.

By the time she'd dried the plates and cutlery, the lone tea towel was sopping wet, so she left the heavy frying pan propped in the empty basin on the table to dry and went back into the house. McRoberts was still drinking and, she suspected, slightly drunk. When she asked if he needed her for anything else, he replied, 'No thank you my dear,' he said. 'Off you go and make yourself comfortable.'

That sounded a bit personal, coming from her employer, but she guessed things were less formal out here. Back in her room, she made up the bed. Surprised to find no chamber pot tucked under it, she regretted not visiting the rough bush lavatory out the back. Not wanting to go back through the room where her employer was still drinking, she hoped she wouldn't need to find her way out there in the dark.

There were no coat hangers in the curtained wardrobe, so she managed to squeeze everything into the carpetbag as she undressed, except her skirt, which she draped over the rail at the foot of the bed. Between worrying about Ned and nervousness about being alone in the house with a strange man, it took her a long time to get to sleep.

It was very dark when Nora awoke with a disturbingly full bladder. Sitting up, she lowered her feet to the ground, felt around for her boots and bent to pull them on. Then, lighting a candle, she slipped through the darkened house and out the back door. Hoping no snakes or scorpions were lying in wait for her, she crept down the pathway to the smelly latrine.

Just as she stepped out again, a gust of wind blew out the candle. She could make out the dark bulk of the kitchen building in the bright moonlight, so carefully made her way back. Knowing there were matches in there, she pushed open the door and felt her way inside, but as she reached out to locate the table, she heard a movement behind her and turned in time to receive a moist kiss from her employer. Imprisoning her arms in his embrace, he pushed her back against the table and started kissing her neck.

'Mr McRoberts! What are you doing! Stop this minute!' Nora cried, struggling to pull away.

'Come on, lovely,' he crooned, moving to hold her with one arm and fumbling at the neckline of her nightdress. 'You know you really want it. You women all come out here looking for a man. No good screaming. No one around to hear you.'

As the flimsy material tore and he clutched her breast, his grip on her weakened. Freeing her right arm, she brought her fist down on his bent head. It was an awkward blow, but in that moment of freedom, her flailing arm struck something hard. With a clatter, the washing up basin tipped, setting the heavy cast-iron frying pan sliding across the table towards her.

'Let me go!' she gasped as his hand closed on her wrist, but he just laughed. No matter how she struggled, he was much stronger, so she relaxed, hoping he'd think she'd given up. Loosening his hold, he was fumbling with his fly, when she reached for the heavy cast-iron frying pan and brought it down on his head.

McRoberts fell like a log, and Nora was running for the door when a new fear entered her mind. Had she killed him? If so, would anyone know she'd been here? They'd find her things. With a gasp, she raced back into the house, where moonlight filtering through the hessian allowed her to find the bedroom. Grabbing her bag and skirt, she headed for the front door but, as she fumbled at the bolt, angry shouts told her McRoberts was not just alive, but coming for her. As he stormed through the back door, the bolt clattered into its slot, the door swung open and she stumbled out.

Chapter 8

'You want a top-up, there, Ben?' Bluey asked.

'No thanks. I'm fine. Might head home soon.'

'Not drinkin, mate?' asked Steve.

'I've had a couple but can't keep up with the real drinkers.'

'Me neither. Don't know how Bluey does it. You wouldn't think he'd had a drop.'

'You off to Southern Cross in the morning?'

'Yeah. It'll be good to get Jeanie and the family safely home. It's a rough trip for a woman with a couple of littlies to take care of.'

'Well, I wish you and your wife all the best, mate,' Ben said, shaking Steve's hand. 'Think I'll wander home now. Hope you don't mind.'

'Not at all, Ben. I'm hoping this lot won't make a night of it. I need my beauty sleep if I'm to be off at first light.'

'Ben,' Bluey called, 'if you're heading off, could you see poor old Harry home. He's had a few too many, an' I'm worried he'll end up falling down a mineshaft if we let him go wandering around by himself.'

'Sure, Bluey. It's not much out of my way.'

'Hey, Harry,' Bluey called. 'Here's Ben about to head home too. He's got a lantern. You'd better go home with him.'

'I'm all right, mate,' the old fellow mumbled as he staggered towards them.

'Of course, you are, Harry,' Ben said, taking his arm. 'Goodnight all,' he called, leading the inebriated old man off down the track.

'Wha's his wife's name again?'

'Jeanie.'

'I dreams of Jeanie wit' the light brown hair,' he warbled, 'floatin' like a vapour ... Knew a girl called Jeanie once ... lovely girl ... married another bloke. Why d'y think they always marry some other bastard?'

'Don't know, Harry. But here's your place,' Ben said.

'Tha's fine, mate. Here, y'wanna stop an' have another drink?'

'No thanks. I'd better get on my way.'

'Think I'll turn in, then,' said Harry fumbling with the tent opening as Ben held up the lantern to light his way inside.

'You all right now, mate?'

'Never be'er,' came the slurred response. 'Jus' need a bit of a lie down. Me legs is feelin' funny.'

As his voice merged into a loud snore, Ben headed home, reassured the old fellow wasn't going to wander off.

Reaching the shelter of the nearest group of stunted trees, Nora tried to remember which way she had come. A cluster of lights ahead suggested the town centre, until she heard the call of 'Come in spinner' and saw a large group of men playing two-up by the flickering light of kerosene lanterns. Circling around them, she headed for the dark shade of a bigger stand of trees where she intended to stop and pull her skirt and blouse over the ripped nightie. But, as she reached the trees, angry shouts rang out and the two-up crowd erupted into a brawling mob.

Startled, Nora turned to look over her shoulder, tripped and fell to the ground. As she lay gasping, trying to catch her breath, strong hands grasped her shoulders, pulling her upright.

'Oh, ho. What have we here? Hey, fellas,' the man cried. 'Come an' see what I just caught.'

Nora struggled to no avail. Laughing, he grabbed her wrists and dragged her into the darkness under the trees.

'Come on sweetie,' he said, 'Where you goin' in y' nightie? Looking for a man, eh? Well you've sure found one who's ready, willin' and able. There's a couple of other blokes too, but I get first go. Come on, give us a kiss. To keep it all friendly-like.'

'Let me go,' Nora gasped. 'Please, let me go.'

'What y' got there Alby?'

'Where'd y' find her?'

'Wasn't really lookin'. She just ran inta' my arms. Say, it's handy I'd not done my fly up after pissin'.'

'Well get on with it, mate. I'm already stiff.'

'Let me go!' Nora screamed at them. 'What sort of men are you?'

'Just the usual sort, love,' laughed her captor. Trying to hold both her wrists with the one hand, he tore the tattered nightdress down off her breasts and bent to slobber on her nipples as he lifted the hem to fumble at her.

As Nora fought against his attempts to push her to the ground, a flash of light from a lifted lantern shone in her face, and the other man yelled, 'Shit, Alby, someone's comin'. I'm outa here.'

In the moment of confusion, Nora pulled away, but Alby wasn't ready to give up. He stumbled but never loosened his grip.

Screaming and fighting, Nora was being inexorably dragged back among the trees, when a man appeared out of the darkness to grab her attacker. A right hook between the eyes felled Alby and Nora, tossed over a muscular shoulder, was carried away into the darkness.

Chapter 9

She'd just caught her breath and decided to scream, when the man lowered her to the ground. As she tried to force her shaking legs to run, he said, 'Forgive the rough handling, Mrs Patterson.'

'Do I know you?' Nora stuttered, her teeth chattering. All she could see was a dark shape towering over her.

'Probably not. But you are Mrs. Patterson, aren't you? I was in the post office when you asked for mail from your husband. I'm Ben Drummond.

'Here, you'd better put this on,' he went on, taking off his coat and handing it to her.

Nora wrapped the coat around her but couldn't stop shivering.

'You've had a bad shock. We need to get you somewhere safe. Do you have any friends here?'

'No! No! No one.'

'Mary O'Callaghan might take you in. She's a friend of mine.'

'I couldn't impose on a complete stranger. And in the middle of the night, too!'

'Well, I could take you up to the Salvos place, but they mightn't understand your lack of clothes. Mary's about your size so she might have some things you can borrow.'

"

'Oh, my bag,' she gasped. 'I dropped it when those men... and my skirt. I was looking for somewhere to get dressed.'

'Oh,' was all the comment that brought, but she almost giggled at the impression she received of raised eyebrows.

'Please don't ask me to explain.'

'I'll go and have a look if you like, but I'd better take you to Mary's first.'

Like most Hannans homes, Mary O'Callaghan's cottage was little more than a humpy. After her husband's accidental death, his friends and workmates had rallied around and finished her little dwelling, part tent, part bough shed. She and her son lived on what she could earn cleaning at the pubs or mending miners' clothes, and the pennies he got from doing odd jobs. As was to be expected in the early hours, all was dark when Ben guided Nora along a winding track away from the town's rough buildings and knocked on a door, calling out quietly.

'Mary! Mary! Are you awake?'

'Who's there?' replied a lilting Irish voice.

'Don't be frightened, Mary. It's Ben Drummond. There's a lady here who needs help.'

After a few minutes, the light of a candle flickered past the one little window and the door was pushed open to reveal a pale face and a cloud of dark hair.

'What is it, Ben?' the woman asked, hugging a grey blanket around herself.

'I'm sorry to bother you, Mary. This is a respectable lady named Mrs Patterson. She's been attacked by some ruffians and hasn't any friends here. Can I leave her in your care for tonight?'

'A respectable lady, you say!' the woman asked, raising the candle to expose Nora's state of undress. 'What's she doing running around in her nightie, then? I don't want any of them bad women in my house, Ben. I've got a young boy and I won't expose him to that sort of company.'

'Please Mrs O'Callaghan,' Nora whispered, 'please believe me. A man attacked me in the middle of the night. I hit him, grabbed my things, and ran away, but there were other men out there. I don't know what would have become of me if Mr Drummond hadn't come along when he did.'

When the candle Mary held lit up the tear-stained face of the other woman, her heart softened.

'Oh, well, I'd better get you inside before all the neighbours know about it. Come on in, dear. And you can take yourself off, Ben Drummond.'

'Thank you so much, Mary,' Ben replied. 'Mary will look after you, Mrs Patterson. I'll be back in the morning to see if I can help.'

'Oh, but Mrs O'Callaghan, I've lost all my money. I can't pay you...'

Nora was still protesting as she was dragged through the door.

'Shh!' came an angry whisper. 'You'll be waking my Joey!'

Nora shut her mouth and followed the other woman into the tiny shack. By the light of the candle she saw a tumbled bed, a cluttered table and a couple of rough wooden stools. Mary pushed her shivering visitor down onto one of them, and was wrapping a blanket around her, as a tousled ginger head appeared in the other doorway.

'Mum? I heard voices. Is everything all right?'

'Yes, my dear. Go back to bed. It's only a lady come to visit. You can meet her in the morning.'

She shooed the boy out of the room, then turning to the rough cupboard beside the bed, dragged out a worn nightdress.

'Here, put this on,' she said, 'it's pretty tatty but better than yours.'

While Nora stripped and pulled the borrowed garment over her head, her hostess struck a match to light a little kerosene stove.

'I think we might both be needing a cup of tea, Missus,' she said. 'You'll have to share my bed if you want to get some sleep. Sorry I can't offer you better, but there's only this one and Joey's little bed in the lean-to.

'While the kettle's coming to the boil, maybe you can tell me how you come to be arriving on my doorstep in the wee small hours wearing only a torn nightie and Ben Drummond's coat.'

'I'm s-so sorry, Mrs O'Callaghan,' Nora sobbed, 'I don't know how to thank you for taking me in. Thank God that Mr Drummond was a good man. I thought I'd fallen out of the frying pan and into the fire when he tossed me over his shoulder and carried me off. But he was so kind. And you are so kind too. Oh, what am I going to do? I have nothing left and nowhere to go. And I can't find Ned. Oh, God. I think he must be dead.'

'There, there,' said Mary, putting her arms around the distraught woman. 'You go ahead and have a good cry. Is Ned your husband?'

'Yes. He sent me money to come over. Wrote that he'd found gold and we were going to be rich. I was to write and say when I was coming and he'd meet the coach. But he didn't. And no one knows where he is.'

'Didn't he tell you to wait till after summer?'

'He did say it would be better weather in autumn, but I couldn't stay there. Everything had gone wrong, so I wrote to say I was coming, and caught the first ship I could get on.'

'Didn't you wait for him to answer your letter?'

'I thought he must have written to my old address. I'd sent him my new address, but that's one of the letters that he didn't get. Something must have happened to him.'

Mary handed her a tin mug of black tea with a couple of spoonfuls of sugar. 'Get that into you, Missus. Sorry there's no milk. So what happened when you couldn't find your man?'

'I only had enough money for three nights at the boarding house, so I went looking for work. But no one wanted me except a man at one of the mines, and he didn't just want housework. To get away, I hit him on the head with the frying pan, took my things and ran away. I was looking for somewhere dark to hide and get dressed, when this other man grabbed me. His mates were w-waiting their turn to have me,' she whispered.

'Would you know them again?'

'It was too dark. I just remember the one who grabbed me had a lot of whiskers, black I think.'

'Well, you've had a trying time of it Missus. You need to get some sleep, and so do I. What's your first name? I'm Mary. If we're to share a bed we can't go on calling each other missus, can we?

'No, of course not,' her visitor laughed shakily. 'I'm Nora.'

'You go next to the wall, and I'll try not to wake you when I get up. I've got to go do some cleaning at the pub first thing, but I'll be back about eight. Joey goes out early too, but he doesn't make much noise. If you're hungry there's some damper in that crock on the table.'

'Aren't you scared, here by yourself at night?' asked Nora, as she watched the other woman drop a board across the inside of the door.

'Well, the door's pretty solid. I guess anyone could walk through the hessian walls, but I've got the shotgun and Paddy's old shillelagh. I was nervous at first, but I think the fellas let it be known that it wouldn't go well with anyone who bothered Joey an' me.

Nora didn't expect to be able to sleep and, at first, lay stiffly beside Mary in the rough wooden bed, but exhaustion soon overcame her worries, and she slept.

Chapter 10

Ben wasn't sure if he could face Mrs Patterson. The touch of her soft woman's skin had called up feelings he'd had under control for years. There'd never been another woman for him after Millie, and where he'd spent most of the last eight years quickly taught him to keep a firm rein on his emotions and urges. So except for a couple of depressing visits to brothels, he'd managed to practically suppress his sexuality.

So, the arousal he'd felt while holding Nora's lithe young body in his arms had taken him by surprise. Furthermore, he'd relived that moment in a dream and taken it to the obvious conclusion.

This is a married woman, he told himself, sternly. How could he even dream of taking advantage of her misfortune. The poor thing was in desperate straits and he'd promised to help her. God knew what she'd thought when he grabbed her.

Just another whiskery Hannans bastard, he grimaced, running his hand over his face. Better tidy up a bit. Hanging up his little shaving mirror, he trimmed his black beard and had just sneaked half a mug of hot water from the billy to shave the rest of his face, when Danny emerged from the tent.

'Shavin' again?' he asked, 'On Thursday?'

'Mmm,' Ben replied, stretching his neck to slide the cutthroat razor under his chin.

'Must be a woman', the old fellow muttered to himself. No one on the fields, except for a few silvertails, bothered shaving other than on Sundays.

'Got to go down to Mary's,' Ben explained. 'She's helping out a lady that's in trouble.'

Ah, so there is a woman involved. He'd never bother shavin' to impress little Mary.

✎

'Mmmmm' Nora murmured, snuggling into the dream's embrace. 'Neddy?' she murmured. But had it even been Ned who's dream caresses awakened her? Trying to ignore that question, she sat up. Sunlight streamed through cracks in the limed hessian walls and she had no idea where she was. Last night's events seemed like a bad nightmare.

Then the reality of her situation struck her and she let out a howl of anguish, which brought young Joey O'Callaghan rushing into the room, crying out, 'Mum! Mum! What's the matter?'

But it wasn't his mum sitting up in the bed wailing. It was strange woman.

'Who are you?' he blurted out. Then remembered waking in the night and Mum saying something about a lady visiting. But he didn't expect to find her in Mum's bed, wearing Mum's old nightie.

'Oh. I'm sorry,' Nora said. 'You must be Joey. I think your mum has gone out. She said she'd be home soon.'

'Are you the lady that came in the night?' asked Joey.

'Yes, and your mother very kindly took me in. I hope I won't have to stay here long.'

'Don't worry. Mum'll look after you,' said Joey, snatching a hunk of damper from the crock. 'Got to go now' he mumbled, rushing out the door to the annoyance of a crow that flew off complaining loudly.

Timmy was just coming out of the dunny when Joey got to his place.

'I gotta get back to work,' he said. 'Pa Kenny's on the warpath.' But Joey couldn't wait t' tell him about last night.

'I woke up an' heard people whispering. So I poked me head inta the kitchen an' there was this strange lady, all bedraggled, with just a man's coat on over a scruffy-lookin' nightie. Mum shooed me back to bed an' I went back t' sleep. But this mornin' she was still there.'

'So, who is she?'

'Dunno.'

'I'll come over later, if I can get away. Do y' think she'll still be there?'

✁

Nora sat with her head in her hands, trying to think what to do. Knowing no one in Hannans, she was completely reliant on the good will of Mary O'Callaghan and that Ben Drummond. If Ned didn't turn up, what could she do? Her purse, with its paltry five shillings was probably lost.

If her trunk had turned up at the coach office, perhaps could sell some of her clothes for a few pounds. Mr Drummond might go and see if it was there. He said he'd come back in the morning. *Oh, but what if he comes before Mrs O'Callaghan gets back and finds me only wearing a nightie, again?*

Fortunately for Nora, Mary arrived first.

'Hello, how are you feeling? I got some old clothes from Mrs Grant at the pub. They're clean. I washed them myself yesterday. Everything out here gets stained from the red dirt, but at least they don't stink of sweat.'

There was a dark brown skirt that needed a safety pin to tighten the waist and a blouse that didn't look too bad, though it was stained pink at the collar and under the arms.

'Good thing you've got your boots. Don't think my good shoes would fit you. You said your trunk should have come on the coach. Maybe it's there now. We can get Ben to go and find out.'

Nora couldn't help wondering about her rescuer. It seemed strange that she had no idea what he looked like, despite him having seen, or at least felt, her near-naked body. The thought that a strange man had touched her should have been shocking, but it all felt so unreal. Thankfully, she'd managed to get into the ill-fitting clothes before there came a knock on the door. Nodding in reply to Mary's questioning glance, she braced herself to meet this stranger.

She was relieved to see he was carrying her bag. He was tall and strongly built. Well, she'd guessed that from the way he tossed her around. She knew she was no featherweight. Removing his hat, he stooped and entered the small, cluttered room, saying, 'Good morning, ladies.'

A quick glance showed dark hair and a neat beard, with the ghost of newly-shaved stubble shadowing his cheeks. Grey eyes, she thought, but was too embarrassed to study him more closely, and could only peek from under lowered lids, as Mary said, 'Well, I don't suppose you two need to be introduced, but Nora, this is Ben Drummond. He and his mate, Danny have been good friends to Joey and me.'

'Pleased to meet you,' Nora murmured, blushing a brilliant rose pink, 'And thank you so much for helping me last night.'

'It was…' Ben stammered as he swallowed the words, "my pleasure" in time to substitute 'no trouble.'

She'd only had time to bundle her hair up into some sort of knot on the top of her head, leaving errant tendrils to curl around her face. Despite her ordeal, she looked so wholesomely pretty that he found himself blushing, very aware of the soft female flesh hidden by the unprepossessing clothing.

'I found your bag, but there was no sign of the clothing you said you'd dropped,' he went on, handing it to her.

'Oh, thank you,' she said, opening it and scrabbling inside for her purse so she could offer Mary her last few coins as board money. But it was gone.

'Is something missing?' Mary asked, seeing her distress.

'Yes, my money purse and Ned's photo.'

'Was it in a silver frame? Guess the lousy sods thought it was worth money. Anything else gone?'

'I don't think so,' Nora replied, quickly checking that nothing else had been taken and that the key to her trunk was still pinned to the bag's lining.

'Ben,' Mary said, 'Nora's trunk got left behind at the railhead. Would you mind going down to the coaching office to see if it's arrived?'

'Oh, for sure,' he mumbled. 'I'll do that straight away.'

'Have a cuppa first,' said Mary, 'I cadged a cup of goat's milk from Mrs Grant. So we can have it with milk if you like. Did you get something to eat, Nora? No? Well, I've only got damper with a scrape of treacle, but you'd better have some. Maybe you should go to the police station, too, Ben, and tell them what those bludgers did. Did you recognise them?'

'It was too dark.'

'Do we have to tell the police?' Nora asked, remembering reading sensational reports of an attempted rape in the newspapers at home.

'I guess y' wouldn't want the story all over the papers,' Mary said. 'But those sods shouldn't get away with it.'

'I could have a word to a policeman I know, sort of unofficially,' Drummond said. 'If you don't report it, I don't think there's anything they can do.'

He quickly drank his tea and left, saying he'd bring her trunk back straight away if it had arrived.

'Thank you,' Nora said, still not able to look him in the eye.

'You were lucky it was Ben who came along,' Mary said, after he left. 'He's one of the good, steady blokes. As you found, there are some nasty bastards out here. Oh, most men treat us women with respect, but that's when we have all our clothes on.'

Nora's spontaneous giggle caught in her throat and turned into a sob. She was trying to keep from breaking down when she felt Mary's arms around her.

'Don't cry. I'm sorry, I shouldn't have made a joke about it.'

'It wasn't funny at the time,' Nora hiccupped between sobs, brushing away tears.

'I think another cup of tea might help,' Mary said, turning to check how much water was in the kettle. 'And you haven't eaten any of the damper. I know it's not the most elegant breakfast, but you need to keep your strength up.'

Nora was still dabbing at her eyes, when Mary placed another mug of tea in front of her, along with a slab of treacle-spread damper on a rose-patterned plate. She stroked the pretty plate, surprised to find something like that in Mary's shack.

'Part of my glory box,' Mary said. 'Had a whole teaset, but the box fell off the camel. Only that plate survived. I keep it for when I need to remind myself of happier times.'

'It's lovely. You must miss having pretty things.'

'Well, we were never well off, but Ma and Gran always tried to keep things nice at home.'

'Where did you live?'

'Out near Bathurst in New South Wales. Ma and Pa had a little farm and we lived with them at first. They didn't like Paddy bringing me over here. Maybe they were right.'

'What happened to him?'

'He decided his claim here was a dud and went to work on Brookman's lease. He was down the shaft when a rope broke and dropped a bucket of ore on top of him.'

'Oh, God no. Was he...?' Nora asked reaching out to take Mary's hand.

'He was already dead when someone got to him,' Mary's voice broke as she went on, 'When they let me see him, I knew that was God's mercy. He couldn't have lived like that.'

'Oh Mary, how terrible for you. And here I am weeping all over you, when you're grieving yourself.'

'I don't usually go to pieces,' Mary said, choking back sobs. 'I've got used to keeping a stiff upper lip. The blokes don't know what to do with a weeping woman. Anyway, poor Joey needed me, so I couldn't let myself fall apart. It was hard explaining to him what had happened.'

'Is he all right?'

'Well, he was pretty broken up, as you can imagine. He misses his dad. Paddy was always such a happy person, laughing and joking. It's been a dreary, mournful home without him. I think Danny helped Joey. Him having the same Irish sense of humour.

'Let's have another cuppa,' she went on, wiping her eyes.

She was just about to pour the tea when Ben Drummond arrived, balancing Nora's trunk on his shoulder.

'Oh, thank you so much,' she said, jumping up, 'I feared I'd lost everything.'

'It was on the last coach,' he told her, 'Seems it got overlooked for a couple of days.'

He's got nice hands, she thought irrelevantly, as he bent to place it on the floor. Then felt a quiver run through her body at the thought of those hands touching her bare skin. Shocked, she pushed the disturbing thought away, before kneeling to unlock the trunk. Searching through the stuff in the removable tray, she lifted out a large, framed photograph, relieved that the glass was unbroken.

'Here's a photograph of Ned,' she said handing it to Mary, just as young Joey arrived home. He leaned over his mother's shoulder to see what she was looking at.

'It's a picture of Mr Patterson. Him that's gone missing,' she told him.

'I seen him! Him and his brother.'

'Ned doesn't have a brother!'

'I thought they was brothers,' the boy said, turning away to liberally spread treacle on a slab of damper. 'They was in Courthope's buying a lot of stores. I remember the man in the photo, 'cause he gave me a whole shillin', just for minding his horse and cart.'

'When was this?' asks Ben.

'Oh, a while back,' he said, stopping to chew, 'Would of been before Pa died, because I'd just bought his baccy for him.'

'That's a long time ago,' said Mary, 'Are you sure?'

'Of course, I'm sure. Haven't seen him since, but I seen the other Mr Patterson. The one I thought was his brother. A coupla weeks ago. He was back at Courthope's.'

Nora's spurt of hope died; as Joey continued to insist that there were two Mr Pattersons. The boy was obviously confused or else he'd made up the story.

'Do you recognise him, Ben?' Mary asked, handing him the photograph.

'Not really,' he said, though the black and white image sparked a vague memory of someone from the distant past. 'Pretty sure I've never seen him around here. Is his hair fair or ginger? And what colour are his eyes?'

'He's got fair hair, and his eyes are ... well somewhere between blue and green. Kind of speckled, if you know what I mean.'

'Yes,' he said, turning to study her own, 'eyes are rarely all one colour.'

His, she saw weren't just grey, as she'd thought. More the colour of a stormy sea.

'Anyway, I'd better head home or Danny will try to do too much on his own. Goodbye, Mrs Patterson. I hope he turns up soon.'

'Goodbye Mr Drummond, thank you for all your help.'

'Mum, is it alright if I go an' see Timmy?' said young Joey.

'Yes, off you go. Don't get into any mischief. Here,' she said, following him outside, 'take this old sugarbag an' pick up some dung on the way back.'

'Do you want to change into your own things?' Mary asked, when she came back inside. 'Go into Joey's room, in case someone drops in.'

When she emerged a short while later, wearing her own skirt and blouse, Mary smiled and said. 'I bet that feels better.'

'Yes it does, but thank you so much for finding me something to wear earlier. It was embarrassing enough meeting Mr Drummond after what happened last night. I was afraid he might catch me in your nightie.'

'He's a good bloke. Not that I really know anything about him, except he's English. Never talks about himself. But then, a lot of blokes out here seem to have things in their past they don't want anyone to know. The rule is "don't ask".'

'I only know I'm so glad he came along when he did. Even if I'd got away, everything was so dark and I had nowhere to run to. Thank you again for taking me in, Mary. But, with my purse gone I can't even offer you a couple of shillings for board. Unless Ned comes soon, I'll have to find a job.'

'Well, in the meantime you can stay here for a few days, but I have to go out now. A barmaid friend asked me to stand in for her this morning. She's got her monthlies and isn't at all well. I'll be back about midday, I expect.'

Left alone, Nora could no longer pretend to be coping. No longer tell herself that Ned would turn up. Burying her face in her hands, she let go the tears that threatened to drown her. But she couldn't afford to just go to pieces. Fighting for calm, she scrabbled in her bag for a handkerchief to dry her streaming eyes and blow her nose.

Thank God she had found a sanctuary, even if it was only for a few days. There was no one back east who could help. It would take weeks to get an answer to a letter anyway. She must stand on her own two feet and face whatever the future brought. But where should she start?

It seemed that Mary was happy to do barmaid work and considered the real barmaid a friend. It wasn't thought a respectable job back home, but here things were different and she couldn't afford to be fussy. Even the singing barmaid job didn't seem so degrading after the alternative she'd been offered by McRoberts, but a shudder ran through her at the thought of men like that Alby leering at her, touching her.

She jumped, choking back a scream when a dog barked outside, followed by a scuffle, a loud cawing and a knock on the door. Shakily rising to her feet, she peered through the little glassless window as the dog returned with a happy grin after chasing off the crows. A sturdily built old man with a wild, white beard stood outside. Her first instinct was to hide. Could she pretend no one was home?

'Mary,' he called, knocking again, 'Ben got us a roo on Tuesday. Thought y' might like some.'

Realising he was one of Mary's friends, she reluctantly opened the door, saying, 'I'm afraid Mrs O'Callaghan isn't here just now.'

'Oh, you must be the lady that's staying with her, then. I'm Danny O'Hara, Ben Drummond's mate. Mrs Patterson, isn't it?'

'Yes,' she replied, hesitating about inviting him in.

'I've got a piece of roo meat here Mary could maybe use.'

'Oh, maybe you'd better come in,' she said.

'It needs to go in the meat safe. I think she usually sits it in that tin dish,' he said, pointing to one hanging on the wall. He was obviously a regular visitor, Nora thought, as she reached for the dish. Between them they managed to get the meat into it and squeezed into the hessian-covered safe that hung from a rafter.

'Would you like to sit down, Mr O'Hara?' she said, indicating the seat near the door. She wanted to keep the table between them, in case he wasn't the kindly old fellow he seemed.

'You work with Mr Drummond, you said,' she began, blushing to think what his friend might have told him.

'To be sure,' Danny replied, seating himself, 'Been a good mate to me.'

'Have you known him long?'

'Only since the rush started. We was both leggin' it to the fields from down Albany way. Sure was glad when he happened along and offered to push my wheelbarrow in exchange for putting his swag aboard it. Big strong fella, Ben. Got to know each other on the track and decided to team up. We was lucky and found ourselves a nice little lead. You been here long?'

'Only a few days. I came to join my husband. He sent me the money to come. Said he'd found gold, but he's not here and nobody knows where he's gone.' Her voice broke on the last words and she dashed tears from her eyes, embarrassed to have broken down in front of a stranger.

'Oh, that's real tough. I'm sure he'll turn up. Meantime, you got good friends in Mary and Ben. And me. If you need any help, just ask for Danny O'Hara. Our mine's up the hill a way.'

Mary still hadn't returned and Nora was wondering if she should offer the visitor a cup of tea, when the door flew open and in rushed Joey, along with a pungent odour. 'Oh, hello Mr O'Hara,' he said throwing a sugarbag on the floor.

'Hello young fella,' the old man said. 'What you got there?'

'Just some horse an' camel shit. Mum wants to start a garden when the rains come.'

'Better leave it outside then mate.'

'Oh, yeah, it's a bit stinky, isn't it.'

He took it outside and then poked his head back in, 'We havin' a cuppa?' he asked, giving Nora an accusing look.

'I was about to ask Mr O'Hara if he'd like one, but was worried about using up your mother's kerosene.'

'Don't worry,' the lad replied, 'I'll get the billy on outside.' Nora felt foolish that she hadn't thought of lighting up the outside cooking campfire.

'Better wash y' hands, mate,' the visitor said, and Nora was relieved to see Joey complying as she reached up to get three cups from the open shelf.

'There's some damper bread, Mr O'Hara,' she said. 'Would you like some with your tea?'

'Wouldn't mind a piece, lass, if there's enough to go round.'

'Of course there is,' Joey said as he came inside. 'If Mum's not back soon, I c'n make another one. The water won't be long, Missus. It were still warm. You found the tea an' sugar?'

'Yes. We don't have any milk, do we?'

'No, Mum got a bit this mornin' but it's all gone,' he replied giving her a reproachful glance.

'Oh, I'm sorry, Joey. Did I use your share?'

'It's all right. You was needin' it. Y' better put a bit more in than that,' he added as Nora carefully measured out the tea, the teamaker's mantra 'one for each person and one for the pot' playing in her mind.

'Really?'

'Mum says another one for the stranger at the gate. Some of these blokes c'n smell a cuppa from a long way away.'

'Like me an' Ben, y' mean?' said O'Hara, in a hurt tone. Nora feared he'd taken offense, till she saw the wink he threw at her.

'No, of course not. You're our mates. But I don't like some of them blokes what come hangin' around. Mum's too nice to tell them to bugger off. Beggin yr' pardon, missus.' he said taking the teapot outside to fill it.

'He's a good lad,' O'Hara said. 'Gettin' a bit rough round the edges. Shame there's no school here yet. He's a bright boy. Been readin' Sherlock Holmes in the paper, y' know.'

Nora wouldn't have thought that was suitable reading for a boy his age. Perhaps her disapproval was obvious, as he added, ''Tis not all blood and guts, y'know. There's lots of interestin' information in them stories.'

'Y' talkin about Mr Holmes?' said Joey, placing the teapot on the table. 'Do y' think the next bit's out yet?'

'Should be in the latest edition, Joey.'

Nora was pouring the tea when Mary pushed open the door and tossed her hat on the bed.

'Hello, Danny,' she said, 'I see you've met my new friend. Did Ben tell you what those bastards tried to do to her?'

'Not really, only that she was in some trouble and you were helping. I guess he thought 'twas none of my business.'

Conversation was easier with Joey there. He had a lot of questions about O'Hara's experience at other gold rushes, but some of his innocent observations about members of the Hannans community made Nora blush.

'Joey,' said his mother, 'You and Timmy must stop pokin' your nose into other people's business.'

'We're just playin' at being detectives like Mr Holmes.'

'You need to wait till you've got a crime to investigate, Joey,' said the visitor. 'Can't go around investigating innocent people.

'Well,' he continued, picking up his hat, 'I'd better be on my way. Thanks for the cuppa. It's been nice talking to you, Mrs Patterson. Remember you got some good friends keeping an eye out for you now.'

Chapter 11

Later that day, Ben headed for the police tent, hoping to find Purkiss on duty, but it was Corporal Williams behind the desk.

'Yes, sir. What can I do for you?'

'Hello, Corporal, I was wanting to speak to Constable Purkiss. Is he in?'

'Yes, but if it's a police matter, I will handle it.'

'No, not really,' Ben replied. 'I just wanted to ask him about something.'

'Well, he'll be going off duty in ten minutes, if you'd like to wait.'

'Thanks, Corporal. I'll be out the front having a smoke.'

Ben breathed a sigh of relief as he stepped outside. Despite it's ramshackle structure, the interior looked and smelt like a police station. And he'd been in a few of them. He was just finishing his smoke, when the young policeman joined him.

'Hello mate,' he said with a friendly grin, 'the Guv said you were looking for me.'

'Yes. Can we go for a bit of a walk? There's something I need to ask you about.'

When they were far enough away from any inquisitive police ears, he still found it hard to raise the subject. Purkiss might feel impelled to report it to his superior, no matter how Mrs Patterson felt.

'Righto, mate,' said his companion, 'spit it out. I hope you're not going to confess to some heinous crime.'

With a nervous laugh, Ben launched into an account of last night's happenings.

'What did she hit him with?'

'A frying pan, I believe.'

'So, she ran outside in her nightdress, and these other bastards grabbed her. And that's where you came in. Did you recognise them?'

'No, it was too dark.'

'How did you come to recognise her, then?'

'Well, when I held up the lantern to see what was going on, it lit up her face. The men were turned away.'

'You'd met her before?'

'No, but I've seen her around town, asking after her husband. I think she arrived about a week ago expecting him to meet her, but he never turned up.

'Mrs Patterson?'

'Yes.'

'She's been into the station a few times. We've got him listed in our missing person's book. So, who's the other bastard that attacked her then?'

'McRoberts out at the Golden Orb. I should have gone and sorted him out last night.'

'Not on your own mate. I can see why Mrs Patterson doesn't want to make a fuss. If word got out that she was running around with nothing on but her nightie, some of these blokes haven't seen a woman for months. They might get the wrong idea. But, hey, I'm off duty. Let's go visit this McRoberts.'

'You fellas managed to nab any gold thieves?'

'No. It's almost impossible. Nobody knows anything, or so they would have us believe. Anyway, the latest is we're looking for a fugitive from the east, a murderer who arrived on one of the steamers and slipped past the officers sent to intercept him at Albany. They think he headed out here. A message came up from Perth that we need to investigate anyone who arrived since October last year.'

'They've got to be joking. There must be hundreds. And more arriving every day.'

'Well, no. Deadly serious stuff, this. I'm sure the city bosses have no idea what it's like out here. Anyway, you're in the clear as you've been here longer. To make our job really easy,' he laughed, 'he's described as medium height with fair or light brown hair. Oh, and he wore a moustache when last seen.'

'Well, you've got your job cut out. That would describe at least a third of the blokes out here. And the moustache will have long ago disappeared under a bunch of whiskers. Anyway, he might have just passed through to one of the other finds.'

'Oh, we're supposed to check them all as well.'

'Do these blokes have any idea of the distances and conditions out here? So, who did he murder?'

'Killed a British major in Port Melbourne, pinched his clothes, his steamer ticket, and his name. They thought they'd catch him at Albany, but he slipped ashore wearing prospectors' clothes.

Dropping in at Mary's on his way home, Ben found the two women sitting under the shade of the bough shed. Mary was chopping meat while Nora peeled potatoes.

'Hello, Ben,' Mary said, 'I'm making a big stew out of that roo meat Danny brought. Nice change from tinned dog. Got time for a cuppa?'

'No thanks, Mary. I'd better get on home. Just came to tell Mrs Patterson I talked to the policeman I know.'

Turning to her with a fleeting smile, he said, 'we visited that McRoberts bloke. Unfortunately, because you went there of your own free will, there's not much the police can do, but the constable gave him a warning. I don't think he'll bother you again. As for the other blokes, as we can't identify them, the police couldn't do much even if you did report it.'

'Thank you, anyway, Mr Drummond,' Nora said.

'I guess they're going to get away with it, then,' said Mary. 'We need more police here.'

'Well, at least we've got a few now, but they're badly overstretched. Well, so long for now.'

It seemed to Nora that she'd only just got to sleep that night, when a dingo howling close by aroused her. Then, an owl hooted and some wild creature went scurrying across the roof. But it was the sound of gunshots and distant shouting that kept her wide-awake worrying about Ned until, towards dawn she dozed, drifting in and out of disturbing dreams until Mary stirred at first light.

'I'll boil the kettle on the kero stove,' Mary said as they both got dressed, 'No time to boil the billy outside. I've got a whole day's work at Grant's pub, so need to get cracking.'

They were just sitting down to their breakfast of damper and tea when there came a knock on the door and Mary went to open it, saying, 'Hello Johnny, what did you want?'

'Mrs Lindsay sent me to ask if you can come in and cook for us today. Our cook, Ah Lim, is sick.'

'No, I can't. I'm working at the big pub all day.'

'Could I do it, Mary?' asked Nora.

'It's only plain cooking, Missus,' the young man said. 'Ah Lim sometimes cooks what he says is special, but the blokes don't always like it.'

'Well, if they're happy to take someone else, I can do with the work,' said Nora.

'I'm sure you'll manage, Nora. If I went, they'd just have to eat what I cooked or go without. Anyway, I've gotta be off.'

'What's the matter with the usual cook?' Nora asked as she accompanied the young man back to the hotel. 'I hope it's not typhoid. I hear there's a lot around up here.'

'No. Last night, he an' Ah Sam from the club, got celebratin' some special Chinese holiday. Here's the pub, Missus. I'll take you around t' the kitchen. We got a proper oven and all. I don't know what Ah Lim gets up to in there. There'll be lots of rice anyway. I think he lives on the stuff.'

Nora was pleased to find the kitchen clean and tidy. There was plenty of rice, but also bags of potatoes, onions and flour. She was wondering if she should make a damper, when a man's voice called out, 'Baker,' and she found a large fellow at the door with a basket of real bread.

'Mornin' Missus,' he said, 'Where's Ah Lim?'

'He's sick today. I'm doing the cooking in his place,' said Nora, placing the loaves on the table. 'Do I need to pay you?'

'No, Missus. Pub's got an account. So long.'

Deciding she'd better talk to the publican, she tracked him down in the bar and introduced herself.

'Mrs O'Callaghan was busy, so I've come in her place. How many are here for the midday meal? What do they usually have?'

'Pleased to meet you, Mrs Patterson. Thanks for coming at short notice. Maybe eight or ten for lunch. Something like soup and bread will do as long as there's plenty. Great appetites, these blokes. We get about ten more coming at night, and they'll want a big meal, but it doesn't have to be fancy.'

'I'll do my best, sir,' she answered.

'Oh, I can pay you three and six for the day's work.'

Back in the kitchen, Nora searched in a few more of Ah Lim's hidey-holes and discovered some withered carrots and turnips. Soup should be easy, but she had no stock. Cutting a hunk off the flitch of bacon hanging in the big meat safe, she chopped it small and set it to boil in one of the big copper pots, then added chopped vegetables and some barley to thicken it a bit. By midday, the soup was ready and, with the baker's fresh bread, it seemed to go down rather well.

She guessed dinner would have to be something made with canned corned meat but, just as she was trying to think what to make, there was a knock on the door and a whiskery gentleman stood there with a bulging sugarbag.

'Hello missus,' he said. 'Bill O'Reilly. I'm lookin' for Ah Lim. I brought him this turkey I shot this mornin'.'

'He's sick today and I'm doing the cooking,' Nora said. 'I'm Mrs Patterson.'

'Oh well maybe you can use it. Not a real turkey, y' know. One of them big birds called bastards, begging your pardon, Missus. I already gutted it, so you won't have to do that but you'll need to pluck the bloody thing.'

'Thank you very much, Mr O'Reilly,' she said, relieved not to have to remove the bird's innards. It would be just the thing for dinner, but she'd seen some of those native birds and they were very big. So, worried that there mightn't be enough time to cook it, she got straight into the unpleasant job of plucking the fowl, and had it and a pile of potatoes in the oven by mid-afternoon.

The finished meal, all roasted to golden perfection, was quickly demolished by the hungry hotel guests. But night was closing in by the time she'd served the second course, a steamed pudding. As she was contemplating the great heap of dishes, the publican stepped into the kitchen.

'Congratulations, Missus. That was a fine dinner. Don't worry about the dishes. I'll get Freda the housemaid to do them. Here's your wages.'

Feeling guilty, because she was sure the housemaid had quite enough to do, Nora took the money, quickly noting it was the correct amount. She hung up her apron, tidied the kitchen, put on her hat and slipped out into the glow of sunset, attracting the attention of the drunken men standing around the hotel door. Ignoring several slurred invitations to buy her a drink, she hurried up the road.

It was only a short walk to Mary's place on the edge of Danny and Ben's lease, but as darkness gathered and heavy footsteps echoed behind her, Nora's pace increased until she was almost running before she reached the gate. Waiting to catch her breath, she knocked on the door.

'Is that you, Nora?' Mary called. 'Come in, you don't have to knock.'

Mary had just arrived herself, but Joey had the outdoor fire lit, the billy boiling and the pot of stew simmering on the edge of the fire.

'Hello, Nora, how did your day go? You look like I feel. I'm glad we've got leftover stew for dinner.'

'I'm not sure I can face food anytime soon, and my feet are killing me.'

'Take off your boots and put your feet up. I kicked mine off as soon as I got in the door.'

'Oh, and Mary, here, I owe you this for feeding me,' Nora said handing her the money she'd earned.

'How much did the old skinflint pay you?

'Only three and six. I'm sorry, but it wouldn't get me a day's board at the boarding house.'

'That's all right. Here, two bob'll do. You can keep the rest for yourself.'

Nora gasped in alarm when a man's voice called, 'Mary, are you all right?'

'Yes, Ben,' Mary said going to open the door.

'Sorry to disturb you,' he said, his eyes seeking Nora in the dimly lit interior, 'Danny was a bit worried when no one seemed to be home today.'

'Oh, I was working at the club all day and Nora got a day's work too, cooking for Lindsays. I guess Joey was off hunting clues with Timmy. But we are all fine.'

'I'll be off then. Goodnight.'

'Just one of my guardian angels checking up on me,' Mary laughed, closing the door. 'If Danny had come, he'd still be talking. You might have noticed, Ben doesn't say much.'

She had noticed. And he seldom smiled. Did some secret sorrow lurk behind those storm grey eyes? Well, she had enough troubles of her own without worrying about what that might be.

<h1 style="text-align:center">Chapter 12</h1>

As soon as breakfast was over on Saturday morning, and Joey set off with a list of things to buy from the general store, Mary cleared everything off the table except her sewing machine and spread out a worn pair of man's dungarees.

'Joey's bum's almost hangin' out of them pants. I been putting off cuttin' up Paddy's old britches,' she said, wiping her eyes, 'but needs must when the devil drives.'

'You must miss him terribly.'

'Yes,' Mary replied, attacking the trousers with the scissors. 'Paddy wasn't just my husband, he was my best pal. It's been hard, but I had to keep going for Joey's sake. He's such a good boy. I fear I leaned on him too much for support when he was grieving for his dad too. Sometimes I forget he's just a young lad.

'It was terrible hot,' she went on, 'so he had t' be buried the next day. We were so short of water here that the miners were given an exemption from working their claims. Most of them left for Southern Cross or somewhere cooler. Those who could afford it went all the way down to Perth. Burying Pat took all my money, but the fellas all chipped in to help Joey and me have a holiday down at Fremantle. Being by the beach helped take Joey's mind off what had happened. I couldn't forget, though. I'd have been terrible lonely down there, except that Danny and some of the other blokes came down. It was good having someone there that I didn't have to explain to if I burst into tears at the drop of a hat.'

'Couldn't you go home?'

'Well, with the money they gave me I'd have had enough for the fares if we'd gone straight away, but I couldn't go. My Pat's buried up here, so I came back. Ben and Danny were about to put in for their lease, so they included this plot where my house is, so no one can throw me out. Then, along with some of their mates, they finished this little house Pat had started building. I've got good friends here. Someone's always dropping in to see if I'm all right. As you've seen, Ben and Danny keep an eye out for us.'

'Did you know them before?'

'They were at Coolgardie. I think they met up on the track. I know Danny's been all over the world chasin' gold, but Ben's not one to talk about himself. Paddy palled up with Danny and some other fellas, then we all came over here after Hannan's big find.'

'Did you get any help from Pat's employer?'

'Not really. He'd only been there one day. But we get by. I earn a bit working at the pub and mending shirts and patching dungarees for the blokes. Now there are more women here, I'm hoping to get some proper dressmaking jobs. I'm glad I talked Paddy into buying a sewing machine. It's earned its keep. I'd love a treadle machine, but they cost a pound more and would have been too heavy to bring out here.'

'My mother was a dressmaker, but she didn't live long enough to teach me. I wouldn't know where to start. But I'll need to find some sort of work. I can't afford to pay board, so it'll have to be live-in. Are there many jobs for women?'

'I'll ask around, but for now, you can stay here. If you don't mind sharing the bed.'

'But I can't stay here, sponging off you,' Nora replied, tears starting in her eyes. 'Oh, what on earth will I do?'

'Just stay here a few days while you try to find something. I think I might enjoy the company. There are so few women, I've even started talking like one of the blokes. And you're more respectable than some of my friends. It will do me good to mix with a lady for a change.'

'I don't think I'm quite a lady,' Nora laughed. 'But thank you.'

Later that morning, Ben walked down to the post office as he'd been doing several times a week. He'd been in the west for almost a year before he finally found the courage to write home after years wasted carrying his swag around outback New South Wales, trying to forget. After burying those memories for so long, it had been hard to drag them out into the light. To cleanse them of all the horror and shame and put them into words the folk back home could understand.

'Sorry, Ben. Nothing for you, or for Mrs Patterson. She's staying with Mrs O'Callaghan, you said. Her husband not turned up yet?'

'No.'

'I hope he does. It can't be good for a young lady out here on her own.'

Coming out of the Post Office, he ran into Joey and his mate Timmy O'Rourke.

'Hello there boys,' he said. 'What've you young fellas been up to?'

'Hello Mr Drummond. I been tellin' Timmy about Mr Patterson and how he's disappeared.'

'We think maybe someone done him in,' Timmy put in.

'Please don't tell Mrs Patterson that. She's worried enough already. You know, lots of things might have stopped him coming to town. Maybe his horse strayed, or he's sick, or has hurt himself.'

But Timmy wasn't to be put off; 'They coulda dropped 'is body down a mineshaft. Hey, maybe he's at the bottom of his own mine.'

'Well, if something's happened to him, the police will find out. They're going to look for his mine when one of them goes out that way.'

'There's not enough policemen, though, is there?' said Joey. 'We heard Corporal Williams tellin' Mr Humphries at the post office that they can't keep up with all the crooks comin' into town.'

'Yeah,' added Timmy, 'Lots of spivs and bludgers starting up gamblin' an' sly grog places. Whorehouses too. Anyway, I gotta go, Joey. See y' tomorra.'

'Timmy's s'posed to be workin',' Joey explained.

'So am I,' Ben said. 'Better get back to camp. You heading home now, Joey?'

'Yes, Mum's expectin' me.'

'I reckon Mr Holmes could find Mr Patterson,' Joey said, as they walked up the road.

'Maybe. But we don't know if he's really missing, do we?' Ben was saying as they reached the boy's home.

'Hello Ben,' Mary called from where she and her guest sat in the bough shed.

'G'day, Mary, Mrs Patterson.'

'Come in, Ben. Nora's been helping me with some sewing.'

'I can't stop, Mary,' he said, hanging his hat on the gatepost as he followed Joey into the yard. 'We got a lot of work on today. How are you today, Mrs Patterson?'

'I'm fine, thanks to you and Mary, Mr Drummond,' she said with a smile that soon faded, 'But I don't know what I'm going to do if Ned doesn't come soon,' she added, unshed tears glistening in her eyes.

'I've been telling her she's welcome to stay here. I'm enjoying the company.'

'Well, I'd better get home,' he said, disturbed by Nora's distress. 'If you need anything, remember we're just up the hill.'

As he approached the camp, Seamus bounded out to greet him, and Danny called out, 'Time for another cuppa before we get back to work?'

'Sounds good, Danny. I'll make it. I met young Joey and his mate down town,' he continued, tossing tea into the billy. 'Maybe we shouldn't have said it's no good looking for clues unless a crime's been committed. Young Timmy reckons Patterson's been murdered. I hope Joey doesn't tell the poor lady that. He's probably just sick or something.'

'Odd that he didn't get her letters, though. Most blokes get to town occasionally.'

'I guess he'll turn up soon.'

Later in the afternoon, however, Ben's mind returned to the subject. Why would a man ask his wife to come, then not even check if she'd replied to his letter? If he wanted to run out on her, he'd never have written that letter. And no man in his right mind would want to leave a lovely woman like her, anyway. Something must have happened to the bloke. He wouldn't be the first to die of typhoid or snakebite out in the bush.

'Time to pack it in don't y' think, Ben?' Danny's voice cut across his musing, and he was surprised to see the sun had begun its slide towards the horizon.

'Righto,' he replied. 'I'll go get some wood for the fire. I'm cooking tonight, so you've got a choice of tinned beef or tinned mutton.'

'Maybe we could live dangerously an' have the mutton,' Danny laughed. 'Seamus can have the beef.'

'He's not very happy with tin meat, I think. I'd better go get another roo.'

With dinner over, while Danny sat reading by the dim light of the lantern slung from the boughshed's rafters, Ben attempted to sketch him. Unhappy with the result, he rolled himself a smoke and sat watching as burning embers sparkled in the campfire smoke drifting towards the starry sky. Beautiful but dangerous, he thought, like this harsh country. Perhaps part of what called to him was that constant awareness of danger. Many men had succumbed to the unmerciful conditions on this goldfield.

That was hardly likely to have happened to Patterson, though. He wasn't still out prospecting, and he'd have had neighbours once word of his find got out, so why was there no news of him? He looked like a decent sort of bloke in his photograph, not that you could tell by that. *But who the Hell does he remind me of?* Someone from the past. Not back at home. Must be in Queensland. Well there were a lot of people in Brisbane.

'Think I'll be turning in, Ben,' Danny said, pulling himself up out of his chair.

'Me too,' Ben replied, yawning. 'See you in the morning.'

Towards morning, the dream came. But it was different. Millie was there, as usual. Her mouth moved but he couldn't hear her voice and, as her figure faded into a turmoil of hoof-beats and screaming, the horseman came towards him, sabre swinging. As it arced downwards, he lurched to the side and found himself on the ground, wide-awake and gasping. Sitting up, his pulse a drumbeat in his head, he found himself vainly trying to wipe away phantom drops of blood.

Where the Hell did that come from? The sabre-wielding maniac had never attacked him before. But it was the man's face that stuck in his mind. Now he knew where he had seen Ned Patterson before. 'Don't be ridiculous,' he told himself, but the idea persisted.

Chapter 13

A cool breeze whispered through the mulgas as Ben rode out on Sunday morning. Drawn to the glowing colours of the claypan and breakaway country to the northwest, he'd tucked some paper, and the little wooden paint box that had shared his wanderings, into his tucker-bag.

'Not goin' far today, mate,' he told his horse.

After an hour or so, he found what he was looking for. A clump of gimlet trees clustered at the base of a towering red and white breakaway. Dismounting, he loosened the saddle's girth strap and poured water into his hat for the horse before having a drink himself, leaving some in the mug for painting.

'Off you go, mate,' he told Walter, with a pat on the rump. 'Go find yourself something to eat, but don't go too far.'

Finding a suitable rock to sit on, he quickly sketched the rough outlines of the scene, before opening the battered little paintbox. The soft blues and greens of an English spring were barely worn, but little remained of the strong reds and ochre colours of the outback and he'd begun using the red dirt itself as a pigment.

It was only after almost poking himself in the eye with the brush while shooing the flies away, that he noticed that his bum was numb from the hard rock seat. That's why he liked painting.

He could forget everything, all the old pain and sorrow, even the whereabouts of his horse. Brought back to the present by that thought, he jumped up and was relieved to see Walter nibbling at the scrub on the far side of the flat.

'C'mon, fella,' he called waving the horse's nosebag. Walter lifted his head and, aware that the bag contained not just chaff but a liberal amount of oats, turned to amble back as Ben scouted around for firewood and kindling to make a small campfire near the shade of a gum tree.

'Here, mate,' he said as the horse wandered up, 'Let's get the old nosebag on.'

While the water came to the boil, he examined his morning's efforts. He was rarely satisfied with his work, but this wasn't too bad. *Maybe I should get some new paints*, he was thinking as he skewered a slab of damper on a stick to toast over the fire. Washed down with strong black tea, it was an adequate, if not inspiring, midday meal.

'Righto, Walter, me boy, time we got moving,' he said, removing the nosebag and offering the horse another drink, before kicking sand over the remains of his fire to extinguish it.

Back in the saddle, he decided to ride to the top of the breakaway before heading home, to see what sort of country extended further north. So it was mid afternoon before he cut the Broad Arrow track and turned towards Hannans. Then, seeing a horseman approaching from the direction of town, he sat waiting, despite the urge to retreat into the bush as he'd have done once.

Recognising the police uniform the man wore, Ben was relieved to see it was Constable Purkiss. He looked a bit lost, peering into the bush as if looking for a track. Then, on seeing Ben he rode up, calling out, 'Hello there, Drummond. Nice meeting a friendly face out here. I'm looking for a track off to the east. Do you know it?'

'I think there's one a bit further on. It's pretty overgrown but it might be what you're looking for.'

'I've been sent to investigate a dead body someone found out this way. The directions are very vague.'

'Do you know anything about the bloke?' Ben asked.

'No, just another poor devil overcome by thirst. The third this month. A couple of prospectors came across him lying in a dry creek bed. Which way are you heading? I don't suppose you could come along. You've been around these parts a while. You might be able to identify him.'

'Righto. I was on my way back to town but I'm not in a hurry.'

'By the way,' the policeman said as the rode on, 'we've got more information about that murderer we've been looking for. He's a deserter from the British army in India. Killed a fellow officer a couple of years ago and escaped to one of the ports. They reckon he came to Australia and decided a gold rush would be a great place to disappear.'

'Should we be worried he'll do someone else in?'

'No, they don't think he'll be a danger to the public unless he's cornered. Apparently, he and that Major knew each other, so it was probably a personal grudge.'

✺

'I think word's got around that there's a new woman staying with me, Nora,' Mary laughed. 'So, I expect all the fellas will want to come have a look this afternoon. We often get a few visitors on Sunday. It's the only day the blokes take time off scrabbling for gold.

'Oh, and I told Joey he could bring his pal Timmy over for lunch,' she added. 'I gave him money for some real bread so we can have sandwiches. Timmy's mum makes cool drinks and sells them in her shop. Hers are better than the dishwater some places are selling. I don't like her husband though. Seems a surly sort of bloke. Timmy talks a bit rough, but he's all right.'

It wasn't long before the boys turned up, accompanied by a scruffy little dog.

'Hello Timmy,' Mary said, before introducing him to Nora.

'G'day, Mrs Patterson,' he said, politely pulling off his shabby old hat. 'Ma thought you ladies might like some lemon drink, Mrs O'Callaghan.'

'Oh, that's nice of her, Timmy,' she said, taking the corked bottle. 'I'll make us some sandwiches and we can have the cool drink with them.'

The lemon drink was delicious, and surprisingly cool. 'That's really nice,' Nora said. 'Just like my auntie used to make.'

'I used to make it, but couldn't get any lemon essence,' Mary said.

'Mrs Kenny makes chili wine too, like Gran used to,' Joey put in between mouthfuls of canned beef sandwich.

Timmy was very quiet, obviously finding her presence inhibiting, Nora thought. He was taller than Joey, with thin bony legs and arms, and a serious expression that made him seem older than his friend. She was amused to see his straight, brown hair was still standing on end long after he removed his hat. Then she noticed something else.

'What happened to your ear, Timmy,' she blurted out, without thinking.

'Dog bit it,' he mumbled, flushing as his hand shot up to cover it.

'Oh, I'm sorry,' she said, 'That must have hurt.'

'It was ages ago.'

'My husband chopped off his big toe when he was a boy.'

'Did you know him back then?' asked Joey.

'Yes, we were school pals. I tried to stick it back on but that didn't work.'

'Of course it didn't,' Timmy said.

'Well, I was only six at the time. What's your dog's name, Timmy?' Nora said, trying to make amends for embarrassing him.

'Splinter. It weren't her what bit me. She's a good little bitch. It were a nasty big dog Pa had when he came t' live with us. I were glad when someone shot it.'

'I shouldn't have asked about Timmy's ear,' Nora said, when the boys had wandered off. 'I didn't stop to think he might be touchy about it.'

'I think he's got sick of being asked about it, so mostly keeps it hidden under that old hat.'

A little later, when Mary started mixing dough to make fried scones, Nora remembered she was expecting visitors. All male, it seemed. At the thought of having to meet new men after what had happened, she wondered if she could hide in Joey's little room, but before she could suggest that, a little man with pale eyes and giant ginger moustache knocked on the open door. 'Good morning, Mrs O'Callaghan,' he said in a squeaky voice.

'Hello Bert,' Mary said, then turned to Nora, introducing him as Bert Bowden.

'Pleased to meet you, Mrs Patterson' he said in response to her mumbled greeting.

Nora breathed a sigh of relief when Mary shepherded him out to the campfire, saying, 'Take a seat Bobby, the billy's on and I'll make some tea when the other fellas arrive.'

Seeing two more men at the gate, Nora lurked inside. But when Mary saw her cowering in there, she said, 'Look, I know these men. They're decent blokes. No one's going to embarrass or hurt you while you're under my roof. So come out and meet them.'

'Oh, Mary, I know it's silly, but I feel all panicky.'

'You need to eat something. Here, Freddie Chapman brought us some shop biscuits. Have one yourself and put the others on a plate and take them out there.'

A few minutes later, she took a deep breath and stepped out the door, the biscuits rattling on the plate as her hands shook.

'Do have a biscuit,' she said, after Mary introduced the newcomers.

Bluey Longmore, a tall redhead, helped himself to one, saying, 'you probably don't remember me, but I was there when you arrived on the coach and were looking for your husband. Did you find him?'

Nora was saved from answering when Mary cut in, 'Mrs Patterson is staying with me while waiting for her husband to join her.'

'Oh, good,' he replied. As he still showed an annoying level of curiosity, Nora was glad to see Mr O'Hara coming through the gate. With him was a tall man with a drooping grey moustache.

'Hello Danny, Charlie,' Mary greeted them.

'Good afternoon, ladies,' said O'Hara. 'Mrs Patterson, meet Charlie Osmond.'

'How do you do, Mr Osmond,' she said.

'Howdy, Ma'am.' the American replied with a slow smile.

'Hello there, Danny,' called Longmore, 'Ben off wanderin' again?'

'Yep. Think he planned on riding out towards the breakaways.'

Nora was surprised at the depth of her disappointment and realised she'd been hoping to see him again, despite her embarrassment about how they met.

'Oh, here comes another visitor,' Mary sighed and Nora turned to see a man in a very large hat swaggering up. A holstered gun hung from his belt.

'Oh, No, not Texas Tom,' muttered Danny.

'Hiya fellas. Good afternoon, Mrs O'Callaghan,' a twangy nasal voice called, 'and who is this other lovely lady?'

'Mrs Patterson,' Mary said, then, turning to Nora with a grimace on her face, 'meet Mr Tucker.'

'Pleased to meet you,' she said.

'The pleasure is all mine, Ma'am,' he replied with a flamboyant bow, before turning away to call out, 'Hey there, Danny. Where's y' limey pardner got to? Ain't seen him around much.'

'Well we've been workin' hard and Ben's busy today.'

'How come he rides off outa town on his big ol' bronc every Sunday? Goin' prospectin' is he? You running out of colour in that there little ol' mine of yours?'

'No, Tom, the mine's still payin' us wages.'

'Just likes to wander over yonder, does he? Odd that. Puts me in mind of a fella I knew back in Californie. Quiet hombre like that, didn't mix much. A bit of a mystery man till the U. S. Marshall came callin'. Seems he was wanted for murdering someone back east.'

'Waal,' came a slow drawl from the back corner of the bough shed, 'If you ever really was in California, my friend, you should mebbe have learned tain't healthy to stick your long nose into other fellas' business.'

Into the sudden quiet, Danny said, 'I guess you're not acquainted with my old mate Charlie Osmond, Tom. Wonder you never ran into him back there in the States. Meet Tom Tucker, Charlie.'

With the nosy American put in his place, the conversation moved on, but Nora was left wondering about Ben Drummond. Maybe he usually stayed away these gatherings. She'd thought he might be avoiding her.

'Joey, be a good lad and put some more wood on the fire,' Mary said, then called Nora to meet a new arrival, a handsome young man called Bill Thompson. Flashing her a toothy smile, he took her hand, though she'd not offered it. Holding it for longer than was polite, he expressed his delight in meeting her.

Nora mumbled something in reply and pulled away. After her recent experience, such close contact from a stranger was unwelcome. Flustered, she escaped inside to regain her composure, not emerging until she noticed Mary looking for her.

Smiling to reassure her friend, she sat by the fire listening to the men talking. About camels, it seemed.

'... reckon they can go days without water,' someone was saying.

'All the big prospectin' parties are usin' them.'

'Better than horses when there's no sure supplies of water,'

'Well, horses were lucky to survive out here that first summer.'

'Yes, some bastards rode the poor things till they dropped, then ran off to scrabble for gold, leavin' them to fend for themselves.'

Nora was only half-listening to the discussion about camels, until it began to get heated. Some of them, including the opinionated Tom Tucker, disliked the Afghans. But Nora had enjoyed seeing them in their colourful costumes that brought a touch of the exotic to the ragged, dusty town.

'A man needs a horse. The God-damned Afghans can keep their stinkin' camels.'

'Y' wouldn't say that, Tom, if you were out somewhere with y' poor horse dyin' of thirst.'

'We'd be hard up for tucker and even stuff to build our camps without the camel trains,' someone said.

'I hear they've sold that Londonderry mine down at Coolgardie,' said Bluey Longmore in an obvious attempt to change the subject. 'Some big English outfit buying it.'

'Yeah, another big company movin' in. Soon, there'll be no room for the little bloke.'

'There's still plenty gold for us little miners if we could dig closer to these bloody big mining leases.'

'Yeah, I hear some of the alluvial miners are talkin' about forming a union.'

'Oh Moran, the MP? He's a bit of a stirrer. Troublemaker, they say.'

'Who says? He's got the right idea. We need to unite, stick together to fight for our rights against the big companies. He reckons every man over twenty-one should get a vote too.'

'What about the women? They'll be wanting a vote too, now South Australia looks like giving in to these suffragettes.'

'And why shouldn't we have a vote?' said Mary.

'That shut them up,' she murmured, sitting next to Nora. 'If they keep getting hot under the collar, I'll have to break up the party. I don't know why that Tom Tucker turned up. I hardly know him. Danny can't stand him. Seems he's a friend of one of his mates.

'Oh, good, it looks like he's leaving. Charlie too,' she said, rising to farewell her guests.

'Thank you for your hospitality, Mrs O'Callaghan,' said Osmond. 'Nice meeting you Mrs Patterson.'

Slapping his hat on his head, he hurried away as if to avoid the company of the other man, who took both women's hands, saying, 'Farewell my lovely ladies. Sure was a pleasure to meet you, Mrs Patterson.'

Everyone seemed glad to see him go. Mary got up to make another cup of tea and Nora was surprised when the man named Thompson took her place on the log seat, sliding close. Too close, she thought, frowning.

As she ignored him, he patted her hand, saying, 'Please don't frown, Mrs Patterson. You have such a lovely smile.'

Snatching her hand away, she glowered at him, but was saved from having to respond by Mary, who asked him to move so she could sit there. Reluctantly, he gave up his seat and went to join the other men who were arguing about protectionism versus free trade.

'You all right now, Nora?' Mary asked.

'Yes. I'm sorry to have been so silly. Your friends are real gentlemen'

'Not so sure about Billy Thompson. Thinks he's irresistible to women. But he'd not step out of line.'

Chapter 14

Several crows flew off as Ben and the policeman dismounted and approached the body. The man must have been there for several months, the extreme heat and dryness having dried the carcass out, so the smell was not too bad. Any identifying marks had been obliterated by decomposition, but he appeared to have been fair-haired, of medium build. He seemed to have only four toes on the left foot, but Purkiss reckoned dingoes had been at the body and dragged the bones about.

A Miner's Right certificate was in the pocket of his coat, along with a few shillings and a couple of poor quality specimens of ore.

'Well, at least we know who the poor bastard was,' the constable said, looking at the Miners' Right. 'Name's Alexander McCaig.'

There was no way the remains could be removed, so they set to work digging a shallow grave in the sandy creek bed. When it was as deep as they could make it, they rolled the body into it, covered it with sand and piled rocks on the top to deter dingoes from disturbing the poor man's resting place. While Purkiss muttered a prayer, Ben scratched the man's name on a piece of fallen mulga to mark the grave.

'I guess all these blokes just lost their way and ran out of water,' Ben said, as they rode away, 'but it would be a great way to get rid of a body. By the time anyone finds them there's not much left to identify.'

'Well, did you find any suspicious clues, Sherlock?' Purkiss laughed.

'No, but I doubt if even Conan Doyle's smart detective would find anything after so long with the wind blowing dust over everything.'

'Good yarns, aren't they. He sure runs rings around the poor London bobbies. Are they really as stupid as he makes out?'

'Scotland Yard are pretty good, but the ordinary police aren't really trained to solve crimes.'

'So, you were in the force over there, hey?'

'Once upon a time.'

'Uncommunicative bugger, aren't you? Why'd you leave?'

'Migrated.'

'You know, we could use a bloke like you,' Purkiss said. 'You fellas are doing all right so far, but if the gold runs out and you're looking for a job, think about it. We need more men here. Since the railway got close to Southern Cross, there are dozens arriving every week on the coach. Mostly good folk, but always a few bad eggs. We've got brothels and sly grog shops opening up nearly every day. We no sooner pin one down, than another pops up.'

Ben shook his head. *They wouldn't touch me with a bargepole if they knew about my past*, he told himself with a grim smile.

'Well, keep it in mind, mate,' the young constable said, before going on to grumble about the problems confronting the handful of officers trying to keep the peace in the new town.

'How are we supposed to do our job working in a tent? A bloody willy-willy whisked all our paperwork out the door and across town the other day. A real dust storm would blow the whole box and dice away. And so much of our time is wasted chasing blokes who've wandered off into the bush. How are we supposed to find them? There must be thousands of men out here.'

'Probably are,' Ben told him, 'In the first few months, we had about fifteen hundred men here, four hundred at Coolgardie and another five hundred out prospecting. The place was like an ants' nest when we arrived. It's quietened down a lot. Some made a fortune and went off to live the high life. Others gave up and went home.'

'Anyway, mate, thanks for your help,' the policeman said as they reached the main track. 'I've got to see a bloke out at Broad Arrow. I'll see you around.'

Waving farewell, Ben rode back towards town sadly remembering his days as a young bobby, pounding London's cobbled streets with his mate, Jim. They joined the force at the same time and ended up marrying each other's sisters.

Jim was an easy-going bloke, but Ben had ambitions. The police force was changing, with a special detective branch at Scotland Yard, where ordinary constables could be posted to work with the detectives. Ben enjoyed the work and dreamed of becoming a detective himself. 'Getting ideas above your station,' grumbled his father-n-law, still a constable at sixty. He was right. There was no chance of promotion in London. Moving to the colonies might bring advancement, he was told. Instead, it brought disaster, grief and shame.

So it wasn't hunger for gold that drove him to join the thousands rushing to the new goldfields, but an attempt to escape the past. With hundreds of men crowded onto the steamship, all he wanted when they reached Albany was to get away from his fellow travellers, all making their way to the goldfields, nearly 500 miles away.

Those with enough money travelled partway by train, then bought or hired horses or wagon rides for the long trip, over rough tracks, to the new goldfield. But for Ben, like many others, the only option was to walk.

The weather was lovely that first day, and the bush bright with flowers, as he stepped out along the railway line, heading north to Broomehill, from where a man named John Holland, with the two Krakouer brothers, was blazing a new 230-mile 'short cut' to the goldfields. The sugarbag slung over his shoulder contained flour, tea, tinned meat and a panning off dish, while his rifle, prospector's pick and shovel were rolled up in his swag, from which dangled a waterbag and billycan.

The next day dawned dark and dismal, with a soaking drizzle that hung about all morning. Fighting off waves of melancholy, he kept on, to be rewarded in the afternoon, when the sun came out, bathing everything with a golden light. That afternoon, he caught up with a white-whiskered prospector pushing a wooden wheelbarrow bigger than himself, loaded with mining tools and supplies. After making friends with the man's dog, Ben introduced himself and offered to push in exchange for room on the barrow for his swag.

Looking him up and down, the old fellow addressed the dog, 'What do y' think, Seamus? Y' reckon that might be a good idea?'

Seeming to receive an affirmative reply, he turned to Ben.

'Pleased t' meet you, I'm Danny O'Hara, and I'd be glad to take a break from pushin' this load, so pile y' stuff on.'

'Thanks, Mr. O'Hara,' Ben replied, taking up the barrow handles. 'You pushed this all the way from Albany?'

'Well, I'm used to travellin' this way. Been chasin' gold for a long time. California, an' the Victorian rush in the 50s.'

'Have any luck?'

'Enough t' keep me lookin,' he chuckled. 'It becomes a habit, this gold seekin'. I was thinking of goin' t' the South African rush, when I heard about the big find here.'

Looking back, Ben was surprised that he teamed up with the Irishman when for years he'd travelled alone. Maybe it was simply that Danny and the dog were prepared to take him on trust.

Reaching Coolgardie, hard on the heels of Holland and his mates, they decided to go into partnership. Danny to supply the mining know-how, and the six-foot Ben providing the muscle.

A month later, they heard that three Irish prospectors, Hannan, Flanagan and Shea had made a rich find about thirty miles east of Coolgardie, so joined the hundreds who rushed to peg mining claims at Hannan's Find. Ben, like most of the new arrivals, was dazzled by the easily-found alluvial gold, and set to work to provide them with a substantial stake, while Danny was casting an experienced eye over the lay of the land and investigating the promising quartz outcrop that had provided them with a decent income for nearly two years.

⚬⚬⚬

About dusk, Nora was washing her hands after a visit to the little dunny behind the cottage, when she heard hoof beats and looked up to see the silhouette of a tall man on a tall horse at the gate. Scurrying to the door, she whispered, 'Mary, there's a man out here.'

'Probably just Ben on his way home,' Mary said, stepping outside. 'Hello Ben. You an' Walter have a good day?'

'Yes thanks Mary,' he replied doffing his hat, 'I shot a couple of ducks on the way home, Mary. Thought you might like one.'

'Ooh, I certainly would. Thanks Ben. We're getting spoiled with all this real meat.'

'Nice to get a change from tinned dog,' he said, with a wry smile that seemed to fade when he saw Nora looking at him. She quickly looked away, embarrassed to be caught watching his face.

Chapter 15

Nora had been lying awake for hours worrying about Ned, and how she could survive with no money and no job. She was still awake at dawn when Mary yawned and sat up.

'Sorry if I disturbed you,' she said when Nora stretched her cramped legs.

'No, it's all right. I was awake.'

'Better get dressed before I call Joey.'

By the time the boy emerged, yawning, Mary had tea and toasted damper ready.

'Don't you dare go out until you've combed this mop,' his mother said, tousling his ginger hair.

'I tried Mum. But it's got all knotty.'

'Well eat up, then I'll see what I can do. You need t' comb it every day. You eat up too, Nora. Better grab some before Joey eats it all.'

'Thanks Mary,' Nora said, taking a slice of toast.

'D' you need me for anything this morning, Mum?' Joey asked, his mouth full of damper and treacle. 'Me an' Timmy was goin' speckin' for gold down the creek if he can sneak out. We're sure to find a nugget if we keep lookin'.'

'I didn't know there was a creek,' Nora said. 'Everything seems so dry.'

'Well, there's no water in it, just rocks an' sand 'cause we don't get much rain here. Mr O'Hara says a long time ago there was lotsa rain, an' it washed gold down from the hill where the mines are and into the creek. Gold's worth a lot of money, so we gonna keep lookin'.'

'Watch out for snakes down there, an' scorpions under the rocks.'

'We always do, Mum. Did y' hear a bloke got bitten by a snake out at Burdong. His mate cut it an' sucked the poison out, an' he was all right.'

'I'm surprised more men don't get bitten,' Mary said, 'I guess they've learned t' be careful.'

'Are there lots of snakes?' Nora asked.

'Yes, you were lucky not to meet one the other night. Good thing you had your boots on. More tea?'

'Yes, please, Mary.'

While the two women sipped their tea, Joey consumed the last piece of toast, before saying, 'Mum, y' know Mrs Malley what has the grog shop down past the blacksmith's? Her husband must be dead, 'cos she was kissin' the fella from the bakers. D' you think she's goin' t' marry him?'

'I'm sure I haven't the faintest idea, Joey. Anyway, it's none of my business. Or yours either,' she replied, reaching for her hairbrush. 'Here let's have a look at your hair.'

As soon as she'd tidied his tangled curls, Joey slapped on his old hat and made his escape.

'I worry he and Timmy will get into trouble wanderin' around Hannans. The miners are mostly good blokes, but all sorts are comin' in now.'

'Shouldn't he be at school?'

'We haven't got one yet. There aren't enough children here.'

'I guess there's no chance of getting work caring for someone's children, then,' Nora sighed, looking around the small, cluttered room. 'I must find work and somewhere to stay, Mary. You've been so kind, but I can't go on sponging off you.'

'Oh, Nora, don't cry,' Mary said, seeing the tears in her eyes.

'Don't tell me Ned'll come back, Mary,' Nora sobbed. 'He must be dead. He'd never have abandoned me out here after asking me to come.'

'I'm afraid you might be right. Even if he was sick, surely someone would have brought a message.'

'I keep seeing him lying out there somewhere. And I can't help thinking maybe he took his own life, Mary.'

'Now, why would he do that?' her friend asked. 'Here he was looking forward to you coming and joining him. And he'd found gold. He must have been really happy.'

'Not if he knew I'd betrayed him,' Nora sobbed. 'What if he'd heard about that? No, No! He couldn't have.'

'Do you want to talk about it?' her friend asked.

'I was unfaithful, Mary. I had an affair. He was one of the doctors at the hospital. I was ready to divorce Ned and marry him, but he was married too, and he didn't really love me anyway.'

Soon the whole story poured out. He was one of those grand creatures who strode through the wards while the nurses stood to attention, scared that something wrong with their uniforms, the set of their veils, or the folded corners of the bedcovers, might attract Matron's disapproving eye.

'I'd heard the other nurses sighing over handsome Dr Carruthers, but I was a happily married woman. I shouldn't have listened to the things he whispered while pretending to ask about the patients, but I was so lonely after Dad died.

'I thought I was in trouble when I was told to report to the Registrar in his office, but it was him. Before I had time to resist, he was kissing me. I did try to pull away,' she said, blushing at the memory.

'He was such a good kisser. And such a good liar,' she laughed, wryly. 'I don't know what came over me. He got me a live-in job looking after one of his patients, an old lady named Mrs Riordan. He came to see her every day, but she couldn't get out of bed, so had no idea that we were carrying on under her roof.'

After a brief visit to his patient, he'd whisk Nora away, ostensibly to discuss the treatment. But no sooner were they out of the room than he was pulling off her white veil and undoing the ties of her starched apron. By the time they reached the parlour she was lost. After he'd gone, Nora would do her best to return her clothing to the standard expected of a nurse, but the old lady soon noticed what was going on.

'One morning, she said, "You need to watch that one, girl. Only interested in one thing. Better to make 'em pay for it." As she started getting better, James and I had less time together. I should have seen it was all over when he started rushing off after a quick kiss, but I was too busy worrying about how to tell Ned I'd found someone else. It wasn't until I confessed to James that I was married, and he just laughed and said, "That makes two of us!" that I realised he'd never meant the things he'd said about us being together.'

'So, what happened,' Mary asked when she'd been quiet for a long time.

'He stopped coming to see Mrs Riordan. Sent another doctor. Then I got Ned's letter. It was Mrs Riordan who said I should come. Hearing about him going to West Australia and finding gold, she told me she'd been at the gold rush in California and gave me some advice about what to expect out here. Oh Mary, it's such a relief to tell someone. The guilt has been gnawing away at me.'

'Well, you need to put it behind you and get on with your life, whether Ned comes back or not. But you never said you were a nurse. We've got a hospital of sorts here now. You might get work there. They're desperate to get some nurses. One of the shopkeepers' wives, Mrs Alderdice, is the temporary matron. I'm not sure if they've got any money to pay you, but you would have somewhere to sleep, even if it's just a tent.'

'I didn't know there was a hospital.'

'It's only a few tents up towards the big mine.'

'I did see some big tents out there when I was looking for work, but there was no one around.'

'It's just opened. I know Mrs Alderdice. I'll take you to see her this afternoon. Anyway, let's have another cuppa.'

'Oh Mary, thanks for listening to me wailing. I feared you would throw me out when you heard what kind of a woman I was.'

That afternoon, Mary took Nora up to the hospital. There was a huge tent, two smaller ones, a corrugated iron kitchen with a tin chimney, a partly-built hessian building and a tiny tin outhouse in the bushes to the right. Further away, two men worked on another small building.

When a lady stepped out of the kitchen, Mary called out and ran to intercept her. After a few words, the woman nodded, glanced at Nora, and walked over to the main tent.

'That's Mrs Alderdice,' Mary said as she came back. 'Come on, she wants to talk to you.'

As they entered the large tent, Nora saw it was set up as a hospital ward.

'Mrs Alderdice, this is my friend Nora Patterson,' Mary said, as the matron came to meet them.

'Pleased to meet you, Mrs Patterson. Come into my elegant office,' she laughed, indicating a corner partitioned off with pine planks.

'I'll be on my way, then,' Mary said. 'Got to get down to Windells.'

'Mary, before you go,' said the older woman, 'I hear you do some sewing. I've ordered several bolts of cloth. We are going to need it made into sheets, aprons and caps. If you can do the work, I'll let you know when it arrives.'

'Oh yes, I'd be very interested,' Mary replied, before almost skipping out the door. Nora knew how much that work would mean to her.

'Now, Mrs Patterson,' Mrs Alderdice said, sitting behind the rough plank table and waving Nora to the other chair, 'Mary said you're a nurse.'

'I worked at the Melbourne hospital for nearly a year. I was still only a trainee, but I did help in theatre a few times.'

'Your friend said you've found yourself stranded here. What happened?'

'I don't know. My husband wrote asking me to come, but he's not here. I've been here over a week. Mrs O'Callaghan kindly took me in, but I have no money left.'

'So, you're available until he turns up?'

'Yes. I'm sorry I can't say how long that'll be.'

'Well, I'll be glad to have you on board for as long as you can stay. We can't get trained nurses to come out here. As you can see, this isn't like a real hospital and the living conditions are primitive. We're hoping for government help to set it up properly. But in the meantime, we're needed here so sick men aren't being dragged off to Coolgardie over rough roads. Some died on the way.

'So, for now it's only these tents and the tin kitchen. The new hessian fever ward will be finished soon. Oh, and we hope to have a morgue of sorts by next week. Sadly, we really need one. Some of our patients are too far gone when we get them. I could really use someone with hospital experience, but we can't pay you a proper wage. Just your keep and a small allowance. And I'm afraid the nurses' quarters is just another tent.

'I really need somewhere to live, so I'm not fussy, Mrs Alderdice.'

Standing up, the matron said, 'Come, and I'll show you around. You'll find it's nothing like what you've been used to. This tent is our only ward at present. It has room for eight patients. At least it has a real floor, but there's no way of keeping the dust out, so we are constantly sweeping. Often, I can't even spare the water to dampen the dust.

'This is the nurses' tent,' she continued, leading the way to one of the smaller tents. Inside, Nora glimpsed four stretcher beds covered in grey blankets. 'I'm afraid it has a dirt floor and you'd be sharing with the other nurses. Also, if we're very busy some of the other shopkeepers' wives come in to help and they might need to take turns in the beds. How soon could you start?'

'Tomorrow, if you need me,' Nora said.

'Oh, good. Welcome aboard. Have you got much luggage?'

'No, not really. A little trunk. I could leave it with Mary if there's not enough room.'

'That might be best.'

'I'll have to ask her. She doesn't have much room in her place.'

'Well, there is a sort of storeroom here, but it's not very secure.'

Mary would still be working so, nervous about waiting out in the road with so many strange men milling about, Nora spent a few of her last pennies on a cup of tea and a currant bun at the little teashop over the road from Windells' Hotel. Among the passersby, she recognised one of Mary's friends, the redheaded Bluey, on the far side of the road. Watching him hail someone and stride across towards her, she was wondering why redheads got that nickname, when she saw Ben Drummond step out to shake his hand.

She couldn't hear what they were saying but while the redhead waved his arms excitedly, she found herself watching Drummond's profile. When the other man finished his story and laughed out loud, a fleeting dimple flickered in his cheek as a slow smile transformed his serious expression.

When the two men walked on, she saw Mary emerge from the pub to head home, so hurriedly finished her tea and left the teashop.

'Mary,' she called, running to catch up.

'Oh, hello, Nora. How did you get on?'

'I've got the job, Mary. I start tomorrow. There's not much room in the nurses' tent. I wonder if I could leave my trunk at your place.'

'I don't mind. It's out of the way under the bed.'

'I'll need to decide what to take,' Nora was saying as Mary pushed open her gate.

'Well, you can do that while I get dinner on. You home, Joey?' she called.

'Yeah, Mum. I got the fire lit. What's for dinner?'

'Just more tinned corned beef an' spuds, I'm sorry t' say. Can you peel the spuds, Joey?'

'Sure Mum. I kinda like corned beef an' spuds.'

'Do you mind if I spread my stuff out on the bed to sort it, Mary,' Nora asked, 'I don't know how much will fit in my bag.'

'Go ahead.'

'I guess I won't be needing my one good dress. I'm so glad I brought practical clothes. Oh, here's our wedding photograph.'

'You look lovely and your Ned's very handsome.'

'We were so happy that day,' Nora sighed, laying the photograph on the bedcover, and lifting the next item from the trunk's tray.

'What's that?'

'Oh, it's a gun', Nora replied, opening the box to show her the little weapon.

'It's almost pretty with that engraving,' Mary laughed.

'That old lady who'd been out on the American goldfields gave it to me. Said I should carry it for protection here. But I've not needed it. Good thing I didn't have it on me when that McRoberts got out of hand, I might have shot him instead of just flattening him with a frying pan.'

'Do you know how to use it?'

'Well, she did show me, and I've fired a shotgun. But to be honest, I'm a bit scared of it. She said to wear it under my dress and make a slot in my skirt so I can reach it. I did do that, but I'm afraid I'll shoot myself in the foot, or worse.'

'Danny knows a bit about handguns. Maybe leave it here an' I'll show it to him next time he drops by.'

Chapter 16

After working hard all morning, Danny collapsed in his chair with a plate of bully beef stew. He'd never admit that he was too tired to keep working, so Ben was pleased when, having finished his meal, he said, 'I'm thinkin' I might wander over and see poor old Fred Thomas. I hear he's been sick for the last few days. I'm a bit worried about him.'

'Maybe take him the rest of that stew. There's not enough left for tonight's meal,' Ben said.

'Yes, I might do that,' his mate replied, bending to pick up the pot, 'I'll see you later, Ben.'

'Righto. I'll just go on with the dollying then, shall I?'

'That'd be good. I don't intend to be long, just checkin' up on the old fella.'

Taking up the iron bar they used to crush rock in the big dollypot, Ben set to work. Despite the physical effort, the rhythmic action took little conscious thought, and he found himself once again thinking about Mrs Patterson's missing husband. Surely, he wouldn't have asked his wife to come if he didn't want her here. Could the boys be on the right track? Well, maybe not murder, but he might be lying dead somewhere out there. *Look at that poor bugger we found the other day. I guess his folks must be worrying about him.*

Seamus, who usually gave plenty warning of anyone approaching, had gone with Danny, so Ben, still lost in thought, jumped when he heard a scuffle of footsteps close behind him.

'Hello, Mr Drummond.'

'Oh, hello, Joey. For goodness' sake, don't creep up behind people. You frightened the life out of me.'

'Sorry, Mr Drummond. Is Mr O'Hara here? I brought back the paper with the Sherlock Holmes story.'

'He's gone to visit a friend. I think he meant you to keep the paper, Joey.'

'That'd be bonza. I really like reading about Mr Holmes. He's real clever findin' all them clues. Knows lotsa big words too, like alimentary.'

'Isn't it elementary with an E? Alimentary's to do with your guts.'

'Oh.'

'Finding clues isn't really as easy as it seems in those stories. When he finds a footprint, he always knows who made it. How can he be sure? What if we found prints made by someone with a peg leg. Would you know if it was Mr Cartwright from the Six-mile, or that bloke from the saloon? They're great stories but Sherlock Holmes isn't a real person you know.'

'Doncha think Mr Conan Doyle is writing about someone real? I mean he's obviously Dr Watson, so Mr Holmes must be someone.'

'Perhaps you're right Joey. I hadn't thought about that, but the London police are smarter than he makes them. They find lots of clues, but they don't always add up. A fella, in France, I think, reckons if someone leaves a handprint on the wall, you can tell whose it is by the patterns on their fingertips. Seems we've all got different ones.'

'D' you think that's right?' Joey asked, examining his grubby fingers.

'I don't know, and the experts pooh-pooh the idea, but it makes more sense than the other idea that you can tell criminals by the shape of their heads.'

'Maybe if Mr Holmes was here, he'd find out what's happened to Mr Patterson.'

'He's still not turned up, then?'

'No. Mrs Patterson's been doing a lot of cryin' on Mum's shoulder.'

'How do you think Holmes would go about looking for clues? The trail will have gone cold, don't you think?'

'They need to find the man I saw with him that I thought was his brother.'

'You've seen his picture. Are you sure the other man was just like him?'

Joey screwed up his face in concentration. 'No, not 'zactly. He had one squinty eye and his beard was more ginger. Well, the nice bloke I think must have been the Patterson fella had yellow whiskers.'

Chapter 17

Next morning, Nora was awake before dawn, eager to get to the hospital and start work, but worried about coping with the strange conditions. It would be nothing like working in a well-ordered hospital. Could she bumble through, finding her way without appearing completely incompetent? By the time she had got dressed, she'd worked herself up into a state of anxiety.

'Are you all right, Nora?' Mary asked.

'No, just worried I might do something wrong, like poison someone.'

'Now, don't be silly. Mrs Alderdice will be there, and the other nurses. You'll be all right.

'Anyway, you'll need a proper breakfast. Nursing's hard work and you mightn't get a chance for a meal. I'm opening a tin of canned beans for Joey. You should have some too.'

'Just a little bit on a piece of damper then, thanks,' Nora said, as Joey wandered out of his room, yawning.

'Wakey, wakey, Joey,' said his mother. 'Didn't you sleep well, love?

'I dreamt about Sherlock Holmes. Prob'ly because I been wonderin' what he'd do to find Mr Patterson. Can't remember what happened,' he said, frowning, 'But it got scary and woke me up.'

'Maybe I should stop you reading that stuff,' Mary said, placing a heaped plate in front of him.

'Mrs Patterson,' said Joey through a mouthful of beans, 'Did Mr Patterson have whiskers?'

'Just a moustache, but he probably grew a beard here.'

'Yeah, all the blokes have got whiskers, except for new-chums and silvertails. I'm sure that was him I saw. He gave me a whole shillin' for minding his horse and cart. But that other man looked a lot like him.'

'Maybe he was just a mate, Joey,' put in his mother.

'The men I showed Ned's picture to seemed to think there were a lot of fellows who looked a bit like him. One had a wooden leg,' Nora said with a shaky laugh, getting to her feet. 'I guess I'd better be on my way.'

'Good luck,' Mary said as Nora pinned on her hat and picked up the bag of clothes. 'Come and see us whenever you can. There'll always be a cuppa in the pot.'

'Thank you, for everything Mary,' Nora said. 'I don't know what I'd have done without your help.'

Stepping out into the cool morning, she was relieved to find very few men on the street. Most were already hard at work. She had almost reached the hospital when someone called her name. Startled, she turned to see a black-bearded stranger approaching, touching his hat.

'I'm Jim Blake' he said. 'We met on the coach. Remember?'

'Oh, yes Mr Blake. How do you do?'

'Very well, thank you. Just not getting rich as quick as I hoped,' he laughed. 'How about you? You were coming to join your husband if I remember rightly. Are you living in town?'

'I'm helping out at the hospital while waiting for him,' she said.

'There aren't many ladies here. Have you got to know some of them?'

'Yes,' she replied.

'The reason I ask is that my family has come up to join me. My wife would like to meet some other ladies.'

'I'd be delighted to get to know her of course but, until my husband arrives, I'm living at the hospital so have nowhere to entertain friends.'

'Would you come to our place if she invited you? It's not much of a house. Just the usual Hannans hessian mansion.'

'Yes, that would be nice. She could contact me care of Mrs Alderdice at their shop. She's running the hospital.'

'Thank you,' he said 'Well, I won't hold you up. It was nice seeing you again, Mrs Patterson,' Blake said, touching his hat as he turned to go.

Hurrying on her way, Nora arrived at the hospital to find it in chaos. When the matron saw her, she rushed over, saying, 'Mrs Patterson, thank God you're here. Can you start straight away?'

'Yes, of course.'

'It's been quite a night. Four new cases. We have a crushed leg, and three men came in with dysentery. It could be a symptom of typhoid, so I've isolated them in the other ward, though it's not properly finished.'

Handed a big apron and a sort of mobcap, Nora was set to work sponging down the bedbound patients with some of the hospital's scarce water supply. Hearing Matron call her name, she thought she must have done something wrong. But Mrs Alderdice, who'd seen that the new nurse really was more experienced than most of her helpers, said, 'Nurse Patterson, leave that for Nurse Briggs to finish. You said you'd helped in theatre?'

'Yes, but only a couple of times.'

'Well, doctor needs to amputate young Mr Nelson's leg. It can't be saved. I will be assisting him, but I'd like you to stand by in case of an emergency. For now, could you stay with the poor young man until doctor arrives? He's in a lot of pain but I can't give him morphine before the anaesthetic. He's in the kitchen. It will have to serve as our theatre.'

'Of course, Matron,' Nora said, heading for the one iron building, where the table was spread with a clean sheet. A dish of water, strongly redolent of carbolic, lay on a chair ready for the doctor to wash his hands. The patient was very young, and very pale.

'How are you feeling, Mr Nelson?'

'Not real good, Nurse. Please call me Johnny.'

'Did Matron explain that we can't give you something for the pain because you'll be having chloroform, Johnny?'

'Yes,' he grimaced. 'I'm all right.'

He obviously wasn't, so she tried to keep him talking hoping it might take his mind off what was going to happen. For someone so young to lose a leg would be devastating.

'Have you been at Hannans long?' she asked.

'We came in the first rush. We've done pretty well, but Dad can't work the mine on his own.' Then, his voice breaking, 'And I'm going to be useless.'

Nora was saved from replying, as Dr Martin hurried in.

'Righto, young John Nelson,' he said, bending to wash his hands. 'I'm sorry we can't save your leg. If we leave it, it'll go rotten and kill you, so it's got to come off. Here Nurse, You're new, aren't you?'

'Yes doctor.'

'Well, please lay out my tools on the end of the table. Where's that wardsman got to? We need to get on with this. Ah, Matron, here you are. And our missing wardsman. Here, Dunne, let's get the boy on the table.'

Nora felt herself wincing in sympathy with the patient's groans as he was lifted. It was all very different from the operating theatre in Melbourne.

In the end, Nora wasn't needed. Matron obviously knew how to administer chloroform and as soon as the patient lost consciousness, Dr Martin got to work to remove the badly damaged limb, then cauterise and stitch the wound.

Some time later, Matron called her into the office. 'Thank you for mucking in, Mrs Patterson,' she said. 'Are you still happy to stay?'

'Yes, Mrs Alderdice. I need the work and somewhere to live until my husband turns up.'

'Oh, good. I think we've earned a tea break, then I'll let you get settled,' she said, leading the way out to the kitchen, where a young nurse was stoking the wood stove. 'Nurse Briggs,' said Matron, 'This is Nurse Patterson. She will be sharing the tent with you girls. Can you show her around. And yes, you can make us all a cup of tea.'

Nora had been worried about suggesting Mr Blake's wife contact her through Mrs Alderdice, but the matron seemed in a more approachable mood, so she diffidently explained that there might be a letter.

'Don't worry, Nurse,' she replied. 'If one turns up, I'll pass it on to you.'

Conversation was stilted until the matron left, then Nurse Briggs let out a sigh of relief, whispering, 'She's in a surprisingly good mood, after all that fuss.'

'When did the urgent cases come in?'

'I got dragged out of bed about two, when the first bloke with dysentery came in. We got the young man with the crushed leg about six. Doctor had to cut it off. Of course, you know that. Matron is worried the dysentery cases might have typhoid. It's a horrible, sneaky thing. They think they've just got a cold or it's something they ate, so it's too late by the time we get them. I hope these blokes have just got the scutters. Anyway, I'm supposed to be showing you around, so better get moving or she'll be after my tail.'

'I've got a bag of clothes I left outside. I didn't expect to be working straight away. I'd better go and get it.'

'Yes, and I'll show you where you'll be sleeping. I'm Molly, by the way.'

'And I'm Nora.'

Leading the way into the small tent that served as nurses' quarters, Molly said, 'there are four beds. Aggie Spence sleeps there, she should be sleeping now. She did night shift. I'm here, and the one in the corner is for other ladies who come to help, so you'll have the one in the other corner.'

There wasn't much space, only the four beds, a little cupboard and a curtained hanging rack in the corner.

'The curtain keeps some of the dirt out, unless we get a dust storm,' Molly said, 'but we find it's best to keep most of our stuff in our bags or cases under the beds. Now, we'd better get back before Matron comes to check up on us.'

'Thanks for showing me around,' Nora said, tossing her bag on the bed.

Back on the ward, it was time to give the patients their midday meal, then the nurses took turns to have their own.

⚓

Ben was stooping to swing the heavy bucket of ore away from the windlass, when Joey reached the camp.

'Hello, Mr Drummond,' he called as Seamus bounded out to greet him. 'Mum mended your shirt. Here it is,'

'Oh, that was quick.'

'Mum said it was just a seam comin' undone. Yours'll take a bit longer Mr O'Hara, she said,' he went on, as Danny climbed out of the mine and joined them.

'Well, thank her from me, Joey,' Ben said.

'How you all been gettin' on?' Danny asked. 'I dropped in yesterday afternoon but no one was home.'

'Oh, Mum took Mrs Patterson up to the hospital.'

'What's wrong with Mrs Patterson?' Ben asked with a worried frown.

'Oh, nothin's wrong. It's just that she's a nurse. Going to work there. She went up there this morning.'

'That's good,' said Danny. 'It was kind of y' mum to take her in, but you don't have a lot of room to spare.

'Mum's asked her to come an' see us sometimes. I think she liked havin' another lady to talk to. Her husband's still not turned up.'

'It's good that she's found somewhere to live,' Ben said, stooping to sprinkle tea into the bubbling billycan.

'Can you join us for a cuppa, young Joseph, or is Mum expectin' you home?' Danny asked, as Ben handed him a mug.

'Mum's workin', so I can stay.'

'I thought so, Joey,' Ben said. 'Here's your tea. You can help yourself to some damper an' treacle, if you like.'

'Yes please.'

'Ah! Nothin' like a nice cup o' tea,' Danny said, leaning back in his bush timber armchair.

'Mr Drummond,' Joey said after a few minutes, 'you know when we was talkin' about Sherlock Holmes and you asked if I could tell which peglegged fella made the tracks. Well, I can. Mr Jones from the saloon leaves a kinda square track, but Mr Cartwright's peg is round.'

'They wouldn't want to be up to no good with a smart detective like you on their trail,' Danny laughed.

'I hope they didn't see you tracking them,' Ben said. 'I'd be very annoyed to find some young fella following me around looking at where I've been. You boys got to be careful where you go snooping. Detective work isn't a game.'

Chapter 18

Nora was relieved that the afternoon was relatively quiet. Except for keeping watch on young Johnny Nelson, it was routine work. The dysentery cases showed no sign of fever and Matron was satisfied that it was food poisoning.

'They shared a meal last night,' she said, 'It's a wonder we don't get more cases of that with no way to keep food cool and away from vermin.'

Later, with the evening meal over, Nora was helping settle the patients for the night, when Mrs Alderdice said, 'Nurse Patterson, do you think you could do the early morning shift from three am? Nurse Spence will take over now, so you can get some rest. I'm sorry to load the work onto you on your first day, but I think young Nurse Briggs needs her sleep, she did an extra three hours today. Oh, here's Nurse Spence now.'

The other nurse was a tall, stern-looking young woman with a surprisingly sweet smile. Nora wondered how she managed to keep her apron and cap so white.

'You can knock off now, Nurse Patterson. Three o'clock, remember.'

'I don't have an alarm clock, Matron.'

'I'll come and wake you,' the other nurse told her.

'Wake up. Wake up,' came the whispered command. A guttering candle flame flickered in the darkness.

'What's wrong?' Nora gasped, sitting bolt upright on the rickety bed.

'It's time for your shift, Nurse Patterson.'

'Oh, I'm sorry. I didn't know where I was for a few seconds there. What time is it?'

'Nearly three. Hurry up. I'll light your candle from mine, then I must get back to the ward.'

'Thank you for waking me,' Nora whispered.

Still half asleep, she fumbled with the fasteners on her clothes, ran out to the lavatory, washed her hands and gulped down a cup of water.

Maybe there'd be time for breakfast later.

'Oh good,' said Nurse Spence, as Nora hurried into the ward. 'Everything's pretty quiet. Johnny Nelson will probably wake up soon and you can give him two drops of morphine. Good luck. If you have any real trouble, come and wake me, but Matron will be along in a few hours.

'Thank you, Nurse Spence,' Nora said.

'Call me Aggie when Matron's not around.'

'And I'm Nora. Sweet dreams and I hope I don't need to bother you.'

With all the patients asleep, there was time to catch her breath and find out where the few supplies and utensils were kept, before she heard the young amputee moaning. He was barely awake, but obviously in pain.

'Mr Nelson, Johnny,' she murmured, taking his hand to reassure herself that his pulse was normal, 'Would you like a drink of water?'

'Yes please,' came the whispered reply as his pain-filled eyes fluttered open.

'How are you feeling?' she asked, holding the water bottle for him to sip.

'My leg hurts, nurse. When I move my foot, my leg hurts. My foot hurts too. How can it when it's not there anymore?'

'I think sometimes that happens. I can give you something to help with the pain.'

Carefully measuring out the dose of morphine, she brought it back to find the young man in tears.

'What am I gonna do, Nurse?' he sobbed, angrily wiping his eyes. 'I can't work with one leg, can I? I'll be another poor pegleg wandering around lookin' for handouts. Oh God.'

'I'm sure there'll be some sort of work you can do,' Nora said, aware that she was probably offering him false hope. 'Here drink this. It'll make you feel better. Isn't there a man with one leg who works at one of the saloons in town?'

'Yes. And there's Mr Cartwright. He's got a mine at the Six Mile. But his mate's got two legs.'

'How did you get on at school, Johnny? If you're good at writing or sums you could work in an office.'

'I didn't do too bad. But I left when I was twelve to come out here with Dad. Does he know what's happened? Has he come to see me?'

'He was here yesterday but you were asleep. He'll be back to see you later.'

'Poor Dad, I must have given him an awful fright.'

'What happened?'

'The rope snapped, and the bucket of rock fell on my leg.'

'Perhaps I shouldn't be making you think about it.'

'Oh, it's good talkin' to you, Nurse. Makes it easier to put up with the pain. I think that medicine's making it a bit better, too.'

'Well maybe you might be able to sleep for a while. Doctor will be in later to see how you are.'

When the morphine had done its job and the boy slept, Nora began her rounds checking on the other patients. It was too early to wake them for the usual hospital routines, but old Mr Howard was awake.

'How are you feeling?' she asked him, taking his pulse.

'A lot better, Nurse. I'm hopin' the doc might let me go home today.'

'Well, he'll be in later, but I'm not sure you're ready to go home.'

Soon the other patients were stirring, and she was kept busy until Matron arrived.

'I'll take over here Nurse. You go and get yourself a cup of tea and something to eat.'

Not wanting to spoil the good impression her efforts had made, she didn't tarry over her breakfast but hurried back.

'Nurse Patterson,' Matron said, some time later, 'There's a letter here from that Mrs Blake.'

'Thank you, Matron,' she replied, slipping it into her apron pocket, where it stayed until she had knocked off and was enjoying a quiet cup of tea in the kitchen.

"Dear Mrs Patterson," she read, "I am newly arrived in Hannans and don't know any other ladies. My husband suggested that you might join me for afternoon tea one day. At present, I am staying at the Club Hotel. Yours sincerely, Alice Blake."

Back in the nurses' tent, she wrote a quick note to say she could come on Monday afternoon, if that was acceptable, delivering it at the hotel on her way to Mary's. She found her friend balanced on a stool, hammering a nail into one of the posts of the wall.

'Hello, Nora,' she said, climbing down from her perch, 'Sit yourself down. I'll only be a minute.'

'What are you doing?'

'Hanging up my picture of Paddy,' she said. 'I got it framed while I was in Perth. Ben drew it, y' know. An' that's my Paddy. He looks so serious in photographs, but he was always laughing or singing.'

Nora was surprised by the quality of the little sketch. 'It's very good. Did he go to art school?'

'I don't know where he learned to do it. But then, he never talks about the past. Can you stay for a cuppa? Billy's boiling.'

'Yes, please, Mary.'

'How did your first two days go?'

'All right. But it's nothing like working at a big hospital. We were very busy yesterday, and today I started at three o'clock. The other nurses seem nice, and Mrs Alderdice isn't as stiff and bossy as my old matron. I think she wants me to do the early morning shift for a while.

'Well remember to drop in for a cuppa in the afternoons, if you can.'

'Thanks Mary. Oh, I've been invited to afternoon tea at the Club Hotel,' Nora said, 'I don't suppose it's very flash, is it?'

'Maybe a little bit for Hannans,' she laughed. 'They've wallpapered the hessian walls. Why, who's inviting you? Some handsome fella?'

'Nothing like that. I ran into a chap I met on the coach. His wife has just come to join him and knows no one here, so he asked if I would meet her.'

'That's nice,' Mary said. 'If she's not too hoity-toity, bring her here one day. It would be nice to get to know some ladies. I love having the fellas drop by, but I've almost forgotten how to talk to respectable women. You're an exception, why's that?'

'Because I'm not really respectable, that's why.'

Mary sighed as they sat drinking their tea.

'What's the matter?' Nora asked.

'Bluey's been onto me about trying to get some money from Brookman,' Mary said, 'But I don't think they're legally responsible for Pat's death, and I don't want people pitying the poor little widow and thinking they've got to give me money.'

'Well, sometimes bosses do help if someone is killed at work.'

'But it just brings it all back. I think I knew, you know, because my heart stopped beating for a moment when I heard there was an accident. I ran all the way and was there when they brought him up, Nora. It was horrible. I'm glad Joey never saw his dad lying there all broken. He'd been a big, strong, good-looking fella,' she sobbed as Nora's arms closed around her.

'Oh, Mary,' she said. 'I don't know how you can be so brave.'

'I'm all right,' Mary replied, wiping away her tears. 'It's good to talk to someone about it. I think the blokes don't like being reminded of what could happen to them, workin' down the mines.'

'It must be very dangerous. Yesterday Dr Martin amputated a young fellow's leg that got crushed in a mine accident.'

'Is he going to be all right?'

'Well, the doctor's pleased with how he's doing, but so many things can go wrong. I guess, I'd better be getting back,' she was saying as the gate squeaked and Danny O'Hara's big grey dog lolloped up to peer in the doorway.

'Hello Danny,' Mary said, as he appeared, shooing the dog away from the door, 'There's some tea in the pot, if you'd like some.'

'That'd be grand, Mary. Just thought I'd drop in to see how you were going. G'day, Mrs Patterson. Joey told us you're working up at the hospital.'

'Yes, I started yesterday. I was just about to go back.'

'Oh Danny,' Mary said, 'I was telling Nora yesterday that you know a bit about guns and might have a look at her little one.'

'Thinking' of taking up shootin' as a trade, lass?' he asked with a twinkle.

'Someone gave it to me. They thought I might need it out here in the wilds of West Australia,' Nora laughed, opening her trunk to retrieve the gun.

'Ah, a little Colt New Line. Well made, and lovely engraving. I think they were the first pocket revolvers that used proper cartridges. One of the earlier ones might have been a problem, but you shouldn't have any worries with this one. Have you fired it?'

'No, I was worried that I'd load it wrong, and it might blow up or something.'

'Let me have a look at the cartridges. Well, they seem all right. It might need a bit of a clean. Would you mind if I showed it to my friend, Charlie?'

'Not at all,' she replied.

'Charlie's a Californian so knows all about guns. They all carry handguns over there.'

'A lot of men do, here, too,' put in Mary.

'I used to have one but decided I was more danger to myself than anyone else. Gave it to Ben. He doesn't like carrying it either. But Charlie, well, I've seen him pull it in a flash when some bastard - beggin' your pardon ladies - when some bloke started getting obstropolous.'

'Oh!'

'No, he never shot anyone, but it sure quietens them down to suddenly be facing a sixgun. He's a steady fella, Charlie. Not like that other Yankee, Tom Tucker.

'I'll be off then, ladies,' he went, picking up his old hat as he rose to his feet. 'I see you've put up Paddy's picture, Mary. Looks just like him. I reckon Ben could make a crust out of drawin' folks if the gold runs out. I told him he should order some proper paints and paper from the east.'

Chapter 19

Ben was on his way to town the following afternoon when he saw Constable Purkiss knocking on Mary's door.

'Hello Constable,' he called, 'you looking for Mrs O'Callaghan?'

'Yes, do you know where she is'?

'Working at the Club, I believe. Is something wrong?'

'I just wanted to talk to her about her boy. I found him and his mate sneaking around one of the brothels. "Looking for clues," they said.'

'Really? I'm afraid Joey's been reading the Sherlock Holmes stories in the paper and getting ideas. Have you heard any more about Mrs Patterson's husband? If he turns up it might stop the boys playing detective. They think he's been done in.'

'The corporal's going to track him down when he goes out on patrol. Tell Mrs O'Callahan what I said. I'm sure she wouldn't want her boy hanging around whorehouses.'

'Righto, Constable, I'll tell her. And if I see young Joey I'll give him a talking to.'

'I hope I put the fear of God into them,' Purkiss laughed. 'I said they could be sent to the reformatory on Rottnest Island.'

As the two men strolled down the road, Ben asked, 'You fellas found that murderer yet?'

'No,' Purkiss replied. 'It's like looking for a needle in a haystack. He's supposed to have arrived about six months ago, but a lot of those blokes have gone home or up the Murchison. Or just disappeared. Our man could be one of the unidentified blokes who've perished out in the bush. The groups who came here together vouch for each other, but it's hard to find out much about the rest.'

'Well, good luck with it. Not nice to think we've got a killer hanging around. Are you sure he's not dangerous to anyone else. What about the ladies? Are they safe? Shouldn't people be warned?'

'We don't think he's likely to attack anyone, unless he's cornered, and don't want to alert him that we're on his trail. I'm not supposed to have told you blokes, so keep quiet about it, will you? But warn the ladies not to trust strangers.'

'Maybe he's not a stranger. If he's been here that long, he could have made himself at home in the town. Could be hiding in plain sight.'

'I guess you're right. Anyone you can think of?'

'Not really.'

On his way home, Ben dropped in at Mary's place. No one answered his knock, so he followed the sound of chopping around the shack to find Joey hard at work.

'Hey Joey,' he called.

'Oh, hello, Mr Drummond. Mum's not here.' Leaving the axe embedded in the log, he wandered over, saying, 'Mum won't be back till later. Would you like a cuppa? The billy's boilin'.'

'That would be nice, thanks Joey.'

Watching the boy bustle around making the tea, Ben decided he didn't seem too perturbed by the policeman's warning and decided he'd better reinforce it.

'I hear you and Timmy have been bringing yourselves to the notice of the police. Not a good idea, Joey.'

'But we wasn't doin' nothin' wrong.'

'Well, what were you doing, poking around those brothels?'

'We was wonderin' if maybe them ladies might remember Mr Patterson.'

'Really?'

'Well, I thought ...Timmy said ...we thought maybe he'd of gone there, y'know. With Mrs P. far away, maybe he, y'know, needed... y'know.'

'Joey, what goes on in those places isn't something young boys should be talking about.'

'But don't y' think he might of, y' know? Timmy says blokes go there all the time, because they gets lonely on their own.'

'Yes, it is lonely for a man on his own. But they don't all visit those ladies. And if they do, it's none of your business. You and Timmy better make sure the constable doesn't catch you there again. They've got a place they send bad boys to.'

'That's what the p'liceman said.'

'How would your poor mum get on if you got sent there?'

The boy's face fell, 'Does she know about it?'

'Not yet, but Constable Purkiss asked me to tell her. Perhaps you'd better tell her yourself. And tell her the police are chasing a bad bloke who's supposed to be out here, so don't trust strangers. You and Timmy should be careful, too. Anyway, I'd better be getting home.'

Seamus ran out to welcome him when he reached the camp, and Danny asked, 'Did y' get them onions?'

'Yes, and the latest Coolgardie Miner. Do you want to have a look at it while I get dinner on.'

'Saw you talkin' to that police fella down at Mary's. Somethin' wrong?'

'No just Joey an' the O'Rourke boy getting carried away playing Sherlock Holmes. They were poking around behind one of the brothels. Seems Timmy thought Patterson might have gone there. Purkiss warned them about getting sent to a reformatory, so I don't think they'll go there again.'

'Maybe I shouldn't have encouraged him to read those stories. I didn't expect him to read them all, but he'd such a bright little fella. Did the bobby tell you any more about that bloke they're chasin'? Is he dangerous?'

'They haven't found him, but don't think he'll murder anyone else. I hope they're right. Seems they've not put out any sort of warning because they don't want him to know they're after him. So Purkiss shouldn't have told us and asked that we keep quiet about it. Apparently, he's only killed a man, but maybe we should warn the ladies.'

Later, as he lay watching the stars, Ben tried to recall what he'd learned about investigating crimes during those few weeks attached to Scotland Yard, but there was nothing to fit the problem facing the police out here. Well, to start with, there was no crime scene and no body, though there seemed to be a regular supply of corpses out in the bush. Had they all died from natural causes?

All the rules he remembered for conducting a manhunt were designed for English conditions, so he doubted even the top detectives would know where to start in a place like this with an itinerant population. Many, like him, wanted to hide their past. He was sure he could have invented one and no one would have questioned it.

There must have been hundreds of blokes arriving back then. It was the height of the gold rush. And probably about a third answered to the murderer's description. What was it? Medium height, with fair or sandy hair. Nora Patterson's husband, for one, fit that description and time of arrival. He might even have come on the same boat as the killer.

What on Earth had happened to him? And what was she going to do if he didn't turn up. Probably go back east, he thought sadly, as the image of her lovely face faded leaving just the ghost of her smile to linger in his mind as he slept.

Chapter 20

Corporal Williams was glad to finally see signs of mine workings. But the place looked deserted, eerily unwelcoming. No sign of anyone working the mine, and only abandoned diggings nearby. *If this is the place Patterson reckoned was going to make him rich,* he was thinking, *I'm surprised it's the only mine still here. The windlass is wound up, so he can't be down below. Guess he might have gone into town to meet his wife.* 'A bit late, mate,' he muttered.

Usually, any visitor, even a copper, was welcome at these bush camps, and could count on some billy tea and a bit of conversation, but Williams couldn't shake off the feeling that he was not wanted here. Most of the prospectors were decent blokes, but you never really knew what sort of reception you'd get, so he approached with caution, calling out 'Hello, the camp!'

At the second call, a scruffy, sandy-bearded man emerged from the canvas and brushwood structure, cradling a rifle, and Williams felt suddenly very exposed. There'd been no real animosity towards the police on these diggings, but there was something about the bloke's stance that made the hair on the back of his neck prickle. So he was relieved when the man lowered the gun and stood waiting for him to approach.

'Edward Patterson, I presume?' he called as he rode closer.

The man just grunted, but his grip on the gun tightened.

'Got a message from your wife. She's in Hannans looking for you. Says she was expected.'

'Damn!' the man muttered, before replying, 'Er, I wasn't expecting her yet. What's the date anyway?'

'February the thirteenth. Seems she wrote and wired you.'

'I'll be in town in a few days, then,' the man said, running his hand over his bewhiskered face, before turning and re-entering the shack, to the surprise of Williams who had been hoping for the customary offer of hospitality.

'Surly bastard,' he muttered, 'If I had a wife like that, I'd not be wasting my time out here.'

The wife! Here on the fields, the miner mused as he stood watching the policeman ride away. He'd not had a woman since he was thrown out of a Hannans brothel months ago, and though tempted by the enticing near-naked black girls who occasionally wandered by, they were always in groups, shepherded by other women. Besides, he was sure the men weren't far away with their spears.

So, the woman's photograph had become the focus of his wildest fantasies, and now she was here. Throwing himself on his narrow bed, he let his thought dwell on finding her on Hannans' dusty streets, seeing the alarm in her eyes as he ripped off her clothes and took her by force, then and there. It was the most exciting fantasy he'd had in a long time. Of course that could never happen.

A loud 'Cooee!' startled him and he remembered the buyer who was coming to look at the mine. Quickly tidying himself up, he emerged in time to see two men approach, riding camels and accompanied by a young black man on foot.

'Good afternoon, gentlemen,' he called, striding forward, hand outstretched, to meet the two men as they climbed off the crouching camels.

'Are you satisfied with the agreement, Mr Patterson,' Cyril Hawthorn asked some time later, wiping his perspiring face. With a grimace of disgust at the red-dirt stains blemishing the snowy cloth, he cast a critical eye over the interior of the shack, thinking, *how can men live like this?* Of course, this fellow would probably hightail it back to civilisation as soon as he had the money. He seemed to be an educated man, despite his unkempt appearance.

'It is a generous offer,' said his partner, John Hargraves. 'You understand that we are prepared to take the chance that the mine lives up to expectations.'

The third man frowned, as he carefully perused the fine print. 'Yes,' he finally said, dipping the pen in the bottle of ink to sign as the mine owner for the last time.

Chapter 21

Nora sighed with pleasure as the kiss brushed her lips, and her breasts responded to soft caresses. 'Neddy?' she murmured, waking. But that gentle touch hadn't belonged to Ned. Or to that other man with his smooth doctor's fingers. Throwing off the blanket, she sat up in bed. What sort of woman would have such dreams about a man she hardly knew, when her husband might be in danger, or even dead?

Guessing it was time to get up anyway, she lit a candle and quietly got dressed so as not to disturb Molly. Tying on her apron and pulling the unflattering cap over her hair, she slipped out to the kitchen for a cup of tea and a slice of toast before reporting for her early morning shift, determined to put those guilty feelings behind her and concentrate on her work.

'There's a new patient,' Aggie told her. 'Mr McRoberts. Badly lacerated leg from a fall in the mine. His wounds have been dressed and we gave him some morphine as he was in a lot of pain.'

Nora wondered if it was that Mr McRoberts. *Serve him right if it's him*, she thought uncharitably as she walked into the ward.

She was pleased to find Johnny Nelson's pulse and temperature were normal.

'I'll be back to change your dressing, Johnny, as soon as I check on the other patients.'

She started with McRoberts. It was him. Snoring, open mouthed like a landed fish. None of the other patients was seriously ill. So, after dressing Johnny Nelson's stump, she spent the next hour tidying the beds and sweeping. One of the first chores she'd been given as a little girl was sweeping. The dust made her sneeze, but she liked to swish it off the verandah and watch it float away. But that was nothing like the red dust of this place. It seeped into the layers of her clothes. Her corset was turning orange, and her petticoat hems were stained dark red.

Outside, when mining operations were in full swing, you could hardly breathe and a film of red soon covered everything. Even the newspaper squares in the lavatory were coated. She'd just finished mopping the floor, when Dr Martin arrived. He was pleased with Johnny Nelson's rapid recovery, and agreed that Mr Howard could go home.

Rejecting the doctor's suggestion that he try walking with crutches, McRoberts refused to get out of bed and kept Nora busy over the next few hours. When he was unable to deposit anything in the bedpan he'd demanded, Nora enjoyed seeing him wince when she suggested an enema. Having tucked him back in bed, she was scrubbing the bedpan with carbolic and hadn't realised that her shift was finished until Matron appeared.

'I've just been helping Mr McRoberts,' she said. 'I've checked on everyone else.'

'Good work, nurse,' Matron said, 'Now off you go, and tell Nurse Briggs she's late. Ah, here she is.'

Giving the other nurse a sympathetic smile, Nora slipped out. Making herself a cup of tea, she went outside and stood sipping it as she gazed across the distant plains. Was Ned somewhere out there sick, or even dead?

⤞

She was a bit nervous about meeting Mrs Blake that afternoon. The dainty note had suggested someone with fashionable tastes. So, she took extra care getting ready before heading down the dusty road, watching her step for ankle-turning rocks. Dogs ran here and there, chasing carts, barking at camels and leaving stinking deposits ready for the boots of unsuspecting ladies.

The Club Hotel was the best that Hannans could offer. Mainly constructed from hessian, it sported a corrugated iron roof that extended out into a verandah, and a separate entrance for guests and ladies. Women were not welcome in the public bar.

As Nora stepped inside, unsure where she should turn, she was greeted by a young woman wearing a blue and white striped gown. A flower-trimmed hat perched on top of her fair hair.

'Hello,' she said. 'You must be Mrs Patterson. I'm Alice Blake. Won't you join me in the ladies' lounge?'

'How do you do?' Nora said as she followed her hostess into a small room furnished with a table and a few bentwood chairs.

'I've ordered tea and cake, but I'm not sure what we'll get. This is definitely not the Palace Hotel,' Mrs Blake said with a giggle, just as a young boy's voice was raised outside the door, 'You wait till I tell Mum.'

'Billy!' her hostess jumped up, flustered. 'What's going on?' she called. 'Come in here at once.'

A dark-haired boy about ten burst into the room, followed by a girl a little younger who was poking at him with a stick.'

'Lenore! Stop that this minute,' their mother said. 'Where's Donny?'

'I don't know. He was with us a minute ago.'

'Billy, you go and find him. Now! And Lenore, sit down and behave like a lady.'

'I'm so sorry,' she said, turning to Nora. 'I don't know what's got into the children since we've been here. This young miss is Lenore. She's eight, Billy's ten and little Donny is only three. They were supposed to be looking after him. I'm terrified he'll wander off and fall down a mine or something. That's why we're here. I told Jim I won't stay in the house until he builds a fence around it.'

'I can see why you would worry. There are holes everywhere.'

Just then the door swung open, and a girl backed into the room, carrying a tray.

'Here's y' tea an' cakes, Missus,' she said, plonking the tray on the table. 'It's just rock cakes.'

'Thank you,' Alice said.

As the girl left, Billy came rushing in, dragging a very dirty little brother.

'Oh Donny,' his mother sighed. 'Where was he, Billy?'

'Down at the stable playing in the dirt, Mum.'

'Me was havin' fun, Mummy.'

'Well, just look at you. Take him and wash his hands, please Billy.'

As they left the room, Alice sank down on the chair with a sigh.

'I'm sorry about all that,' she said, lifting the teapot. 'How do you like your tea? We've only got goats' milk.'

'I'll have some, please.'

'And a rock cake? I guess we're lucky to get anything, but I did want everything to be just right and make a good impression, Mrs Patterson. You'll think the Blakes are a rough sort of family.'

'No, of course not. I'm not used to anything flash. My folks were farmers. I've eaten many a rock cake in my time. Not to mention damper and johnnycakes. Please call me Nora.'

'Oh, and I'm Alice. I do hope we can be friends. I was so lonely in Perth, not knowing anyone. That's why I agreed to come. But I hear there's no school.'

'Not yet. There needs to be fifteen children. Your three should help.'

'Donny wouldn't count. He's too little.'

'I like it here,' put in young Lenore, 'It's fun not having to go to school.'

Before her mother could tell her to be quiet, the door opened, and Billy pushed Donny ahead of him into the room.

'I is all clean now, Mummy,' the little boy shouted, running to lean on his mother's lap.

'This is Mrs Patterson, children. Now please sit down and be quiet so we can talk.'

❧

'There's a steady breeze, Danny. Do y' think we should start dryblowing this lot?' Ben asked later that day.

'To be sure. I reckon we should see a bit more colour than what we've been gettin' lately. Unless you want to leave it till tomorrow.'

'No. It'll be good to see what we've got.'

Danny couldn't do the heavy lifting involved in dryblowing, so it was Ben who repeatedly raised the dish of dirt above his shoulders, to slowly and carefully allow the contents to fall into another dish on the ground, while the wind whisked away the lighter dust, leaving only the heavy gold-bearing particles behind.

Though he'd never admitted it to his mate, Ben had thought the work would kill him at first. Now, the only effect was to occasionally ensure a good night's sleep, free of the nighttime horrors he'd endured for years. But not this night. In the darkest hours, as usual, the old dream returned.

But it was getting less disturbing. Each time the man with Patterson's face attacked him, he woke shaken, but free of the old soul-freezing terror. What had changed? He hadn't been the target of that insane attack before. And Millie wasn't there. Of course, she never had been. She was alone in Brisbane. Where he should have been, by her side.

A wave of pure grief, untainted by that other horror, swept over him, and he wept for the girl he had loved.

Chapter 22

The skinny horse heaved a great sigh as the driver pulled up his wagon outside the Coolgardie livery stable on Friday afternoon.

'I want to sell this rig,' he told the man leaning on the fence.

'The wagon don't look up to much and the nag seems done in,' he replied, lifting the horse's lip to examine its teeth. 'Been livin' on scrub, has he?'

'Yeah, so whatever you think is fair. Need to get rid of the lot. I'm heading back home. Had enough of this prospecting lark. I'd like to leave my suitcase here for a while, if that's all right and come back for it later?'

'Come inside and I'll see what the boss says.'

The deal was soon done. The seller pocketed the money, picked up his carpetbag, and strode down to the West Australian Bank. Filling in a deposit form, he handed it, along with a passbook and cheque, to the teller.

'Thank you, Mr Patterson. That all seems to be in order. But this is a substantial amount, so it may take a week or more to be cleared before we can transfer it to the account with the Bank of New South Wales. You should check with us next week.'

The customer's face wore a worried frown as he left the bank. He hadn't been prepared for the delay. He needed to get away. The longer he stayed, the more he'd be drawn back to

Hannans where she was. He wanted her. But he'd need to change, become a different man for that to happen. Preoccupied with his thoughts, he stepped out into the wide red dirt road.

Hearing the frantic cry of 'Whoa, there!' and a clatter of hooves, he swung back. But, stumbling on the loose gravel, he wasn't quick enough. A glancing blow from the slow-moving horse sent him and his heavy bag tumbling to the ground.

'My dear sir,' cried the young man who leapt from the closed buggy to help him up. 'I trust you are unhurt.'

As the other man climbed to his feet, he took in the red side-whiskers, the black suit and white clerical collar.

'Thank you', he muttered, bending to retrieve his bag. Then, casting another quick look at the young minister, he staggered, allowing the other man to support him.

'It's just my ankle,' he said putting on a pained expression. 'It'll be fine. I just need to rest up.'

'Can I take you home, or to a doctor?'

'No, no. I just need somewhere to rest for a while. Unfortunately, I don't live in Coolgardie. I just arrived in town.'

'Let me help you inside this hotel, where you can sit down. I must take care of the horse and equipage, but I will return and see if you are recovered. I will need to book a room here anyway.'

'Perhaps I should too,' said the other man, 'I'm not going to be up to doing much today.'

<h1 style="text-align:center">23</h1>

Nora helped Johnny Nelson get back into bed. With his wound healing, he was learning to get around on crutches but could only stay up for a short while.

'You're doing really well, Johnny,' she told him.

'I'll be glad when I can go home. I won't be much use, but I can do some jobs around the camp to help Dad.'

'You'll be here for a while yet, I think, young fellow,' Dr Martin said, coming into the tent, accompanied by Mrs Alderdice. She turned to Nora, saying, 'Nurse Patterson, I have a message for you. Corporal Williams said to let you know that your husband has been contacted and is expected in town in the next few days. I suppose this will mean you'll stop working. I'll be sorry to lose you. Can you stay on till the end of the week?'

In the rush of relief that flooded her mind, Nora didn't know what to say. 'I can't say until he comes, but I'm sure he will understand I can't just leave you in the lurch.'

As soon as she knocked off, she hurried over to Mary's. Seeing her friend outside, she called out, 'Mary, Mary, Ned's alive. The policeman saw him. He'll be here soon.'

'Oh, Nora,' Mary replied, coming to the gate, 'that's good news, after all your worrying.'

'I need to talk to the policeman who saw him. I'll just run down to the Police Station and see if he's there.'

'Come back for a cuppa. I've got a couple of visitors. They are barmaids, but nice girls.'

'I'll be right back,' Nora replied.

Hurrying down to the police tent, she was pleased to find Williams behind the desk.

'Thank you so much for letting me know that my husband is all right, Corporal,' she said, 'I was really worried. How was he? I'm sure he must have been sick or something not to have been here sooner.'

'I don't know, Missus. He appeared to be well enough. Just seemed to have forgotten you were coming. Said he'd be in town in a day or two. Didn't seem in any great hurry. Is he always so unfriendly?'

'Ned? No, he's not like that.'

'Maybe I caught him at a bad time, but I got a strong feeling that he wanted me gone. Maybe he doesn't like policemen,' he laughed. 'Would he have any reason for that?'

'No.'

'Well, I was out there on Wednesday, so he should turn up soon. I told him you were at the hospital.'

Thanking him, she headed back to Mary's, confused by his comments. Ned unfriendly? If anything, Ned was too friendly, too trusting. And as for having reason to be wary of the police, except for a few escapades with his mates before they were married, he had never been involved in anything shady.

As she stepped through the gate, Mary called, 'Come and meet the girls, Nora.'

Two young women were sitting in the shade of the bough shed. Marge, with the hennaed red hair, was older and more reserved, but the pretty blonde Nellie jumped up and surprised Nora with a hug.

'Any friend of Mary's is a friend of mine,' she gushed.

'Sit yourself down, Nora,' Mary said, 'Marge brought us a real cake.'

Mary was pouring the tea when Joey arrived.

'Hello, young Joey,' Nellie asked. 'Did you smell the cake from way down town?'

'No. I just come home t' tell Mum about Mr Rutherford's windlass,' he replied indignantly.

'Oh, you don't want any, then,' said Marge. 'Not even a little piece?'

'I'll try to force it down,' he replied with a wide grin.

'So, what's the matter with Mr Rutherford's windlass?' his mother asked.

'One of the posts broke an' the lot fell over. The bucket crashed right down the bottom of the shaft.'

'Are he and his mate all right?'

'Yes. Some of the fellas are going t' give the poor old buggers a hand to fix it up tomorrow.'

'Language! Joey,' Mary said.

'Sorry, Mum,' he mumbled through a second mouthful of cake, 'Want me to go an' chop some wood? '

'That'd be nice, love,' she replied, sending him off with a quick hug.

'You've done a good job bringin' him up, Mary,' said Marge. 'It must be a worry having him wanderin' around with hundreds of men here. Most are good blokes, but all sorts are turning up since the railways started getting closer. I heard a rumour the police are lookin' for a murderer that's supposed t' be out here.'

'Yes. They don't think he's a danger to women, but said we should be careful of strangers.

'Another cup, anyone?' she went on, picking up the teapot.

'Not for me Mary,' Nora said, turning at the sound of the gate squeaking as Ben Drummond appeared. She'd forgotten how nice-looking he was when he smiled. Seeing the other women, he stammered, 'Good morning, ladies. Hello, Mary, I didn't know you had company. Danny sent you the Illustrated News.'

'Thanks,' she said, taking the magazine. 'You might know Marge Johnson from the Club, Ben, and this is Nellie Parker who's just started at the Exchange. Have you ladies met Ben Drummond?'

'Don't think I've had that pleasure,' Nellie said with a giggle, fluttering her eyelashes.

'Pleased to meet you ladies,' he said, but went on, 'I'm sorry, Mary. I can't stay. Need to get back. We're putting in a costean, and if I leave Danny on his own, he'll try to do too much.'

Before he could escape, Nellie rose and sashayed towards him. 'Please tell me, Mr Drummond, what's a costean?' she simpered.

'You know anything about mining, Miss Parker?'

'No, but I'm sure you could teach me a lot, Ben.'

As her fingers reached out to touch his shirt, he stepped back, his expression grim.

'A costean is a pit we dig away from the main shaft to try to find where the lode goes. If you want to know more about mining, I'm sure you'll find others eager to enlighten you, Miss Parker. Now, I must really be going, goodbye, ladies.'

With a quick nod to the others, he strode around the corner and was gone, much to the disappointment not only of Nora, but obviously of the two barmaids.

'The one that got away,' murmured Marge with a laugh. 'You shouldn't be so obvious Nellie.'

'Ooh, I don't know. I've not seen him around, Mary. Is he a friend of yours?'

'Yes, Ben and his mate Danny were very good friends to me when I lost my Paddy. You leave him alone.'

'Why? You want him for yourself?'

'No, Nellie. As I said, just a good friend.'

'Well, I wouldn't mind having him for a 'friend'. He can park his boots under my bed anytime he likes.'

'He's Danny O'Hara's mate?' Marge asked. 'I've seen him around, but not often in the bar.'

'I don't think he's really one for the booze,' Mary said, 'but he sometimes joins Danny and his mates at the saloon. Will you girls get time off to go to the races tomorrow?'

'Maybe earlier in the afternoon, but we'll be rushed at the pub as soon as it's over. I guess it'll be the same for you, eh, Nellie.'

'Yes, maybe we can go together. What time is it starting?'

'About one o'clock. Can you come, Nora? What time do you knock off?'

'I could come, but maybe I should stay there in case Ned comes looking for me.'

'Just ask someone to tell him where you've gone.'

Nora gathered the empty cups and took them inside. The discussion of Ben Drummond had made her uncomfortable, especially the idea of his boots under Nellie's bed, and him in it.

Stop it this minute, she upbraided herself. *It's none of your business where he puts his boots.*

The two barmaids left soon afterwards, needing to get back to work before the evening rush, and Nora decided she should go too.

'If you decide to come to the races, come here first so we can go together. You'll need a shady hat. You can borrow my good one. It's not black so I can't wear it while I'm in mourning.'

'That would be nice, thank you. I've only got a little boater and it doesn't keep much sun off. I might get my best blouse out of the trunk too. I can wear it with this skirt. I don't want to look too dowdy when Ned comes, anyway.'

Chapter 24

Half a mile off the road from Coolgardie, a black, enclosed buggy stood in the shade of a clump of gum trees. Though the distance could be travelled easily in a few hours, an overnight stop had been necessary.

A crow that had been grumbling in one of the trees flew off with a weary cry when the man in black climbed out about sunrise. Peering into a hand mirror, he examined his neat moustache and side-whiskers, before attaching the pristine clerical collar.

Some time later, he was kicking sand over the dying campfire, when a low moan drew him to his fellow traveller's bedside inside the horse-drawn van.

'Ah, waking up, are we?' he said unctuously. 'Time for your medicine my dear fellow. Must keep you alive until we get to town.'

Chapter 25

Now she knew Ned was alive, Nora could look forward to enjoying the bush races that afternoon. Wearing a frilled white blouse and the pretty borrowed hat, she drew admiring glances from male onlookers as she strolled across to Mary's.

'Hello Mrs Patterson,' Joey said when she opened the gate. 'Mum's around the back. You want a cuppa?'

'Yes please, Joey,' she replied.

Walking around the house she was surprised to see a square patch of the hard red soil had been turned over. Then she stopped short, whispering, 'Ned?'

But of course, the fair-haired man wasn't him. He turned as Mary called, 'Hello Nora. Meet Clint Sutcliffe. He's an old friend of Paddy's and mine. Clint, this is my friend Nora Patterson.'

'Pleased to meet you, Mr Sutcliffe.'

'G'day, Mrs Patterson,' Sutcliffe greeted her with a wide smile.

'Better knock off, Clint,' Mary said, 'if you're riding this afternoon. Joey's making tea.'

'I'll just finish grubbing out that last stump and be right with you.'

'I've wanted to make a garden for a while,' Mary said as they walked away. 'Joey and I have been picking away at the ground, but hadn't got far. Then Clint turns up out of the blue, and he's got it all done this morning.'

'I better get more horse an' camel dung for the garden,' Joey said. 'Mr Sutcliffe's got a camel, Mrs Patterson. Her name's Salome.'

'That sounds like a good name for a lady camel,' Nora said.

'I don't think she can dance, though,' Mary laughed. 'Oh, hello Danny,' she continued, as the Irishman pushed open the gate.

'G'day, ladies. You all set to go t' the races?'

'Well, I'll need to change. Danny,' she went on as the other man joined them, 'Did you meet Paddy's friend Clint Sutcliffe back in Coolgardie?'

'Yes, hello mate. You were headin' up the Murchison, if I remember rightly. Any luck?'

'Made enough to feed myself and my camel. And put a bit by. Thinking of maybe settling down.'

'Ben off out bush, Danny?' asked Mary, pouring the tea.

'Not today. I talked him into entering Walter in the races. He an' Bluey been helpin' old Jimmy Rutherford fix up his windlass this morning.'

'Joey says it collapsed the other day,' Mary replied. 'Lucky the old fella wasn't under the bucket.'

'You all going to the races?' asked Sutcliffe.

'I guess just about everyone'll be there.'

'A few of my mates are trying to set up a camel race. Thinking of challenging the Afghans, so I'll be off now, ladies. Need to get old Sal ready to show what she's made of.'

The racetrack was on a cleared patch of flat ground northwest of the town, surrounded by a rudimentary post and rail fence. A few thatched shelters had been built on the western side, one housing a makeshift bar that was already doing a roaring trade. The others were furnished with some rough seating. The Blakes had already arrived, and Nora introduced Alice to her friends.

'You'll not want to be next to the bar, ladies,' Danny said, leading the way to the last shelter.

'This will do nicely, Danny,' Mary told him. 'Now I'm sure you want to go off and lay some bets. Oh, is that Bluey's mate, Steve? That lady must be his wife.'

'It is, to be sure. Hello Steve, Mrs Hoskins.'

By the time the introductions were over, and the four women had seated themselves, it was time for the first race. Walter didn't disgrace Ben or himself, coming second. So, after taking care of the horse, Ben meandered down to join Danny and the women.

'Old Walter put up a good effort, Ben,' Danny said. 'Maybe you should train him up for the next time.'

'I hope you didn't bet on him, mate.'

'Well, I only bet on a place, so he did me proud. I've got a few bob on Charlie's horse in the next race.'

'You reckon it's got a chance?' Ben asked.

'Well it looks more promising that the other nags.'

But Danny was to be disappointed as a scruffy roan gelding won by a nose.

'Might do better in the next,' he said. 'I went for a place with Willie Jacob's black.'

'Damn. Should have gone for a win,' he muttered as the black came in first.

'Would you ladies like a lemonade or something?' Bluey asked. 'They've got ginger beer too if you'd rather.'

'I'd like a ginger beer, please,' said Nora.

'I'll have the same, thanks Bluey,' said Mary. 'I think they're just about to start the camel race.'

As the crowd moved away towards the bar, they saw a ragged bunch of camels milling around at the far end of the track. Then a distant tinkling evolved into a melodious ringing as three tall, elegant camels came pacing up the track from the town end, their colourful trappings matched by the exotic costumes of their riders.

'Uh, oh,' chuckled Danny, 'maybe our fellas have bitten off more than they can chew. Those aren't pack camels.'

'No, they're certainly not,' put in Bluey, handing the women their drinks, 'the bloke on the tall one is Faiz Mahomet. That's his new riding camel.'

Similar comments came from others in the crowd, as the camels were marshalled into some sort of orderly line. Though many of the diggers treated Afghans with contempt, Faiz Mahomet commanded a level of respect withheld from his compatriots. Maybe it was money that made the difference. He and his brother were successful businessmen.

The crack of a pistol shot, and they were off. That Mahomet's camel would take the lead was a foregone conclusion, but a few of the miners, including Clint, were giving the other Afghans a run for their money.

The crowd's cheers and catcalls turned to coughing and sneezing as they thundered by in a cloud of red dust. By the time the air cleared, it was all over.

Then Clint Sutcliffe came whooping back, 'Came third' he shouted, just as his tired camel decided it was time to prop, catapulting the rider over her head. He hit the ground heavily and lay still. But, as Nora rushed forward, expecting the worst, he sat up groggily and started to laugh.

'Are you hurt?' she asked.

'Don't think anything's broken,' he said, clutching at his shoulder. 'Sorry, I'm not hysterical. It just struck me as funny. Me showing off and old Sal deciding to put me in my place. Where is she? Didn't run off, I hope.'

'No, I think Ben caught her,' said a white-faced Mary. 'What's so funny? I thought you were dead, you idiot.'

A soft padding announced the arrival of the camel, with Ben in tow.

'You all right, mate?' he called. 'Better let your camel know if you are. She's very worried.'

Sutcliffe scrambled to his feet to embrace his furry friend's head, as Ben, relieved of responsibility for the animal, said, 'I guess we can presume he's unhurt.'

'Silly bugger's lucky he didn't break his neck,' Mary muttered.

'You ladies been enjoying the races?' Ben asked.

'Until Clint pulled that little stunt,' Mary laughed.

'He could have concussion,' Nora said. 'I should have made him go to the hospital.'

'How are you settling in up there, Mrs Patterson?' Ben asked.

'It's strange working in a canvas ward that feels like it would blow away in a strong wind,' she replied, flashing him a smile, 'but I'm getting used to it.'

'Damn you Ned, why aren't you here?' Nora muttered, angrily next morning, as she pushed the heavy broom across the ward floor. It was five days since Corporal Williams spoke to him. Surely that was enough time to ride into town.

As she finished sweeping, Dr Martin arrived with news that three badly injured men were arriving and that patients well enough to manage back at their camps were to be discharged forthwith. One of them was McRoberts, who was able to walk with the aid of a walking stick.

Before leaving, he followed Nora into the office, saying 'Er, Nurse Patterson, Mrs Patterson, I owe you an apology for the other night. I'd been drinking and mistook you for … er …a different kind of woman.'

'Oh, you did, did you?' she replied angrily, 'Am I suddenly more deserving of respect because I'm not your servant? Treat all women with respect and you might avoid being crowned with a frying pan. Or worse.'

Mumbling something about profound apologies, he hurried away. Glad to see the last of him, Nora set about preparing beds for the newcomers, who were being carried in by their mates. One man had suffered a head injury requiring immediate surgery and Nora once again assisted during the operation. The other two had been badly cut up in a drunken brawl, one still so inebriated that he passed out, and never felt the stitching of his jagged wound.

It was well after midday by the time Nora knocked off. After a bite to eat, she put on her hat and wandered over to Mary's place to find Danny O'Hara just arriving. 'Hello, Mrs Patterson,' he said, 'I'm glad you're here. I brought your little gun back. Charlie gave it a going over. Says it's in fine condition, but I need to give you some lessons in using it.

'Now's as good a time as any. What do y' reckon?' he went on, 'you got an old bully-beef tin, Mary?'

Danny set up the empty can on a stump in front of the heap of spoil around Paddy O'Callaghan's abandoned mine.

'Now Mrs Patterson, here's your little gun. It's not loaded, so you can't do any damage while you get used to handling it. First rule is, never point it at anyone unless you want him dead. And don't look down the barrel to see what's there.'

Nora laughed nervously, as he added, 'you wouldn't believe the idiots who've shot themselves doing that. Later, I'll show you how to keep it in good nick, but for now, show me how you'd go about tryin' to put a hole through that old tin.'

Nervously, Nora took the weapon, cradled the butt in her hand and aimed at the target.

'Not bad for a beginner,' Danny told her. 'At least you're pointing it the right way. Would you mind if I put my hand around yours to show how to get a better grip?'

'No.'

'You need to relax your hand, or you won't get your trigger finger to work when you need it.'

'That's better. Curl your finger around the trigger, but don't squeeze it yet. Now, try pointing the gun again, and when you're ready just squeeze.'

'Like that?' Nora asked.

'Yes. You've got the idea. Now let's load it and see how you go.'

After he showed her how to load the little weapon, Nora took it back, being very careful to not put any pressure on the trigger.

'That's the way. Now aim at the target and squeeze the trigger. Be ready for the recoil. It's not too bad with a little gun, but it can be a shock if y' not expecting it'

Carefully, Nora took aim. As she expected, she didn't hit the can, but dirt flew up from the embankment to the right of it.

'Not too bad. We'll make a shooter of you yet. Ready to try again? You saw where that went. Try to correct it.'

This time the impact sent a few small rocks rattling down the embankment on the other side.

'You can see that you've gone too far the other way. Just keep trying.'

Nora's next two shots shaved the bark off either side of the stump.

'You're gettin' closer, lass. Now if that was fella, you'd have winged him for sure.'

'I'm not sure I really want to shoot anyone, Mr O'Hara.'

'Call me Danny, lass. Well, only real maniacs want to kill, but if someone means you harm, you might need to protect yourself.'

'You've done very well, Nora,' Mary called. 'I think she needs a break from it, Danny. How about stopping for a cuppa.'

'That's a good idea. Then you can have a go at cleaning and reloading and we'll try again.'

After they finished their tea, Danny showed Nora how to open the gun, clean and load it. When she could do that without too much fumbling, she had three attempts to hit the target, getting closer each time.

Chapter 26

The gruesome story ran like wildfire through the crowd outside the pub next morning, '... some bloke just out of town with half his head blown away' Ben heard.

Probably another suicide, he thought sadly. They'd been a regular occurrence at the height of the rush.

'A travellin' parson found him an' roused a couple of fellas. They're taking him to the morgue,' came another voice as a bunch of excitable diggers rushed up the street with the corpse bouncing on a folded camp stretcher. The leg that dangled over the side lost a boot as they turned towards the hospital

Well, so much for not disturbing the scene before police can investigate.

'They know who he is?'

'Some bloke named Patterson. Blew his head off.'

'Patterson, you say?' Ben asked.

'Yeah, I think they said Edward Patterson.

My God. I've got to warn Nora. Pushing his way through the jabbering crowd, he set off at a run towards the hospital.

Nora was helping Matron get a patient into bed, when Dr Martin poked his nose in the door.

'I'll be back presently, Matron,' he said, 'need to go down to the morgue. Some idiot's blown his head off. Suicide they're saying.'

'Anyone we know?'

'Some bloke named Patterson. Edward Patterson.'

With a gasp, Nora dropped the patient and ran after the doctor, tears streaming down her face. As she caught up with him at the door of the tin shed that served as a temporary morgue, he turned in annoyance, grabbing her arm as she tried to push past him.

'What are you playing at, woman! You can't go in there! It's the morgue,' he blustered.

'I know! It's my husband. I want to see him,' she sobbed, pulling away and rushing inside, gagging as the stench of blood and putrefaction hit her. Then Ben Drummond was trying to get between her and the corpse, crying, 'Nora! You mustn't look!'

But she'd already seen the mangled mess that had been the man's face, and ran outside, retching. The doctor got to her first and tried to get her to sit down on the ground, but she was soon recovered enough to gasp.

'That's not Ned. It can't be.'

'My dear lady, you've had a bad shock. It may take some time to take it in,' the doctor said. It was a common reaction to suicide. But she repeated, 'It's not Ned! It's not my husband. He's got all his toes.'

'Who, Ned?' asked Ben.

'No! No! That poor man! Ned cut off his big toe when he was a boy.'

'Well, if this isn't that Edward Patterson, who is he?' asked Constable Purkiss, who'd followed them out of the morgue. But Ben was remembering a skeletal foot in a shallow red-dirt grave. *No,* he thought, shaking his head. *That can't be Patterson. Williams saw him last week.*

'You don't need me to tell you the cause of death, Constable,' the doctor called. 'I'll take Mrs Patterson back to her quarters.'

'I am quite all right now, doctor,' Nora said, 'and would prefer to go back to work.'

'Maybe she should go to Mary O'Callaghan's place,' Ben said, catching up with them.

'Yes, that might be for the best. If you can accompany her, Mr Drummond, I have visits to make in the town.'

'Of course.'

Nora, annoyed at being handed over like a parcel, waited until he was out of earshot before turning on Ben.

'I assure you, Mr Drummond, that I am quite capable of taking care of myself.'

'Of course,' he replied, but she'd seen the elusive dimple flicker in his cheek.

'Don't you dare laugh at me,' she stamped her foot. 'It is broad daylight.'

'And I see you are fully clothed,' he couldn't help saying before, seeing tears glinting in her eyes, he went on, 'Oh, Nora, I'm sorry ...er ...forgive me Mrs Patterson.'

'Don't worry. Danny's stopped calling me Mrs. You might as well, too.'

'Do you want to go to Mary's?'

'No, thank you. I was a bit shaken, but I'm all right now and I need to get back to work,' she said hurrying away, hoping to quietly slip back into the ward.

'Ah, there you are, Nurse Patterson,' came Matron's voice as she flitted past the office.

'Yes, Matron. I'm sorry I left the ward without permission.'

'I understand you've had a bad shock. Are you sure you should continue working?'

'Yes, yes. It wasn't him. It wasn't my husband,' but tears, perhaps of relief, overflowed as she crumpled onto a spare bed.

'I'll be fine in a minute, Matron,' she mumbled, trying to control the overwhelming emotion.

'A cup of tea, that's what you need. All is right and tight here. We will have a cuppa and a sit down.'

'I'm sorry I ran out like that,' Nora said as they walked to the kitchen. 'But you know my husband's been missing. I thought ... they thought ... that it was him. But it wasn't.'

'Are you sure?'

'Yes. He chopped his big toe off cutting wood when he was a boy. This man had all his toes. I'm glad I saw his feet first,' she said stifling a damp giggle. 'I didn't really have to look at his face. I don't think he had one anymore.'

'Oh dear,' said Matron 'Maybe you should take the rest of the day off.'

'I think I'll be better to keep working. If I'm busy I might not have time for worrying about what has really happened to my husband. He told Corporal Williams that he'd be in town in a few days. And that was last Wednesday. He should have been here by now.'

Despite her good intentions, Nora couldn't stop thinking about that man who might have been Ned. She even started to doubt she'd seen all his toes. Dr Martin arrived as she was finishing her shift.

'Why is Nurse Patterson working? Didn't you know she'd had a disturbing experience?' his too-loud whisper drifted across the tent.

'She insisted on working, Doctor, and has shown no signs of being unable to do so.'

'Nurse Patterson,' he called, and she came across, fearing a reprimand, but he just wanted to express his concern.

'How are we feeling after this morning's events?' he asked in the jovial bedside voice he adopted with patients, a sudden change from the furious whisper.

'I'm quite well Doctor,' Nora told him, 'I think it was best to keep working.'

'Well, what you saw may prevent you from sleeping tonight. Matron, please give Nurse Patterson some of that sleeping draught.'

'Yes, of course, Doctor.'

Taking the cup of foul-smelling medicine with her, she was just entering the nurses' tent when a voice called, 'Mrs Patterson? I'm Reverend Simpson. Hearing that you had a bad shock today, I come to offer some comforting words,' and she turned to see a red-haired clergyman approaching.

'Oh, I'm quite over it now, sir,' she said, 'although I was a bit shaken at the time. I'm not sure if I'm allowed to invite you in. Maybe we could go and see if there's a cup of tea available at the refectory tent.'

'Unfortunately,' he said, stroking his neat side-whiskers, 'it was I who found the poor man who was thought to be your husband.'

'It wasn't him and I don't know why they thought it was,' she said, as they walked to the other tent.

'I believe his name was on a Miners Right the man carried.'

'Maybe it's someone with the same name. Patterson's not uncommon and there are lots of Edwards. The kettle's still hot. Would you like a cup of tea, sir?'

'That would be delightful,' he said. Seating himself at the table, he asked, 'So, have you heard from your husband?'

'Corporal Williams brought a message that he was coming to town, but that was a week ago.'

'I'm sure he'll turn up then.'

He was not at all like the other parsons she had known, who couldn't have a conversation without bringing God and Jesus into it, but she didn't like the way he kept patting her hand or arm. Forcing herself to be polite, she tried to make small talk, but found some of his questions a bit too personal. When Matron arrived, ostentatiously looking at her watch, he rose to leave, saying, 'Farewell good ladies. I intend holding a service of praise on Sunday under those trees near the post office. You would be most welcome to come.'

Back in the nurse's tent, Nora threw off her cap and apron and collapsed on the bed. But her mind was too disturbed to rest for long. So, she got up, tidied her hair, put on her hat and went to visit Mary. When she was nearly there, she saw her friend hurrying towards her.

'Nora,' she called as she approached, 'Are you all right? Ben just told me what happened.'

'I'm fine, Mary. It wasn't Ned. I was just coming to tell you about it.'

'Well come and have a cuppa. Ben said something about his feet,' Mary said, pushing open the gate.

'Yes this man had all his toes. Ned didn't,' she replied.

'It must have been an awful shock,' Mary said, putting the billy on the fire. 'Are you sure you're all right?'

'I got a terrible fright. But I knew straight away that it wasn't Ned. It was pretty awful seeing that poor man, though. And why would he have Ned's Miners' Right? It must be some other Edward Patterson.'

'Maybe he lost it, or someone stole it. Well, he'll be here soon and you'll be able to find out all about it.'

It was good to talk to Mary, who insisted she stay for the early evening meal. Walking back in the last glow of sunset, she felt ready for bed. But the doctor was right. She no sooner closed her eyes, than that gruesome image crept into her dreams. But this time it really was Ned. He sat up with his ghastly face and accused her of infidelity.

Finally, in desperation she swallowed the sleeping draught.

⚯

There was little sleep for Ben that night, either. There'd been a disturbance in the town earlier on, with shouting and pistol shots. Hoping it was just drunks letting off steam, he'd turned over and tried to get back to sleep, but owl hoots and dingo wails, even the duet of snores from Danny and Seamus, sounds he'd usually sleep through, kept him awake.

The creaky stretcher frame dug into his shoulders as he tossed and turned, trying to make the thoughts of Nora Patterson go away. It was not just remembering the feel of her near-naked body in his arms. At odd times during the day, he found himself recalling her sweet smile and the tears she tried to hide, that melted his resolve to never let himself care about someone; never let down his guard. But today, thinking that poor bloody suicide was her husband, his only thought had been to protect her, to take her in his arms and comfort her.

Where was her husband, the man who should be there for her? Was the man mad? Why would he ask her to come if he didn't want her here? Surely, he could have been here by now. Something must have happened to him. He might have been bitten by a snake or tossed off his horse.

The strangely satisfying image of Ned Patterson lying out there dead was wiped away by the thought of Nora left a widow, all alone with no one to console her. *Poor Nora. Poor sweet Nora,* he murmured, dreamily imagining comforting her, wiping away, no, kissing away, her tears.

A dingo's mournful wail pierced the silence and Ben leapt out of bed, still wrapped in the dream. The dream of holding Nora close. A dream that could never be.

As Seamus growled and went to investigate, Ben sat, head in hands, trying to suppress the urge to weep. She was a married woman. He had no right to have such thoughts about her. *Stop it, you silly bastard,* he told himself. *No woman would want a man like you.* A man with a history he couldn't share; lost years he couldn't speak of.

Chapter 27

'Nora, wake up. Hey, wake up!'

As Aggie Spence's voice finally pierced the fog of sleep, Nora's eyes blinked open.

'Is it time to get up? But I just went to sleep,' she murmured drowsily.

'Yes. Wake up,' the night nurse said, shaking her again. 'You're due on the ward in ten minutes. Are you all right?'

'I think so, but Matron gave me a sleeping draught.'

'I know. Are you sure you're all right?'

'Yes. I won't be long.'

Forcing herself to concentrate, Nora dressed quickly and ran to the ward, pulling on her cap. She still felt foggy-brained as she went about her work but slowly, as the effects of the drug wore off, worries about Ned took over.

Why hasn't he come? He's had days to get here. Surely, it's not that hard, she was thinking as she spooned gruel into the mouth of Mr Jameson, one of the new patients. A falling rock had struck the left side of his face, and the injury was too much of a reminder of yesterday's bloodied corpse. He could only eat some of the food so, putting it aside, she dosed him with morphine linctus and tucked the blanket back around him. With that task finished, the worries re-emerged. Maybe Ned was ill. But when the policeman saw him, he'd been well.

After helping the other patients with their midday meal and settling them back in bed for the afternoon rest period, she was looking forward to finishing her shift when Molly Briggs stuck her head in the door.

'Matron wants you, Nora. You've got a visitor.'

Thinking it must be Ned, she rushed to knock on the office partition. But her heart sank when she saw it wasn't him, just Corporal Williams.

'I'm sorry to bother you, Mrs Patterson,' he said, 'Would you mind having a look at this Miners' Right. Do you recognize the signature? Is it your husband's?'

Taking the stained and crumpled paper, Nora was assailed by the smell of blood.

'Yes,' she whispered, 'that's Ned's signature.'

'This was on the body of the man who died yesterday. I regret you had to witness the remains. I have confirmed that he is not your husband. I remember his hair was fair, not ginger.'

'Yes but, how did he get hold of Ned's certificate?'

'That's what we want to find out. When I visited your husband, he said he would be here in a few days. I assume he hasn't arrived yet.'

'No, and I'm really worried.'

'Well, when he does turn up, please ask him to drop in at the station. He might be able to help us identify the dead man.'

'Oh yes, of course,' Nora replied.

'I'll be on my way then, ladies,' he said, touching his cap as he turned to leave.

'Good afternoon, Corporal,' Matron said. Then, turning to Nora, she went on, 'Nurse Spence's father is ill and I'm allowing her to go home. I'll take over her shift tonight. Try to get to bed early, please, as I may need to call you earlier than usual if fatigue catches up with me in the early hours.'

'Of course, Matron,' Nora replied.

She awoke sometime in the early hours and couldn't get back to sleep. The narrow stretcher creaked and groaned in rhythm with the muttering and moaning wind that rippled the canvas tent, flapping the fly and bringing down drifts of red dust. She turned the other way, but sleep refused to come until, exhausted, she drifted into a dream where the sheets she was hanging out to dry became a ship's sails being buffeted by storm winds.

A persistent clanging dragged her back to an alarming reality. The wind no longer moaned. It howled. The tent flapped so wildly it seemed about to fly away as dust swirled about and into her eyes. Hearing shouting, and a loud crash nearby, she leapt out of bed and rushed to the door to peer out into dark, dust-driven chaos. A flash of lightning showed the big ward tent rocking wildly, with Matron and Molly trying to hold it down while Mr Dunne, the night warder, jumped around clutching at the flailing guy ropes. Wearing only her nightie, she ran to help. Fortunately, Matron was too busy to notice before the white garment faded into the darkness, stippled red by the dust.

All they could do was stop the tent from blowing away until a lull in the gale allowed Dunne to catch and secure one of the ropes, just as several other men came running out of the swirling red darkness. Nora was glad when two of them took over from Molly and Matron, but kept hanging onto her rope until someone grasped it higher up, shouting, 'Let go miss. You ladies better go find shelter.'

As they ran to the sleeping tent, which had so far withstood the buffeting of the wind, lightning flashed and rain came pelting down, turning the dust on their clothes to mud. Once inside, Molly crouched on the muddy floor and Matron slumped on one stretcher with her head in her hands. Nora didn't know how long they'd been trying to hold things together before she awoke, but both were shivering, so she wrapped blankets around them.

'Thanks, Nurse,' the matron said. 'Oh, but I must go to the patients.'

'I'll go, Matron,' Nora said, pulling her dressing gown over her muddy nightdress, 'I wasn't out there as long as you. Sit there and try to relax. It's getting lighter now. I'll be back to report soon.'

Not waiting for a reply, she ran out and fought her way back to the main tent, where the men were finally getting things under control. In the dim light, she was surprised and relieved to see at least one of the patients had got out. Despite his bad leg, Mr Truscott was holding one of the corners down.

'Is anyone else inside?' someone shouted.

'Yes,' Nora called as she ran up. 'I've got to get in and see to our other patients. Are you all right, Mr Truscott?'

'Yes, but I'm not sure about the others. There was a lot of stuff blowing around. I hope they stayed in bed.'

'You can go in now, Missus,' one of the other men said, holding the tent door open.

Inside, she could just make out the pale faces of the bed-bound patients glimmering through the darkness. 'Is everyone all right?' she called.

'I think so', said Mr Lyons, 'but Jameson got a bit wet when the rain drove in. Couldn't see what happened t' the other fellas.'

'We're fine, nurse,' came Rowntree's voice. 'The rain didn't get in down this end.'

'Reassured that they were safe in their beds, she pushed her way through the debris, to Jameson's bedside. At least he hadn't had time to get too chilled in the rapidly decreasing temperature, and the dressings on his wound weren't wet. She helped him up and supported him as they struggled to walk to the bed recently vacated by Mr Truscott. At least it was still dry. After wrapping him up as best she could, she was wondering what most urgently needed doing, when a figure shrouded in soggy hessian appeared in the doorway. Tossing aside his wrappings, Mr Alderdice shouted, 'My wife? Where is she? I came as soon as I could.'

'She's resting in the nurses' tent, Mr Alderdice. What's it like out there now?'

'It's easing off a bit, but your kitchen roof's gone and the hessian walls of the new building are in tatters.'

'Please let Matron know our patients are all safe,' Nora said.

'Thank you, nurse. I'll tell her,' he called as he left.

Shouts from outside suggested more helpers had arrived, so Nora concentrated on taking care of the sick men, but it was hard to make herself heard over the drumming and clattering on the roof. It sounded like gravel raining on the canvas.

Suddenly, several men pushed their way in, shouting what sounded like apologies, but the only word she understood was 'hail'. Well, that explained the clattering on the roof and the sudden chill. Scrabbling in the blanket box, she found extra dry blankets to wrap around the men. They really needed warm drinks, but she didn't dare light the kerosene stove with violent draughts swishing through the tent.

It seemed like she'd gone deaf when the noise suddenly stopped, leaving only a steady patter of rain. The wind was gone too. The flapping of the canvas diminished to a gentle quivering and the ropes' creaking lulled to a soft hum. Suddenly they could hear each other speak.

'Do you have any pain, Mr Jameson?' she asked. At least he'd stopped his shivering, but she needed to get him out of his wet clothes. Her nose suggested he may be wet with more than rainwater, as his shamefaced murmur soon confirmed.

'Don't worry, we'll get you changed as soon as everyone leaves.'

Going to the group at the door, who were still peering out questioning the lull in the weather, she said, 'Excuse me gentlemen, I appreciate all your help, but now, I would like you to leave.'

With mumbled apologies, they left, just in time for a bedraggled Dr Martin to appear.

'Are the patients safe, nurse? I can only see four. What has happened to Mr Truscott?'

'He was out helping, doctor. He hasn't come back. I hope he's all right.'

'He's here, Dr Martin,' Mrs Alderdice said, pushing the door open. 'The men sent him to us in the nurses' tent as soon as more help came. He doesn't seem any the worse for wear.'

'I'm fine doc,' the man called as he entered. 'Never felt better in me life.'

'Well go and sit down. I'm not discharging you until I am convinced of your recovery.'

As the doctor checked the other patients, Nora got Mr Jameson into a clean nightshirt and dry blankets in a dry bed, while Molly lit up the little kerosene stove and made tea for everybody.'

'Sit down and drink your tea, Mrs Patterson,' Matron said. 'We've had a rest and can take over now. I suggest you go and get dressed then.'

'Oh,' Nora blushed as she remembered throwing off the wet bedraggled dressing gown leaving her clad in just the filthy mud-spattered nightdress. Gulping down the last of her tea, she was about to run out when Matron took off her own coat and handed it to her.

Wrapping it around her, she ran outside. The rain had settled to a gentle patter, but the ground was covered with slippery red mud. One wrong step was enough to send her feet sliding away. With a startled shriek she fought to regain her balance until a hand grasped her arm, hauling her upright against a solid body.

'Careful,' Ben said, as he held her close just a shade too long, before regaining control of himself and offering her his arm.

'Thank you, Ben,' she said. 'You're a lifesaver. Matron loaned me her coat. It would have been ruined if I'd hit the ground.'

'You might have suffered some harm yourself,' he said. 'I came to help. We've not had any damage, and I checked on Mary's place. As we're on higher ground, most of it ran through the camps and down the hill. You'll have a big clean up here, though.'

'Yes, the men who were helping have gone to get some breakfast and collect brooms and shovels.'

'Where are you heading?'

'Oh,' she said, clutching the coat around her as she remembered she wore only her nightie under it. At least the blush warmed her cold skin, as she went on, 'Just here, thanks.'

With a quick smile, she escaped into the refuge of the tent.

Why does my sense desert me when he's around? She was quite at ease with Danny and the other men, but Ben Drummond's presence left her floundering. *Stop thinking about that man*, she told herself sternly. But questions about him crept in when she wasn't on guard against them. Was he married? Maybe a widower. So many women died in childbirth. That might explain the sadness that blighted his rare smile.

Carefully folding Matron's coat, she laid it on the one dry and mud-free bed. Then, with a quick peep out the door to make sure no one was likely to walk in, she stripped off the soggy nightdress. It would never be white again.

Finding a towel, she rubbed herself dry, then climbed into dry camisole, drawers, petticoat, blouse and skirt. Thank God she'd not been wearing stockings. In her bag, she found some warm ones she'd not needed since last winter and dragged then up her cold legs before forcing her feet into the wet boots. Then, putting on Matron's warm coat, she headed back to the ward, taking extra careful steps. She didn't want to need rescuing by Ben Drummond again, or by any of the other men working to sweep away the remaining water and mud. He wasn't among them, and she half hoped he'd gone home. But there he was inside, helping Dr Martin and Mr Alderdice to re-hang the green baize lining of the tent.

'It's pretty wet,' the doctor said, 'but it helped keep most of the rain off the beds.'

'It should dry out by tonight,' Ben put in, 'we're not likely to get much more rain.'

'Well, as soon as it stops, can you fellows put up some ropes to hang the wet bedding out to dry. Can't have sick people lying in wet beds, and it's on the cards that we'll get an epidemic of typhoid after this.'

'Why is that, do you think, doctor?' asked Molly, who'd been watching them.

'Well, nurse, the pompous old medicos insist it's airborne, but we people here on the front line know damn well it's carried by contaminated water. So, as half the population of Hannans do their business under the nearest tree, all that, plus rubbish and dead animals, will have been washed into every hole or hollow. Please tell all your mates to boil any of that water before they drink it.'

'We mostly do. Tea's the favourite drink around here. Or beer.'

'Better get to the pubs and saloons quick if you want some,' said Alderdice. 'With all the washed-out diggers camping on the bar room floors, there won't be much left. We aren't charging the blokes to stay there, but we're doing a roaring trade in booze.'

'The beer should be safe,' the doctor put in, 'and water straight from the condensers, but avoid anything being sold as cool drink. Some dodgy brews around.'

'I'll pass that on to the blokes outside,' said Ben, heading for the door.

'I'll be off now you ladies have everything under control here, Matron. I'm glad we only had these five patients, but I'm concerned about the Nelson boy. I shouldn't have let him go home.'

'We didn't know this was going to happen. He might need to come back if their camp has been damaged,' she replied, as he took his hat and left.

'I'd better be going too, dear,' said her husband. 'Don't overdo it. You and the nurses all need to get some rest. If you need help, send me a message. I'm sure the other ladies will help out once they've got their own places sorted out.'

Matron gave him a bright smile and waved as he left, but then her face fell as she allowed her fatigue to show for a moment, before jumping up and clapping her hands.

'Nurses, we need a proper schedule. Thank God we haven't got any seriously ill people to look after among this mess, Nurse Briggs, you should have knocked off hours ago, so go and sleep because we'll need you back on the ward this afternoon. Nurse Patterson, can you work through till then?'

'Yes Matron, I'm fine. But the patients need some food. There's no sign of the cook and the kitchen's damaged. Do you want me to go and try to make something?' she was saying when, there came a call from outside and Molly opened the door to see two smiling Chinese men carrying large pots.

'Soup Miss, soup for you ladies and sick people. Mr Grant and Mr Lindsay send soup. Here comes boy with some bread. Where we put this?'

With the kitchen out of action there was only the matron's plank desk, so it was quickly cleared to make room for the two pots of soup, the thickly-sliced bread, a heap of china bowls, a ladle and soup spoons.'

'Oh, thank you, gentlemen,' said Mrs Alderdice. 'And thank your employers. We are all starving here.'

Bowing, the two men left for their respective workplaces.

Except for Mr Jameson, the patients could feed themselves, so Matron took care of him, while Nora and Molly served soup to the other four. With them fed and tucked back in bed, the nurses were able to get their share, after which Matron shooed Molly off to bed, before saying, 'If you can manage without me for a while, Nurse Patterson, I might have a nap on the spare bed in the nurses' tent. Just do what's really necessary and call me if you need help.'

Chapter 28

Outside, the men were nearly finished cleaning up the worst of the mud, when the parson turned about ten o'clock.

'Ah, here comes our neighbourhood God-botherer, just in time to avoid any work,' Jim Blake muttered before raising his voice to call out, 'Hello Reverend, come to give us a hand, have you?'

'It seems you gentlemen have it all under control, so I will go and offer my support to Matron and her helpers,' the preacher replied, before entering the hospital ward.

'I'll go too, and see if Mrs Patterson needs any help in there,' said Ben. 'I saw the other nurses head for the sleeping tent a while ago, so she's on her own.'

'I'll come too,' said Bluey.

Nora was relieved to see them. She was too tired to deal with the parson, who wanted her to wake her patients so he could pray with them. That she didn't intend to do. Even Mr Truscott, tired out after his early morning efforts, was snoring quietly in his bed.

'I'm sorry, sir, but you will have to leave. These patients have had a hard night, and I've just got them settled down. You'll have to come back later.'

As the other men came in, he capitulated, handing her some pamphlets. 'Perhaps you could give them these to peruse when they awaken.'

'I'm afraid I was rather rude to him,' Nora said after he'd gone. 'He wanted me to wake the patients, but they need their rest'

'Are they all right?' asked Bluey. 'I saw one fella out in his nightshirt trying to help.'

'Mr Truscott. He was almost ready to go home, but doctor's worried all this might bring on a relapse, so he's got to stay. His mate sent a message that their camp's awash, so he's better off here. Mr Jameson is the one we're worried about. His head wound was beginning to heal, but he got very chilled when the rain soaked his bed this morning.

'The other blokes have gone to sort their own camps, but our places are all right,' Bluey said. 'We'll see if we can fix up your kitchen roof.'

By midday, when Nora hung the last of the wet bedding on the ropes strung up outside, the clouds had disappeared, the sun shone and, but for the muddy evidence of its passing, the storm may have never happened. She was standing outside, enjoying the warmth and the fresh smell of rain-soaked earth, when Mary arrived.

'Hello Nora,' she called, 'How are you after this morning? I'd have come sooner, but Ben said you were all right here, and a couple of my neighbours got completely flooded out, so I had two big, wet blokes cluttering up my place during the worst of it.'

'I was relieved to hear you and Joey were all right. It got a bit hectic here. We thought the ward was going to blow away.

The hessian walls of the new fever ward got all torn up and our kitchen lost its roof, but Ben and Bluey fixed it. One sheet of iron had blown away down the gully.'

'I'm wondering what I can do to feed the patients,' she went on, 'we got some lovely hot soup from the hotels this morning, but our cook hasn't turned up.

'Ah, here she is,' she continued as a very round lady came hurrying up from the main street wearing mud-encrusted rubber boots and carrying two over-stretched string bags packed with tins and parcels of food.

'Hello, Mrs Campbell. How did you get on in the storm?' called Nora, going to take one of the bags.

'We're all right,' she puffed, 'But one side of the shop got blown in. Everything got soaked, so I couldn't get away. I heard that the fellas were helping up here and Mrs Fagan told me the hotels had sent food, so I thought I'd wait till now and see if I can put some sort of meal together. How many patients are there now?'

'Just the same gentlemen we had yesterday,' Nora told her.

It was a long day, and it was dusk before Aggie came to take over.

'Did you get some sleep?' Nora asked her.

'Finally, when the men finished cleaning up outside. Can you put Phenyle in the dunny before you knock off, please. I've just washed my hands.'

'I guess it's my turn,' she laughed, stepping out into the gathering gloom. No one liked the job, but Dr Martin insisted that the disinfectant be added night and morning.

It was already dark inside the lavatory, so hoping no spiders were lurking, she carefully lifted the lid. Though she held her breath as she poured the strong coal-tar disinfectant into the pan, the fumes stung her eyes. Outside, she took a few deep breaths of fresh eucalypt-scented air and was about to hurry back to the ward, when a sound behind had her swinging around.

No one was there, but the chill of fear lingered as something whooshed overhead. *Just an owl,* she told herself. But as she turned towards the ward, she glimpsed the dark shape of a man in black, watching her. Heart pounding, she turned to face the threat, but it was gone.

Telling herself it was just her imagination, she hurried inside.

Chapter 29

The brief storm caused chaos in the town. Like the hospital, the camps up on the high ground avoided serious damage. The water didn't accumulate, just washed over the dirt floors and away down the hill. Joey and his mother had rushed to put out buckets and pots to catch the leaks in the roof, but the beds stayed dry. Just about everything else got soaked, including the wood in the wood heap. Clint Sutcliffe had arrived to help spread it out in the sun to dry.

The camps on the flat and the businesses in town got the worst of the flooding. The water dug a deep gully in front of the Post Office and the Warden's office and flooded the hotel cellars.

'Our cellar's full of shit,' Timmy told Joey, 'Pa Kenny didn't fill in the cesspit like he was s'posed to. We had t' dump the cool drinks that were down there. It'll take days to get rid of all the water.'

Maybe that's why Timmy turned up with a black eye. He wouldn't say how it happened, but it wasn't the first time.

Pa Kenny's a real bastard, Joey mused as he walked home. The worst Pa ever did was smack my bum if I done somethin' bad. Gee I miss him.

On Friday night Danny, as usual, joined a few mates at the Black Swan saloon. Despite flooding in the cellar, the place had escaped any real storm damage, though some lingering debris still clung to the limed hessian walls. Inside, light from a couple of hanging hurricane lanterns showed a rough bar constructed from packing case pine, supported by three large barrels. A motley collection of characters lounged on the benches along each wall, while Danny and his cronies had commandeered the one rickety table with its six mismatched chairs. Ben seldom joined them, but he wandered down there about seven.

As he pushed the swing doors open, Jack Morrison, the son of one of Danny's mates called to a long-haired fellow leaning on the bar, 'G'day Sandy, haven't seen you for a while.'

'Hello Jack,' the man said. 'Grand t' see you. How's your dad?'

'Fine, he's usually here with us, but was a bit tired tonight. Feelin' his years. You getting any gold?'

'Enough to get by, but I canna see myself gettin' rich any time soon. Might have to give it away and go work on one of the big mines. Canna fancy working for one o' those English companies that are buyin' up everything. Guess I'll just stick with chasin' this bloody gold that seems to be everywhere but where I'm looking.'

'Well as long as you're gettin' enough for tucker. Remember y' got mates if you need a hand, mate.'

'You an' your dad makin' wages?'

'Yeah, we get enough, an' he reckons there's still good gold down there.'

As he turned from the bar Jack recognised Ben and raised his glass in greeting.

'Hello, Ben,' he said, 'Have y' met Sandy McCaig? We met him down near the Cross on our way up to the fields.'

'Good day, Mr McCaig.' Ben said as they shook hands, 'Did you have a relative out here somewhere? An Alexander McCaig?'

'Not that I know of, but that's ma name,' he replied, warily, taking in the size of the other man. 'Maybe it's me you're lookin' for.'

'No, unfortunately this fella's dead. He perished out in the bush. You sure he's not a relative of yours?'

'I dinna' think so. I haven't any family out here that I know of. How did you find out his name? Him bein' dead?'

'Had his Miner's Right on him. Nothing else.'

'I say, Sandy,' put in Jack, 'If this bloke had a Miner's Right with your name on it, maybe he's the one who hit you over the head and stole yours.'

'Well, much as I wouldna wish dyin' like that on anyone, it'd sure serve that bastard right.'

'Yeah, Ben, this nasty piece of work cracked Sandy's scone and left him for dead.'

'They reckon the swine hit me with a shovel, sliced ma ear clean off,' he said, putting up a hand to smooth his fair hair forward to hide the lack. 'I'd have been dead if Jack an' his dad hadn't found me.'

'Really?' Ben asked, 'When was this?'

'About five months ago,' Jack replied.

'Maybe you could drop in at the Police Station. They're still holding the Miners' Right, I believe. You could let them know if it's yours.'

'Righto. I will do that.'

'Hang on a minute, mate' Danny called next morning, scuttling away. 'Gotta go for a leak.'

'Righto,' Ben replied, lowering the dish of dirt to the ground, then stretching his back ready for the next stint of dryblowing. *Wish we could afford one of those fancy dryblowing machines*, he was thinking.

He was ready to set to work again, when Danny appeared from behind the hut with a worried frown, saying, 'Just spoke to that young bobby. Blake's little boy's gone missing. They're afraid he's fallen down a shaft. The blacktracker says he came this way. We'd better check the costeens. Maybe the shitehouse shaft, too.'

While they rushed to make sure there was no sign of the boy, young Joey came running up from his place, red-faced and puffing.

'What's wrong, Joey? Is your mum all right?' asked Danny

'Mum said t' tell you,' he gasped, 'little Donny Blake's run off. He mighta fallen down a mine.'

'We just heard it from the constable,' Ben told him, 'and we've checked our shafts. Old Walter's in his paddock. I might saddle him and go help with the search, Danny.'

'Righto, mate.'

'Joey,' he said, as Ben rode off, 'when you catch your breath, go tell Mum that Constable Purkiss and the tracker just passed this way, heading east. If the tracker reckons the boy's not down one of the town mineshafts, he won't be. But there's more mines out this way, and plenty dangers in the bush for a little fella.'

Ben didn't know what he could do to help, but even he could follow the police horse's tracks and it wasn't long before he saw the horse standing off the track to the right. As he reached the spot, the policeman stood up holding the still form of a small child. A little dog sat gazing up at the boy.

'Oh, dear God. Is he...'

'No. No. Just half asleep.'

With relief, Ben saw that the boy was crying.

'He's all right,' the constable went on. 'A few scratches and bruises, but he'll survive. Went to sleep under the trees. The dog's barking led us straight to him. It had a snake bailed up. Here, you hold him, while I mount. Better get him back to his folks. They'll be frantic.'

As the constable handed the child to Ben, his sobs rose to a wail, 'Mummy! Mummy! Want my Mummy!'

'It's alright, Donnie,' Ben said, patting the boy on the back. 'The nice policeman's going to take you home to Mummy on his big horsey. See? Won't that be fun?'

'Come on little fella. Let's get you home,' the constable said, leaning down to lift the wide-eyed child up onto the horse.

'Want Boofy!'

'Bugger! I forgot the bloody dog. Can you hand him up, mate?' Then to the boy, 'Can you hold onto Boofy so he doesn't fall off?'

'Yes. Me got Boofy.'

'We'll be off then,' the policeman laughed, wrapping his arm around both boy and dog. 'Better take it slow in case we lose Boofy. Can you find your way back to the police camp, Dom?'

Seeing the quizzical expression on the black man's face, he laughed, 'Silly question. Ben, meet Dom, the best bloody tracker in the force.'

'Pleased to meet you, Dom,' said Ben, turning to the other man who hesitated before grasping the offered hand. It was not often a white man shook his hand. He was also surprised when the whitefella walked beside him instead of mounting and riding away.

'Is that your real name, Dom?' Ben asked as they strolled back towards town.

'Near 'nough. Bit of it anyhow. Whitefellas can't say real name. All blackfellas just Jacky to them, or Jacky Jacky,' he snorted. 'Silly bugg'rs.'

'I got to know a few black stockmen over the east. Great horsemen. That's strange, seeing you had no horses here till the settlers came.'

'Well, we like the whitefellas' horses,' he said patting Walter's neck. 'They don't mind what colour face you got.'

'I guess you know this country very well.'

'Not like them fellas,' he said with a nod to the blacks' camp on the edge of the lease. 'Their country, not mine. Tough place. Gold diggers come, dig up grain grass, yam plants, kill roos, cut down bush tucker trees. Don't plant whitefella plants for tucker. Just gold. Mad for gold, you fellas. Can't eat it.'

'Or drink it, as some prospectors have found. So where's your country, if you don't mind my asking.'

'Down Perth way. Me Noongar, Whadjuk man from Swan River.'

'You must miss the river and the sea.'

'All time,' he said sadly. 'All time.'

Both men fell silent as they wended their way back towards the town.

'Well, here's our camp, Dom,' Ben said. 'Danny will have the billy on. You got time for a cuppa?'

'He not mind blackfella come?'

'No.'

'Righto. Thanks. If I'm late boss just think I gone walkabout. Whitefellas think we just wander around like sheep,' he laughed. 'Can't follow old ways here. My country too far away.'

'Hello, Danny,' Ben called. 'The boy's safe. Dom here found him, and the constable's taken him home. You got the billy on? Our tongues are hanging out for a cuppa. Oh, meet Dom.'

'Good to meet you, Dom,' said Danny. 'Had he gone far?'

'Little fellas travel quick on little legs.'

'Well, take a seat, mate. I'll just go and unsaddle Walter.'

'Nice horse that one.'

'Can you talk to them local fellas?' Danny asked Dom.

'Not much. Got a few words. Them fellas ... different. Talk different. All blackfellas not same, you know. Noongar not come way up here. Three hundred miles a long walk just t' say hello.

'I never thought of that,' said Ben, as he returned. 'A bit like expecting an Englishman to understand someone from Spain or Italy.'

'Yeah. Whitefellas say Sydney words and 'spect us to know what they talkin' about. Kangaroo? What's that? Oh, Yongka we say. Whitefella call baby piccaninny. Silly name for black baby somewhere else. Not blackfella word.

'Good you let them old fellas camp here,' he went on, sipping his tea. 'This special place. Good tucker till all dug up for gold. And them hills special too. Some are ... what you say? Holy place, like church. Whitefella not give a damn. Just dig it all up. Blow it up, Boom! Chasin' gold.'

'What about where you come from?' asked Danny.

'Noongar country buggered. Whitefella dig up to grow wheat, apples, cabbages. Fence off water for sheep. Blackfella come around. Bang! Bang! No more blackfella. Er, me talk too much. Thanks for tea. Gotta go.'

After he'd hurried away, Danny said. 'Sounds like a lot of blacks were just shot down over here like happened in the early days in New South Wales. Poor buggers didn't stand a chance.'

'It was happening not that long ago, back in Queensland when the squatters moved out into the bush. I saw it,' Ben replied. 'Guess we better get back to work mate.'

But what Dom had said sparked a clear memory, free of the tangled dream images that haunted him. That rider, standing tall in the saddle, shouting orders to the ragtag bunch of armed stockmen just before the attack. And he still wore Ned Patterson's face, but a lot younger. He shook his head. Of course it wasn't him.

Chapter 30

Matron called Nora into the office just before she knocked off. 'Have you heard from your husband, Nurse Patterson?'

'No, Matron,' she replied, trying not to show the worry that kept her awake at night.

'Nurse Spence will be leaving us in a few days to get married,' she said, 'so I would like you to do the night shift. Would you be able to start on Monday night?'

'Yes, Matron. If you think I'm experienced enough to take that on.'

'You've shown yourself to be capable and reliable. I'm sure you will cope,' she was saying, as Dr Martin arrived.

'You haven't seen a little boy wandering around, have you?' he said. 'The child of one of my new patients, Mrs Blake. Seems he's gone missing.'

Hearing the news, Nora quickly finished up for the day and hurried over to the Blake's new house to offer her help, though there was little she could do to comfort the distraught young mother except hold her hand and ply her with cups of tea. When the Reverend Mr Simpson arrived, offering to pray with Alice, Nora got little Lenore to help hang out the washing Alice had been doing when Donny disappeared.

They heard Boofy's excited barking even before the policeman arrived. Dismounting, he lifted the little boy down from the horse.

'Mummy! Mummy,' he cried, his earlier distress gone. 'Me ride big horsey, Mummy.'

'Oh, thank God,' Alice whispered, running to sweep him up into her arms. 'Are you all right? You naughty, naughty boy. Why did you run off like that? Oh, Constable. Thank you so much for finding him.'

'Just part of the job, Mrs Blake. Very glad I could bring him back safe. And Boofy, of course,' he laughed.

'Praise the Lord, who has answered our prayers,' the preacher intoned.

'Bloody dog,' came Jim Blake's angry voice as he came running up. 'He must have followed it. Should get rid of the mongrel.'

'Now hold on, Mr Blake,' said the constable. 'Don't blame the dog. Our tracker reckons the dog followed the boy not the other way around. It was Boofy barking at a snake that led us to him. Dom would have found him, but it might have been too late. So maybe Boofy's a hero,' he laughed as he swung up into the saddle.

'I must away, dear Mrs Blake,' the preacher was saying, 'I leave you and your little family in God's care.'

'I'll be off, too, Alice,' Nora said, pinning on her hat.

'Thank you, Nora. I really appreciate your coming. Won't you stay for a cup of tea?'

'No, thanks. I'll leave you to look after your little boy.'

'I would be delighted to escort you back to the hospital, Mrs Patterson,' Simpson said.

'That won't be necessary, sir,' she said, 'I'm only going to Mrs O'Callaghan's place.'

'Allow me to accompany you that far, then,' he said, offering her his arm.

Ignoring the gesture, Nora walked on. She would prefer to be alone with her thoughts but, feeling obliged to make conversation, she asked how long he'd been on the goldfields.

'Only a short time. I had thought to take the word of God to the heathen blacks, but such were the reports of ungodly men congregating out here in the wilds, that I was called to this ministry.'

'And are you enjoying the work?'

'God's work is always rewarding. And how are you keeping, my dear lady. Has your husband finally arrived to claim you?'

Somehow the idea of Ned 'claiming' her seemed offensive, but she replied that she was expecting him any day now. Glad to reach Mary's gate, she farewelled her unnecessary escort, stepped through the gate and knocked on the door.

'Hello, Nora,' Mary said, 'Come on in. I'm just about to make a cup of tea. Did you hear about Blake's little boy going missing? Ben just dropped in to say they'd found him.'

'Yes, I went over as soon as I heard. Poor Alice was in a state, but the constable just brought him home. I hope you don't mind me dropping in again. You must be sick of me always here under your feet.'

'Don't be silly. It's nice having a woman friend to talk to.'

'Well, I've got tomorrow off, and Matron just asked me to start doing the night shift on Monday night. Aggie Spence, who's been doing it, is leaving to get married.'

'Why don't you come and have lunch with us tomorrow. We'll probably see Danny and some of the other fellas in the afternoon, and maybe Ben if he's not out prospecting, or whatever it is he gets up to out in the bush.'

'That would be nice,' she replied. Not sure if she would be relieved or disappointed if he didn't turn up. That man was too much on her mind.

Nora awoke about three A.M next morning, before remembering it was her day off. But the pleasant prospect of a lie-in was quickly destroyed by worries about Ned. It was ten days since the policeman visited his mine, but there was still no sign of him. Corporal Williams had returned within a couple of days, so Ned's mine couldn't be that far out. Why wasn't he here?

At dawn she was still awake, her mind inventing increasingly bizarre explanations for his absence. So, donning her dressing gown and boots, she crept out to the kitchen. Finding the teapot still hot on the side of the stove, she poured herself a cup of the strong brew and wandered out to watch the sunrise. As its fiery red glow outlined the trees and shrubs, a movement down the slope drew her delighted gaze to a family of kangaroos grazing on the soft grass that had sprung up after the rain.

The storm had filled the hospital tanks so, after a proper breakfast with the cook, Mrs Campbell, she took great pleasure in washing her hair and having a shower bath in the new corrugated iron cubicle behind the kitchen, despite being limited to half a bucket of water.

Feeling cleaner than she had in weeks, she headed down town to go to church. It was a few weeks since the Anglican vicar of Coolgardie had last come to Hannans and Nora enjoyed the service, despite its being held in a bare corrugated iron building that bore no resemblance to a real church. But listening to the sermon aroused her feelings of guilt. God might forgive her, but would Ned?

Still in a subdued mood, she wandered over to Mary's in the late morning.

Clint Sutcliffe was already there, helping Mary dig manure into her garden plot, accompanied by a chittering little wagtail searching the newly turned soil for worms. They both put down their tools when she arrived.

'Look, Nora,' Mary said, 'I've got a proper garden. All it needs is some plants, but it's no good putting anything in until we get some real rain.'

'It looks good, Mary,' Nora replied. 'How are you keeping Mr Sutcliffe?' she went on as he put away the shovels and joined them.

'Very well, thank you. I've been working for Mr Nelson. You know his son lost his leg.'

'Yes, Dr Martin's arranged for him to go to Coolgardie. There's a chap there who can make proper peglegs.'

'That's good. I hope the young fella can learn to get about on it.'

'Clint brought us some real corned beef,' Mary said, 'and I cadged some of those Chinese greens from Ah Sam. Thought they'd make a change from just spuds to go with it. Ah, here's Joey. I guess his belly told him it's dinner time.'

'Hello Mrs Patterson, Mr Sutcliffe,' Joey said. 'Where's your camel today?'

'G'day, young Joey. Old Sal's over at Nelson's place. Not sure their horse is happy about sharing the paddock with her, though. Grumpy old nag it is. Y' know, I'm glad I got a camel. With horses, no matter what you want to do, they always just say "Neigh".'

Mary laughed at the horsey sound, but Joey just looked puzzled. 'What's funny?' he said, 'That's just what horse say.'

'Yes, but it sounds like "nay",' Mary explained, 'and that's an old word for "no". You'll have to do better than that, Clint.'

'Righto. What do you think Sal said when he met a kangaroo?'

'Prob'ly just grunted. Camels can't talk.'

'That's right. But what's this about grunting. Sal would be hurt to hear you say that. She's a very intelligent camel.'

'I like Sal. When I grow up I'm going to have a camel. As well as a horse, of course.'

'All right, you two. Enough of this talk about camels. Go and wash your hands, Joey.'

'I think she means me, too,' Sutcliffe said, following the boy.

'Can I give you a hand, Mary,' Nora asked.

'Well, we'll eat out here in the bough shed. Perhaps you could spread the cloth over the table and put out some knives and forks. Clint brought a bottle of hop beer so we can have that with our meal. The flies don't seem so bad today, just try not to swallow any with your dinner.'

There was something very likeable about Clint Sutcliffe, and Nora enjoyed the meal and the company. He and Mary's husband had been boys together and his tales of their boyhood pranks made Mary laugh and left Joey wide-eyed.

'I say, Joey,' Sutcliffe said, 'did y' hear about the big cricket games over east?'

'Yeah. Some English blokes have come out here to play against our fellas. Pa started teachin' me t' play cricket, but I never got the hang of it. Then he was gone.'

'We used to play as boys, and Paddy was pretty good at it. Did you have a bat and ball, then?'

'He made a little bat for Joey out of a bit of packing case, an' one for himself, too.' Mary said.

'If you've still got them, maybe Joey and I could have a go.'

'I think that's a grand idea. What do you think, Joey?'

'That'd be bonza.'

By the time the two women had the dishes done and put away, Joey had progressed to being able to hit the ball occasionally. The shouts of laughter suggested both were enjoying themselves.

'Clint's good for him,' Mary said, as they sat watching the game, 'with his riddles and jokes. Paddy said he was always like that even when they were boys. He reckoned Clint should have gone on the stage. Some of the jokes are so old they must be growin' whiskers, but Joey's not heard them before. I heard him catch Timmy out with one of the riddles the other day. He was real chuffed. Timmy's usually one jump ahead. He's not a bad young fella seeing the sort of family he comes from. I guess poor little Mrs Kenny's all right, but her husband's a nasty sod.'

'The little bugger's worn me out, Mary,' Sutcliffe said as he staggered theatrically over to collapse on the wooden bench.

'Ah, here comes another victim, Joey,' he added, as Bluey Longmore opened the gate, saying, 'G'day, ladies, hello Sutcliffe.'

'Hello Bluey,' Mary said. 'Do you play cricket? Poor old Clint can't keep up with Joey.'

'I used to play a long time ago,' Longmore said. 'What about it, Joey? Want another game?'

'Yes please, Mr Longmore. I'm just startin' t' get the hang of it.'

'You got a great young bloke there, Mary. Paddy would've been real proud of him,' Sutcliffe said, as they watched the play resume. Bluey's bowling suggested more than a passing acquaintance with the game and soon it was Joey needing to call a halt.

'You're doing real well, there Joey,' Longmore said. 'Keep practising and you might end up playin' for Australia one day.'

'Do you think we'll really be able to call ourselves Australia some day?' the other man asked. 'Instead of bein' just a bunch of squabbling colonies.'

'Oh, I'm sure federation's going to happen. Don't take any notice of the West Australians. With all the t'othersiders here on the fields, we'll soon outvote the bloomin' isolationists. As long as everyone registers to vote, of course.'

'Nora, come and have a look at the dress Nellie wants me to alter for her,' Mary said, leading the way inside. 'I've got it wrapped in a sheet to keep the dust out. I don't know where she got it. It's far too big for her and all the frills are tattered. Lovely material, though.'

'It looks a bit fancy for Hannans.'

'I'll have to do something about the neckline, or she'll look like a floozy. Maybe she is. But I can't help liking her.'

'She's a pretty little thing, isn't she?' Nora was saying as they stepped outside where the two men were discussing the relative merits of horses and camels. Bluey agreed about the benefits of camels for remote prospecting, but felt the bond between a man and his horse was something special.

'Well, I've never had a horse who was as much fun to travel with as my old Sal. That camel has a real sense of humour. She always laughs at my jokes. Oh, here come a couple more visitors, Mary,' he called.

'Just in time for a cuppa, fellas,' Mary said, as Ben and Danny joined them.

'Not off into the wilds, today, Ben?' Bluey asked.

'No, that new tank we ordered arrived yesterday, so we've been setting it up.'

'Shame it hadn't come before that storm,' Danny put in, 'It was hard watchin' all that water run away down the hill.'

Turning to Nora, he went on, 'How're you goin' up at the hospital? Got everything straightened out?'

'Pretty much. They've fixed up the new fever ward.'

'How do you like working up there, Mrs Patterson?' Bluey asked.

'Oh, I'm getting used to it. A bit different from where I used to work.'

'You're not from Queensland, are you?' Ben asked.

'No. From Victoria.'

'What about your husband? Did he ever live in Queensland?'

'No. Why do you ask?'

'It's just the photograph of him reminds me of someone I met back there.'

As the conversation moved on, Ben wasn't sure if what she'd said was a relief, or confirmation that he was crazy, thinking that man could be Patterson.

As Mary poured the tea, Bert Bowden arrived with the unlikeable Tom Tucker, his shy greeting drowned out by the American's loud, 'Hiya, fellas. And how are our lovely ladies today?'

'No better for you asking,' Mary whispered to Nora as, not waiting for an answer, he joined the men, saying, 'You fellas heard about this Mt Catherine find? Do y' reckon it's as rich as they're sayin'?'

'Sounds as if it's pretty big,' Clint replied. 'Lots of blokes dropped everything and headed out there.'

'Maybe not quite a mountain of gold, though. Did y' hear Robinson reckons the others murdered a bunch of blacks?'

'Yeah. They've been arrested. Seems odd he never reported it until he'd had a row with Fitzgerald about the lease. And they only found a coupla bodies.'

'Seems like a lot of fuss about someone shootin' a few blacks. Goddamned country would be better off without them,' said the American.

'I don't know,' put in Bluey, 'you can't just go around shooting people, even blackfellas.'

'Don't worry, those blokes will get off,' said Ben, suddenly standing up, 'a black man's life's not worth tuppence in this country. I think I'll be off back up to camp, Mary. See you later, Danny.' Picking up his hat, he strode away leaving his half-drunk pannikin of tea forgotten on the log.

'Funny bloke,' said Bowden in the ensuing silence. 'Seemed upset.'

I guess Ben is a funny bloke, Danny was thinking, as he wandered down town later. After working together for more than two years, he still knew little about his partner, but suspected there was something tragic in his past. Even drunk he never loosened up, just got quieter and quieter. Himself, he found booze helped when sad old memories started to harass him.

Poor old Ireland! He wondered if his family back there survived that awful famine in the forties. He was long gone by then. Maybe the English saved his life when they shipped him out to Botany Bay when he was fourteen.

He had plenty scars to remember the bastards by, but after the first few whippings he got smart, kept his head down, pulled his forelock, said "Yes sir, no sir" to the master he was assigned to and found himself a free man just in time to catch the gold fever that drew hundreds to California in '49. Though he'd hoped from there to sneak back into Ireland, the lure of gold drew him back to Australia's Victorian rush, and later to South Africa, before news of these new rich finds brought him to Western Australia.

Wrapped in old memories, he bumped into young Constable Purkiss near the pub.

'Sorry mate,' he said, stumbling back.

'You all right, Mr O'Hara?' the young man asked, helping him regain his balance.

'Not watchin' where I was goin'. You had any luck catching that murderer?'

'There's some characters we're keeping an eye on. This Sutcliffe bloke, what do you know about him?'

'He's an old friend of Mrs O'Callaghan's. One of her late husband's mates from way back, I believe.'

'Had you met him before?'

'Yeah, back in Coolgardie in '93. I think you'll find Sutcliffe is all right. Paddy O'Callaghan wouldn't have been friends with a killer.'

Chapter 31

After lying awake half the night, worrying about Ned and the whining of the wind testing the tent's frame, Nora slept in. So it was quite late by the time she wandered down town. Some respectable tearooms had popped up in the main street, and she was thinking of buying herself some morning tea, when a high-pitched cry of, 'Coolgardie Minerrrr!' pierced the baritone rumble of massed male voices, and she looked across the street to see young Joey, a hessian bag of newspapers on one shoulder and a leather moneybag slung on the other. He was doing a roaring trade with the news-starved crowd as she crossed over, fumbling in her purse for the right change.

'Hello, Mrs Patterson,' he said, with a big grin, handing her the paper.

'How do you like selling papers, Joey?' she asked.

'It's a bonza job. I get a farthing for every paper I sell.'

'Well, best of luck with it, Joey. Your mum must be really proud of you. Is she home this morning?'

'No, she's workin' all day,' he replied as more eager customers crowded around.

Waving goodbye, Nora took the paper with her into Mrs Cornell's hessian tearoom. Ordering her tea and a slice of seedcake, she took a seat near the window and watched the men passing by or stopping to hail friends. They were much less alarming now she'd met some of them socially.

The paper was full of reports about that big gold find and the arrest of some men for killing Aboriginal people, but it was hard to tell what had really happened. Some men had caught typhoid and died before they could get to the hospital. She guessed it was the start of the epidemic Dr Martin had predicted.

Finishing her tea, she decided to stroll down the street to see what new businesses had opened up. There were a couple more general stores selling anything from water tanks to needles, a bootmaker and even a little hessian bookshop, where she enjoyed a browse before buying a copy of Lorna Doone. As she emerged from the bookshop, looking forward to an afternoon of reading, the reverend Simpson appeared, all smiles and solicitation.

'Good afternoon, Mrs Patterson,' he said, walking beside her. 'I see you are a reader. What have you got there? Ah, a harmless story. Do you read a lot of novels? Some are most unsuitable for ladies. I would be happy to suggest some improving reading.'

'Thank you, sir,' Nora replied, 'I prefer to make my own choices.'

'Are you returning to the hospital? Let me accompany you. It is not safe for a lovely young woman to wander these streets unescorted.'

Unable to shake him off, she continued walking, trying to ignore his annoying comments and was glad to reach the hospital grounds and say goodbye.

Nora was glad when her shift finished just before dawn next morning. With only five patients, all on the mend, she'd had little to do but try to ignore the big tent's scary creaks and moans, and worry. Ned told the policeman he'd be in town in a few days. Maybe he wasn't coming. Maybe he's found someone else.

But that's not like Ned. He'd tell me if he didn't love me anymore, she was telling herself, as Molly arrived to relieve her.

'I just made pot of tea, Nora,' she said as Nora was stepping out the door, 'if you want a cuppa.'

'Thanks Molly,' she called, heading for the kitchen to pour herself a cup and wander out into the coolness and birdsong to watch the rising sun paint the distant hills with gold.

Shivering a little in her light clothing, she was about to go inside when a magpie alighted on the nearest tree and, after a few practice notes, launched into glorious song. Within minutes, four more arrived to join the chorus. One landed almost at her feet and she dared not move for fear of disturbing them. In a brief break in the song, echoes of the same melody came drifting across the parched red earth from several directions, before a different call sent the birds winging away into the sunrise. Yawning, she headed for her bed.

Awakening about midday, she got herself some lunch, and was strolling down town to see what the newest general store had in stock, when the Reverend Simpson appeared alongside her.

'Good afternoon, Mrs Patterson,' he said, 'Let me accompany you. A lady alone might attract the attention of the hotels' more disreputable clientele at this time of day.'

'Thank you, sir, but I am quite capable of taking care of myself,' she said as they reached the new shop, 'If you will excuse me, I'm going in here.'

Quickly stepping inside, she was confronted by the usual jumble of pots, pans, picks, shovels and bags of produce, but to one side was a table piled with ladies' clothing, some of the more intimate kind. As she lifted a pair of frilled drawers to examine a camisole top, she heard someone say, 'Very fetching, indeed,' and turned to find Simpson had followed her. Blushing, she was searching for something more appropriate to pretend to want to buy, when she glimpsed Bluey Longmore in conversation with a man about to enter the shop.

Quickly squeezing between two customers, she slipped through the door and ran to catch up with him just as Simpson followed her out the door.

'Hello Mr Longmore, 'she said, 'I was wondering if you are going to visit Mary. That's where I'm heading. Mr Simpson offered to escort me but perhaps you might save him the trouble.'

'Certainly, Mrs Patterson,' he said, tipping his hat, before continuing, with a twinkle in his blue eyes. 'We wouldn't want to keep the reverend gentleman from his pastoral duties.'

'Goodbye, Mr Simpson,' she called to the angry parson.

'He annoying you?' Bluey asked, offering her his arm.

'He seems to think I need him to watch over me. Maybe he's the same with all the ladies. Just feels it's his duty to protect us, I suppose, but I find it really irritating. I'm not a young girl, I'm a married woman who's used to taking care of herself.'

'Well, you do need to be careful out here. There are hundreds of fellas hanging around, and not all of them are good blokes.'

'I know that. But it's not as if I'm wandering around town at night. It's broad daylight.'

'Have you known Mary long?' she asked as they strolled up the hill.

'I met her and Paddy in Coolgardie before we all came here. It was very sad when poor Paddy got killed.'

By that time, they'd reached Mary's gate, to find her pouring used washing-up water on the pumpkin plant by the door.

'You two must have smelt the fruitcake I've just made in the camp oven. I was hoping someone would help us eat it.'

Feeling she had to explain why they were together, Nora said, 'Mr Longmore rescued me from the Reverend Simpson. Every time I walk down the street, he seems to pop up out of nowhere wanting to protect me from what he calls undesirable elements, but there's something about him that makes me nervous.'

'I don't like the man, either. Smarmy, sneaky character. A priest shouldn't look women over like he does.'

'Oh well, he's allowed to marry. Maybe he's hoping to find a wife.'

'Hannans is hardly a good place to start looking, is it?'

'Timmy an' me reckon he dyes his hair an' whiskers,' said Joey.

'Why do you say that?' his mother asked.

'He tossed a little box in the bush. I thought it might be good to keep stuff in so picked it up. An' it's got Hair Dye written on it.'

'Why were you looking at his rubbish?'

'We was just walkin' past when he threw it out of his buggy. But why would anyone wanna have red hair if he didn't have to? I'd swap mine for any other colour tomorrow. Got sick o' being' called 'Carrots, an' worse things at school.'

'Your hair's lovely,' Mary said patting his curls. 'But it's none of your business if Mr Simpson dyes his hair. I bet you two were sneaking around, lookin' for clues again. People don't like being spied on, Joey. Please stop it. Now, run out and see if the billy's boiling.

'I wish he and Timmy would stop poking their noses into other people's business. You will stop for a cup of tea, won't you?'

'Of course,' Nora said, 'the fruitcake smells delicious.'

'Just wish I had real butter to put on it. Ah, here comes another one with a good nose,' Mary laughed as Ben pushed open the gate.

'What's so funny?' he asked.

'Oh nothing, really. You're just in time for a cuppa.'

'Thanks Mary. I've just been down to the Post Office.'

'Any news from home?'

'No,' he said sadly. 'Maybe they're all dead.'

'Oh, I'm sure they're not, Ben.

'I just had a visit from that policeman,' she told him, 'asking questions about Clint. I said I've known him since before I was married. He was Paddy's best man. He went bush after that, and I don't know where he got to for a while. He visited us when we were in Coolgardie, then headed off up the Murchison. I hope he's not in some sort of trouble.'

'Purkiss was asking Danny about him too,' Ben told her. 'I don't think he's in trouble. Remember us telling you that they're looking for a bloke who arrived about six months ago, a murderer from the east.'

'Surely they don't suspect Clint.'

'They're checking up on all medium-sized fair-haired men. They don't think this bloke's a danger to the public. He just killed someone he had a grudge against. They kept quiet about it so as not to alert him that they are on the hunt. Purkiss shouldn't have told us, and asked us to keep it quiet, but we're worried about you and Joey here by yourselves, and the ladies up at the hospital, too. Danny thinks you ought to start carrying your little gun, Nora.'

'You've got a gun?' asked Bluey, raising his eyebrows.

'Yes. An old friend gave it to me, but I'm afraid to use it.'

'Danny will have to give you more lessons, then,' said Mary. 'If there are murderers getting around, maybe you should wear it under your skirt like the old lady said. And I'll be making sure the shotgun's loaded.'

'You've got some stuff growing in your garden already,' Nora said, after the two men left.

'Yes, I put a few seeds in after the rain and a few are starting to shoot, but most of that green is just grass,' Mary told her. 'It springs up after rain all along the creeks and in sheltered places. Mostly dies off when it happens this early in the year. There won't be the wildflowers we get later in the year, but it'll be nice out in the bush.

'You know what,' she went on, 'it's Joey's eleventh birthday on Friday and I've been trying to think of something special to do. Maybe we could have a picnic. I'm sure Danny and Ben would take us out in their cart. Would you like to come? It might be a bit rough.'

'That sounds nice. I loved bush picnics when I was a girl.'

'Don't say anything to Joey yet. Do you think Alice and her family might like to come?'

'Maybe, if Donny's adventure hasn't made her too scared of the bush.'

'But you'll come, won't you?'

'Yes, I'd like to. I'll be on night shift so will have the day off. But perhaps I should stay in town in case Ned comes looking for me.'

'Well, it'll serve him right if you're not here. It's all of two weeks since Corporal Williams told him you had arrived.'

'I know, and I'm worried that he's sick or something. Anyway, I'd better go. I had a snooze this morning, but need a nap before tonight's shift.'

Her hopes were dashed, however, when she reached the hospital. The place was in an uproar with the unfinished fever ward being readied for the admission of three typhoid cases. Seeing her arrive, Mrs Alderdice called out, 'Oh, Nurse Patterson, I know you're not on duty, but could you give Nurse Briggs a hand to make up the beds in the fever ward, please?'

Of course she couldn't refuse, so spent the next hour helping get the new ward ready, then Matron called the staff together in the kitchen to explain how they were going to manage the extra workload.

'Dr Martin will arrive shortly with the new patients. They'll be isolated in the fever ward. I will care for them, with the help of Mr Dunne. Nurse Spence has agreed to stay on a couple of days, so she and Nurse Briggs will handle the day shifts in the main ward, while Nurse Patterson takes the nights. We are expecting a new nurse soon to take over from Nurse Spence.'

Chapter 32

Danny was dollying the following morning, while Ben worked on dryblowing, until the wind changed, sending clouds of red dust across the campsite.

'Hey, Ben,' called Danny, 'Better pack it in, mate, or everything will be covered in dirt.'

'Sorry Danny.' Ben called, removing the cloth masking his face, 'Should I move over the other side to take advantage of this strong wind?'

'No, it'll probably get too strong and blow the bloody gold away and you with it. How's it goin', anyway?'

'Lookin' good,' he said, bringing the container of gold grains to show Danny.

'Not bad for a mornin's work, mate. I think you've well and truly earned a break. I'm a bit buggered myself. I'll get the billy on while you get out of that rigup. You won't be able to do any more today. Maybe later we could do somethin' about clearing the ground for that iron kitchen you been on about us puttin' up. Might be nice to have an inside fire when the cold weather comes.'

As Danny went to stir up the fire, Ben moved to the leeward side of the camp and stripped off the shirt and dungarees he kept for that dirty job, subjecting them to a vigorous shake, before hanging them on a hook in the bough shed. He was heading for the shack to get dressed, when a female voice sent him scurrying inside, as Seamus ran out, tail wagging wildly.

'Cooee,' Mary called, stooping to stroke the dog's shaggy coat and pretending she hadn't seen the naked man.

'Hello there, Mary,' called Danny. 'You're just in time for a cuppa.'

'Yes, I thought I'd about timed it right. I brought some treacle scones I made this morning.'

'Take a seat lassie. Ben's around somewhere.'

'Thanks, Danny,' Mary said, settling herself on one of the log seats by the campfire. 'Actually, I have a favour to ask. Or maybe I should say another favour, after everything you fellas have done to help us.'

'It's been our pleasure to help you and the young'un. So, what's wanting done? Something get damaged in that storm?'

'No, nothing like that. But it's Joey's birthday on Friday and I was telling Nora how pretty the bush will be after the rain, and I thought it'd be nice to have a picnic to celebrate. So, I wonder if maybe you and Ben would take us out to one of the creeks while there's still a billabong or two left.'

'Sounds like a nice idea,' said Ben as he emerged, fully clad, from the shack.

'Better wash y' face, mate. You look a bit piebald.'

'Hello, Ben,' Mary laughed. 'You been dryblowing?'

'Yes, couldn't you guess? If we're going on a picnic, it better be soon. The water might all be gone by next week.'

'What about Friday? We'll have earned a bit of a break, after puttin' this lot through, don't y' think, Ben.'

'Don't see why not.'

'I think Nora will come if she's not working that day.'

'We'll have to take young Timmy.'

'Steve might like to bring Jeanie and the little ones,' Mary said. 'And maybe the Blakes.'

'Bluey an' Steve have got a big dray. All the young'uns could ride on that,' Danny suggested.

'So,' he went on, 'young Joey's turning what? Eleven? Y' know, Mary, he's a really bright boy. Most ten-year-olds couldn't read those Sherlock Holmes stories.'

'I was surprised, myself. He kept asking me what words meant. A lot of them were too hard for me, so we had to look them up in Paddy's old dictionary. I'm a bit worried about this detective stuff he and Timmy get up to, though. Sneaking around watching people might get them into trouble.'

'It could be worse,' Danny said, 'at least they're playing at being on the right side of the law. Up the Murchison, a couple of boys took it into their heads to play bushrangers. They were riding out with their guns to hold up the stagecoach when their fathers caught up with them.'

'Oh, dear. I guess boys will be boys, but I can't help worrying. Oh, you remember they thought Nora's husband might have visited a brothel?'

'Yes, I hope they haven't been back there.'

'No, but I heard something bad that I don't want to tell Nora. One of the madams comes into the pub t' have a drink in the ladies' saloon. She heard me asking if anyone knew Edward Patterson, and yesterday she said they'd had a nasty bloke called Patterson at the brothel a few months ago. "Got rough with my girls, so we threw him out," she told me.

'It mightn't have been him. So better not say anything,' Danny said. But for Ben, the thought of Nora at the mercy of a man like that was chilling.

'Hey, Ben, you comin' to give me a hand?' Danny called a bit later.

'Oh, sure Danny,' Ben replied, flooded with guilt to see his old mate struggling to shift a large rock with a crowbar.

'Sorry, Danny. Didn't realise you'd already started,' he said as he took over from the older man.

'You goin' deaf or something? I called you a coupla times and you're just standin' there like a stale bottle of beer. Where were you mate? Away with the fairies?'

'Sorry mate. Just didn't hear you.'

Bloody hell, he thought. That wasn't the first time he'd found himself standing around in a daze, thinking about her. *Stop it, you silly bugger*, he berated himself. *Never can be anything between you and her, or any other woman.* But it wasn't just the thought of her sweet face, but the secret delight that his heart wasn't completely dead. Nora Patterson's smile had pierced the wall he'd built around it.

'Might be an idea to ride out an' find somewhere to take the ladies for this picnic,' Danny said as they knocked off for lunch.

'There's one place where there was a bit of a billabong last year. I'll go and have a look this afternoon.'

⟶⟵

'Will you be needing me today, Matron?' Nora asked on Friday morning. 'Mary O'Callaghan's invited me to a bush picnic. It's to celebrate her son's birthday.'

'No, Nurse Patterson. You've been working double shifts and we'll need you again tonight. Now that Nurse Bowra has joined us, we can get back to a regular schedule. Go off and have a nice day with your friends. And here's something for Mary's boy,' she said, producing a bag of boiled lollies from her desk.

Nora dropped in to Courthope's store, looking for a present for Joey. When she explained what she was after, the storekeeper said, 'Young Joey? What about this?' handing her a small book. It's soft paper cover showed two policemen chasing a masked man.

'Yes, he might like that,' Nora agreed, fumbling in her purse for the right coins.

As she left the shop, she saw the Reverend Simpson wandering down the other side of the road, so quickly hurried back up the hill to Mary's.

'Happy birthday, Joey,' she said, handing him the book. 'And Mrs Alderdice sent you these lollies.'

'Gee thanks Mrs Patterson,' he said with a big grin.

'We're just about to walk up to Danny's,' Mary told her.

'Can I help carry something?' Nora asked, seeing a basket of food on the table and a heap of rugs on the chair.

'Maybe grab a couple of blankets. Oh, here comes Timmy.'

'Hello, Mrs O'Callaghan. Mum sent some cool drink,' he said, the bottles clinking in the sugar bag he carried.

'That's nice of her,' Mary said, leading the way up the hill, where Seamus greeted them enthusiastically.

'Down boy,' Danny said, 'You'll have to stay home today. We're worried he'll scare the little-uns. Ben's just harnessing Walter. Here, Mary let me relieve you of all that stuff.'

'It's just sandwiches and a cake I made with dried eggs. I don't know how good it'll be. You never know how things will turn out cooked in the camp oven.'

'I'm sure it'll go down a treat, lassie,' he was saying as Ben arrived with the horse and cart.

'Hello, ladies, boys,' he said. 'Bluey and Steve are bringing their big dray. You young blokes can ride on that while the ladies come in the cart.'

'Blakes are bringing their buggy and will pick up Mrs Hoskins,' Danny explained.

The creak of trace chains and the thud of hooves announced the arrival of the dray pulled by a big draught horse. A little way behind came the Blakes in their buggy with Steve's wife, Jeanie.

'I'm glad you could come, Nora,' Mary said, when they were seated in the cart. 'You must have all been flat out at the hospital with all the typhoid patients. I heard a couple had died.'

'Yes, and there was another death during the night. The trouble is, they think they can look after themselves in their camps and we don't get them until it's too late. I'm worrying Ned could have got it and that's why he's not turned up. It's two weeks, now. What if he's out there dying while I'm going picnicking?'

'Try not to worry,' Mary said, taking her hand. 'He'll probably turn up today, just because you're not hanging around waiting for him.'

'I keep telling myself he'll come, but I don't think I know who he is any more. Nothing that's happened makes any sense. The Ned I know wouldn't ask me to come then leave me stranded here.'

'You ladies comfortable there?' Danny asked, settling himself on the seat, as Ben hopped up to take the reins and turned to them with a questioning smile.

'We're fine, aren't we Nora?' Mary said.

'We'll be off then,' Ben said, flicking the reins and calling 'Gee up' to the horse.

Nora was surprised how, soon after they left the town, the dust cleared and the air was filled with the fresh bush smells. Tall, spreading gums stood along the barely defined track, some still covered in cream or yellow blossoms despite the long dry season.

The smaller trees and bushes, though all described as mulga, were obviously not the same. Some had silvery or bright green leaves that stood out from the general olive green.

About half-an-hour later, they followed a gully between white-trunked river gums to a level area beside a winding pool of water and drove along the bank, sending a flurry of birds squawking into the sky. Within minutes, the white cockatoos were back, taking up watchful perches on the branches overhead and a noisy crowd of pink and grey galahs dropped down to forage on the ground. At the far end of the bank was a cleared area framed by the branches of a fallen tree.

'Righto, ladies,' said Danny. 'This is the spot. What do you think? Will it do?'

'It's lovely, Danny,' said Mary.

'I reckon a couple of branches of that tree will make you ladies comfortable seats.'

Pulling Walter to a halt, Ben jumped off the cart and offered Nora his hand to help her down.

'Thank you,' she murmured, annoyed at herself for blushing. *Silly woman. He's just another bloke. Ned will be here soon.* But would he? Every day that he didn't come, he seemed to become more unsubstantial, like a ghost. She shivered at the thought, clutching the solidity of Ben's hand for a moment. To hide her embarrassment, she walked to the creek, disturbing a lizard that scuttled away as the dray arrived, followed by the Blakes' sulky.

While the men unharnessed the horses and hobbled them down the far end of the billabong, the two women walked up to where Nora and Mary were unpacking the food.

'Hello Mrs Blake, Jeannie,' Mary said. 'All you ladies have met, haven't you?

'Who wants a drink?' called Ben, going to retrieve some of the bottles he'd left to cool in the water the day before.

By the time everyone had their drinks, the women had the food ready. There were three types of sandwiches, Alice's real ham and pickles, Mary's canned corned beef with mustard and Jeanie's tinned sardines sprinkled with vinegar. Then it was time for cake.

'The billy's boiling, ladies. Anyone for a cuppa,' Danny asked.

Mary's 'Yes please,' was echoed by the others.

'It's really nice here,' Alice said as they sipped their tea, 'So different from the town. No dust; no thumping rock crusher; no clattering dollypots; no blokes yelling to make themselves heard over the noise. Lovely. Oh, Donny, what's the matter?'

'Wanna play wit' Billy an' Lenny,' Donny whined, trying to escape his mother's hold.

'Billy,' Alice called, 'what are you playing?'

'Hide and seek, Mum.'

'Could Donny go with you?'

'He'll give away my hidey spot.'

'He c'n come with me,' said Joey, but it wasn't long before, with a shout of triumph, Timmy found them hiding behind a tree and it was their turn to do the seeking. Lenore crawled in behind her mother's skirts, as Joey called, 'Coming ready or not.

'Can you see them, Donny?' he asked. 'How 'bout you look under everything an' I'll look over the top.'

That turned out to be a good strategy, as it was Donny who saw Timmy's boots behind the buggy wheel.

'Gotcha, Timmy!' Joey cried.

'Gotcha Timmy!' Donny echoed, running to his mother. 'Mummy, Mummy. Joey an' me, gotcha'd Timmy.'

'That's wonderful Donny,' Alice said. 'Now I think it's time for more cake.'

'Jim's trying to start a game of cricket,' Ben said, as the children squabbled over the last of the cake. 'He brought a ball, but the bat's a piece of dead mulga. Looks like I'm on Bluey's team with Joey.'

Bluey managed to hit the ball away into the scrub a few times but it wasn't long before a lucky bowl clanged on the kerosene can wicket. Then Ben managed to get one run before hitting the ball up into a tree. Timmy retrieved it, tossed it to Jim. Then Ben was out and it was Joey's turn.

As the thwack of the makeshift bat striking the ball echoed across the space, Nora said, 'I'm glad I came, Mary. My life's been such a turmoil since I arrived and it's so peaceful out here.'

'With the noise that lot are making?' laughed Mary.

'Yes, even with that. It's a happy noise.'

'It's been a great success, Mary,' Danny put in. 'Glad you thought of a picnic. Hey, what's all the fuss, now?'

'Someone hit the ball into the billabong,' Alice laughed.

'Probably won't find it in there,' said Danny. 'Reckon they'll be givin' it away. We need to be makin' tracks soon. Young Joey said he's got to go sell papers up at the Croesus when the fellas knock off.'

'Yes,' Mary explained, 'the boy who did it has quit. I'm a bit worried he won't get home before it starts to get dark.'

Chapter 33

Nora had hoped to snatch a couple of hours sleep before her night shift started, but soon realised there was some sort of crisis, so went over to the main ward to find out what was happening.

'Another three very ill patients have just been brought in,' Matron told her. 'We've made the two with typhoid as comfortable as possible in the fever ward, but I'm afraid the other, Mr Morrison, has pneumonia. Doctor is with him now. Would you be able to start work a bit early tonight?'

'Yes, of course,' Nora replied.

'Thank you. Get something to eat before you start.'

As Nora had feared, the sick man was the Mr Morrison she'd met on the stagecoach. He gave her a sad smile, but was too short of breath to speak. Molly had just applied a poultice to his chest and that seemed to ease his distress slightly, but there wasn't a lot they could do for him. As his friends had liberally dosed him with brandy before he was brought in, Dr Martin was reluctant to give him morphine, one of the usual medications. Even young patients often failed to respond to the treatment available, so it was just a case of watch and wait while his aged body battled for survival.

Fortunately, only two of the other general patients needed much attention overnight, so Morrison was Nora's main concern, but it was frustrating being unable to ease his suffering except for giving him regular drinks of water and replacing the poultice. She was relieved when Dr Martin turned up at dawn, but his response to her query about the patient was to sadly shake his head, saying, 'I doubt he'll last the day, nurse.'

The old man was still holding on two hours later when she knocked off and found her way to her bed. She was too tired to lie awake worrying for long, but it was a month since she'd arrived in Hannans, and two weeks since she heard Ned was alive. Where was he?

It was mid-afternoon before Nora awoke on Saturday, hungry and dying for a cup of tea, so after dressing; she headed for the kitchen, where Molly was pouring hot water into the teapot.

'Want a cup?' she asked. 'I hope I didn't disturb you when I got up.'

'No, I slept like a log. Didn't get much sleep yesterday. What's been happening? How is Mr Morrison?'

'Oh, he died a couple of hours ago. Did you know him?'

'Not really, but he came up on the coach with me,' she replied.

'One of the typhoid blokes died too. We're gonna need a bigger morgue if this keeps up. I'd better get back to work. The baker brought us some fresh bread and Matron brought some plum jam. You better get some before it's all gone.'

Saddened by the news, she spread some jam on a slice of bread then took it and her tea out to the bough shed. With a cool breeze wafting across from the west, it was quite pleasant out there, so she got her book, but the old man's death brought back her fears for Ned, so it was hard to keep her mind on the story.

Back at work that night, there was little to do once she got the patients settled down. Unlike last night when poor old Mr Morrison's coughing and wheezing had disturbed the others, it was scarily quiet. She didn't believe in ghosts, but it was hard to forget the men lying out there in the makeshift morgue, with the wind playing eerie music on the taut guy ropes and the flap of canvas echoing like footsteps. Was Ned lying dead out there somewhere, too?

Weariness and worry took their toll and by the time Molly came to relieve her at three o'clock, all she could do was fall into bed.

It was one of those lovely goldfields mornings, but Ben never noticed the scented breeze or the birdsong that Sunday. Seeing Blake and Hoskins with their children brought home to him what he had missed. Would he end up another lonely old man wandering around the outback? Much as he enjoyed the bush, he wanted more. But the future he and Millie dreamed of was never to be and now no woman in her right mind would have him. There was only one woman he wanted, anyway. Turning off the beaten track, he headed into country he'd not explored before, part of his mind automatically recording how to find his way back.

The dark mood still hung over him at midday when he stopped to boil the billy. Giving Walter a drink and a perfunctory pat, he was loosening the girth strap when he received a gentle nudge from the horse's nose.

'Sorry, mate,' he said in answer to the questioning look, 'I'm a miserable bastard today.'

While waiting for the billy to boil, he started to sketch a stand of salmon gums but, instead, found himself doodling a man's face. The face that haunted his dreams; that looked like Ned Patterson. It was crazy to think it could be him. But then, maybe he was crazy. Despite the past, he'd never doubted his sanity. But this obsession with Ned Patterson shook his confidence.

He'd vowed never to be caged again and now his eyes were drawn to the long shape of the gun hanging in its scabbard on Walter's saddle. It would be so easy. But he'd never succumbed to that temptation, even in his darkest days. And now, even if Nora wasn't for him, there was someone he cared about. What's more, he suddenly realised, there were others who cared for him. Danny, Mary and Joey needed him. *I couldn't abandon Walter out here anyway*, he thought, looking around for the horse.

⤙⤙

Nora managed to get a few hours' sleep that morning, before wandering over to Mary's in the afternoon. Young Joey was sitting in the bough shed holding the book she'd given him, but just gazing at the ground and drawing circles in the dirt with his bare toes.

'Hello, Joey,' she said. 'Do you like the book?'

'It's all right. Mum's inside,' was all the reply she got.

'Hello Nora,' Mary called from the door. 'Come inside. I'm busy hemming sheets for Mrs Alderdice. We'll have a cuppa in a minute.'

'Can I make it?'

'That'd be nice. I've only got two hems to do to finish this batch, so won't be long. I asked Joey to put the billy on a while ago, so it should be hot. I've already put some tea in the teapot.'

'Goodoh, I'll take the pot out and see if it's ready.'

She was surprised to see Joey had disappeared. By the time she'd made the tea, Mary had joined her, but still no Joey.

'I don't know what's got into him, he usually likes his cup of tea,' Mary said. 'I hope he's not sickening for something. I wanted him to come to Mass with me this morning. It's the first time for ages that we've had a priest come here. But he wouldn't get up and he's hardly said two words since.'

'He was out here when I arrived. Seemed a bit quiet.'

'I guess he's off somewhere with Timmy, but he usually tells me what he's doing. I'll just top up the billy. A few fellas will probably drop in for a cuppa. I hear you've had a sad time up at the hospital.'

'Yes, we lost another typhoid case last night. I didn't know him, but the old chap who died of pneumonia came up on the stagecoach with me. He was a nice old gentleman.'

'That must have been old Bill Morrison. He was one of Danny's mates. Not sure we'll see him today. He might be nursing a sore head after the wake last night. Still no sign of Ned?'

'No. Sometimes I think he's dead and want to weep. Other times.' she went on with a teary smile, 'I get so angry that if he turned up, I'd probably punch his nose.'

'Oh, Nora. You just have to keep hoping. Ah, hello, Clint,' she went on, as Sutcliffe pushed open the gate.

'G'day Mary, Mrs Patterson,' he replied, 'Where's Joey? I remembered a good joke to tell him.'

'He's off with Timmy, I think.'

'You need to warn them to be careful playing detective, Mary. There's some nasty types around. I just got waylaid by a bobby asking all sorts of questions. Seems a bloke who looked a bit like me has done someone in. I hope I convinced them it wasn't me.'

'Yes, Ben warned us. This bloke murdered someone over the east and took his place on the steamer. The police think he came up here. But it was months ago, and they didn't think he was a danger to anyone else.'

'I don't know, Mary. They seem pretty serious now about catching him.'

While Mary was pouring his tea, Bluey and Freddie Chapman arrived, followed by Danny and Charlie Osmond.

'Ben off out bush again?' Mary asked after they'd exchanged greetings.

'Said he wanted to have a look out east.'

Nora was still trying to convince herself that she wasn't disappointed when, a few minutes later, Bert Bowden arrived bearing a tin of Swallow and Ariell's biscuits.

'Joey'll be sorry to miss out on them bickies,' Danny said. 'Off chasin' clues with Timmy, is he, Mary?'

'I think so,' she replied, with a worried frown.

'I've just been telling Mary the boys need to watch out. The bobbies are lookin' for a murderer,' Sutcliffe said.

'We did hear about it, but they said he only did in a bloke he knew so wasn't likely to be a threat to anyone else,' Danny said.

'I think they're getting more worried now,'

Mary had been too busy to make anything for afternoon tea, so Bowden's biscuits were nearly all gone by the time Joey sidled in, looking furtive.

'What y' been up to, mate?' Danny asked him.

'Nothin' much,' the boy muttered, grabbing a couple of the remaining biscuits.

'You might need t' put some more water in the pot if you want a cup of tea,' his mother told him.

'I'm glad t' see he's not lost his appetite,' she whispered to Nora. 'I hope this lot don't hang around too long. I need to get back to sewing.'

The men, meanwhile, had been having a heated discussion about the big leaseholders at White Feather trying to drive alluvial miners off their claims, until Freddie muttered a morose 'goodbye all' and wandered off.

'What's the matter with Fred?' someone asked. 'Hope he's not sick. Been a lot of bloody typhoid around.'

'No,' said Bluey, 'he's worried about his womenfolk back home. Those bodies were found not far from where they live.'

'That must have happened a while ago, though. Don't you think?'

'But the bastard's probably still hanging around.'

'What's the story?' asked Clint. 'Where's this?'

'Outskirts of Melbourne, I believe. They've found a couple of decomposing bodies. The latest was in a suitcase in the Yarra. These blokes had their boat run aground an' were tryin' to push it off when one fella stubbed his toe on it. Prob'ly thought they'd found buried treasure or summat. Must've got a shock to find a dead woman inside. All chopped up, apparently.'

'Maybe change the subject gents,' Mary said. 'Let's talk about something you can eat.'

'Oh, yes,' Danny said, looking at Joey's wide-eyed face. 'How about roast pork?'

'With lots of cracklin' an' apple sauce,' put in Bluey, 'There've been times when I'd have given all the gold in Hannans for a feed of Mum's roast pork.'

'Couldn't beat my Ma's Thanksgiving turkey,' Charlie added

'My mum made a great jam roly-poly,' said Bobby.

'How about spotted dick?' Clint said with a chuckle.

'Seems a serious condition,' muttered Bluey.

'Talking of food, I'd better head home' said Bobby, 'Got our dinner cooking in the coals. It's probably done by now.'

'What is it? Underground mutton?'

'I wish. I guess the cockies are glad the bunnies haven't got over here yet, but they're easier to catch than those wild critters.

'There were a lot of roos and little animals here at first, but what we didn't eat, we scared off.'

Though the conversation had moved on, Nora was haunted by the words "decomposing bodies". Was that all that was left of Ned? When the men had left and Joey was out of earshot, she asked Mary what the story was.

'It's pretty gruesome. They found one body a while ago. She'd been cut up and buried under the floor of an old shanty. Now there's this one in the suitcase and they think the same bloke did it.'

Chapter 34

Nora pushed away her tear-soaked pillow. Two and a half weeks after Corporal Williams told Ned she was here, he still hadn't come and it was hard to quiet the warring waves of sorrow and anger.

Giving up hope of getting any more sleep, she dressed, got herself a bite to eat and walked down to Paisley's store to buy some hand soap. There was almost nothing left of the cake she'd brought from home. Hearing her name as she stepped out of the shop, she turned to see a neatly dressed young man raising his hat. His face looked familiar, but she had no idea who he was.

'Vernon, from the Warden's office,' he went on, seeing her confusion. 'We met at Mrs Bunning's'.

'Oh, of course,' Nora replied with a smile.

'Am I right in assuming that you will be leaving us soon, Mrs Patterson?'

'Why do you ask that?' was her puzzled reply.

'Oh, I thought, as Mr Patterson's sold his mine, you might be heading back to more civilised regions.'

'No, I don't think we'll be leaving any time soon,' she replied, trying not to blurt out that she knew nothing about the sale. 'And how are you settling in?' she asked, to cover her confusion.

'We've finally got the office sorted. It's a bit hard working in a glorified tent, but everything's pretty shipshape now.'

'Well, goodbye,' she said, hurrying away, her mind in turmoil. The man must be mistaken. Ned had sold the mine? If he had, surely he'd have come to tell her, not leave her here alone thinking he was dead. *Oh, Ned, what the blazes are you up to?*

She'd not really intended going to Mary's, feeling that she was maybe a nuisance always being there, but needed to share this unexpected news. So, after stopping at the bakers to buy half a dozen fruit buns and narrowly avoiding meeting the reverend Simpson, she headed over to her friend's place to find Danny had just dropped in.

'Hello, Nora,' Mary said. 'I'm about to make a cuppa.'

'Oh, that'd be lovely. Hello Danny. I brought some buns,' she said. 'About time I stopped eating you out of house and home.'

'Ooh, thanks. They smell lovely. So, how are things up at the hospital, Nora?'

'Quieter. Sadly, it's not because the patients are getting better. We lost four over a couple of days. They were just too sick when they arrived to be able to do much for them.'

'Is that why you were looking so worried when you arrived?'

'No, it's not that. I heard some news about Ned that I just can't understand. Mr Vernon from the Warden's office told me Ned has sold his mine. Seemed to expect me to be leaving town. I think he must be wrong.'

'Maybe selling the mine's what's been holding him up,' Mary said.

'I don't know,' said Danny, 'He must have done the deal some time ago. The transfer papers need to go to Perth, and could take a week or so to come back to the Warden's office.'

'Well, he should turn up soon,' Mary said. 'Maybe he wants to surprise you with all the money he's made.'

'How you goin' with that little gun of yours,' Danny asked, turning to Nora. 'Been practisin'?'

'I haven't had time.'

'I been thinkin' about you girls up at the hospital. There'd be nothing to stop some bastard wanderin' in.'

'We do have Mr Dunne living up there.'

'He must have to sleep sometimes. I'd feel happier if you had the gun an' knew how to use it.'

'It must be scary up there when you're working nights,' Mary said.

'Mostly I'm too busy to think about it.'

'Is the gun still here?'

'Yes.'

'Well, maybe you could have a go with it now.'

Nora only reluctantly agreed, but began to feel some enthusiasm when, on her first try, she hit the tin can target, sending it flying off the stump. By the time Mary had the tea ready, she'd begun to feel a little bit more confident.

'Where's Joey?' Danny asked, as Mary poured the tea. 'He'll be sorry to miss out on a bun.'

'We'll keep one for him,' Mary said. 'But I'm worried about him. He's been quite odd, the last few days. You know how talkative he usually is. Now he just grunts, eats what I put in front of him and goes off to bed.'

'He's not off his food, then?' Danny said.

'No sign of fever?' Nora put in.

'No, he doesn't seem to be sick or anything. If he was, at least I'd know what to do. He's just not like my little boy anymore. Has he been up your place talking about Sherlock Holmes and all that stuff?'

'No, we haven't seen him since Friday, but young Timmy came looking for him yesterday.'

'Timmy came here too. I was surprised because they're usually together, playing detective or something. I hope that's where Joey's gone today.'

'Well, young fellas can get a bit funny at his age. You know, growing up and all.'

'Yes, I know, Danny. Specially, with not having his dad to talk to.'

Nora frowned, remembering the gossip she'd heard from other nurses about what sometimes happened to young boys. Who knew what any of the men out here were really like? She even had a passing thought that maybe Mary should worry about Joey getting so close to Danny and Ben, before dismissing it immediately.

'I guess he'll turn up soon,' Mary said, 'nothin' wrong with his appetite.'

Nora remembered that conversation next day when she ran into Joey in the main road and he pretended not to see her, slipping away between two shanties. But she was distracted from his odd behaviour by the sudden appearance of the Reverend Simpson, who seemed to leap out of a shop doorway in front of her. Turning with a surprised expression, he prevented her passing on by apologizing profusely, and unctuously asking after her health.

'Very well, sir,' she replied, turning to cross the road so hurriedly that she almost stepped in front of a passing dray. Of course, that gave him the excuse to grab her arm, rather too tightly, she felt, shaking him off.

'My dear Mrs Patterson, I hope you are unharmed.'

'I am perfectly unscathed as you can see, Mr Simpson,' she replied hurriedly, stepped onto the dusty street, after a quick look to be sure it was safe.

Annoying man, she thought, wondering what it was about him that made her so nervous. That was when she began to wonder if it was since he turned up that Joey's strangeness had begun.

'Don't be ridiculous,' she muttered to herself. 'Disliking him is no excuse for accusing him of something like that.'

Chapter 35

Danny was on his way back from picking up some supplies at Courthope's store that Thursday when he saw Joey walking dejectedly up the road in front of him. Remembering Mary's worries, he caught up, saying, 'Hello, there, young Joey.'

'Oh, hello, Mr O'Hara.'

'You too busy these days to come see y' old mates?'

'No, Mr O'Hara, I've just been busy, you know, sellin' the papers and all.'

'Well, how about comin' up for a cuppa? I know your mum's out, an' Ben will be putting the billy on about now, I imagine.'

'Oh, sure. That'd be nice.'

But the boy was strangely quiet as they walked up to the mine.

'I think there's more of the Sherlock Holmes story in the paper,' Danny said.

'I've gone off them a bit. Mr Holmes only finds clues in London. Out here, the dust would cover the bad blokes' tracks in a coupla days.'

'That's why the police have black trackers helpin' them. They see things we new chums miss, because their people have lived here for hundreds of years.'

'I know, but it's not just clues y' need. People tell him stuff, too. What if they're too scared to tell?'

'Mmm, yes. I guess folk won't talk if they fear somethin' bad might happen if they do.'

Hearing a gasping sob, Danny was convinced someone was bullying the boy. When Seamus came bounding out to greet them, Joey threw his arms around dog, burying his face in the shaggy fur.

'Hello Joey,' Ben called.' Then, noticing Danny's hushing gesture, asked, 'Got the sugar Danny?'

'Yes, and look! A tin of fig jam. It just arrived an' sold out in ten minutes. You like jam, Joey?' he asked, cutting thick slices of damper bread. 'I hope so, because I got one for your mum.'

When they were all sitting around the fire with their tea, damper and jam, Danny thought of a way to maybe get Joey to talk about what was troubling him.

'Y' know, Joey,' he said, 'what you were sayin' about people bein' scared to talk, puts me in mind of somethin' that happened when I was about your age. Everyone in our village was hard up. Sometimes there wasn't enough money even to buy tucker.

'Anyway, one day I heard two lads talkin' about breaking into the big house to steal some stuff. When they caught me listenin', the older one grabbed me around the neck. He was strangling me, until the other boy dragged him off. "You won't tell anyone, will y' Danny," he said. But just to make sure, the other one said, "If y' blab, you an' your folks might all get fried when we burn y' house down." I was terrible scared and didn't tell anyone. So they went an' did it. And got caught.'

'What happened to them?'

'Both got hung. They killed someone when they were trying to get away. Maybe if I'd talked no one would have got killed.'

'Was that during that terrible famine in Ireland?' Ben asked.

'No, I was out here by then. We still had potatoes to eat, if nothin' much else. 'Twas when the spuds went rotten in the forties that hundreds of people died,' Danny replied, with one eye on Joey who'd been very quiet since hearing the story. He was still holding his half-eaten slice of damper and gazing into the fire.

Looking up, he cleared his throat and asked, 'Did y' hear blokes are pinchin' gold from the big mines?'

'Yes, the police have been trying to catch them,' said Ben.

'Well, I know somethin' about it, but... I'm scared Mum'll get hurt if I talk,' he sobbed.'

'Who said that?'

'The blokes what put them gold rocks in my bag. They grabbed me afterwards to take them back.'

'Shit! When was this?'

'Friday night when I was sellin' papers up at the big mine. With all the fellas crowdin' around buyin' papers, I didn't notice anything. Then someone shouted an' they all went back to the mine. The sun was going down, so thought I'd better get a wriggle on an' take the money back to the paper-shop. But the moneybag was awful heavy.

'When I heard someone behind me, I thought it was just one of the blokes headin' home, until he grabbed me an' wrapped his arm around my neck so I couldn't breathe. Then another bloke opened my bag and pulled out a piece of rock that glittered in the sunset light.'

'Did you see what the bastards looked like?'

'No. It was gettin' dark an' they kept behind me. All I could do was shut up and let them take their old rocks. Then one bloke said, "That's the boy. Y' never seen us, did you? Keep y' little trap shut and nothing's likely to happen to you. Or your little Ma. Wouldn't want her gettin' hurt, would ya?"

I thought if I just kept quiet it might be all right, but it happened again on Saturday night, an' they said that about hurtin' Mum again. Now I'm scared to go back.'

'Of course you are. When were you supposed to go up there next?'

'Friday night. An' I know it'll happen again.'

'The police need to know, Joey. This is worse than just stealing a bit of gold.'

'I can't tell. They'll find out I snitched an' come after me an' Mum.'

'Joey, the police don't let the crooks know who they heard stuff from. I'm sure they'll keep you out of it. I know Constable Purkiss pretty well. What about I go talk to him? But first you need to tell your mum what's goin' on.'

While Danny went to Mary's with Joey, Ben strode down town, hoping he was doing the right thing. He waited for Purkiss to leave the police station on his evening rounds, then hurried to catch him up.

'Oh, hello Drummond. Got something on your mind?'

'Yes,' Ben replied.

'What about?'

'Gold stealing. It's only small time, as far as I can tell, but there's more to it than just theft.'

'Go on.'

'You know young Joey O'Callaghan?'

'Yes. Him and his mate Timmy O'Rourke have come to my attention,' he laughed.

'Well, Joey's started selling papers, and he went up to the big mine to catch the men coming off shift late Friday afternoon.

While all the miners crowded around buying papers, someone slipped a couple of specimens into his moneybag, waylaid him on his way home to get the stuff and, to silence him, made serious threats against him and his mother.'

'Would he recognize the blokes again?'

'No, he never saw their faces. Same thing happened the next night. Poor little bugger's been scared stiff, but he broke down and told us. The trouble is he thinks if the bastards find out he told, something's going to happen to his mum. Do you think it'd be possible to keep the boy's involvement out of it?'

'I don't see why not. I'm sure Corporal Williams will understand, and we'll work something out. So, leave it with me.'

Ben was hurrying back to Mary's, when Bluey's voice broke into his thoughts as he passed the saloon, 'Hello, Ben, comin' for a drink?'

'Er, not tonight, mate.' he replied.

'You all right?'

'Yes. Just got something on my mind.'

'Not got time for a quick one?'

Ben shook his head and was about to walk on when his friend asked, 'Has Fred asked you about the cricket on Saturday?'

'No?'

'He wondered if you might play. We're short one bloke an' need somebody who can hit the ball in the right direction. Some of them are pretty hopeless.'

'I think that counts me out,' said Ben.

'Well, you did a fair job with that piece of mulga the other day. Let Fred know if you change your mind.'

'I'll think about it mate. Might see you there, anyway. G'night,' Ben said, before hurrying up to Mary's.

'You can see why the poor little fella didn't tell you, Mary,' he heard Danny saying as he lifted his hand to knock. ''Twas only me wafflin' on about something that happened years ago that made him open up. Oh, here's Ben now.'

Inside, Mary sat with her arm around the sobbing boy, tears drying on her own face.

'Danny says you were going to talk to that policeman you know, Ben,' she said.

'Yes, he'll have to tell Williams, but understands why we want to keep Joey out of it. He says they've talked the owners into fencing off the mine entrance so the blokes can be checked before they wander off. So, it shouldn't happen again, Joey.'

Chapter 36

Three weeks after Corporal Williams spoke to Ned at his mine, Nora knew he wasn't coming. Did he sell the mine and go home because he never got my letters? No, the policeman told him I'm here. Even if he didn't believe it was me, surely he'd have come to make sure.

With so many dying of typhoid, could he have caught it and died after he sold the mine? The grim image of his corpse lying somewhere out in the bush was still haunting her when she knocked off in the morning.

After a couple of hours of trying to sleep, she gave up, got dressed and was strolling over to Mary's when the policeman accosted her.

'Excuse me, Mrs Patterson,' he said, touching his cap.

'Hello, Constable Purkiss, do you have any news of my husband?'

Glancing around and lowering his voice, he went on, 'No, I'm sorry. It's something else. Are you going to visit Mrs O'Callaghan?'

'Yes, I'm on my way there just now.'

'Could you give her a message please?'

'Of course.'

'Ask her to send young Joey up to Ben Drummond's place on some pretext in about an hour. I need to talk to the boy, but don't want to visit his home.'

'Oh, is Joey in trouble?'

'No. His mother will know what it's about.'

'All right. I'll tell her.'

'Thank you,' he said, raising his voice as some men approached, 'We'll be in touch if we hear any more about that matter, Mrs Patterson.'

How odd, Nora was thinking as she hurried on, eager to find out what it was all about. The constable's manner was almost furtive. But when she passed on the message, Mary explained about the gold thieves.

'That's what's been wrong with Joey', she said.

'Oh, poor Joey,' Nora said, 'what a horrible thing to happen to him. Is he all right?'

'Still very quiet. He's out in the bough shed reading that book you gave him. I let him sleep in this morning because it was late before he settled down last night. Poor little devil was carryin' all that worry for days. I should've tried harder to find out what was the matter.'

'You couldn't have known it was something like that.'

'No. I just thought he was sickening for something, or he'd had a fight with Timmy.

'I'm glad Danny got him to get it off his chest,' she continued, 'but I'm worried, Nora. Ben thinks he might have to go up there again tonight, so the thieves won't notice anything different. The mine owners have fenced the mine entrance off so the blokes can be searched before they get out. If the police catch the thieves in there, they won't know Joey told them, but he's pretty scared.'

'It'll be very brave of him to do that.'

'Anyway, let's have a cuppa. I'll send Joey up the hill after he's had his and a bit of fruit damper.'

Joey still had his nose in the book when he wandered inside to join them.

'Oh, hello, Mrs Patterson,' he said but there was no sign of his usual friendly grin.

'Hello Joey. Are you enjoying that book?'

'It's all right. Not as good as Sherlock Holmes, though,' he replied, stuffing a slice of damper and jam in his mouth.

'Have another piece, Joey,' his mother said, 'then can you take that shirt I mended for Mr Drummond up to him?'

'Righto Mum,' he said, quickly demolishing another slice, before running off with the folded shirt.

'I didn't want to tell him about the policeman,' Mary said. 'Soon enough for him to worry when he knows what they want. Anyway, what's been happening up at the hospital? I heard another patient died of typhoid.'

'Yes. I hope we don't get any more. Dr Martin thinks it'll ease off when the weather gets cooler. But then we'll start getting people dying of pneumonia. Oh, and Mrs Alderdice was really pleased to get those sheets you made.'

'It's easy work, but my hand was pretty sore from turning the sewing machine handle. I'm getting some nicer jobs now more ladies are here. Alice Blake asked me to make her a brown dress. It's the only colour that doesn't show the dirt. Are you all right, Nora? You're looking a bit pale.'

'We've been very busy and I'm having trouble sleeping during the day for worrying about Ned. I keep seeing him lying out there dead.'

'You don't believe he's just run off, do you?'

'No. I've known him all my life. We were good friends long before we got married. He'd not just leave me here.'

'How long is it now?'

'More than a month since I arrived, and three weeks since he was told I'm here. I don't know what to think. If I knew he was dead, I could maybe grieve properly, but I'm left in this kind of limbo.'

'Have you got tomorrow afternoon off?' Mary asked.

'Yes, I'm still on night shift.'

'Would you like to come with us to watch the fellas play cricket? It might take your mind off your worries. Joey and me usually go along to watch. I'm hoping it'll cheer him up after all he's been through.'

'That would be nice,' said Nora. 'Ned used to play a bit when we were first married.' she said sadly, thinking of that happy time.

'Come here for a bite to eat first. You'll need a shady hat, so you can borrow mine again.'

'Thanks Mary. I guess I'd better head back and try to get my forty winks before tonight.'

Meeting the reverend Simpson on the way home, she went out of her way to be polite. Knowing what had been worrying Joey, Nora blushed to remember what she'd been thinking about the man. Discarding the possibility that Ben might be a danger to Joey, she'd been happy to let her unfounded suspicions rest on someone else.

***

Danny dropped in at Mary's that afternoon to find Joey nervously waiting to go to the paper shop and collect his newspapers.

'I wish I could go with you, love,' Mary said, 'but I'd stand out like a sore toe up there among all the blokes.'

'Ben an' me are goin' to keep an eye on things. I'll suddenly have urgent business with the new blacksmith up that way, an' Ben will walk up the other side of the road and buy a paper off you just before you head for the mine. We won't be far away, mate. If anything goes wrong, run back down there.'

'Thanks, Mr O'Hara,' Joey replied, only slightly reassured.

Danny walked down to the paper shop with him, but after that Joey was on his own and was glad to see Drummond wandering up the other side of the road. But he was so nervous that he jumped when Ben called out 'I'll have a paper, young fella,' and strode across the road.

'You all right, Joey,' he continued in an undertone as he pretended not to have the right change.

'I think so, Mr Drummond.'

'I'm sure they'll catch those blokes, and they won't bother you again.'

'I hope so, Mr Drummond.'

'Well good luck.'

As Joey trudged up the hill, he was startled to see some policemen talking to the mine manager inside a small area enclosed by a hastily-erected fence at the mine entrance. He'd imagined the police would be in disguise. If the thieves saw the policemen there, they might know he'd blabbed. He was poised to run away when he was intercepted by a scruffy-looking miner.

'Give us a paper, lad,' he called, holding out the right money. It wasn't until he asked quietly if Joey was all right, that he recognised Constable Purkiss in dungarees, broken-down boots and a battered old hat.

'Yes,' he whispered.

'Just go on up, like you usually do. The blokes can't buy papers until they've been searched. Come right up, but when the corporal yells at you, just do what he says.'

'Righto,' Joey said, his fear beginning to give way to excitement as a bell rang and men poured out of the mine, some cursing when prevented from leaving. As Joey reached the fence, Corporal Williams' angry-sounding voice rose over the din, 'What's that boy doing here?'

'Selling papers,' the manager replied and the corporal turned to glare at Joey, shouting, 'You, boy! Clear away from there.'

He backed off a bit, but the policeman again raised his voice, 'Go on, off you go. Further down the hill.'

Joey obeyed but would have liked to see what was going on. He soon heard, though, when most of the miners were let out and crowded around buying papers. Two men had been caught with rich specimens of ore tucked inside their shirts.

'Idiots never even tried t' hide the stuff.' someone said.

'Well, no one expected the troopers t' pen us in like chooks,' another man laughed.

'I'm glad they caught them two. Nasty pair of stand-over merchants.'

Hearing some suggestions of better methods of smuggling out stolen gold, Joey thought maybe he should tell the police, but decided he'd had enough cloak and dagger stuff for one day.

✣

'Hello Joey,' Nora said next morning, relieved to be greeted with his usual cheeky grin. 'I brought some of those buns.'

'Ooh, they're real nice,' he said, opening the gate for her, before calling out to his mother, 'Mrs Patterson's here, Mum. An' she's got buns.'

'G'day Nora. Come on in.'

'Hello Mary, here are the buns,' she laughed.

'I wish we had some fresh butter to put on them. This tinned stuff is awful.'

'Mum,' Joey butted in, 'you haven't seen Timmy, have you?'

'Don't interrupt, Joey. No, I haven't. Not since he came looking for you the other day. Did you go to his place?'

'Yeah, but even Splinter didn't come out to say hello when I whistled. I called out too. Timmy woulda come out to let me know if he couldn't get away.'

'Did you ask his folks where he was?'

'Na,' Joey replied, screwing up his nose, 'I don't like goin' there. Mr Kenny's not a nice bloke.'

'Well, I guess he must be busy. You'll probably see him at the cricket this afternoon. Now go and wash your hands.

'He'd been avoiding Timmy, scared he might accidently say something about those crooks, and he really misses him. The billy should be boiling, so I'll go make the tea. I made us sandwiches for lunch. We need to eat up. The blokes are likely to keep playing till nearly sunset, so dinner might be late tonight.

'Can I go now, Mum?' Joey asked after eating a sandwich and two buns.

'Righto. We'll see you down there,' Mary replied.

After a second cup of tea, the two women pinned on their shady hats and strolled down the road to the sports ground. Inside the encircling racetrack, a level area of bare red earth had been cleared of stumps and other obstructions. Nellie was sitting under one of the thatched shelters and they joined her just as the game began.

Chapter 37

Ben already regretted agreeing to play. It must have been something to do with Mary saying Nora would be there. With the other team batting first, he was relegated to the farthest fielding position with nothing to do but chase a few balls into the scrub. As he'd expected, when his team went in to bat and his turn came, he was immediately caught for a duck. But even the good players hadn't done very well, so they were already trailing by a couple of runs when the other team started their second innings.

Back in the outfield, bored stiff, he was gazing across the ground to where a random beam of sunlight lit up Nora's lovely face when, hearing excited shouts from his teammates, he turned as the ball flew straight at him. That he managed to clutch it and throw it at the wicket was a complete fluke, but his team cheered as the opposition tailender walked off.

Still well behind in the scoring, their team's experienced batsmen made a valiant effort to catch up, but they were all out by the time the sun started its decline towards the west, leaving the tailenders to try to recoup the team's losses. Steve put up a good show, making three, but Clint and Bluey, after dodging Jim Blake's furious bowling had only made one run each when Longmore was caught out and it was Ben's turn.

To his surprise, the ball shot up and out, far beyond the cleared area. Clint and he scrambled to add six runs to the score amid cheers from their team and curses from those who had to try to find the ball among the prickly scrub.

But it was the smiling face of Nora Patterson that he saw. Dragging his eyes away, he returned a few back slaps before the other team's bowler came raging back, ready to annihilate him. Unprepared, he just managed to deflect the ball away from the eager fieldsmen. Shaking off the distraction, he managed to keep his teammates happy by hitting a four before being caught out.

He was tempted to avoid going near the women, but couldn't brush off Joey's excited welcome.

'Wow! You said you didn't know how to play. How come you hit a six?'

'Just luck, Joey.'

'Congratulations, Ben,' said Mary. 'I think you've won the game for them.'

'Yes,' put in Nora. 'The chaps on the other side don't look very happy.'

Giving in to temptation, he sat on the ground next to her, asking, 'Are you enjoying the game?'

'Oh, yes. I used to watch Ned play when we were young.'

'He hasn't turned up?'

'No,' she replied, tears in her eyes.

He was wishing he could take her in his arms and comfort her, when a lucky catch by the bowler brought a burst of cheering.

'Well, there's only Clint and Bill Taylor left,' Bluey said, 'We don't need any more runs, but Bill might do all right.'

But Taylor had other ideas. After talking to the team captain, he came over to Joey, saying, 'I say, young fella. I've done me elbow. Could you take my place?'

'Oh yes, please, Mr Taylor. Are you sure?'

'Yep. Here's the bat. Off you go.'

'That was kind of you Bill,' said Mary, as Joey ran out onto the field, 'He's been dying to have a go.'

Joey's first enthusiastic swing sent the ball flying over his head and into the crowd, but he and Clint didn't waste time knocking up a single. Joey couldn't wipe the grin off his face as everyone except the opposing team cheered. When Sutcliffe got bowled out a few minutes later, Joey ran back, crowing that he'd been 'not out' at the end.

Ben had noticed Constable Purkiss watching the game from the other side the field so, after congratulating Joey, he made his excuses to the ladies and wandered across.

'G'day, Ben. Young Joey did very well,' the policeman said. 'Did well last night too. It took lot of guts to go up there and keep cool like he did.'

'Are you sure you got the bastards that were threatening him?'

'Yes, the younger bloke confessed. Told us how they'd done it, before we'd even asked what they'd done with the specimens before.'

'Any luck finding that murderer you're chasing?'

'No. But we've got a bit more information on him. Seems he's a Queenslander who went over to England and joined the army over there. He was posted to India and got himself in a fight and killed a senior officer. The military police believe he hopped on a ship to Melbourne. They think he knew that English major and had a grudge against him. Weird bloke, though. Cuts an ear off his victims to keep as a souvenir.'

'I hope they're right that it was a personal grudge, and he doesn't just go round doing people in,' Ben said.

At the end of the game, all the men, and Nellie, headed for the bar. It was just a board laid across a couple of barrels, but they were doing great business.

Danny was handing Nora and Mary glasses of lemonade when Ben rejoined them. Joey had already drunk half of his.

'Bluey's bringin' the beers,' Danny said, 'I got you one, Ben.'

The conversation was mainly about the game, with Joey excitedly taking part, but Nora was very aware of Ben's silent presence.

Then she thought of something she was going to tell him, 'A while back, you asked if Ned ever lived in Queensland. He didn't, but I think an auntie of his married a wealthy squatter and went to live up there. I wonder if it was a cousin of Ned's you remember.'

'That might explain the likeness. But then again, it was a long time ago, I could be wrong about it.'

'Can you ladies stay for the dance?' asked Bluey, 'we often have a bit of a hop after the game. Jimmy McAdam and his mates play some music. It's just a bit of fun, but we need as many ladies as we can get so the blokes don't have to dance with each other.'

'Oh, I don't know whether I can,' Nora said. 'I need to get back to the hospital.'

'You don't have to stay long. We'll have to finish up before it gets dark. We've got some lanterns but they don't shed much light. Can't have people prancing around in the dark. The boozing will go on all night, and maybe some singing. But not the sort of songs ladies would like. What about you Ben?'

Despite the overwhelming desire to put his arms around Nora, Ben shook his head. 'I think I'll just head home mate. Not really into dancing.'

'You'd better stay so you can carry Danny home,' Bluey chuckled. 'He's already had a few and isn't likely to stop dancing while there's music.'

'I'll stay for a while, then.'

'What about you ladies?

'It might be fun,' Mary said. 'Paddy and I used to love dancing. Please stay for a little while, Nora. I'm sure one of the fellas will walk us home afterwards.'

I probably shouldn't. Oh, why wasn't Ned here? How could she dance with other men when she didn't know what happened to him?

⤙

Ben stood back as Charlie Osmond asked Nora to dance, and Clint swung Mary into the laughing, stomping group, that included some men dancing in pairs. He couldn't take exception to Charlie's gentlemanly way of holding Nora, but walked away so he didn't have to watch. Ordering a beer at the bar, he tried to join in the conversation of the hardened drinkers but, when the dance ended amid cheers and clapping, he was drawn back to Nora's side.

'Hey, Ben,' Danny said, 'If you're not dancing with Nora, I'll ask her myself.'

Watching the laughing crowd stomping, swinging and changing partners, Ben changed his mind. Maybe he could resist kissing Nora in one of those dances. He had just worked up the courage to ask her when a high-pitched giggle drew their attention to Bluey and Nellie whirling around inside the circle of dancers, her flying skirts exposing frilled bloomers. When she let go of Bluey's hand and came staggering towards Ben, he reached out to stop her falling, not prepared for her to clutch his other hand and drag him into the whirling throng.

As she pulled him into an untidy embrace, Bluey stepped up to offer Nora his hand, saying, 'Looks like Ben's been kidnapped. Guess you'll have to dance with me.'

'Thank you, Mr Longmore,' she said, 'but I think I'll sit this out. I need to get back to the hospital and get some dinner. I'm on night shift.'

'I'll see if Mary wants to leave too, now the party's getting a bit rough. Ah, here you are, Ben. I thought Nellie had you hogtied.'

Nora turned to find a very red-faced Ben scrambling out of the crowd, his shirt partly hanging out. 'I couldn't escape till Bill Thompson cut in,' he said as Mary and Clint joined them.

'Mary,' Bluey said, 'Mrs Patterson needs to get back to the hospital and I thought you might be ready to go too.'

'Yes,' she replied, 'I'd better get Joey home. Danny's been trying to teach him the Irish jig. Here they come. Both puffed out, by the looks of things.'

'This young spalpean's got the makings of a dancer Mary. You can't keep the good old Irish blood down,' Danny chuckled.

'He'll be needin' his dinner now, so we'll be off home.'

'Maybe you should call it a day too, Danny,' said Ben, 'I'm not figuring on hanging around.'

'Scared Nellie might get her claws into you again, eh?' laughed Bluey.

'I don't know, she seems happy with Bill. I think they are made for each other,' Mary said and Nora turned to see Thompson planting passionate kisses on the young barmaid's neck.

'I'll see you later, then, Ben,' Danny called. 'You headin' off, Bluey?'

'Well if you can see the ladies home, Ben, I'll stay.'

'I'll come too,' Clint said.

Well, g'night, ladies,' called Danny, as more lively music struck up and he was dragged away by one of his Scottish mates.

'C'mon Danny. We got a jiggin' contest on. You Paddies against us Scots.'

It was a lovely evening, a full moon lending its magic to the fading sunset's glow. Despite all her worry about Ned, Nora had enjoyed herself. By the time she and Ben reached the track to the hospital, the others were quite a way ahead, Mary leaning on Clint's arm, Joey swinging the lantern.

'Goodnight,' Sutcliffe called. 'You alright to see Mrs Patterson home, Ben?'

Though he was left with no choice but to agree, Nora could tell he was reluctant.

Her own 'Goodnight,' was echoed by the others, as Ben took her arm to guide her along the rough track.

'Thank you for walking me home, Ben,' she said, as they got to the hospital gate.

'It looks like you'll need the light for a bit longer. Are you going to the ward, or your tent?'

'I'd better let Matron know I'm here. She might think I've run out on her. But I can find my way from the corner there. She might get the wrong idea if she sees you.'

'Goodnight, then,' he said, turning to towards her. Tentatively, he lifted his hand as if to touch her face, and her breath caught in her throat.

Oh, my God, she was thinking, as he turned and walked away, *I'm the one getting the wrong idea.* She had been sure he was going to kiss her. And she could no longer deny that she wanted him to. Much as she'd loved Ned, what this man did to her heart was something entirely different. And that realisation, on top of the disastrous affair with James Carruthers, made her question her own moral worth. *Maybe I'm just a slut,* she thought sadly. *Like a bitch on heat, or a cat yowling in the moonlight for a mate.*

Smarting from Matron's stern comments about her late return, Nora quickly changed and made herself some toast and a couple cups of tea, before taking over from Molly. The first hours went quickly, with a new patient, Mr Abbott, needing dressings changed and dosing with morphine. It wasn't until he sank into a drugged sleep that the other patients settled down.

She had never been really nervous working the night shift before. She'd got used to the shifting shadows in the corners and the eerie whines and squeaks of the canvas building. But about midnight, repeated stealthy movements outside sent a tingling chill down her spine. Telling herself it was just Dr Martin coming late to check up on the new patient, she went to open the door.

No one was there, but a noise further off in the quiet night drew her eyes to the dense shadow of some trees, where something moved and, for a moment, a figure was standing there, watching her.

Heart thudding, she pulled the door shut, dropping the locking bar into place and stood there shaking, as the thud of heavy footsteps passed by before fading away into the distance. But something about that steady pacing struck her as odd. It didn't really sound like footsteps. Then she remembered. It was the sound of a kangaroo hopping. Was it just a roo she'd seen out there?

'What's the matter, nurse?'

'Oh, I thought I heard something outside, but it was just a roo,' she said, going to the man's bedside. 'Are you all right, Mr Smith? I thought you were asleep.'

'I heard a noise and saw you shutting the door. You looked scared.'

'No. All is well,' she said. 'Are you comfortable?'

'Yes nurse.'

'Well, try to get back to sleep.'

After checking the other patients, she was sorry Smith had taken her advice and was peacefully snoring. She would have welcomed the distraction of some conversation as the long, quiet hours passed, with every flap of the canvas imitating prowling footsteps. So, it was a relief for her, if not for him, when Abbott woke from his drug-induced sleep, crying out in pain. By the time she had dosed him with morphine and checked his wound, Molly arrived to take over.

'Everything seems pretty quiet, 'she said. 'No excitement during the night?'

'Not really,' Nora replied, stifling a yawn. 'They all had a good night except Mr Abbott. He's had his morphine an hour ago.'

'You look dreadful,' Molly told her. 'Better go and get some sleep.'

'Yes, I didn't get much yesterday.

Chapter 38

'It was a good night last night,' Danny said, as Ben slung the waterbag from Walter's saddle. 'You should have stayed, but I guess Nora had to get back. She was working, wasn't she?'

'Yes. Night shift.'

'She's a fine young woman. Pretty too. If I was thirty years younger, I'd give you a run for your money. None of my business, but you seem to like each other, maybe a bit more than a little. If you care for Nora, don't let her slip through your fingers.'

'She's married, Danny.'

'Well, we both know he's either dead or the bastard's abandoned her and doesn't deserve her. Y' know, I loved a woman once. In California, it was. Never thought she'd take a second look at someone like me. Her family were wealthy, and I was a hand-to-mouth dirt miner, so I left without even saying goodbye. But I struck it rich. Came back dressed up fine, my pockets full of gold, but I was too late. I threw that gold into her grave and went on the biggest bender of my life. Woke up broke. But she was still dead.'

'It's no good, Danny. Nora would run a mile if she knew what I am. About my past. You see, I went off my head after my wife died. Something else bad happened too. They locked me uand threw away the key. I spent years in the madhouse. I'd still be there if a new governor hadn't bothered to talk to me.'

'Oh, mate, I'm sorry. But look, I've known you for quite a while now and I'd say you are probably one of the sanest fellas on this goldfield. Whatever it was. It's behind you.'

After watching his friend ride away, Danny meandered down to the town, sadly thinking of that girl in California. He was still immersed in old memories when Jimmy McAdam called out, 'Danny, come an' have a dram wi' us. I've just become a grandpa. Need to wet the bairn's head.'

It was late morning when Nora woke up. Slipping on her dressing gown, she wandered over to the kitchen to find Molly about to make tea.

'I guess you'll be wanting a cup,' she said.

'Yes please, Molly.

'Did you hear a girl got raped last night?' Molly whispered, 'That Nellie from the pub.'

'Is she all right?'

'I don't know. Just heard Dr Martin telling Matron.'

'Oh, poor Nellie. Do they know who did it?' she asked, remembering her dancing with Bill Thompson.

'I don't think so. It could have been any of hundreds of blokes.'

Nora wondered if Mary had heard. So, after a bit of breakfast, she wandered down the road to her friend's place. When Mary opened the door, Nora caught a whiff of the flowery perfume Nellie wore. Guessing she was there but didn't want to see anyone, she just said, 'I heard something had happened to Nellie, Mary. Do you know if she's all right?'

'Pretty shaken and a bit bruised, I'm afraid.'

'Is she here?'

'Yes, but she doesn't want anyone to see her,' Mary whispered.

'I'd better go then.'

'No, hang on. I'll go see if she'd like to talk to you.'

After a few minutes, she called out, 'Come on in, Nora.'

As she went in, Nellie emerged from the other room, her face pale except for a purplish bruise on her cheek.

'Are you all right,' Nora asked.

'Better than I'd have been if Charlie Osmond hadn't heard me screaming and pulled a gun on the bastard.'

'Was it anyone we know?' Nora asked, hesitantly.

'No. Oh, my God. Everyone will think it was poor Thommo. I didn't let him walk me home in case he got the wrong idea, so I went on my own and this drunk followed me. Big bloke, with a stinkin' breath and lots of whiskers. He kept pawing at me, so I yelled at him to leave me alone and tried to get away. That's when he knocked me on the ground and started fumbling with his pants.'

'He didn't succeed then?'

'No, while he was trying to get through all my petticoats, I clambered up and gave him a kick where it would do the most good. Must have hurt, because he yelled. But it made him angry and he hit me. When Charlie heard me screaming and fired a shot over his head, he ran off. Charlie didn't know what t' do with me. I didn't want t' go back t' the pub, so he brought me here and landed me on poor Mary.'

'It's all right, Nellie,' said Mary. 'I was awake an' Joey'd gone t' bed. You're sure you don't want to go to the police. Perhaps you should, it must be all over town by now.'

'Yes, I heard you'd been raped,' Nora said.

'No good going to the police. I'm a bad girl and I was drunk, so I deserved all I got. That's what they'll say. Maybe if I can turn up for work looking cheery the gossips mightn't believe it.'

'That's an awful bruise on your cheek.'

'I can probably cover it up with powder an' paint,' she was saying before a knock on the door sent her scurrying into Joey's room as Mary went to the door.

'It's Marge, Nellie. You want to see her, don't you?' she called, and Nellie emerged as her friend bustled in, carrying a tapestry bag.

'I thought you might have gone to ground here, Nellie. Oh, Hello Mrs Patterson.'

'Good morning, Miss Johnson,' said Nora.

'Gee, look at you Nellie,' the visitor said, 'Charlie told me what happened, so I brought my powder and paint in case you need some patching up.'

'Thanks Marge. I was wondering how I could get hold of mine.'

'Let's have a look at you. We need to cover up that bruise first. I've got just the thing. Lucky you didn't get a black eye. Here, hold still,' said Marge, spreading a thick layer of beige paste over the bruise. 'When that's dry, we can put on some ordinary powder. You want me to do it for you?'

'Yes, please. You're better at it than me. Marge used t' be on the stage,' she added.

'You'll have a cup of tea, won't you Marge?' Mary asked.

Picking up the teapot, she had just stepped outside to fill it from the billy, when the sound of a man's voice sent Nellie scurrying back into Joey's room, until she heard Mary say, 'Hello Charlie.'

'Is young Nellie still with you?' he asked.

'Yes Charlie, and she's all right.'

Relieved to hear who it was, Nellie went to the door, saying, 'Hello, Charlie. Thanks for rescuin' me last night. I don't know what I'd have done if you hadn't been there.'

'I'm just glad I happened along at the right time, Nellie.'

'You might as well have a cuppa while you're here, Charlie,' said Mary.

'Please stay, Charlie,' Nellie called. 'I'll be out as soon as Marge finishes patching me up.'

'Do you want another cup, Nora?' Mary asked. 'You know Charlie, don't you?'

'Hello, Mr Osmond,' she said

'Good morning, Mrs Patterson. How are things up at the hospital?'

'Sadly, we've lost a few patients. Typhoid, you know.'

'It's a killer. We lost a lot of fellas last year,' he was saying as Nellie sashayed out the door,

'How do I look?' she said.

'As good as new,' Mary laughed. 'You're a miracle-worker Marge.'

'You look fine, Nellie, but you should rest for an hour or two before you go back to work,' Nora said.

'Are people really saying I got raped, Mrs Patterson?'

'That's what Molly heard Dr Martin tell Matron. I'll tell them, and anyone else who asks, that a drunk was bothering you and Charlie came to your rescue.'

'I'm glad I could be of help,' he said, 'but with all sorts of nasty types comin' into town, you ladies need to be careful. Specially you nurses, Mrs Patterson. Anyone could walk into the hospital at night. Maybe you should start packin' that little gun of yours. You girls should get one too. The honky-tonk girls in the saloons back home all packed guns under their skirts.'

'I think the old lady who gave me the gun had been one of them,' Nora said.

'Do you still have it, Mrs Patterson?' Marge asked. 'Can we see?'

'Yes. Actually, it's here. I'll go and get it.'

'Ooh, isn't it pretty,' Nellie said. 'Yes, I want one of them.'

'You used a gun?' asked Charlie.

'I have,' Marge said, 'I was in a travelling theatre group an' the boss made us learn to fire his old Colt Forty-five. Never had t' shoot anyone. One look at the gun an' the drunks shot through.'

'This one's a lot easier t' handle than the Forty-five,' Charlie explained. 'Danny was teaching you to use it, wasn't he Mrs Patterson? You been practisin'?'

'Not really. I was supposed to have another lesson, but I haven't had much time.'

'Well, you should think about it. I know you ain't aimin' to be another Annie Oakley,' he laughed, 'but Danny seemed to think you're a natural. The important thing is to get a good grip on the butt before you draw and keep your finger off the trigger until you get it clear. You might need to tie the holster down onto your ... er, lower limb?'

'It's called a leg, Charlie,' Nellie laughed.

'Righto. I tie it to my thigh,' Nora said with a bit of a chuckle.

'Er, yes. Of course. If it's tied down there, it'll stay put when you pull the gun out. I imagine gettin' it out from under all them there petticoats might be harder than actually learnin' to shoot. But you gotta get used to handling it so you're not scared to use it if you need to. Got time to show me how you're goin'?'

'I guess so.'

'Go on, Mrs Patterson,' said Nellie.

'All righty,' said Charlie. 'Now, it ain't much use to you with no bullets in it, so let's see you load it.'

Nervously trying to remember Danny's instructions, Nora inserted the cartridges.

'Very good. You done that well. Now let's do some shootin'. Where'd you do it before?'

'Out the back,' said Mary. 'Here's a new tin can, Nora. You ruined the old one.'

Feeling a bit overawed by the American's obvious expertise, and very aware of the increased audience, Nora felt her hand shaking as she lifted the little revolver and took aim, so was pleasantly surprised that the bullet grazed the stump right next to the can.

'Good,' said Charlie. 'Take a deep breath, count to five and try again.'

This time she hit the can, so Charlie got her to move back five paces. From that position she managed to hit it again.

'Well, you've got the makins of a shooter. A steady hand and a good eye. All you need is practice. Start wearin' it all the time and when you're sure you can draw it safely, start keepin' it loaded.

'Anyway,' he went on, picking up his hat, 'I'd better be off before my pardner comes gunning for me for leavin' him with all the work.'

'Thank you for the gun lesson, Mr Osmond,' Nora said.

'We'll be heading off, too,' Nellie said, throwing her arms round Mary. 'Thanks for everything. Marge says I can have a nap in her room.'

'Ah, Joey's back,' Mary said, hearing him greet the two as they left, 'I let him go looking for Timmy straight after breakfast, so he wouldn't start asking what happened to Nellie. I guess he's hungry and looking for something to eat.

'Want some damper and jam, Joey?' she went on as he came through the door.

'I s'pose so. Have you seen Timmy, Mum? I can't find him anywhere.'

'He'll be busy in the shop,' Mary said.

'He's not there. Mr Kenny said if he saw Timmy, he'd give him another hiding.'

'If things are bad at home, he might want a feed when he turns up, so I'll cook extra dinner. Now you sit down and have some of that nice fig jam on your damper.'

'I'd better be off now,' Nora said, 'I think I'll take the gun and do some practice. I don't want to disappoint Danny and Charlie.'

'I hope young Timmy's all right,' Mary said as they walked to the gate, 'He usually comes here when old Kenny starts throwing his weight around.'

Chapter 39

Ben returned to town earlier than usual. The bush hadn't helped his mood like it usually did. The conversation with Danny had made him face up to the hopelessness of his love for Nora. He was riding dejectedly back through town when, hearing his name called, he was surprised to find himself passing the post office. Bob Humphries stood outside waving.

'You got mail, Ben,' he called. 'From England. Just came on the coach.'

'Thanks Bob, I'll come in,' Ben called, turning Walter's head towards the hitching rail, as Bob came out waving the letter. 'Here, mate. Might be what you've been waiting for.'

'Yes, it is,' Ben said, recognising his sister's handwriting. Not wanting to open it in the crowded street, he rode up to a clump of trees on the outskirts of town. Hitching Walter's reins over a branch, he sat on a log, carefully opened the letter and read:

Dear Ben,

I was glad to get your letter. We thought you must be dead. Jim and his mum are finding it hard to accept that Millie's gone. They blame you for taking her away.

I can't believe you were in that place. No one in our family ever went mad. Auntie Jessie was a bit daft, but she was old.

What are you doing wandering around out there in the wilds? Why don't you come home? Ma wants you to come home. She's getting old, Ben. Jim's dad died, and Auntie Mary. Jim's Uncle Tom, too. We've got four children now. Johnny's ten, Mary's eight, Billy's six and Benny's four. We called him after you when we thought you were dead.

Jim's a sergeant now and gets more money, so we got into a nicer place. I'd like Ma to live with us, but there's not the room.

Next came a few words hidden by a big, smudged blot, before the letter resumed.

Sorry about the blot. There was a lot of shouting next door and I went to make sure the stinking bully wasn't bashing his wife again. Then thought I'd better get Benny inside before the big boys come home. It's rougher around here than when we used to play in the street.

Please write again soon and let us know when you are coming home.

Your loving sister, Bessie.

He couldn't imagine living in London's crowded tenements after knowing the space out here. Besides, Nora was here. But, could he tell her his story? He cringed, thinking of the smile in her eyes changing to fear, distaste or horror knowing what he had been. Maybe he should go back to England. Get away from everything that reminded him of this place and the one woman who had begun to cure him of the misery that had haunted him.

Folding the letter, he pocketed it and headed home leading Walter but, as he emerged from the trees, he saw Danny wandering up the track. Worried that the old chap seemed a bit unsteady on his feet, he hurried to catch up and heard, as he got closer, the mournful notes of an old Irish song. One he'd only heard a few times when Danny was very drunk.

I guess he was about due to fall off the wagon, he was thinking. It was at least three months since his mate's last bender. At least he was a friendly drunk. Not like some of his countrymen who'd given a new meaning to the word 'donnybrook'.

'Hey, there, Danny,' he called as he got closer, 'You been celebrating something?'

Stumbling a bit as he turned, Danny needed a few minutes to focus his eyes on his friend.

'Ah, 'tis ye, Ben. Glad t' be meetin' up with you. Yes, we had a few drinks. Not sure what 'twas… Ah yes. Jimmy Mac, y' know the Scotty bloke who plays the fiddle. His daughter's had a baby and we was wettin' the baby's head. Oops,' he laughed as he staggered sideways and Ben caught his arm. 'Maybe I had a few too many. …Sorry about that. Shoulda known better. Y' know, 'twas thinkin' about that girl in California I told y' about. Feelin' a bit sorry for meself. Then when Jimmy says come have a drink, well I needed it. Just shoulda known when to stop, though.'

'That's all right, Danny. You might need a bit of a lie down, so let's get you home.'

'Might be needin' the shitehouse first. That's why I was headin' home. Never been so drunk that I shat meself, but I seen it happen to other fellas.'

While Danny visited their rough but adequate lavatory, Ben took care of Walter, then got the fire built up and made some strong black coffee.

Ben was getting the fire going next morning, when Danny came shambling out of the shack, shielding his eyes from the glare of the blaze.

'How're you feeling?' Ben asked.

'Bloody terrible. Got a head on me like a forty-shillin' pot. Why the blazes did I go an' get drunk. Devil take Jimmy McAdam and his bloomin' whisky.'

'Here, I made coffee, and you need something to eat. Do you feel up to bacon and beans?'

'I'll just have a slab of damper. My gut's not too happy with me today.'

'That'll do me, too,' Ben said, thinking Danny's stomach might revolt at the smell of bacon. 'Take the day off mate. I'll potter around with what I can do on my own, but I finally heard from my sister back home and need to answer her letter.'

'I'll be fine by tonight. Hey, it's your turn to get sozzled next.'

'I'll try to avoid it. You know what I'm like if I drink.'

Danny did know. Ben was always a quiet fella but in drink, he kind of closed down. He'd never seen Ben fighting drunk but, having heard a bit of his story, for the first time he wondered if his mate had a violent history.

After doing a few jobs around the mine, Ben got out his rarely used writing paper, pen and ink and set himself the task of composing a reply to Bessie, pushing away the thought that he must also write to his brother-in-law and former best friend, Jim. He owed Millie's family an explanation. Millie's mother would never forgive him for bringing her out here to die.

The ink had dried on the nib, so he dipped it into the ink again and made a determined effort to write:

Dear Bessie,
Thank you for your letter. I should have written sooner about Millie. I just couldn't. She bled to death, Bessie, and I wasn't there when she needed me.
We'd been so happy, with a nice little house, and I got promoted. There wasn't much crime in Brisbane, but out in the country, there was a kind of war going on between the settlers and the black people. When a wealthy squatter got killed. I got sent out to help the police. Millie wasn't near her time and said not to worry.

We had a posse of fifty local men with us, and when we reached the blacks' camp, they started shooting, killing men, women and even little children. The local police didn't interfere. Back in Brisbane, I tried to report it, but had to go to investigate a suicide. A woman had jumped in front of a train. Jim will know what that's like. By the time I got home it was too late.

I held Millie in my arms and wept until the undertaker came and asked about burying her and our baby. It was a little boy, but I never even held him. They had to be buried next day because of the heat. The neighbour's wife came to do what had to be done for Millie, and her husband took me to the pub and got me drunk.

It was late when I remembered about the massacre and went back to the police station. The sergeant on duty told me to go home and sober up, so I got angry and started shouting. They said I attacked the inspector when he came out to investigate, but I was just trying to get him to listen.

Someone hit me with a truncheon and I woke up in jail, hung-over and weeping for Millie. When they wouldn't let me out to go to her funeral, I went mad, screaming and yelling. Then I wept for days. No wonder they thought I was crazy.

I was in the asylum for five years. Remember how I liked to draw? Well, I met this artist who only went off his head every now and then. He gave me some art stuff. They let me work in the garden and when the governor saw me drawing plants, he talked to me and decided I was sane.

Even when I got out, I couldn't face up to what had happened. That's why I never wrote. Then I heard about the gold over here and thought I might as well come and see what all the fuss was about. I've been lucky. I've got a share in a mine ...

'You interested in something to eat, Ben?' Danny's question made him realise that it was midday and he'd been writing for hours. Or trying to write, he revised with a wry smile, seeing the blotted and crumpled pages tossed on the ground ...

'Hard letter to write?' asked his mate, settling himself by the fire to toast a thick slice of damper.

'Yes, but I think I've got it beaten.'

'Sometimes it's hard to find the right words.'

'Yes,' Ben replied, folding the letter and tossing the discarded copies onto the fire. 'Do you want anything else. Feeling up to bacon yet?'

'Maybe a few beans, if you are having any.'

Even the tempting smell of frying bacon couldn't take Ben's mind off the memories he'd been reliving. Yes, it was a hard letter to write. Trying to condense all the old sorrow and shame into words that wouldn't upset Bessie too much had left him feeling drained.

When Danny leaned forward to pour himself a second cup of tea, Ben realised he was sitting holding a forkful of cold bacon, several beans having dropped off.

'You all right, mate? More tea?'

'Yes please, Danny,' he replied, surreptitiously picking beans off his shirtfront and tossing the cold, greasy bacon to Seamus.

'Sometimes it helps to talk about it,' Danny said, quietly.

'I guess I owe you some sort of explanation,' Ben replied, after a long silence. 'If it wasn't for you and Fergus, I'd probably have ended up like one of those poor dead bastards we find out in the bush.

'I was a policeman, a London bobby, back in the old country, and they said I'd better chances of promotion out here. My wife and I were happy in Brisbane and had a baby on the way. Then...well, you know what it's like out in the bush. A big squatter got speared, the bush police wanted more men, so they sent me, a mug newchum, out there.'

'Go on,' said Danny, stuffing tobacco into his pipe.

Retelling the story was easier. And Danny's quiet acceptance helped, as he described seeing his colleagues join in the massacre then burn the bodies to cover up the atrocity, and his angry return to the city, only to be ignored and sent to the bloody suicide site. They weren't supposed to drink on duty, but when the other bobby bought him a drink, he'd had to buy the next round. He'd quickly learned the Australian practice of shouting drinks.

'So, with a couple of beers in me, I went home. I was too late. Millie lay in her own blood, white as a marble statue. All I could do was hold her. The baby was dead too.'

Unable to continue, he concentrated on rolling his cigarette. After a few calming puffs, he forced himself to go on, because it was good to let those awful memories go. His neighbour meant well, taking him off to the pub. But he wasn't much of a drinker and was very drunk when he remembered he had unfinished business and staggered off to the Police Station.

'They wouldn't listen, so I made a fuss. Then the inspector came storming out claiming I'd disobeyed orders at the remote station and, what really got my goat, that I'd shown cowardice in the face of the enemy. What enemy? Unarmed women and children?

'I tried to explain but he turned away, so I grabbed his arm to stop him leaving. The sergeant thought I was attacking the pompous bastard and knocked me out. I woke up in jail and when they wouldn't let me out for Millie's funeral next morning, I went berserk and tried to tear down the cell door, so they said I was mad, locked me up and threw away the key. After I got out, I couldn't stand being around people, so went bush,' he was saying when Joey came trudging up the hill.

'G'day, Joey, is everything all right?' Danny said, seeing the boy's worried frown.

'I can't find Timmy. Have you seen him?'

'He was looking for you last week. You not seen him since?'

'No, I can't find him anywhere. His ma thinks he ran off after Pa Kenny gave him a hiding. But we ain't seen him at all,' he said, shakily.

'We'll keep a lookout for him, Joey, but you'd better stay home, in case he comes lookin' for you,' said Ben.

'Wonder where the young fella's got to,' Danny said as Joey headed home.

When Ben went to post his letter that afternoon, he found Purkiss and a strange policeman rifling through the accumulated mail, much to the annoyance of Bob Humphries.

'I've no idea what they're looking for,' he muttered, taking Ben's letter.

'Neither have we,' whispered Purkiss, following Ben outside.

'What's all the fuss, then?'

'Detective O'Connell from Coolgardie's come over here and we're expecting some big shots from the city too. They think the bloke we've been looking for might have killed those women in Melbourne, so we need to warn all the ladies.'

'I'll tell Mrs O'Callaghan. What about the nurses up at the hospital?'

'The matron's been told, and a constable's been sent to tell the other womenfolk. Well, I'd better get back to work.'

'Before you go,' Ben said, 'have you seen anything of young Timmy O'Rourke? Mrs Kenny thinks he's run away, but Joey hasn't seen him either. You know how they always got around together.'

'Well, I wouldn't blame the lad wanting to get away from his old man. Nasty bastard that one. I'll keep an eye out for him, but tell his ma to report him missing if he doesn't turn up soon.'

Chapter 40

Shaken by the attack on Nellie after her own scare the previous night, Nora decided to take Charlie's advice and try wearing the gun. Glad no one else was in the nurses' tent to ask questions, she lifted her skirt and petticoat, buckled the padded belt around her waist, then sat and tied the holster's ribbons around her thigh, before inserting the little revolver. Standing up, she let her skirt fall to her ankles and was relieved to find there was no telltale bulge, though it felt very strange as she walked. *I suppose I'll get used to it*, she thought.

Slipping her hand into the hidden slot in her skirt, she fumbled to find the corresponding gap in her petticoat to reach the gun. But just as her hand closed around its butt, laughter outside warned her of the entrance of Molly and the new nurse, Betty Bowra.

So, it wasn't until late that night on the ward that, having finally got the patients to sleep, she had a chance to practise reaching for the gun. She had just found it was possible, if slow, to get a grip on it, when two patients woke up. One man was in real pain, needing dressings changed and morphine. By the time he'd gone back to sleep, it was nearly dawn. Nora was surprised how quickly the shift had passed. Practising with the gun, she'd almost forgotten her worries about Ned. Until she knocked off and tried to get some sleep, that was. Now they were back.

Perhaps Vernon was mistaken, and Ned's mine hadn't been sold? But that didn't explain why he hadn't come straight to Hannans when he heard she was here almost a month ago. But men died out there in the bush, of thirst, snakebite, accidents or typhoid. Had Ned joined their ranks? Unable to shake off the grim image of his body lying out there on the hard red earth, she gave up on sleep, dressed and headed for the kitchen, just as the other nurses walked in, followed soon after by Mrs Alderdice.

'I didn't want to alarm the patients,' she said, 'but the police suspect that the man who killed those women in Melbourne might be here on the goldfields. They've been looking for a fugitive who killed a couple of men, but now they think he's one and the same murderer.

'Also, as you may have heard, a woman was attacked the other night and now a young boy seems to have gone missing. So, I've been told to warn you girls not to have anything to do with strange men. I need to know where you are going in your time off and who you are going with. We'll be arranging to have a couple of men staying up here at night.'

'The boy who's missing. Is it Timmy O'Rourke?' Nora asked.

'Yes, the police are looking for him.'

'I'll be going over to Mrs O'Callaghan's, Matron,' Nora said, 'Timmy's young Joey's pal. He must be upset.'

'Yes, and tell Mary, and any other ladies you know, what we've heard about that murderer and to take care.'

'I certainly will, Matron.'

She found Mary talking to Ben at her gate and called out, 'Hello, Mary, have you been warned about that murderer?'

'Yes. Ben told me last night and Constable Purkiss was here asking if we'd seen Timmy and he told us a bit more,' Mary said.

'Is there any news of Timmy?'

'No. Joey's off, running all over town looking for him. Oh, here he comes now.'

'Timmy's really gone missing, Mum,' Joey gasped. 'The police have sent one of the blacktrackers to try to see where he's gone.'

'Oh, I hope they find him soon,' Mary said.

'I'm gonna go an' watch the tracker,' the boy said, turning to run off.

'I should have made him stay here,' Mary said. 'He shouldn't be getting under foot, and I wouldn't want him to be there if they find something bad.'

'I don't think we could have stopped him, Mary,' Ben said. 'I'll go and keep an eye on him.'

Joey caught up with the tracker a little way down the hill.

'Hey Mister, you found Timmy yet?'

'Hello young fella,' he said. 'You Timmy's mate?'

'Yeah.'

'Looks like he come up here coupla days ago with his dog. You seen him?'

'No, I was busy. I looked for him yesterday morning. I thought he'd turn up at the cricket in the arvo.'

'You haven't found any fresher tracks, Dom?' Ben was asking as Purkiss joined them.

'No mister, even 'round his place. All old tracks. But, see, he come back downhill. Went that way.'

'Hey Joey,' Ben called. 'Don't go walking around where Dom's trying to look.'

'Oh, didn't think of that.'

'This might take a while, Joey,' Purkiss said. 'You better go home. We'll let you know if we find anything.'

'I wanna know what's happened to Timmy,' Joey muttered.

Seeing the boy was near to tears, Ben said, 'Don't worry, I'll stay with him.'

'Do you have any idea where Timmy might have gone, Joey,' the policeman asked. 'I know you boys were always snooping around looking for clues. Did you find any that we should know about?'

'Not really. Just some things that didn't seem right. Like that Mr Simpson dyeing his hair. Why would someone pretend to have red hair?'

'Maybe he's going grey and wanted to touch it up.'

'Maybe.'

'Anything else?'

'Well, lotsa blokes go to see them ladies at the brothel. An' some fellas hang around ladies whose husbands is away. That's what Timmy says anyway.'

While they were speaking, Dom headed off jogging across town towards the northeast. Eyes on the ground ahead, he followed a trail invisible to the onlookers, across the churned up flat where hundreds of men had been living and digging for the last two years.

Hurrying to catch up, they occasionally saw what might have been the imprint of Timmy's bare sole on a patch of undisturbed soft ground. And the tracks of a small dog.

The tracks wandered back towards town then it looked like he'd stopped in the same place for a short while, before running out to the Broad Arrow road. He'd jogged along it for about a mile then stopped and stood among some trees by the side of the road. Wheel and hoof tracks showed that a buggy had stopped there. Then Timmy's tracks disappeared.

'Must have got a lift with someone heading out to Broad Arrow,' Purkiss suggested.

'Maybe boss,' said the tracker, 'but buggy not just comin' out of town. It come back an' around an' away again.'

Then, jogging away up the track and around a bend he called, 'Buggy stopped here. Man got out, went in bush an' walked back. Then he gets buggy an' comes back. Stops here an' turns around. Then goes again.'

'Maybe saw Timmy and turned back for him. Might have got out for a piss or something, and Timmy hailed him. I'll head back,' Purkiss said. 'Good job Dom. You coming?'

'Be along soon, boss,' the tracker said, still examining the jumbled tracks with a puzzled frown.

'What's the matter, mister?' asked Joey, bending to examine the ground.

'Nothin' young fella,' the black man replied. 'Nothin' to see here. Be headin' back to camp. You go home too, hey?' he went on, turning to walk back towards town.

'All right,' said Ben. 'Come on Joey. Might as well go home and tell your mum what we've found out.'

'We'll send someone to find out if he's at Broad Arrow,' the policeman said as they caught up with him.'

Ben and Joey were about to turn off the road to make a shortcut home, when Joey's sharp ears picked up a sound to one side. A whimper.

'What's that?' he asked, then, not waiting for an answer, dodged between two mulga trees.

'Splinter, Splinter, what happened to you?' he cried as the two men followed him to where he crouched beside the little dog. Splinter lay on her side, gasping, close to the tree she'd been tied to.

'Bloody Hell,' Purkiss muttered. 'Is that the boy's dog? How long's the poor thing been there?'

'Looks like a couple of days,' Ben replied, untying the rope, while Joey comforted the distressed animal.

'Looks like he tied the dog up so it wouldn't follow him,' Purkiss mused.

'He was gonna come back,' Joey said, 'Timmy'd never leave her behind.'

Chapter 41

The tracker wasn't really satisfied Timmy had got a lift. There were too many confused tracks, and it looked like someone had deliberately tried to disguise them.

He caught up with Purkiss near the Police station and shared his concerns.

'Well, I'll go see if the Inspector is happy about us following this up.'

With permission to proceed, the constable and tracker saddled up and rode out of town, Dom keeping his gaze on the churned-up ground. About eight miles beyond where Timmy's tracks were last seen, he slowed his mount, saying, 'Buggy turn off here.'

'Can you follow its tracks?'

'Yeah. No trouble,' the black man replied, leading the way along an overgrown track. Purkiss was just about to suggest it was a wild goose chase when the heaped rocks and broken timber of an abandoned mine appeared through the bush. Here on the cleared ground, even he could see the undisturbed tracks of buggy wheels and hooves. There was also a pile of horse dung where the horse had stood. Tracks led to the old mineshaft.

'Man carry somethin' to mine,' the tracker said.

'Could it be a body?' the constable asked.

'Skinny young fella, not heavy.

'Long way down,' he went on, looking down the hole. 'Somebody hafta go down an' look.'

'We'll need to come back with ropes in the morning. Be too dark by the time we ride back.'

'Buggy man drove back to road,' Dom said leading his horse back along the track.

'An', see here,' he went on as they reached the road. 'Just went back t' town.'

'Did you notice the man's shoes?'

'Yeah. Posh shoes. Bit worn, but not old minin' boots.'

'What about the horse's shoes.'

'Pretty new. No rough bits.'

Early next morning, Ben headed down to the police station and was glad to meet Purkiss tethering his horse out the front.

'Did you find young Timmy,' he asked.

'No, and don't say anything to Joey, but we suspect he's been done away with. The buggy didn't go to Broad Arrow. Dom tracked it out another ten miles or so and it turned off into the bush and went to an abandoned mine. Dom says he carried something to the mine. He can tell by the depth of the footprints. We fear it was a small body.'

'Oh no,' Ben said.

'After what Joey said about Timmy not leaving his dog tied up, it looks very suspicious. It was too late to try to get down the mine last night, so I'm on my way out there now. Just going to get a spare horse and some rope.'

'Better get a lantern too, and some canvas to wrap him up, if he is down there. I could come and give you a hand, if you like.' Ben said.

'I'd appreciate that. I thought I'd have Dom with me, but the boss has sent the trackers off to look for some bloke who's got himself lost.'

'I'll go get my horse and meet you out where we were last night,' Ben said, hurrying away.

'Thanks mate.'

About an hour later, the two men reached the abandoned diggings, disturbing several crows that flew off with mournful caws.

'There's a lot of rubbish down there, and something rotten,' Purkiss commented, peering down the mineshaft. 'Well, we'd better get on with it, I suppose.'

'I might be better to go down,' Ben said as the policeman unrolled the rope and tied it securely around a nearby tree. 'I'm used to climbing down shafts.'

'Officially, I suppose it should be me, but I might take you up on the offer.'

'Well, here goes,' Ben muttered. Tying the end of the rope around his waist, he backed over the lip of the shaft and slowly lowered himself into the dark cavity.

'Sing out if you want me to light the lantern and send it down,' the policeman called.

'Yes, please. It's pretty dark. There seems to be the remains of a ladder, but it might just be old timbers.'

'Here it comes.'

By the lantern's light, Ben could see that the old ladder was still in reasonable condition, so, leaving the lantern hanging, he climbed further down, disturbing a cloud of blowflies.

'Drop the light a bit lower. I'm nearly at the bottom.'

The air was so foul that Ben had a passing fear of explosive gases sometimes found in mines, but then identified the smell as rotting flesh. Surely, Timmy hadn't been there that long.

As he tentatively lowered one foot to what appeared to be solid ground, his boot sunk into something soft, bones cracked under his weight and the appalling smell of putrefaction almost choked him.

'Lower the lamp,' he called, his voice echoing eerily in the narrow shaft.

As the lantern's light illuminated the maggot-infested dark mass below, he was relieved to see the long leg bones of a kangaroo. But beyond the roo's bones was something else. Knowing it was useless, he called Timmy's name and reached out to touch the still, small body, already crawling with blowfly larvae.

'Better send down the canvas and cord we brought,' he called.

It was going to be a difficult task, wrapping the body in the tight space, but it had to be hauled up. There was no way he could climb out carrying Timmy. Unfolding the canvas sheet, he spread it over the dead roo, the only space available, and gently rolled the boy's body onto it. There was no obvious fatal wound, but the side of his head was a mass of dried blood and crawling insects, and Ben's stomach churned to see his whole ear was missing.

With the body securely wrapped, Ben undid the rope from his own waist and tied it around the package.

'Righto, mate,' he called. 'You can raise him up. Then send the rope back down for me.'

When Ben clambered over the lip of the hole, the young policeman was bending over in the bush to vomit. He'd unwrapped and examined the body.

'Should have skipped breakfast,' he said, wiping his mouth. 'Poor little devil.

'Phew,' he continued, wrinkling his nose. 'That smell's not him. What else is down there?'

'Just a dead roo. I stepped right in it. Better stay to the windward of me.'

'I'll survive. It should've been me down there. It's not hard to see that our murderer's been at it again. The missing ear's his calling card.'

'So,' Ben said, 'it seems he's here in Hannans, hiding in plain sight, under the noses of you police.'

'Yes. Obviously pretending to be someone else. Some flash bloke who drives a buggy.'

'But you fellas have been checking on everyone who got here about the time he arrived from the east.'

'Well, as best we can. Hardly anyone's brought documents like birth certificates out here. The best most can offer to prove who they are, is a bankbook or a Miner's Right. And as we've seen, Miner's Rights are unreliable witnesses. The dead blokes carrying McCaig's and Patterson's weren't them.'

The midday sun was beating down by the time the two men reached the outskirts of town, the boy's canvas-wrapped body slung across the spare horse's back.

'So, we're looking for a buggy driver who wears good shoes,' Ben was saying.

'There aren't that many buggies in town,' Purkiss replied.

'More arriving every day, with silvertails and families moving in.'

'Yeah. We'll be checking all of them.'

'What about the preacher? Joey thinks Timmy was watching him, and for some reason the boys were very suspicious of him.'

'He's in the clear. Never arrived from the east until December. Thanks for your help. I'll take the poor little bugger straight up to the morgue before I put in my report. Then comes the hard part, breaking the news to his ma.'

'We'll have to tell young Joey too.'

'Can I leave that t' you? Might come better from someone he knows.'

'Nothing can make it better for him, but I'll do my best. I'd better sneak home the back way first and get out of these clothes.'

Ben had hoped Danny might volunteer to break the news, but he was gone when Ben arrived back at the camp. After attending to Walter, he tipped a bucket of water into the tin dish, added a liberal splash of carbolic and scrubbed his hands and face, before kicking off the soiled boots and washing his feet. Hoping to get rid of the clinging odour of decomposition, he poured the water over the boots and left them to dry out, before dressing in his best clothes and heading down the hill to Mary's place.

'Hello, Ben,' she said. 'Danny said you'd gone to help the constable. It's bad news, isn't it?'

'Yes, Mary. I don't know how to tell Joey.'

But the boy had seen him too and came running out. Then he stopped and said, 'He's dead, isn't he? Timmy's dead.'

'Yes, Joey,' his mother said, going to enfold him in her arms. As his first cries changed to heartbroken sobbing, Danny wrapped his arms around them both.

Regretting the stark way he'd broken the news, Ben was wondering if he should leave, when Joey broke away from his mother's arms to cry out angrily, 'It's that parson bloke who done him in.'

'No, Joey,' Ben said. 'It was the bloke the police have been looking for. It can't be Simpson, he's only been here a few weeks.'

'Well, that's who Timmy was watching. Timmy said he was up to no good.'

'He's a preacher, Joey. He must be a good man,' Mary said.

'You don't like him, though, do y'. I heard you tell Mrs Patterson.'

'That doesn't mean he's a bad person, Joey.'

❦

Mrs Alderdice had called the staff together and Nora cried out in shock when she said, 'Dr Martin has just informed me that the O'Rourke boy was found dead this morning. The police suspect, that he fell victim of the murderer they've been seeking. This man, who they now believe is a danger to women as well as men, is thought to be here, in Hannans. So, you must all be on the alert. Do not leave the hospital grounds without telling me where you are going.'

With the matron's permission, Nora hurried over to Mary's. She and Ben were sitting in the bough shed drinking tea. Both stood up when she arrived and Mary hurried to her, saying, 'Shh,' with her fingers to her lips.

'I just heard about Timmy,' Nora whispered. 'How is Joey?'

'He's cried himself to sleep, poor little bugger,' Mary said. 'Come and have a cuppa. I'll sneak in and get you a cup.'

'Hello Ben,' Nora said taking a seat in the rough shelter, 'How did it happen?'

'We don't really know, but it was the bloke the police are chasing. He murdered those women in the east and when the police got after him, he did a couple of men in, pinched their things and got away by pretending to be them.'

'But why would he go after Timmy?'

'Maybe the boys got too close with their snooping. I wish to God we'd never given Joey those Conan Doyle stories,' he was saying as Mary rejoined them, her eyes brimming.

'I just don't know what to do to comfort him, Nora,' she said. 'He blames himself. Thinks if he'd been with Timmy, it wouldn't have happened.'

'Of course he isn't to blame,' said Nora, 'It won't do him any good to be torturing himself about it, but it'll take time for him to grieve for Timmy. They were very close, weren't they?'

'They spent every spare moment together, getting into mischief.'

'Did Timmy's mum say he could keep the dog?' Ben asked.

'Yes, and she'll be a comfort. He was crying in the night. I was going to go to him but then I heard him talking to Splinter and he quietened down. They were snuggled up in the bed this morning.'

Poor Joey, Ben was thinking as he headed home. *If anyone's to blame, it's me. I should have warned them we had a murderer here. I've been too busy mooning after Nora and feeling sorry for myself to notice what's going on around me.*

'How's the little fella going?' asked Danny.

'Not so good, Danny.'

'It's a good thing he's got the dog,' the Irishman said. 'Lookin' after her might help take his mind off it.'

'Maybe if we'd warned the boys it mightn't have happened, Danny.'

'Well, we didn't want to scare them, Ben. The police gave us no reason to think a boy could be in danger. If it really is the bloke they've been looking for.'

'It looks that way, with Timmy's ear missing. This bastard likes to keep his victims' ears as souvenirs, the police say. We should have kept an eye on what the boys were up to, Danny. Well, I should have, anyway. When I was in the police I got a taste of detective work back home. Wasn't going to get anywhere over there, though. That's why I left. But maybe I can do something now. Would you mind if over the next few days, I did a bit of poking around. I might see something the police miss. They stick out like sore toes even in plain clothes.'

'That's all right with me, mate.'

'You won't go down the mine on your own while I'm away, will you?'

'I'll try not to get into any trouble. Don't know how I got on all those years without you fussin' about me.'

An hour later, Ben stood on the steps of the Post Office smoking. There were a surprising number of buggies in the town, but the police would be checking on them. He wasn't sure what he was looking for. He hoped the casual pose masked his careful observation of the busy street scene, but the glittering stare of the crow perched on the hitching post was unnerving. He was glad when it flew off, though the derisive tone of it's parting caw reinforced the feeling that he was wasting his time, just looking for some way to assuage his guilt over Timmy.

There were a lot of men who would fit the description of the killer, though the new information suggested he would not be one of the rough-looking miners with their unkempt beards. He wore good shoes, so would probably be well dressed. So Ben was looking for men with neat beards and good hats, when he saw the black hat of the preacher moving through the crowd outside the Club hotel. He appeared to be watching someone so Ben turned to follow the line of the man's gaze and recognised the little boater hat moving through the masculine crowd. About to step down and go to meet Nora, he remembered he was supposed to be watching and glanced back across the road.

Simpson stood observing the young woman's approach, a sly smile on his face, before slipping back into the crowd. Knowing the man had been hanging around Nora, Ben was surprised to see the black hat disappear down a laneway. Maybe, the bloke had finally accepted that she didn't like him. But why the smug smile?

Shrugging off the questions the man's behaviour had raised, he went to join Nora.

'Oh Hello, Ben,' she said. 'I've just left Mary. She's afraid Joey might sneak off to look for clues. He still reckons it must have been the preacher. I dislike the man but that doesn't make him a murderer.'

'Well, it seems he only came west in December. Some of the blokes don't like him much, either, but then they just don't like parsons.'

Chapter 42

Shots rang out. Someone shouted. Then came the sound of running footsteps. Taking a deep breath to calm her racing heart, Nora slid her hand into the slit in her skirt. Surprised how easily the loaded gun fitted her hand, she withdrew it and aimed at the ward door, calling out, 'Who's there?'

'It's just me, nurse. Willie Dunne.'

With a sigh of relief, she opened the door, asking, 'What's happened?'

'We disturbed a bloke lurking around. Tom shot at him, and he headed off. I came to make sure you're all safe.'

'Thanks. We've had no trouble.'

'I see you're prepared,' he laughed, nodding to the gun she still clutched. 'Is that thing loaded?'

'Yes,' she replied a little shakily. The news that Timmy's killer was in Hannans had convinced her to take that step, but she was shocked by how calmly she'd been prepared to kill.

'I'll be off then,' Dunne said. 'We'll make sure no one bothers you, but keep the door barred.'

With the door barred and the gun safely back in its holster, she went to reassure the disturbed patients, hoping they didn't notice her shaking. She was tempted to sample a slug of the medicinal brandy but feared it might affect her aim if something did happen.

None of the patients was seriously ill and most slept after they recovered from the alarm, so with nothing to distract her from thinking about Timmy's horrible fate and worrying about Ned, it was a long, unsettling night's work. Though she didn't need to drag the loaded pistol from its nest, every strange noise had her on edge and she was relieved when sunrise came, and the end of her shift. After a quick cup of tea, she headed for the nurse's tent, but found her passage blocked by a large man in a black three-piece suit with a gold watch chain stretched across his paunch.

'Oh!' she cried, startled.

'Mrs Patterson?'

'Yes?'

'Detective O'Connell from Coolgardie. You reported your husband missing some time ago. Has he turned up?'

'No, have you any news?'

'I'm afraid not, madam. But I would like you to answer some questions about him. I believe he might be a person of interest.'

'What do you mean, a person of interest?'

'Is there somewhere we can talk in private?'

Well, there was only the sleeping tent. Matron had expressly warned that no men were allowed in there, but perhaps policemen might be exempt. Nora peeped in to check no one was in there before ushering the detective in. Sitting on her bed, she waved him to the opposite one and was glad when he sat down. It was intimidating to have him looming over her.

'Your husband is Edward Patterson?'

'Yes.'

'When and where were you married?'

'It was October 1893, in Geelong.'

'When did you last see him?'

'When he left to come west in January last year. I saw him off on the steamer.'

'Are you sure about that?'

'Of course I am?' Nora was getting annoyed and scared.

'Did he have a stateroom?'

'You're joking! We don't have that sort of money. He went steerage, of course. Why are you asking these questions?'

'Your husband fits the description of a fugitive wanted for several cases of homicide. He is believed to have arrived on the fields some time ago. And today we have received a photograph of the man. Corporal Williams says it looks a lot like your husband, the so-called Edward Patterson. We suspect he may be one and the same.'

'So, when was Ned supposed to have committed these crimes?' Nora asked, fighting back tears.

'The person we are interested in apprehending arrived in Melbourne in June last year from India, already under suspicion of murders committed both there and in England. We now believe that he murdered the two young women whose dismembered bodies were recently discovered in Victoria. He then killed a man about to travel west, stole his steamer ticket and luggage and boarded the ship masquerading as his victim. Police were hoping to capture him at Albany, but he slipped through the net by murdering and impersonating another victim, a young prospector.'

Nora sat open-mouthed, then gave a snort of laughter, though it wasn't really funny, just ridiculous that Ned should be suspected of being this man.

'Are you saying this man was in India last year? Ned has never been out of Australia.'

'How do you know that?'

'Because I've known him all my life. We were neighbours and went to school together.'

'Can you prove that?'

'Why should I have to prove it? You're the detective. Get in touch with the police in Geelong. His family had a dairy farm about two miles out of town, just across the river. Our farm was over the road from them. It's not a very big place. Get them to check with the schoolteacher.'

'I'm just doing my job madam. Now, may I have a look at your husband's photograph, please?' he said very stiffly.

'Perhaps you should have done that before you started accusing him of murder.' Pulling her carpetbag from under the bed, she handed him the framed portrait, and he took a small print out of the breast pocket of his uniform and compared them, frowning.

'Yes, perhaps I have been over hasty, but here, you look. There is a definite resemblance.'

Nora took the photo. Yes, the man was not unlike Ned, fairish hair and a moustache that partly hid his mouth, smaller eyes with a bit of a droop to the lids that gave him a world-weary look, not like Ned's open countenance. He looked strangely familiar, but she could not place from where she knew him.

'I see what you mean, but I would advise you not to make unfounded assumptions. That is not a photograph of my husband.'

O'Connell rose making flustered apologies and quickly backed out of the room.

Nora's anger cooled leaving her completely exhausted. Throwing herself on the bed she burst into tears. *Oh Ned, where are you?*

Mary had been up since early morning letting down the pants and jacket she'd made for Joey to wear to his father's funeral. He'd grown about six inches since then.

'Here Joey,' she said. 'You better try these on.'

'Do I really have t' wear them sissy pants?'

'You owe it to Timmy to look your best,' she replied. 'There, you look really nice.'

'They won't let me see him,' Joey said, his voice breaking.

'You wouldn't want to see him like that, Joey. I know, because I saw your dad, an' it's hard to get that picture out of your head. It took a long while before I could remember Paddy like he always was and not like that. You need to remember the Timmy you knew and the fun you had together. Oh, my poor boy. You shouldn't have to face this,' she sobbed, pulling him into her arms.

'Would you like to pick some flowers from the gum tree round the back to put on Timmy's coffin,' she went on as she mopped both their tear-stained faces.

'Yeah, maybe. An' I gotta take Splinter,' he said, bending to pick up the dog. 'She wants t' say goodbye to Timmy.'

'I don't know if you should, Joey. She might start barking or running around and upset people.'

'She's gotta come, Mum.'

'All right,' his mother said, fighting back tears. As she wrapped her arms around him and the dog, Splinter licked her hand.

Timmy had liked the Salvation Army's music. He'd always go and sing along to the hymns they played. So, with no Catholic priest available, Mrs Kenny had asked the Salvation Army captain to do the funeral.

'They was always good to me and Timmy,' she explained.

The Salvation Army captain approached Ben and Danny, saying, 'Mrs Kenny asked if you gentlemen would act as pallbearers.'

'Of course,' both men spoke together.

'Mr Kenny will take a front corner, but we need someone else.'

'What about you, Bluey?' Ben asked.

'I'd be honoured,' their friend replied. 'You better go in front Danny. Kenny's about your height. Thank God, he's turned up sober.'

'We will proceed, then, gentlemen. Please take up your positions.'

While the Salvo's embryo band of drum, trumpet and tambourine played *Abide with me*, the four men carried the rough wooden coffin across the red dirt graveyard, followed by Timmy's mother dressed in her best black. Seeing Joey standing back with Splinter in his arms, she called him to her side. 'You too, missus,' she said to Mary. 'You was kind t' my Timmy.'

The Salvationist's graveside service was short and straightforward, with only well-loved hymns and prayers, before the captain spoke the old words of committal, 'Ashes to ashes, dust to dust,' and the coffin was lowered into the newly dug grave.

Nora mopped her streaming eyes, wrapping her arm around Mary's shaking shoulders, as Joey sobbed, 'I'll look after Splinter, Timmy. Don't y' worry 'bout her.'

Danny was openly weeping, while Ben tried to hide his unshed tears by blowing his nose. Hearing the sound echoed behind him, he turned to see Purkiss also surreptitiously wiping his eyes.

'G'day, Ben,' the constable said. 'Well, not such a good one. But it looks like we might soon be on the track of the bastard that did it. His real name's Maximilian FitzJames. Son of a wealthy Queensland squatter who'd been an officer in the British army.'

Ben's heart lurched, and he almost blurted out that he thought he'd met the man.

'Wanted his son to follow in his footsteps, so sent the boy over to some officers' school. Young FitzJames went out to India and killed another officer. To escape, he killed an Indian soldier, took his clothes, stained his face and slipped away, got to one of the ports and sailed to Australia. The father shot himself when he heard the news. Couldn't take the shame.'

The more Ben heard, the harder it was to ignore the idea that this FitzJames was the mad boy with the sabre who'd haunted him for years. Who looked like Ned Patterson and could be his cousin. Or was that all just some crazy figment of his nightmares?

'It seems he kills blokes and pretends to be them. I'm wondering if that's why we've got these blokes turning up with other fellas' papers. We've got a good photograph of him now. Oh, hello, Mrs Patterson,' he said as she joined them, wiping her eyes. 'I'm sorry the inspector went off half-cocked and bothered you.'

'I understand why. That man does look a bit like Ned.'

✻

As the solemn words of the funeral service resonated, Nora's own grief had swept over her, and she knew Ned wasn't coming back. No matter how hard she'd clung to the hope that he was out there somewhere trying to get back to her, her heart told her the laughing boy she knew was gone. That he was dead. He never would have left without a word. Had he already been dead when she was cheating on him with James? That thought and the wave of guilt it brought threatened to destroy her.

Back at the hospital, relieved that no one was in the sleeping tent, she collapsed on the bed and gave way to the tears she'd been holding back for weeks, before drifting into a disturbing dream where Ned kept showing her his Miners' Right. The feeling that he was trying to tell her something refused to go away as she attended to the patients that night. She was sure the dead man who'd had the paper on him wasn't Ned. What was it she'd overheard the policeman say to Ben? That Timmy's murderer killed men and took their papers to impersonate them. Had Ned been one of them? Had he, like Timmy, died violently, his body tossed away like garbage?

Sickened by the images crowding her mind, she ran outside, gasping for air until her stomach settled.

Back at work that night, kept busy caring for the patients, she could put the horror aside and carry out her normal duties. Then later, when all was quiet and those thoughts threatened to overwhelm her, she distracted herself by practising with the little gun. By dawn, not only was she able to extract it without catching it on her petticoat but had decided that she could lift and aim it inside the layers of cloth. Surely a bullet would tear through and do its job.

Once the patients started to stir, she was kept busy until Molly pushed open the door saying, 'Gee, you look like something the cat dragged in, Nora. You need t' get some sleep.'

'Oh, thanks for the compliment, Molly.'

'Sorry, I didn't mean it like that, but you look all done in.'

'I'll be off and hit the hay, then,' she said, slipping away to escape further observations about her red-rimmed eyes. She was terribly tired, but no way could she sleep. Every time she closed her eyes those thoughts returned.

Ned was her last link with her old life. Now everyone was gone. Oh, how she wished her dad was here, remembering his strong arms around her as they comforted each other after her mother died.

Chapter 43

Ben had been awake for hours, the random bits of information going around in his head. As usual, he got up at first light, but the questions continued to plague him as he went through the early morning routine of feeding and watering Walter, lighting the fire and putting the billy among the coals to boil.

Shaking his head to clear it, he took out the writing pad he'd last used to write to Bessie, sharpened a pencil and sat down to try to sort through the conflicting pieces of information.

It was hard to look beyond his anger and horror at what had happened to Timmy, but other questions kept bothering him. Who were the two unidentified bodies with other men's papers? Could they have been earlier victims? If they had missing ears, it was disguised by the state of the bodies.

This FitzJames murdered and impersonated a major to get on the ship and another man to get off it at Albany. With the police closing in, did he need another alias? Out here, a Miners Right was commonly used as proof of identity. So, was he the man who bashed Sandy McCaig? McCaig had lost an ear. Was it deliberately sliced off? If that was true, and FitzJames found out the Scotsman was alive, might he kill again, to become someone else?

Then, the puzzle that had been lingering in the back of his mind surfaced. Ned Patterson. Who was he really? Nora's childhood sweetheart; the kind fellow who gave Joey a whole shilling for holding his horse; or the rude, threatening man Corporal Williams met at the mine?

If FitzJames looked enough like Ned Patterson to confuse the police, was he Joey's other Mr Patterson? Joey said they were together buying mine equipment. If they were partners, it didn't last because Patterson was working the mine alone. Could the Patterson who Williams met at the mine have been FitzJames? If so, Ned Patterson was almost certainly dead.

Then the disturbing thought returned; *am I just wishing him dead because I want Nora for myself?* But, if he was alive, why hadn't he come to her. Unless he was completely insane or terribly cruel, no man would ask his wife to come to a place like this and then desert her, sell his mine and disappear. *Supposing he is dead, where's the body?* Down a mine like Timmy reckoned? The suicide who had his Miners' Right wasn't him. So where was he?

He felt that thought slip away when Danny's voice broke into his reverie, 'Hey, Ben, why'd you not call me. The sun's already up an' we got a heap of dollyin' t' do.'

'Sorry, Danny,' he said, stuffing the paper in his pocket and pushing the problems to the back of his mind, 'I got sidetracked. I'll make the tea.'

Over breakfast, he tried to pick up the threads of his earlier musing. If FitzJames had been impersonating McCaig, he'd get rid of the stolen Miner's Right when he decided to become someone else. Was the desiccated body carrying that document his next victim? Was he Ned Patterson?

But he wasn't the only person thinking along those lines. About mid-morning, he ran into Constable Purkiss outside the Post Office.

'G'day, Ben,' he said. 'You're just the bloke I need a word with.'

'Not going to arrest me, I hope.'

'No. It's just I've been thinking. This FitzJames kills blokes and takes their place. And he looks like Patterson. So, was that really Patterson that Williams saw at the mine? With nothing but a vague resemblance, only someone who really knew him would know it wasn't the same man.'

'I've been thinking the same thing,' Ben replied.

'That means Patterson's dead.'

'Yes, and you know that dead bloke we thought was Alexander McCaig. Remember he was missing some toes. Do you think that could be Patterson?'

'I don't know about that, but I've been thinking about that fella too. You don't remember noticing if he was missing an ear, do you?'

'He might have. All one side of the face was eaten away. Maybe we should go and dig him up.'

'I suggested that to Williams, but he reckons you'd need some pretty strong evidence to justify exhumation, and the bloke looked like he died of thirst like so many others. We're probably barking up the wrong tree, Ben.'

'Hello, Mr Simpson,' he went on as the preacher sidled by with a brief nod.

When he was out of earshot, Purkiss said, 'I don't know how he does it, but that bloke has a habit of popping up whenever I'm talking to a possible suspect. Not that you're one. What was

I saying? Ah, yes. We can't disturb that poor bloke because of a hunch.'

'I suppose not. What about the suicide who wasn't Patterson? I guess there wasn't enough of his head left to check his ears.'

'No, but if FitzJames did him in he must have been pretty desperate to try to ring in a redhead as Patterson.'

'You got somethin' on y' mind, mate?' asked Danny, later that afternoon.

'I was talking to Purkiss today and we both think this FitzJames might have murdered Nora's husband.'

'That would explain why he hasn't turned up.'

'Well, I've got a bee in my bonnet that the dead bloke we found out near the Broad Arrow road was him, so I'd like to have another look at the grave. It's probably too late to find anything suspicious, but would you mind if I head off this afternoon? I'll camp out tonight and be back tomorrow.'

'That's fine by me, mate. Make sure you've got enough water and tucker. You can take the rest of the damper.'

'Bugger off,' Ben shouted, but the crow had been following him ever since he left the road, just flew to the next salmon gum.

The bird's behaviour was beginning to get on his nerves. He'd expected to go straight to the lonely grave, but uprooted shrubs and fallen boughs littered the ground, and parts of the track had been washed away by water rushing along the creek-bed after the storm. He was thinking maybe he was in the wrong place when he glimpsed the rough cross just before the crow alighted on it briefly then flew off, cawing mournfully.

The grave itself was greatly altered by the flood, which had dug a deep channel around and under it. White bones, washed clean by the rushing water, protruded from the heaped soil and rocks at either end.

After standing bareheaded for a few minutes in respect for the dead, he squatted down to examine the skeletal foot. Yes, most of the big toe was missing, and the tip of the next one. But there was no damage to the rest of the foot and the toes hadn't come away at the joint as would happen if a dingo dragged it off after death. They were neatly sliced through at an angle, suggesting an old injury.

Standing, he went to the head of the grave and dropped to his knees. Whispering, 'Sorry, Ned,' he brushed away the sand from the skull. Though remnants of dried flesh and skin clung to most of it, the top and side were exposed. Was that mark across the curving side of the cheekbone normal? Running his finger over the ragged indentation he could tell it wasn't. The bone had been cut. Had that happened as the ear was sliced away? They'd not looked too closely at this side of the man's head before rolling him over and into the grave.

Though he was convinced this was Ned Patterson, murdered by FitzJames, he knew it would be hard to convince the police. It was too late today to do anything about that and, anyway, knowing this was Patterson made it even more imperative to cover his poor bones.

By the time he'd scraped the sand back over the body and arranged rocks to encircle it, the sun was slipping towards the horizon. Remembering a likely camp spot from that previous visit, he made his way back to the main road. Turning off a little nearer to town, he headed west and made camp on the top of the breakaway. Hobbling Walter, he went looking for wood for a campfire, but stopped to gaze out over the wide land rolling away towards the southwest and glimpsed a cloud of dust on the road from town.

Curious about who would be travelling out here in the evening, as soon as he had the fire burning and the billy heating in the coals, he wandered back to the ridge as the dust cloud revealed a closed van pulled by a dark horse.

Recognising it as the one belonging to the reverend, he idly watched its progress and was surprised to see it disappear among the mulgas before reappearing in a small clearing. Parson, recognisable by his black clothes, lifted a bicycle out of the buggy and wheeled it into the lee of the ridge, where the trees, watered by the run-off from the high ground, grew taller. It was all of ten minutes before the man in black reappeared, without the bicycle, mounted his buggy and drove back towards town.

What the Hell was he doing down there? Ben asked himself, as he tossed bacon and beans into the frying pan. If he went into the bush to shit, he wouldn't need the bicycle and what did he do with it?

Finding that out would have to wait for morning.

He woke to the first twitterings of dawn and lay listening to the sounds of day creatures waking and night creatures scurrying home to their beds. A magpie perched in the tree above where he was lying, its lovely song echoed by the others flying in to join the chorus.

The clinking of Walter's hobble-chains chimed in with the birds' song, so he was not too far away, thank goodness. Rolling up his swag, he started the fire and put the billy on. Toasted damper and cold bacon made a good breakfast before he followed the sound of the hobble chains to find Walter nibbling at the grass growing along a dry creek bed.

Back at camp, he saddled Walter, checked his fire was out and swung into the saddle. Determined to satisfy his curiosity about where the man in black had gone yesterday, he rode along the ridge looking for an easy track down. Coming out onto a kind of promontory, he had a clear view of the clearing below, where the buggy tracks stood out against the undisturbed soil.

Finally finding a safe way down off the breakaway, Ben rode back to see what had attracted the parson to that hidden clearing, and was surprised to see a tent, almost covered by a rough bough shed. The brush that covered it was still partly green, so it had only recently been built. It seemed a strange place for a camp and there was no sign of any mining activity, but if it was a camp then maybe somebody was ill and that's why the parson was there. He decided to call in at the tent and see if there was anything he could do to help.

Chapter 44

Nora had managed to put on a cheerful smile for the patients and her fellow nurses, but it was hard not to weep, not just for Timmy and poor little Joey grieving his friend, but for Ned, because now she knew in her heart that he was dead. Needing kindly company, she headed straight to Mary's place early on Sunday morning.

There was usually a cheerful, holiday-like atmosphere in the town on Sundays, with the miners enjoying their day of rest. But today a pall of fear and suspicion hung over the town, as word spread of the killer in their midst.

Reaching her friend's cottage she found the door closed. There was no response to her knock so she decided to wait, hoping Mary would soon return. A clunk as she sat down in the bough shed, reminded her that she still carried the loaded revolver. There'd been no trouble last night, but the weight of the gun had been somehow comforting.

With no one around to ask what was the matter, she rested her head on the rough wooden table and let her tears fall, but quickly wiped her eyes when the gate creaked.

'Hello, Mary,' she started to say. But it wasn't Mary. It was the Reverend Simpson.

'Good morning, Mrs Patterson,' he said, 'I was hoping you might be here. I'm afraid I have sad news. Your dear husband is no more. Forgive me for breaking the news so suddenly, but the police believe a man who perished in the bush is Mr Patterson. They intend disinterring the body for further investigation and I am going out to say the appropriate prayers at the graveside. If you would like to be there, I will be more than happy to take you.'

'Oh,' Nora said, choking back a sob. 'Yes. Are you leaving straight away?'

'I can delay if you need time to get ready.'

'Oh, I can come now. My friend isn't here and wasn't expecting me. It was kind of you to ask.'

As she climbed into the buggy, she caught sight of young Joey running towards her, calling out and waving his arms. She just had time to return his wave, as the reverend gentleman flapped the reins, calling 'gee up' to the horse and they were off.

The confirmation of Ned's death was overwhelming, and tears flooded down Nora's face as she thought of him lying out there in a lonely grave. By the time she'd regained control of herself they'd passed the hospital and the Mount Charlotte poppet head on its hill. The land around Hannans was mostly flat, but a ridge of hills ran through the area towards the northwest. Turning the horse's head in that direction, the reverend soon had the horse trotting along a rough, rocky track.

Once outside the town limits, she had no idea where they were going. She had thought they'd be accompanying the police, but there was no sign of them She was about to ask him about that, when he unclipped a whip from the side of the buggy.

As he brought it down across the horse's rump, the animal leapt forward into a stumbling canter and Nora felt herself about to fly out of her seat until a hand clamped down on her thigh. Gasping, she turned to thank her companion, but the hand stayed there, even after he had pulled the horses back to a trot.

When she glared at him, he patted the leg apologetically but the smirk he gave her sent a shiver up the spine. Berating herself for overreacting, she nodded in acknowledgement, just as a deep, distant rumbling drew her attention to the western sky, where lightning flashed against a dark bank of clouds.

'Is it going to rain?' she asked.

'Probably not. Doesn't rain much here.'

Chapter 45

'Hello, the camp,' Ben called, as he approached the hidden tent, but there was no response, so he went closer and called out again. Still no reply. Maybe the man was too sick to get out of bed.

Telling himself it was concern not just curiosity, Ben walked right up to the tent, popped open the flap and looked in. Nobody was there, but the bicycle leaned against the far wall, loaded with a swag and pannier bags. Someone planned on travelling.

There was a rough table and a straw-filled palliasse on the floor, but it was the tools lying on the table that drew his eyes. They weren't miners' or carpenters' tools. More the sort he'd seen in a butcher's shop. There was also a box that looked like one of those used by anglers to store their lures. *What possible use would fishing tackle be to anyone out here?* he was thinking as he tentatively lifted the hinged lid. Neatly arranged in small compartments was what looked like a collection of locks of human hair. Only able to imagine they were to be used to make lures, he flipped the box completely open.

The right side was also divided into small sections, each cradling what at first glance looked like dried apricots. But as the lid flopped open he recoiled in horror to see, pinned inside two compartments, what were obviously human ears. One was slightly shrivelled and attached to some dried skin covered in red hair while the smaller, fresher ear was missing part of the rim. In the moment it took to recall where he'd seen it before, he noticed a tattered photograph pinned to the table by a knife. As every hair on his arms prickled and chills ran down his spine, he saw that the girl in the photograph was Nora.

'Oh God,' he whispered as the full significance of the tools sunk in. The parson had been here. Maybe Joey had been right all along that there was something odd about him. Not just odd, but terrifying. Nora was in danger. Dropping the tent flap, he ran back to his horse and leapt into the saddle to ride straight for town.

Feeling fresh after a good night's rest, Walter was keen to go, so as soon as they reached level ground, Ben let him set his own pace, which soon settled into an easy canter. When he stretched his long legs into a gallop, though, Ben pulled him back.

'Whoa, mate,' he said. 'I'm in a hurry too, but you don't need a broken leg.'

Even at a canter, Walter's long stride couldn't cover more than about twenty miles in an hour, and in places he was slowed to a walk, so Ben forced himself to control the panic that had assailed him when he realised Nora was in danger.

He's not going to do anything to her today, he kept telling himself. Just get back to town and convince the police to act. Then she'll be safe.

It seemed hours before he sighted the poppet heads of the big mine, and the short cut to town. Galloping between the miners' tents to reach the street and the police station, he was unaware of the commotion he was causing. His one thought, to get to the police and tell them that the redheaded man was not a man of the church but a murderer, and he had his eye on Nora.

As he tossed Walter's reins over the hitching rail and stumbled towards the police tent, someone called his name, and he turned to see Joey running towards him.

'Mr Drummond. It's Mrs Patterson. I just saw her get into that parson's buggy and he drove out of town. I'm worried. I don't like him.'

'Yes, Joey. You were right to not like him. Now you run home. I've got something important to tell the policemen.'

Relieved that Joey accepted his suggestion, Ben went inside. A pompous-looking gent at the counter complaining about something was deeply affronted when Ben cut across what he was saying.

'Alf, Constable Purkiss. I've got information about the murderer. I believe it's the parson and he's got Mrs Patterson.'

'Hey, Ben, slow down. Take a breath while I get the inspector.'

Leaving the other customer in mid-complaint, Purkiss ran into the other tent, returning almost immediately accompanied by Williams and a detective inspector. Several other officers soon arrived, while Ben gasped out his story and Purkiss tried politely to get rid of the other man.

'You are claiming that the reverend Simpson is the wanted man,' said O'Connell. 'That seems a far-fetched story. How did you come to find this isolated camp and on what grounds do you believe it is the probable site of some nefarious activities, by that gentleman?'

'I've already explained,' Ben replied, raising his voice in frustration. 'There's no time to waste. He has Mrs Patterson and what I found suggests he means her harm.'

'Excuse me, sir.' A young officer burst into the room. 'We've just received a telegram that does cast doubts on the identity of the parson. He hasn't reported to his superiors or contacted his wife.'

'That doesn't make him a murderer.'

Ben had had enough, 'Well if you want to catch him before he kills again, I suggest you get off your arses and follow me.'

With that, he ran from the tent, gave Walter a quick hug as way of apology, swung back into the saddle and galloping up the street.

Without waiting for the spluttering Inspector's opinion, Corporal Williams took control, 'Riddell, get us all horses. We need to get out there as soon as we can get mounted, sir. That lunatic looks set to take the law into his own hands. Purkiss, if you know where he's talking about show us on the map.'

Chapter 46

The track was becoming even more rugged, and Nora gave up any more attempts at conversation after biting her tongue when her teeth clacked together after one bounce. When they came to a smoother stretch along the base of a rocky breakaway, it was the reverend's time to talk.

'Have you been married long, Mrs Patterson?' he asked.

'Only three years.'

'Oh, but your husband left you to look for gold, didn't he?'

'Yes, he came west about eight months ago.'

'Were you happy about that? It seems neglectful to have left a lovely woman like you all alone.'

'You know about the depression we've been having in Victoria. We hoped if he found gold it would give us a new start.'

'Did you miss him? Did you miss married life?'

'Of course, I missed him,' she replied, becoming annoyed.

'Were your relations satisfactory? Some women find that side of marriage unpleasant.'

'That is a very personal question, sir. You have no right to ask that.'

'Oh, I just wondered if he was the sort of man to satisfy a woman like you.'

'You know nothing about the sort of man my husband was, sir. I'm afraid this conversation is unseemly, and I wish to return to town.'

'Too late now. Look at the weather,' he laughed. Pointing to the darkening western sky, pierced by ragged flashes of lighting, he raised the whip.

As the horse responded to the lash, Nora could only hang on tight and pray that she wasn't about to be thrown out onto the rocks, as thunder rumbled, and lightning flashes lit the approaching cloudbank with a lurid red glow.

'What is that?' Nora cried.

'Dust storm,' he replied with a laugh, 'but I'm taking you somewhere out of the dust.'

The horse whinnied in fear and Nora's heart echoed the sound as red dust billowed around and the sky darkened to blood red. Then, just before the gory light faded to black, out of the darkness loomed the shape of a brush-covered tent. Pulling the horse up under the shelter of a bough shed beside it, the man leapt out and ran around to her side to roughly pull her from the buggy. As he dragged her into the tent's dark interior, Nora expected his grip to loosen and change to one of support. Instead, he pushed her so she sprawled face down on the dirt floor then, ignoring her cries, struck a match and lit a candle.

'Ah, that's better,' he said, bending down to pull her upright and swinging her off balance so she stumbled back against him. Then, with one arm imprisoning her arms, he clamped his other hand on her throat.

'Just a little squeeze,' he crooned as she coughed and struggled. 'Now, if you behave, I don't have to hurt you. Yet!' That was accompanied by an insane cackle. 'And you can scream as much as you like. No one will hear you out here.'

'Who are you? Why are you doing this?' Nora gasped.

'Haven't you guessed, little Nora?' he said stroking her breast. 'Ned talked about you all the time. How beautiful you are. So, when I decided to be him, I wanted you.'

'Oh, God! You killed Ned,' she screamed, starting to struggle, but his hold just tightened, and the hand was back on her throat, forcing her head back until her ears popped and her vision dimmed. She fought back against the faintness, but it was hard to breathe as the whining wind swirled dust in through the canvas walls.

*

'Bugger,' Ben muttered when he recognised the signs of an approaching dust storm a few miles out of town. *They'll be driving right into it. I hope that bastard knows what a dust storm can do and takes cover.*

It wasn't long before he realised that he also needed to find shelter. The breakaway wall swung away to the east. That might lend a bit of protection from the howling gale and blinding dust, so he turned Walter's head in that direction. Darkness was already beginning to engulf horse and rider as they reached the lee of the bluff.

Sliding off Walter's back, he went to the horse's head, murmuring reassurance as the choking air spilled down over the cliff and the red sky turned black. Sick with fear for Nora, he tried to remember how to pray.

Chapter 47

The man eased his grip as Nora stopped struggling, so she feigned unconsciousness. She could feel the pistol pressing against her thigh. If she could escape his grip, maybe she could reach it.

Feeling her body go limp, he laughed. So much easier to get her where he wanted her. As he bent to slide his free arm under her legs to lift her, she brought her knee up sharply into his face. Feeling a satisfying crunch as her kneebone made contact with his nose, she pulled away, heading towards the door.

'Argh! You bitch!' he shouted, stumbling towards her, but now she had her hand on the gun. Without attempting to pull it free of her skirt, she fired. And missed. But the passage of the bullet extinguished the candle flame. As everything went black, Nora headed for the dim, reddish glow that lit up the open doorway.

Stumbling through the choking darkness, thick as a mist of red porridge, Nora prayed she wouldn't run into trees or rock outcrops. But she couldn't avoid the stones and fallen branches littering the ground. Time and again, she tripped on some obstacle, and could only hope the roaring of the wind through the mulgas covered her choked-off cries and the scrabbling sounds of her desperate recovery. Twice she fell heavily and lay gasping until fear propelled her into action and she pulled herself up to stagger on.

He couldn't be far behind, and she saw no escape until the red haze began to thin and she made out, some distance away, the cliff-like face of the breakaway. Hoping to hide among the toppled boulders at its base she scurried that way, the pulse pounding in her head and the sound of her own laboured breath masking the feared pursuit of her murderous hunter. Suddenly he was there, in front of her, lit up by a blinding flash of lightning.

'You can't get away, bitch,' he shouted, 'I know where you are.'

Choking back a scream, she slipped between two boulders, but he was close behind, his hand clutching at her skirt. Pulling away, she climbed higher, hoping to find a refuge among the free-standing boulders clustered along the top of the breakaway.

Chapter 48

As the dust began to clear, Ben heard a man shouting. It seemed to be coming from the base of the breakaway. Remembering the place where he'd ridden down that morning, he pulled the rifle from the saddle scabbard and loaded it.

Checking the revolver was also loaded, he left Walter safely hidden by the bluff, climbed up onto higher ground, and began working his way along the ridge to where the cliff rose above the site of the hidden tent. It was hard to control the urge to run, but the man mustn't know he was there. Keeping low among the stunted trees and taking care not to dislodge any pebbles to go rattling down the bank, he was making headway when a clatter of falling stones, and a loud curse indicated the position of his quarry. But where was Nora?

⤝⤚

The pall of red dust was thinning, but nature was not quite finished its tantrum, and the electrical storm was inevitably drawn to the highest point in the flat goldfields landscape. A brilliant flash of light engulfed the scene, a deafening explosion of sound reverberated among the rocks, and Nora, blindly turning to run from the apocalyptic terror, fell forward into a star-spangled darkness.

'My God,' Ben whispered, as the lightning strike shook the rocky ground and he momentarily glimpsed two figures clambering up the rock wall, before the skies opened and everything disappeared in a pink-tinged downpour.

Gauging the distance and angle that would bring him within firing range of where they seemed likely to appear on the top of the breakaway, he abandoned caution, hoping the rain would cover any noise he made, and ran as fast as was possible given the uneven ground and scattered boulders.

Chapter 49

Pulling herself up, Nora pushed her wet hair out of her dazzled eyes and peered into the glittering curtain of red-toned water. Seeing a gap between two leaning rocks, she crawled through to find herself in a cave-like space among a group of boulders. Hoping he wouldn't know where she had gone, she cowered there gasping until her heartbeat slowed. Then, when the roar of the storm eased, she heard his shoes slipping and sliding on wet rocks nearby.

He must see the place she'd crept through. Maybe he was too big to get through there, but she could not escape back that way. Even if she evaded him, where could she run to, on foot, miles from the town. He would soon find her anyway. She had no hope. Then she remembered the gun. It was still there. Still loaded.

Hearing his footsteps crunching the rock outside her haven, with one last, desperate act, she reached for the gun. When his image filled the opening, she pulled the trigger, the recoil driving her elbow back to strike the enclosing rock wall. As her fingers spasmed with shock, the gun dropped onto the slippery red rock and slid away. Deafened by echoes of the report reverberating among the rocks, she didn't know she'd missed until she heard him laughing.

'Ah, so that's where you got to, little bitch. You can't escape, you know.'

Desperately, she squeezed further back between the rocks, emerging on the other side to peer up the slope, where the newly washed rocks shone with a lurid light. Water gushed around their bases, in one place making a little waterfall. Might there be space for her to crawl through there? As the rush of water slowed, she crept forward, one hand, one foot at a time, terrified of dislodging a stone to go clattering away, giving away her position.

It was a very tight squeeze, but she pulled herself through by clutching the sharp rocks. Her hands and knees were bleeding, her dress coated in red mud, by the time she dragged herself out onto a sloping piece of ground below a giant triangular boulder that rested precariously on the rugged cliff top.

Keeping low, Nora crawled around to the other side of the great rock. From there she could see a long way and somewhere in the distance a light flashed. Could that be the sun flashing on harness, or a gun. The surge of hope died away. No one would come looking for her. They wouldn't know where the man had taken her, even if they had reason to think he meant her harm. Pausing to catch her breath, she listened but all was quiet. Scarily, misleadingly quiet because, suddenly, he was there below her.

'You might as well give up, little Nora,' he gloated. 'You shouldn't have made me angry, my dear. I'm so going to enjoy giving you the punishment you deserve. Then, when I'm finished, I'll chop you into juicy little bits and toss them away for the dingoes to chew on. No one will ever find what's left of you.'

Gathering her failing strength, Nora side-stepped along the cliff edge, clinging to the face of the boulder, expecting every moment for her foot to slip on the wet rock underfoot and send her tumbling over the edge. Breathing a sigh of relief, she rounded the rock to find solid ground but as a pebble rolled away under her foot, she went sliding back into the clutches of her tormentor.

'Ha! Got you.' The triumphant yell reached Ben when he was still not close enough for real accuracy with the rifle, so he kept moving forward.

'Not the hoity-toity lady now, are you?'

Grabbing Nora's mud-encrusted hair, he dragged her up onto the level ground, forcing her down across a low rock despite her desperate struggles. Holding her with one hand on her throat, he pulled a knife from his belt. Nora screamed and clutched his wrist as the tip of the blade swooped towards her throat, but it wasn't time for her to die. Shaking off her grip, he dragged the knife through the high collar and thin fabric of her blouse and hacked her light corset open. Her futile attempts to cover her nakedness were stopped by a quick stab to each forearm.

'Very nice,' he commented, pushing her clothing aside with the knife. Feeling the sting of the knifepoint outlining her breasts, she dared not move and drive the blade deeper.

'The dingoes will really enjoy those tender morsels,' he cackled revelling in the terror in her eyes.

'But first things first,' he went on, using the knife to lift her skirt and petticoat. Now, the pressure on her throat increased and she struggled to breathe as he dropped the knife on the ground and began fumbling one-handed with the buttons of his fly. Nora involuntarily squeezed her thighs together at the sight of his erection but when, possessed by lust he relaxed his grip, she frantically fought to escape. Tearing at the hand that held her throat, she kicked out at his legs, feeling her sturdy boot make contact with a knee.

Snarling, he grasped her neck in a two-handed stranglehold and banged her head on the rock on which she lay. As her sight dimmed, a rifle cracked, the bullet whining overhead to go ricocheting away between the rocks.

Released as he jumped back and dropped to the ground, Nora slid off the rock, gasping for breath and scrambling to reach the knife. But he was too quick. Using her body as a shield, he dragged her towards the cliff top, the sharp blade pressed to her throat.

'Drop the gun,' he yelled, 'or I'll cut her throat.'

Chapter 50

As the chilling words echoed off the surrounding rocks, Ben dropped the rifle.

'Come out where I can see, you, or the bitch dies now.'

Ben had no choice but to stand up, stepping to the side where he had a clear run to intervene.

'That's far enough. You're dead!' the man cackled, momentarily releasing Nora. Suddenly a revolver appeared in his free hand, aimed at Ben.

'No, no,' Nora screamed. Throwing her weight back, she brought her heel down on her captor's foot and swung her right arm up to spoil his aim.

Ben was already on the move, hauling the heavy Colt from its holster, when the bullet struck. But it barely slowed his onward rush as Nora's action swung her across the killer's body, still holding his arm. With a shout of rage, he stepped back raising the knife he still clutched in his left hand. With a clear line of fire Ben squeezed the trigger.

✴

'There, sir,' Purkiss yelled, pointing to figures struggling on the rim of the breakaway.

'My God, that's a woman,' the inspector shouted, as a skirt swirled, there was a sudden flurry of movement, and the struggling figures tumbled over the edge. A scream rang out, and a man's anguished cry resounded across the distance as the remaining figure rushed to the precipice. The policemen spurred their horses towards the still figures at the base of the rock.

Ben got there first, sliding down the loose scree at one side of the cliff.

'Nora, Nora!' he cried, stumbling over the rubble to where she lay still on top of her assailant's unmoving body.

'Oh my God, Nora. No, no,' Ben whispered, as he fell to his knees next to her body, clutching her in his arms and burying his tear-wet face in her bloodied hair.

'Ben?' she whispered, and the blood flowed back into his heart.

'You're alive. Thank God. Oh, my darling. I thought I'd lost you too.'

But again, she lay still, and there was so much blood. Desperately, he fumbled to find a pulse. There it was. When a quick investigation showed no major wounds other than bloody gashes on her shoulder and head, he gathered her in his arms and stood up, just as the police arrived.

'Is she ...?' Purkiss said, seeing traces of tears on Ben's face.

'She's alive. I think most of the blood's his,' he indicated the other figure who groaned as one of Purkiss' fellow policeman roughly turned him over.

'Gunshot's just a flesh wound, but it looks like he fell on his own knife,' he said. 'Don't think he'll last to meet the hangman.'

'Hey, Ben, you don't look so good, yourself,' Purkiss said. 'Looks like he winged you. Let's have a look.'

'It's nothing, mate. I've got to get her to hospital.'

Chapter 51

Nora had been watching the play of afternoon light across the green baize lining of the hospital tent for some time before it occurred to her that she shouldn't be lying down on the job. 'Got to get back to work,' she told herself, but was too drowsy to put that thought into action.

Then Mrs Alderdice was bending over her, saying, 'I'm glad to see you are awake, nurse.'

'Oh Matron, I'm sorry,' Nora mumbled, trying to sit up. 'I was about to get back to work.'

'No. Just lie there and rest, my dear, while I check your dressings.'

'Why am I here?' she asked, for the first time becoming aware she was lying in a screened-off part of the main ward, her head and arm heavily bandaged.

'You have some injuries that needed stitches. Go back to sleep now.'

Some time later, Molly's voice aroused her from a confusing dream of mud-slicked rocks ... fighting for her life ... falling, falling, falling ... then Ben's arms around her.

'Nora, do you think you could eat something? It's just soup.'

Blinking, she tried to hang onto the dream, but it slipped away as she became aware of a delicious smell and that she was very hungry.

'Thanks, Molly,' she whispered. 'It smells good.'

'Can you sit up by yourself?'

'I think so,' she said struggling to pull herself up. 'My head's aching and I'm sore all over, but I'll be fine if you put some pillows behind me. I'm having trouble remembering what happened to me; putting all the pieces together.'

'Matron says you've got concussion so might be a bit fuzzy. Is it true that man tried to murder you?'

'Yes. He had a knife.' she shuddered as the full memory returned ... the buggy drive, red dust swirling, the sudden storm. And expecting to die ... 'I pushed him away and he fell, but I tumbled after him. It's what happened after that I can't be sure of.'

I must have dreamt that Ben was crying, his tears wetting my face as he kissed me. It couldn't be true. It was so unlike him to show any emotions.

'Well, it's good to know that the horrible man is dead,' said Molly.

Nora had just finished the soup when Matron and Dr Martin appeared.

'I see you are feeling more yourself now, Mrs Patterson,' the doctor said, as Matron unwrapped the bandages to check her wounds.

'All looks well,' he went on when they had finished. 'Now, if you are up to it, Corporal Williams has been waiting to speak to you.'

After asking how she was feeling, the policeman said, 'Firstly, I must convey the inspector's and my condolences. It is

now confirmed that your husband was one of FitzJames'
victims.'

'I think I already knew he was dead. Then that man said ...
he was crowing about it,' she said with a shudder.

'You'll be pleased to know FitzJames died at the scene and
is no longer a danger to anyone.'

'How did he die? He raised his knife to stab me, then there
was a gunshot and he fell over the edge of the breakaway pulling
me with him.'

'Mr Drummond shot him as he fell, but that's not what
killed him, is it doctor?'

'No. It seems he fell on his own knife and it penetrated the
liver,' the doctor said. 'It took a while to prove fatal.'

'He lived long enough to confess to all the murders. Seems
he needed to brag about outwitting us.'

'Timmy, too?'

'Yes, and the real Reverend Simpson.'

'But how did you know to come, Corporal?'

'Mr Drummond alerted us, after he stumbled on the man's
secret hideaway.'

'That tent?'

'Yes. And that's where we found documents linking him to
previous murders. Among them was this bank passbook, Mrs
Patterson. Can you confirm it belonged to your husband?'

'Yes,' Nora replied, flipping through the pages that showed
regular amounts deposited and withdrawn. The last entry,
however, was a different matter.

'This last one can't be right. Ned never had that much
money.'

'We believe FitzJames has been masquerading as Edward
Patterson for some time and that's the proceeds of selling your

husband's mine. He tried to transfer it to another bank but the Victorian police had already traced that account to him, the transfer never went through.'

Matron returned after seeing the men out, saying, 'All the staff send their sympathy, Mrs Patterson. It seems you had a lucky escape yesterday, and we are all so thankful you've been spared to us. Your friends have been very worried, too. Mary O'Callaghan has called several times, and we couldn't get Mr Drummond to leave last night until Dr Martin told him your wounds weren't life-threatening. I must ask you about him. He seems to care very much for you. Do you return his regard?'

Do I? I think the answer might be yes.

'Matron, I assure you that nothing unseemly has occurred between us, but he has been a good friend to me.'

'Well,' she replied, rising to leave, 'He has been haunting the vicinity of the hospital on and off since dawn. I will allow him to visit you, but only for a few minutes.'

Nora hardly had time to worry about how she looked before Ben hesitantly stepped around the screen. She was disappointed when he came no closer.

'Oh, you're hurt,' she said noticing his arm in a sling. 'Did he shoot you? I hoped I'd spoilt his aim.'

'The bullet just clipped my shoulder. Danny sends his love and sympathy for your bereavement. You have mine too, of course. They say you've suffered no serious injuries. How are you feeling?'

'Glad to be alive. And I have you to thank for that. I'd be dead if you hadn't come. How did you know I was in danger?'

'It was what I saw in the tent. And Joey saw you leave in the buggy.'

'Time's up,' Matron said, clapping her hands as she came into the cubicle. 'You'll have to go now, Mr Drummond. Mrs Patterson needs her rest. Visiting time is tomorrow afternoon. You can come back then.'

With a smile and a quick 'Goodbye,' he was gone, and Matron was fussing over her dressings.

'All seems well,' she said. 'Mary O'Callaghan was here earlier and has taken the things you were wearing to wash. She will try to repair them, but I think they may be beyond help. She will be in to see you tomorrow. In the meantime, you must have complete rest, so doctor has prescribed a mild dose of Morphine. Here is nurse Briggs. I will leave her to get you comfortable.'

'I'm glad it's you Molly,' she whispered when the older woman had gone. 'I'm dying for a pee. Can you get me a bedpan, please?'

'I've got one right here, Nora. I thought you'd be needing it. Here, do you need help to sit up?'

'No. I can cope.'

'I must look a fright,' she said, realizing for the first time that she was wearing one of the men's nightshirts.

'We didn't want to ruin one of your nighties. You've got a lot of cuts on your body. They didn't need stitching, but you're all painted with Iodine. And we had to shave your head around the wound and cut your hair a bit. We sponged most of the blood off, but it needs a proper wash when you're better.'

As Molly tucked her back in bed, Nora wondered what Ben had thought when he saw her.

'Do you have a mirror, I could borrow. There's one in my bag, but I don't know where that ended up.'

'I think the police brought it back, so I might be able to bring it to you. But first you had better drink this.

It was late afternoon by the time Ben reached Mary's gate. He didn't feel like talking to anyone, and intended walking past, but she called out to him.

'Did you get to see her, Ben? Is she all right?'

'Yes. I spoke to her, but I think she was still affected by the anaesthetic. They say she's got concussion too, but they've stitched her arm and the head wound.'

'You look terrible Ben. Did you get any sleep last night? I'd ask you in for a cuppa but by the look of you, you need to get home and go to bed.'

Back at the camp, Danny said nothing, just told him to sit down, handing him a plate of stew. Taking it blindly, he sat gazing at it for minutes before spooning some into his mouth, the savoury taste reminding him that, except for a slice of damper for breakfast, he hadn't eaten since the previous morning.

'Thanks, mate,' he mumbled as Danny plonked a mug of tea next to him. 'Good tucker. Didn't know I needed it.'

'You saw Nora?'

'Yes, she's going to be all right they say.'

'Good. Can we visit tomorrow?'

'Maybe. I'm not sure I should.'

He'd not thought about what people might think of him insisting on seeing her, until he overheard Mrs Alderdice asking Nora about him, and her reply. The last thing he wanted was to embarrass her or injure her reputation. Men could be worse gossips than a bunch of old women. So, he'd better stay away.

'I imagine Mary will go and let us know how she is. She brought back Nora's clothes. She thinks she can mend them, but I don't know how she'll get the mud off them. Maybe you could go get her some extra water.'

'Yes. Good idea,' Ben murmured, his mind filled with images of water washing away the caked mud and bloodstains as exhaustion took hold of him and he slept.

'You going to bed? Or are you goin' to sleep there all night?' Danny's voice broke into the jumbled dream.

'Uh? Sorry. Must have dozed off.'

'Better get to bed, Mate.'

Chapter 52

'Are you awake enough for a visitor, Nora?' Molly asked the following afternoon. 'It's a gentleman.'

'Oh, I can't see anyone looking like this,' she said thinking it must be Ben.

'I'll help you get presentable. I brought my shawl. Let's put that around your shoulders to hide that nightshirt, and I'll brush your hair.'

After Molly had brushed what of her hair showed below the unflattering bandage, and draped the shawl around her, she felt a little better but was very disappointed when a dapper stranger entered, removing his bowler hat.

'Good afternoon Mrs. Patterson,' he said, 'I am Mr Barker from the West Australian Bank. I have some information that may be of interest to you. As you know the inquest into the happenings of the other day are proceeding and it seems likely that your husband's death will be confirmed'

'I suppose so,' she whispered, finding this blunt reference to Ned's death unnerving.

'The bank holds in safe deposit a copy of your husband's will which names you as his sole heir. It was entrusted to us when he opened the account with us last year.'

'Oh, I didn't know he'd made a will.'

'We advise clients to do so when they take up promising claims. There is s a substantial balance in the account, including proceeds of the sale of Mr Patterson's mine, deposited with us by the man masquerading as him. He didn't intend it to stay in the account but the transfer to another bank was stopped. So that amount is still there and though there may be some formalities, I believe it will come to you.'

After he had bowed himself out, Nora lay back, too weary to stop the tears that flowed down her face. While Ned was making sure she'd be all right if he died, she had been cheating on him. Groaning, she turned to bury her face in her pillow.

'Are you all right?' Molly asked rushing to her side.

'Yes,' she mumbled. 'Just leave me alone.'

She was wiping her face and blowing her nose when Molly came back to check on her.

'Are you up to having another visitor, Nora? It's Mrs O'Callaghan."

'Yes. I'd like to see her.'

'I'll leave you to talk, then.'

'Well, you're certainly looking more like yourself,' Mary said. 'Are you too sore for a hug?'

'No, of course not,' Nora replied, leaning into her friend's embrace.

'We were so worried for you.'

'I've got stitches in my head and arm, and lots of cuts and scratches, but nothing that shouldn't heal soon. Matron said you were going to try to mend my clothes. I thought they'd be ruined.'

'They're in a pretty bad state, but I managed to beat the dried mud off your skirt and jacket, and I've washed them. Maybe I could dye them black. You'll need mourning clothes now we know what happened to Ned, and it will hide any stains I can't get out.'

'I think they might be beyond help but if you can fix up the skirt and jacket that would be wonderful. Yes, please dye them. I hadn't thought about needing to go into black.'

'Maybe just for a few months. You could probably borrow my black hat. I think I can probably come out of mourning now. Ben went and got a tank full of water so I could wash the stuff. Has he been to see you today?'

'No. I suppose Danny and he might visit me sometime,' she said, 'but I don't know how many visitors they'll let in. I'll be glad when I'm well enough to get out of here. They might let me go and sleep in the nurses' tent soon and get back into my own clothes. I must have looked a fright when Ben came last night.'

'I doubt if he would have noticed. He's in love with you, you know'

'Of course not. He just feels he needs to keep rescuing me.'

'I wonder why that would be, then,' Mary said with a chuckle, rising to leave.

'Thanks for trying to fix up my clothes. I've only got a few things, so really need them.'

It was only later that she remembered the money. She wasn't sure how much, but it was in the thousands. What could she do with thousands of pounds? She'd never imagined owning anything like that. Maybe she should buy some sort of business. Perhaps a dress shop with Mary, selling pretty dresses for ladies, but in lovely Autumn colours like orange and russet that wouldn't show the red dirt. *But why am I only thinking about living here with its red dirt when I could go home, or buy a house in Perth?*

She knew she should leave. Get away from Ben and the disturbing attraction she'd tried to resist. She mustn't make the same mistake she'd made rushing into that affair with James. Remembering the lust he'd awakened in her, she wondered if this was just some animal thing. Some mating instinct that demanded she find a mate... any mate? But Ben wasn't just any man.

But what did she really know of him, beyond his kind eyes and handsome face. He was a good friend. But he was closed. Hiding something behind a sombre face. No, she mustn't rush into anything. Besides, she needed to properly mourn Neddie and the young dreams they'd shared when she was a different woman.

Despite her good intentions, when she saw Ben next day, she had to know if what she remembered was real.

'It's good to see you, Ben. Come and sit down,' she said, patting the bed.

'That's better,' she said, as he perched on the edge of the bed.

'There's something I need to ask you,' she murmured. 'After I fell, did you hold me in your arms and call me your darling? Or was it a dream?'

The look in his eyes told her it was true, but he shook his head, 'Forgive me, Nora. I had no right. I'm not fit to say those words to you, or any woman. There are things in my past ...'

'Tell me about it, Ben. Let me decide if you have that right.'

'I don't think I can.'

'Try. It's something about losing your wife, isn't it?'

'Partly. How she died, but that's only a part. It's worse than just grieving, Nora.'

'Tell me about it, Ben,' Nora whispered squeezing his hand as he rose to leave.

✒︎

Could he really begin to tell her? Writing about it to Bessie had been hard. This was far harder. Maybe he should just leave. Go bush. But she'd asked him to tell her, and his heart longed to let go of the secrets that had haunted him all these years. But the hospital visiting hours would never be long enough to tell her. Maybe he could write her a letter. Then he wouldn't have to face her disdain. If she didn't want to see him again, she could just ask Matron not to let him in.

Chapter 53

The letter arrived just as Nora was finishing her breakfast next morning.

"Dearest Nora", he began, "you asked me to explain, and it's all too long and confusing to talk about in the short time we'll have in visiting hours. It's not an easy story to tell."

He'd been a policeman in London, she read. Married his best friend's sister. Hearing there were chances of promotion in the colonies, they came to Australia. Queensland. Then he was sent outback to help local police after a squatter was killed by the blacks.

The squatters and their men rode straight into the black's camp, guns blazing. It was a massacre, and the bush police joined in. I tried to intervene but got knocked off my horse and a crazy bloke waving a sabre rode over me. One of the horse's hooves hit me on the head. I came to as they were burning the bodies. When I protested, the sergeant poked his revolver in my face and said, 'Keep your mouth shut. This is how we do things in the bush."

She read of his return to the police station in Brisbane without stopping at home, then being sent to investigate a suicide. He didn't mention the body parts strewn along the railway track, but her imagination filled in the details.

Nora wept as she read how he got home to find his wife had died in childbirth, holding her in his arms until someone came to lay her out and a neighbour took him to a pub and got him very drunk.

It was late when I remembered the massacre and returned to the Police Station. When they wouldn't listen, I started shouting and the inspector came to investigate. I tried to explain what happened, but he turned away, so I grabbed his shoulder to stop him leaving. The sergeant knocked me out and I woke up in gaol, and remembered Millie was gone. When they wouldn't let me go to her funeral, I started shaking the bars and screaming for them to let me out. They decided I was insane and sent me to the asylum. I was there for five years, until they decided I wasn't mad and let me loose. I went bush, carrying my swag around the outback for nearly two years before I decided to come west.

His final words were: "I love you, but I'll understand if you don't want to see me again."

Nora hurriedly wiped her tear-stained face on the bed sheet, as she heard Matron and the doctor talking to the other patients, hoping the distress aroused by Ben's letter didn't show, as they pushed aside the curtain and came to her bedside. 'I think our Nurse Patterson is making a good recovery, doctor,' Matron was saying.

'Good morning, Mrs Patterson,' the doctor said. 'I think we can let you get up today.'

'Do you think I could go back to the nurse's tent now?' Nora asked. 'I'd like to get dressed and maybe sit outside for a while.'

'Yes, I think that would be appropriate, but you must take it easy. I'm sure you are aware of the effects of blood loss and concussion.'

It was a relief to get back to the privacy of the nurse's tent. She was surprised to find how weak she felt after walking there, but after a brief lie-down, was able to get dressed. When Ben came, maybe they could sit out in the bough shed to talk.

With great misgivings, Ben returned to the hospital next day, and headed for the main ward, half expecting to be turned away.

'Ben,' Nora called, and he turned to see her standing in the shade of the bough shed. As he approached, she stepped forward to take his hand. 'Thank you for your letter,' she said, drawing him into the shade.

'I've been trying very hard not to fall in love with you, Ben,' she went on when they were seated. 'But I need to sort out my feelings. I did love Ned dearly, but I've known in my heart for a while that he must be dead, or else he'd changed from the sweet boy I married. Now I know what happened, I need to grieve properly, before I can feel free to love someone else. Are you prepared to wait?'

'Of course, my dear. I'd wait till the end of time. My heart has been dead all these years, and you've brought it back to life. I wanted to die when I thought I'd lost you.

Epilogue

October 1895

'So, when's the big day?' Danny asked, looking up from the newspaper he'd been reading.

'What big day?' asked Ben, who had been singing quietly to himself as he prepared their dinner.

'Whatever it is that's had you grinning like the Cheshire cat all afternoon.'

'No date yet, but Nora's said she'll marry me.'

'That's a relief. I'm sick of you mooning around the place. She goin' to be happy here? Might want to go down to Perth, or back east,' Danny asked, turning the newspaper to a new page.

'She's talking about opening a dress shop here in Hannans with some of the money Ned left her. Wants Mary to make the dresses.'

'You happy for her to do that? Some blokes wouldn't want their wives running a business,' said his friend

'After arriving here with no money, I think she needs her independence.'

'You'll need a proper house. Gonna live here on the lease?'

'Yes, if that's all right with you. She doesn't want to live in town,' he replied. He'd already decided on the site for the house. A lovely spot with a view of the distant hills, far enough away from the mine and camp to be private. He was dreamily picturing the little house he would build for Nora, when Danny's voice penetrated his reverie.

'Hey mate, remember you talkin' about a young bloke with a sabre? Well, listen to this. They've found out more about FitzJames. We knew his old man was a wealthy squatter who'd been in the British army. When he gave the boy his army sabre, he started chasing the blacks an' threatening neighbours with it. The father packed him off to England and he went to India with the army. Sounds like he could be your man.'

The End

GETTING TO THE GOLD RUSH

This map gives some idea of the distances prospectors travelled to reach Western Australia's eastern goldfields. In 1895 the railway had only reached Southern Cross. It didn't reach Kalgoorlie (Hannans) until the end of 1896. Those from overseas or, like Nora, from the eastern states of Australia, had long sea voyages just to reach the ports, Fremantle and Albany.

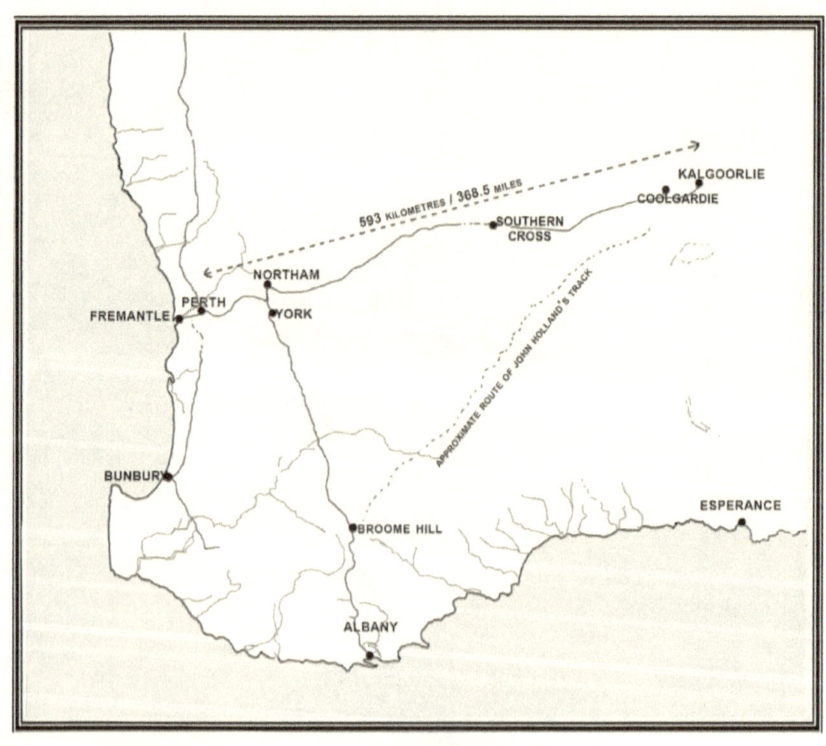

THE HISTORICAL BACKGROUND

Australia ranks second only to China as a gold-producing country. Much of that gold still comes from Western Australia, but it was still an isolated British colony, less than sixty years old, when the first gold finds were recorded.

About thirty years earlier, in the middle of the nineteenth century, gold was discovered in America's west. Local workers walked off their jobs and sailors deserted their ships. When word got out, men from all over the world headed for California.

Those from Australia might as well have stayed home. In 1851, the Australian gold rush began with rich finds at Bathurst in New South Wales, and Ballarat and Bendigo in Victoria. Scenes like those in California followed. Work stopped as men abandoned their jobs and headed for the fields, often leaving wives and children with no support. Again, ships were deserted in the harbours.

By 1860, Australia's population increased by over 207 percent and eastern Australia boomed, especially Victoria and its capital, 'Marvellous' Melbourne. As the easy gold ran out, some were tempted to head for South Africa's rich Transvaal finds, or Western Australia's new Pilbara and Murchison fields, but most were happy to stay put and enjoy the good times.

But, in 1891, came the inevitable bust. Banks closed, businesses failed, and unemployment soared. Men walked the street in ragged clothes or headed bush on the Wallaby Track, to live off the land and do odd jobs for meals on struggling outback properties.

Then, in June 1892, in Western Australia's dry interior, Bayley and Ford struck gold at Coolgardie, collecting two thousand pounds worth in one evening. And the rush was on. Men from all over the world converging on the isolated colony and its even more isolated interior. Newchums from Britain and the

Australian cities joined tough old veterans of the Victorian and Californian gold rushes, to answer the lure of gold.

As it was to be September 1896 before the railway line from the capital, Perth reached Coolgardie and Kalgoorlie, it was no easy journey from the ports of Albany and Fremantle. Some could afford to buy horses or rides on wagons, but many walked at least some of the way, carrying their worldly goods or pushing wheelbarrows, often knocked together from bush timber.

Then, in 1893, Coolgardie was eclipsed by Paddy Hannan and his mates' rich find at what was to become Kalgoorlie, about 30 miles further east. Next day, some 400 men rushed to Hannan's find. Within two months, fifteen hundred miners were reported to be at Hannans, four hundred at Coolgardie, and another five hundred or so prospecting other parts of the fields.

Today, seeing the barren plains, dotted with ghost towns, that surround Kalgoorlie, one would suppose that anyone who set out on foot with no air-conditioned, four-wheel-drive vehicle, no refrigeration and only the water he could carry, must have been insane.

Most of these men were completely rational, however. But, unlike previous gold rushes, water was even scarcer out there than gold. Even veterans sometimes underestimated the semi-desert conditions. So, from time to time, prospectors would come upon the decaying remains of men who had perished of thirst. But these gruesome finds deterred few of those afflicted by gold fever.

In this time long before power tools, mining was hard, dirty, pick-and-shovel work so, with no water to wash clothes, the men could only try to beat the red dust out of them. Most took Sunday off and tried to tidy up a bit, trimming beards, washing faces and hands and shaving in tiny amounts of water.

During the first waterless summers, miners were granted an exemption allowing them to leave their claims without forfeiting them, so they could head for the cooler coast. But even in the winter, when the creeks ran, clean water was in short supply because the diggers muddied the creeks, so cleanliness was difficult. Sewage was not disposed of in a sanitary fashion, and disease was common. Many people died of diseases like dysentery or Typhoid Fever. It was to be another nine years before, thanks to the genius of C Y O'Connor, water was piped the 530 kilometres from Mundaring Weir in the hills near the capital, Perth.

In 1894, Hannan's was still little more than a camp, with canvas or hessian-covered buildings, and some made from local timber, straggling along either side of the road from Coolgardie. And, until the railway finally reached Coolgardie in 1896 and Kalgoorlie in 1897, everything, food, building materials, and - after the big mines got going, heavy mining equipment - had to be transported hundreds of kilometres into the dry interior from Fremantle (618 km away), Albany or Esperance by camel or donkey trains, or wagons pulled by horses. The extra width of Hannan's Street and Coolgardie's Bayley Street echo the problems of turning camel trains.

Of course, with so many diggers streaming into the new goldfields, it was hard to keep track of them all, and government agencies were soon stretched to the limit. The postal service trying to cope with letters and parcels, often simply addressed 'care of Post Office, Hannans', while the few police assigned to the area were continuously asked to trace missing men.

But the places prospectors headed were yet to be found on any map. I remember finding, in a Post Office Directory of the time, an address listed as 'Harder to Find'. I assume it was a humorous name for a gold find, but perhaps it was simply the truth. At best it would have been like trying to find a needle in a haystack, and there were some who didn't want to be found. A late nineteenth century gold rush, with no phones, no electronic media, few newspapers and very slow travel, was a perfect place to hide from your wife, your creditors, or from the Police themselves.

Real People

Constable Alfred Purkiss was a young South Australian who joined the West Australian police force. He was appointed as a probational officer in in March 1894 and temporarily promoted when sent to the goldfields in mid 1894. There is an incorrect report that he died in Hannans in 1895, but that was his brother Albert who was visiting and caught Typhoid. Constable Purkiss was posted to Kanowna in October1895 and was promoted to corporal in 1899 while based at Bulong.

Mrs Alderdice was matron of the first makeshift hospital. She was the wife of one of the shopkeepers. I don't think she had formal qualifications but must have had some experience of nursing. I don't know what she was like, but assume she would have needed to be businesslike and probably a bit bossy. Her contribution gets lost in later records when the hospital structure was formalised and a qualified matron, Miss Way, was appointed in September 1895.

Dr Martin was the doctor who serviced the hospital. In February 1895, he advertised that he was a physician and surgeon and could be consulted at his residence in Hannan Street.

Corporal Williams had been stationed at Southern Cross and was posted to Hannan's Find to take charge of the new Police Station in July 1894.

Constable Charles Riddell appears to have been second in charge, as he took over when Williams took a six-month holiday in June 1985.

H.G.Vernon was draughtsman in the Warden's Office. The Warden, who we don't meet, was Maynard H Jepson, who had multiple responsibilities.

Faiz Mahomet was an important businessman of the goldrush. Towns were reliant on the food and water transported by the camel carrying business of Faiz & Tagh Mahomet. By 1896, the firm was worth £50,000, with branches across WA.

Courthope , Grose and Co. A general store set up when the town was so new that an advertisement of September 1893 still describes it as 'Hannan's Rush', 30 miles from Coolgardie.

Lynne Cairns is an Australian author, artist and historian. Her first historical novels were set in the first years of white settlement in Western Australia. But, with *Gold Town* we move forward to the exciting gold rush years of the 1890s. Lynne also writes poetry and short stories, and is author or co-author of maritime history books about shipwrecks and submarines.

You can learn more about Lynne and her books at her webpage: lynnecairns.com

Other Novels by Lynne Cairns

Where Wild Black Swans are Flying.

Life was tough in Western Australia's Swan River Colony. Little Becky Lees arrived as a baby and has known no other life, but things are about to get worse. Not yet ten, she finds herself lost and alone, far from white settlements. Rescued by indigenous Noongar people, she is taken in by a young widow battling to raise her small sons on a remote farm. Becky grows up and finds love. But life is no fairy tale, and fate has much more trauma in store before she can finally find happiness.

Cast Away

A tale of shipwreck, survival and treasure, for children 10-14. Katie O'Donoghue, an eleven-year-old Irish servant girl, is the sole survivor of a shipwreck on an unexplored part of the south coast of Western Australia. Alone and lost on a lonely shore where few white people have ever walked, she searches in vain for a farm or village where she might find shelter, food and water. Can she survive in the wild? Can she trust the few people she meets, and escape the evil men who think she knows where treasure is buried?

Both books are available (paperback or eBook) from Amazon, Booktopia and other online bookstores

Real History

Secret Fleets

The true story of the World War II Allied submarine base in Fremantle, Western Australia. The book includes sections on the development of submarines, Australia's submarines, the impact of the war and the influx of American troops on Western Australian society. Published by the Western Australian Museum, it is available from the museum's bookshops, or online.